A DANGEROUS PASSION

STEAM! ROMANCE AND RAILS, BOOK 3

E.E. BURKE

Cover Design by Erin Dameron Hill
Train photography by Matthew Malkiewicz

Published by E.E. Burke
ebook ISBN 978-0-9898192-4-4
Paperback ISBN 978-0-9898192-5-1
www.eeburke.com

This book is dedicated to the memory of my father.
My first hero.

CHAPTER 1

March 3, 1873,
Parsons, Kansas

*A*n ambitious man could expect to make enemies. Success bred jealousy, which gave birth to resentment, in extreme cases, violence. If a man didn't keep a knife handy, another man's knife might end up in his back. Of primary concern at the moment wasn't the length of Henry's growing list of adversaries. It was the names he needed to add.

A crowd already filled the Rail Yard Saloon when he strode into the narrow, smoke-filled room. His gaze skittered past an off-duty crew hunched over the bar. Burly tracklayers played cards beneath a sign that warned, *No Sharps Allowed*. Meaning gamblers, not the popular rifle, standard issue for railroad employees traveling through Indian Territory—or anywhere along the Katy line for that matter.

Henry shook out his damp overcoat before draping it over an iron spike, which had been hammered into the wall as a coat rack. He hung up his new bowler hat and adjusted his suit coat over the handle of a Colt, which he carried when he was awake and put next to him when he slept. He didn't anticipate needing the gun in here. One street over at a place that catered to sodbusters, the story might be different.

"Evening, Sean. Mack. Lloyd..." Henry greeted the men he passed. It was part of his job to know his men's names, as well as the names of their wives and kids. These men weren't his enemies. The railroad workers weren't his friends, either. He didn't invite that kind of relationship. What they gave him, he valued more. Respect and loyalty. In return, he worked hard to ensure they kept their livelihood amidst a poor economy.

His opponents included local farmers, competitors, most of his peers. Apparently, members of the railroad's Board of Directors had also turned against him.

Henry made his way to a corner table where his assistant waited with a bottle of whisky and two empty glasses. George Caldwell had been a good hire for more than proper etiquette. His ties to the railroad elite would prove to be immensely helpful when it came to identifying the skunks amongst them. "Pour us a drink, Mr. Caldwell. Let's celebrate our new depot's grand opening."

"Yes sir. Thank you, sir. Very generous." Caldwell measured two shots with care. The younger man's hands, slender and pale as a girl's, hadn't seen the kind of hard work that put callouses on Henry's palms. Still, the dapper New Yorker was punctual, efficient, willing to do whatever his boss required. What more did one need in an assistant?

"Is there something you wanted to discuss?" Caldwell had his pencil at the ready. His dark eyes snapped with curiosity.

"We'll talk business later. Let's have that drink first. Here's to Mr. Parsons." Henry lifted his glass in a salute to his boss, one of the few people who seemed to like him. Or, more specifically, the old man liked his *hard work and ingenuity*. Plus the fact he'd won a construction race when pitted against a bigger, richer rival.

A year ago, Judge Parsons had appointed him General Manager

over the Missouri, Kansas & Texas Railway—*The Katy*, as everyone called it. The old man had promised to promote him to President.

What had prompted the directors to launch an investigation against him? Couldn't come at a worse moment.

"To Mr. Parsons' success in Europe," Caldwell added, before the glasses clinked.

Surprisingly, the potential for an infusion of foreign funds didn't improve Henry's mood. He took a swig. *Irish whiskey. Imported.* Might do the trick. Although he could think of better uses for expensive liquor than getting drunk. Loosening tongues, for one.

"Drink up," Henry urged.

Caldwell tipped his glass a little higher. A flush stained his cheeks. Another drink, he'd be primed for questions.

The well-connected Easterner kept up regular correspondence with his wealthy family, which included two of the Katy's biggest investors. He might've picked up scuttlebutt about the board's intentions.

Henry let the smoky whiskey linger on his tongue. He ought to relax more often. Appreciate the finer things in life. If he could take the time. He worked at such a furious pace to finish the railroad, he hadn't paid enough attention to politics—especially the dirty kind.

Henry stared through the amber liquid to the bottom of his glass. His shrewd, canny boss must've seen this investigation coming. Yet, Parsons hadn't warned his righthand man before setting sail for the Continent. Forced him to rely on a greenhorn assistant for family gossip. It galled Henry to no end. "Any news from home?" he inquired casually.

"My sister has a new son."

"We'll drink to her fecundity." Henry poured a generous second round.

Caldwell drained his glass without further encouragement. At this rate, he'd soon be tossing back drinks like an Irish tracklayer. Hopefully, he'd become just as gabby.

Henry leaned back with his arms folded. "Any business-related news?"

His assistant blinked like a mechanism winding down. "Regarding the Katy?"

No, regarding the price of tea in China.

"The board," Henry clarified. "Any idea why they hired that investigator from Boston?"

This drew a puzzled frown. "To write a report?"

Henry held off on the third shot. Caldwell's cheeks were as red as a signal light, and he'd started to sound like a nincompoop. He might drink like an Irishman, but couldn't hold his liquor like one. "Of course, they want him to write a report. I'm asking if you know why?"

Caldwell gazed into his empty glass as if he'd find the answers there. "Rumors, I suppose."

Tension pulled Henry's shoulders. The hesitant tone in his assistant's voice set off alarms. Members of the board might've deduced the railroad's true financial picture. In one word, *bleak.*

He leaned forward, kept his voice low. "What rumors?"

"The usual. That Mr. Parsons is incompetent, and you're an insufferable ass."

Henry stared at the idiot who didn't value his job. "Is that an attempt at humor or a quote from your father?"

The startled alarm on his assistant's face might've been funny, had Henry been in a mood to be amused. "Oh, no sir. Neither. Only vicious rumors. I wouldn't give them credence."

"I don't. If being an *insufferable ass* could've gotten me fired, I would've been gone years ago. As for Mr. Parsons, the railroad wouldn't be here without him." Henry corked the bottle. Waste of time and good whiskey. Caldwell hadn't told him anything he didn't already know.

The board would replace him if they could find a better man.

There wasn't a better man. Not to lead the Katy.

He fished in his waistcoat pocket for his watch. *Six-fifty.* The time would be different on the railway clock in St. Louis, which was different from the one in Chicago, and at every hamlet in between. Towns set time according to the sun. The Katy ran according to Henry's timepiece.

He'd meet the railroad investigator. Greet him, size him up, decide how to get rid of him. "Better get going. Train is due in ten minutes."

Caldwell straightened, surprisingly attentive for a man who moments earlier had been about to fall into his glass. "Sorry, sir. It's been delayed."

"Delayed?" Henry glowered. "Why didn't you tell me earlier?"

His assistant's face reddened at the chastisement. "I found out before I came over. It's due to a barricade on the tracks south of Fort Scott. Could take them all night to clear it."

"Damn squatters." Henry snapped his watch cover shut. "If those vandals spent half as much time behind a plow, they could afford to buy their land twice over."

Loud shouts from across the room drew his attention. A soot-stained fireman leapt onto a table and danced a jig to the delight of the crowd.

Amazing, how these men could celebrate, no matter the situation. They'd endured every imaginable hardship to build the railroad, faced danger every day to keep it running, yet neither the president nor the board of directors acknowledged their sacrifices. Instead, they complained about the cost. There wouldn't be a railroad without those men. They were worth every penny they were paid, and more.

Henry withdrew greenbacks from his inside coat pocket. He handed the money to his assistant. "Buy a round of drinks for the house. Announce it's on the Katy.

Caldwell did as he was told.

A moment later, a roar went up from the crowd. Men surged to the bar. Several turned and lifted glasses in Henry's direction. "The Katy!" they cheered.

Henry dipped his chin in acknowledgement. His cash. He'd let the company take the credit. These men needed to believe there were others besides him who appreciated them.

He slumped in his chair, growing morose. Once he became president, he'd be in control. He could make changes as he saw fit. More money would be poured back into the railroad to be distributed among its employees, instead of filling the pockets of a few rich men and greedy politicians.

His assistant returned with a smile. "You know the right levers, Chief. Those Irish boys will heave ho all winter for free whiskey."

That wasn't why he'd done it. This time. Henry couldn't claim charity had motivated him in the past.

A shrill whistle pierced through the commotion in the saloon. That train was nearly at the station! Its engineer must've run full steam to make up time.

Henry shot to his feet. He threw more money on the table, instructing Caldwell. "You pay. I'll go meet our guest."

Outside, a brisk reminder of winter sent snowflakes swirling over the muddy street. Recently installed street lamps bravely held off the encroaching darkness.

With a firm hold on the brim of his favorite hat, Henry leaned into the wind. He strode down the sidewalk toward the new depot, an impressive brick and stone structure that ought to convince anyone, even that investigator, of the Katy's financial soundness.

The locomotive let loose with another long whistle. Out in the darkness, its headlamp flickered. Henry searched for the red signal light directing it to a new depot. Why wasn't the damn thing lit to point the way? He'd given explicit instructions.

Breathing fire, he shot across the street. Did he have to be a signal operator, too? One more blasted ball to juggle, as if he didn't have enough to do.

The train's whistle shrieked, twice more, louder this time. Then the roar of the engine became deafening as it charged *past* the new depot, headed for the *old* depot, another fifty yards away. Next to it, a signal had been lit.

Henry released a stream of profanity. He veered off across a field between the two buildings, lost his footing in the slippery mud, barely righted himself. By the time he neared the ramshackle building, he was seething.

A lantern mounted atop a pole illuminated the weather-beaten walls. The ugly shack had served as the Parsons depot since the town's inception two years ago. It wouldn't make a good impression on an indiscriminating hog.

Henry passed four men on horseback, who sat in the shadows beyond the reach of a light mounted below the eaves. He took the steps up to the platform two at a time, slammed open the station door. "Floyd!"

What the hell? It was dark as pitch in here.

Henry fumbled in his pocket for a packet of matches. Struck one. No station agent stood behind the small window that separated the waiting room from the office. No porters were around. Nobody.

A loud squeal came from outside. The train had come to a stop. It would soon release its passengers.

Into a dark building.

Cursing, Henry shook out the match. Lit another. He touched it to the wick in a kerosene lamp, which he secured on a hook attached to the ceiling beam.

Better get the stove going or the passengers would freeze while they waited. He squatted down to open the grate.

The door behind him struck the wall with a loud bang.

A cold gust swirled into the room, as four men stepped inside. The same ones he'd passed outside. The ponchos they wore dripped melted snow. Wide hat brims were pulled low over their eyes. Heavy scarves concealed their faces from the cold—and recognition.

Henry came to his feet, unbuttoning his coat to get to his gun. At the sound of a hammer being cocked, he froze. Despite being a fairly good shot, he was no quick draw. Whoever cocked that gun could kill him before he cleared leather. Worst case, they were here to rob him. Best case, they'd reacted after seeing him go for his gun.

"Sorry, you startled me." He held his hands away from his sides so the men could see them. "Are you here to meet someone on the train?"

He hoped so. Otherwise, he was in trouble.

"You Stevens?" one of the men asked.

Big trouble.

The voice wasn't one Henry recognized. In fact, nothing about the men looked familiar. He hadn't even heard their spurs. He looked down at the heavy brogans on the speaker's feet. Drifters, outlaws, men who lived in the saddle, all wore boots.

Henry's anger reignited. *Blasted sodbusters.* Did they think they could scare him into giving in to their demands?

From outside came the hiss of an engine letting off steam. Soon, passengers would come pouring through that door behind him.

A chime sounded. The conductor's call distracted the four men for a second.

A second was all Henry needed. He bolted out the door toward the train. Those farmers wouldn't take on an armed railroad crew.

Shots rang out. Wooden splinters flew off the doorframe an instant after Henry had dodged to one side. The conductor, who stood next to the train, staggered, apparently struck by a bullet.

Henry gaped in shock. Those crazy settlers would *kill* to get what they wanted. He hadn't expected that.

On metal steps leading from the parlor car, a young woman stood with one foot poised, as if ready to leap off the train and bound onto the platform in her eagerness to disembark.

Henry glimpsed her startled expression. His heart convulsed. Outgunned or not, he couldn't run. He had to protect that woman, the other passengers, the crew.

He jerked his revolver from its holster.

CHAPTER 2

"Get back!"

A man's shout startled Lucy out of her frozen shock. She struggled to make sense of what was happening.

Where had the gunshots come from?

Who had issued the warning? It must've come from the bearded man in a bowler hat, who crouched beside the depot door.

He fired his revolver at someone inside, who returned fire.

The moment had a surrealistic quality, as if she'd stepped into a Ned Buntline tale. The only thing missing were the painted warriors.

Behind her, a woman screamed. Other passengers who'd crowded the exit panicked. They crawled over each other in their haste to retreat.

Lucy couldn't move. In her eagerness to start her new life, she'd rushed out to be the first off the train. Now, she'd be the last to reach safety.

"Lucy! Where are you?" Her father's worried cry came from behind the frenzied crowd.

"I'm all right." Actually, she wasn't, but what could he do about it?

Another loud crack resounded, then a *ping*.

Lucy dropped to her haunches, hugging her satchel. *"Mon Dieu!"* Those devils inside the depot were shooting at the train.

"For God's sake, get back inside!" The command came from the man crouched beside the depot door. He was defending the train from whoever was attacking them.

She scurried up the steps.

"Help..." The strained voice stopped her. Heavens, it was the conductor. He clung to the rail, his face twisted with pain. He'd been shot!

With a groan, he collapsed onto the platform.

How could she leave the poor man in harm's way, possibly bleeding to death? She couldn't live with herself. Before she changed her mind, she dropped the heavy satchel and crept down the steps to go to the aid of the wounded man.

His face, which had been pink with health when he'd taken her ticket, now looked pasty white.

"Miss," he gasped. "Save yourself."

Honestly, she wanted to. Her heart pounded so hard it felt like it would explode out of her chest at any moment.

"Sir." Her voice wavered. She forced more strength into it. "We shall go back inside the train together. I'll help you." Lucy grasped the portly conductor beneath his arms and strained to help him to his feet.

"What the *hell* are you doing?" The bearded man who'd held off the attackers moved backwards, holding his revolver aimed at the depot door. Like a guardian angel, he positioned himself between her and the gunmen inside.

He motioned to a space between the platform and the train's massive wheels. "Jump down. Crawl underneath to the other side."

Lucy squelched a fierce desire to flee. She shook her head. "This man needs our assistance."

Her guardian angel swore an oath. "I'll help him. You get away."

He hoisted the conductor's arm over his shoulder. The wounded man's knees sagged. His considerable weight pulled the taller man down. Though he appeared to be strong enough to manage, they wouldn't be able to move out of danger quickly.

"You need my help." Lucy wrapped her arm around the conductor's waist, encountering a wet, sticky warmth.

She pulled her hand back, stared at his blood on her fingers. Her stomach did a slow flip. She swallowed a metallic taste in her mouth, then met the dark gaze of the bearded man who'd come to their rescue.

His expression reflected understanding, and determination. It inspired her to conquer her fear.

"I can do this," she whispered. She didn't want to, she had to. She covered the conductor's wound with her hand to stop the bleeding.

Another shot rang out. The bullet ricocheted off the railing on the steps. Frightened faces disappeared from the windows of the train.

"Hurry," the tall man urged. "Over there. Keep your head down."

Together, they dragged the conductor away from a bright light illuminating the train to the shadows below the eaves of the station house. The toes of the wounded man's shoes scraped over the wooden platform. The sound sent shivers across her skin.

Her rescuer didn't wear boots like the Western luminaries featured on the covers of dime novels. He had Congress-style shoes, which were popular with politicians and businessmen. What an odd detail to notice, much less care about, in the midst of a life-threatening situation.

They deposited the conductor behind a large rain barrel. He fell to his knees with a groan then curled up against the clapboard wall.

Worried, Lucy knelt beside him. She touched his shoulder to let him know he wasn't alone.

"Stay here." The tall man used his forefinger to indicate *here*. Maybe he thought she was slow. Like the little neighbor boy back home, the one who had a bad habit of wandering into the street in front of carriages.

Her rescuer flattened his back against the side of the building. He inched toward the depot door. From inside came the heart-stopping crack of another gunshot.

Lucy bit her lip to stifle a cry. Screaming wouldn't help him. If she had a weapon, she might be useful. Although people weren't cans. Her hands would shake. She could hold her fear in check long enough to tend to the conductor.

"Let me see how badly you're hurt." She undid the buttons on his vest. Blood soaked the side of his shirt and had congealed in the fabric.

Her head grew light. She took a deep breath to clear it. During the war, she'd volunteered at the Union hospital in Boston. Those soldiers had already been patched up, and she'd read to them. This man was bleeding. He didn't need to hear a story.

She used her clean handkerchief to press against the wound in his side.

He grimaced. So did she.

"I'm so sorry."

"Don't be. Owe you my life." He covered the makeshift bandage with his fingers. His lips quavered when he attempted to smile. "Not sure what you were thinking to come after me."

She hadn't been *thinking* at all. Reacting, mostly. Reality struck with a sickening punch. She could've been killed, or that brave man when he'd shielded her with his body.

Where was he now?

Lucy leaned forward on her hands and knees to peek around the barrel. Her protector remained next to the depot door, single-handedly holding off multiple shooters. Every so often, he'd cast a fearful glance in her direction.

Her brother had written to her after he'd *seen the elephant* in his first battle. Courage wasn't the absence of fear, he'd told her. It came from doing what one had to do in spite of fear.

"That man, whoever he is, shows remarkable valor," she said.

The conductor murmured *aye* in reply.

"I shall write a story about him." She took a shuddering breath. "If I live long enough."

Three burly men in railroad denims, with rifles hoisted, dashed past her hiding place. They crouched next to the bearded man. A light hanging from a pole near the end of the building illuminated his rounded hat above the men around him. He made an easier target because of his height.

A few minutes passed. No more shots came from inside.

The tall man dared to look inside the door, then yelled, "They went out the other side."

All four men dashed to the end of the platform and trampled down a set of stairs. Lucy couldn't see past the corner of the building. In fact, she couldn't see much of anything beyond where the light shone.

Soon, more shouts. More shooting. Then, the gunfire stopped.

After a moment, so did the loud voices.

Her shaky legs gave out. She sank into a clump of skirts, then rested her head against the side of the barrel. Exhaled the breath she'd been holding. The poor conductor remained curled around his wounded side. His chest expanded, which let her know he still lived.

"I believe the shooting is over." Her voice sounded calm, considering the uncontrollable tremors in her limbs. "That gentleman who came to our rescue told us to wait here."

For once, she was content to obey.

An hour ago, she'd been seated in a stalled train, impatient, chomping at the bit, eager to reach her destination: Parsons, Kansas. Dubbed by newspapers as *The Infant Wonder of the West*. For weeks, she'd anticipated a great adventure, the kind of spine-tingling excitement heralded in her favorite books. Reality turned out to be grittier, bloodier, utterly terrifying.

At last, help arrived in the form of an engineer and a soot-stained fireman. They moved the conductor atop a door removed from its frame and carted him away. Another man in a railroad uniform ushered her into the interior of the depot, where she was reunited with her worried father, who'd picked up her satchel. They were instructed to wait with the rest of the passengers.

Her newfound hero hadn't returned. She tried not to be disappointed.

In the small, cold room, men spoke in comforting tones to their wives. Mothers shushed fretful children. Soon, more railroad workers arrived. One doled out blankets, another shoveled coal into a pot-bellied stove.

Squeezed onto a crowded bench, Lucy observed the proceedings with a strange sense of detachment. Odd, how close she'd felt to that brave man who'd shielded her. She didn't even know his name.

Her father gave her shoulder a comforting squeeze. Thus far, he hadn't fussed at her for putting herself in danger. No doubt he would, at a more opportune time. "If you are recovered," he said in a low voice, "I'll go ask where we can find Mr. Stevens."

Henry Stevens. The man her father had been sent to investigate. She'd forgotten all about him. She rubbed her forehead. Irritation flicked at her raw nerves. "Why isn't he here? He was supposed to meet us."

Her father didn't reply. The doubt on his face said enough. The Katy's general manager, reported to be a scoundrel, might also be a coward, who'd run at the first sign of danger. Unlike that courageous man who had risked his life to protect them.

Lucy hunched over, shivering. She hugged her cloak tighter. Normally, the cold didn't bother her. With family roots in New England, she came from hearty stock. She clamped her jaw shut to keep her teeth from rattling and stared at the ground. Capitola, the heroine in her favorite book *The Hidden Hand*, never fell apart.

A pair of shoes appeared in her line of vision. Congress-style, polished leather, caked with mud. "Miss?" His deep, cultured voice matched his shoes.

Her gaze followed gray trousers upward. The matching suit coat, drawn back over a holstered gun. A thrill shot through her. Her rescuer had returned.

He studied her with concern. "Are you all right?"

"I-I'm fine." Nervous, stammering, her mind blank as a chalkboard. One of the feathers adorning her bonnet drooped over her right eye. She brushed it aside, flushed with excitement, a flutter in her chest. "My hat could use some help."

His lips curved slightly at her poor joke. Oh, what fine lips they were. Well-shaped, firm, yet with a hint of softness. She didn't care much for facial hair. Surprisingly, this man's close-cropped beard didn't detract from his handsomeness. Neither did the mud, which had spattered all over his overcoat and trousers. Had he chased after their attackers, gotten filth flung at him by retreating hooves? Her imagination ran wild.

"Any other injuries?" he inquired solicitously.

"No, nothing."

"Good." He exhaled a sound of relief, then straightened to his impressive height. When he removed his hat, his dark hair stuck up every which way. She must've been staring because he hesitated, then smoothed his mussed hair.

How disarming, that this supremely confident man would experience a moment of self-consciousness. It made her feel less nervous.

"You're the young woman who went to the aid of Mr. Kelly?" he asked.

Lucy stood to get a better look at his eyes. Were they the same warm brown color as his hair? It was hard to tell in the dim light. She could see well enough to notice he now stared at her as intently as she stared at him. Then it struck her why. He waited for her answer.

"Mr. Kelly? Is he the conductor?"

"Yes. And you are?"

"Lucy." Her voice came out absurdly breathless. Her hand trembled as she offered it. She'd never been so giddy over a man. That might be because the ones she fancied were fantasy creations, heroes in books. This one might seem larger than life, yet he was *real*.

He appeared unaware of her stricken state when he grasped her fingers. "Lucy...?"

Her name on his lips sent shivers racing across her skin.

"This young lady is my daughter, *Miss Forbes*."

Her father chose the *most* inconvenient moment to reappear.

"Forbes?" Her rescuer's dark eyebrows winged upward. He released her fingers as if they'd caught fire. "*Major* Forbes?"

"Yes?" Her father's shoulders went back. Curt. Unsmiling.

15

Oh no. Other hopefuls had tried and failed to meet his lofty standards.

Lucy rushed to explain before her father could decide this potential suitor wasn't acceptable. "This gentleman came to my aid. He protected me at risk to his own life."

Her father's expression turned decidedly pleasanter. "Ah, I see. Please accept my thanks, sir, for assisting my daughter."

He returned her father's handshake. His gaze soon returned to her. She couldn't tear her eyes away from him, either. "Your daughter, Miss Forbes, should be congratulated. For her bravery."

Courageous, charming and humble. Why, he was nearly perfect.

She laid her hand over her rapidly beating heart, did her best to look dewy-eyed. "Me? I didn't do anything remarkable. But you, sir, you were very courageous to hold off those men who were shooting at us. Were they after money? Jewels?"

The low murmurs in the room died down as her question caught everyone's attention, which put a frown on her rescuer's face.

"I have no idea what they were after. We didn't catch them."

"Why did you let them get away?" blurted the salesman in a plaid suit, a loud, obnoxious fellow Lucy had met on the train.

"Were they bushwhackers?" a soldier sitting nearby chimed in.

"Train robbers?"

"Outlaws?

Passengers fired questions at the bearded gentleman, as if he had the all the answers.

Indeed, he looked and acted like someone in charge. He'd recognized her father's name, so he must work for the railroad. Only, he was wearing a suit, not a uniform or bib overalls common to the crews. He looked to be somewhere in his mid-thirties. Older than her brother would've been had he survived the war. Much younger than her father.

The answer came to Lucy in a flash. He had to be the general manager's *assistant.* His boss couldn't be bothered, so he'd sent his underling. A very handsome and capable underling.

He raised his arms in a gesture meant to soothe the nervous

passengers. "Stay calm, everyone. The attackers have fled. The sheriff is tracking them. You're safe here."

Lucy certainly felt safer with him around.

"Cots are being set up over at our new depot. We'll hand out blankets, food, whatever you need."

"What we *need* is to find our families." A grizzled man wearing a straw hat circled an arm around his plump, white-haired wife, who appeared pale and frightened.

"That's right. Our son said he'd meet us here," she added.

Other voices joined in, each filled with concern. They all wanted to know, as Lucy did, if anyone else had been around when the shooting started.

Her handsome rescuer smoothed his hand over his beard in a gesture that could indicate nervousness. Or it might be a tic. "We were told the train wouldn't arrive until morning. Our station master apparently sent everyone home. A slight miscommunication."

"Slight? I'd say more'n *slight*," someone grumbled.

"You sent them away?"

"Where've they gone?"

"How are we supposed to find them?"

As the passengers' fear subsided, anger took its place, all of it directed at the tallest man in the room. Someone ought to help him.

Lucy touched her father's arm to get his attention. She whispered in his ear. "I think that man must be the general manager's assistant. His boss certainly put him in an awkward spot."

Her father took her cue to step up. "Listen to me, all of you," he boomed. "I am Major Robert Forbes. I'm here on behalf of the Katy's board of directors. You'll be well taken care of. We'll get in touch with whomever you were meeting to let them know you're here..."

The waves of anger ebbed to a murmur, as her father continued.

"Those with wives and children will find lodging. We will spare no expense to see to your comfort. The Katy takes care of its customers." He emphasized that last bit.

Several people began to nod. Others smiled with relief.

How adroitly her father had handled the situation. He already looked and acted like a general manager or vice president. Lucy couldn't be prouder.

The man in the bowler hat didn't appear pleased. In fact, he was positively scowling, which made no sense at all. This confrontation could've turned ugly, if not for the intervention of a more experienced man.

He spoke to her father in a low tone, yet loud enough for her to hear the irritation in his voice. "Let me handle this."

"You?" Her father's frown telegraphed confusion. "Exactly *who* are you, son?"

The stranger drew up to his full height. Every taut line in his face and body conveyed supreme confidence. No, there was a better word: *arrogance.* "I am Henry Stevens, the general manager of this railroad."

Lucy gasped. "*You're* Henry Stevens?"

No, he couldn't be. She'd pictured Mr. Stevens as an older man, balding, with beady eyes and a round belly. Having never seen him in a photograph, she'd used her imagination.

His haughtiness softened as he looked at her. He dipped his chin in acknowledgement. "Indeed, Miss Forbes. Pardon me for not introducing myself earlier."

"Stevens." Her father extended his hand. "We have much to discuss."

The general manger gave her one last questioning glance before he focused his attention on her father, the investigator who'd come to town to topple him off his pedestal. "A carriage is waiting outside. I'm sure you and your daughter will be more comfortable at the hotel. I must see to our passengers. We will talk in the morning."

He turned on his heel and walked off.

Her father leaned over, while she stood there, still stunned. "Lucy, my dear. I believe we've been dismissed."

CHAPTER 3

*T*he next morning, Henry returned to the hotel, exhausted after an all-night search, and no closer to discovering the identities of the men who'd ambushed him.

The attackers had vanished into the mist. If their purpose had been to frighten him away from the upcoming negotiations, it hadn't worked. He was more determined than ever to resolve the railroad's land dispute with the settlers.

Over the past twelve hours, the only positive occurrence had been a change in the weather. Clear skies meant trains would be running on time, which meant the railroad might recoup what it had cost to put up twenty passengers in hotels, thanks to Major Forbes.

As Henry entered the hotel lobby, a bell jangled. His sister glanced up from behind the registration counter.

Her eyes lit with pleasure. "Good morning, Henry."

"Good morning, Claire."

His youngest sister had blossomed since he'd brought her and her invalid husband to Parsons. Claire had proved to be a smart, savvy businesswoman. Something Henry hadn't known about her, having not been around while she grew up. It pleased him to be able to help her get a fresh start. As an added benefit, he got to see her every day.

He rested his elbow on the smooth mahogany surface of the registration table, which he'd ordered from New York. He'd designed The Belmont House to resemble one of the finer hotels one might find back East. His personal rooms had been fashioned after the Presidential suite at the Fifth Avenue Hotel. The investigator should find his lodgings impressive. "Have you seen Major Forbes this morning?"

"He's dining with his daughter." Claire leaned over, smiling. "We served his favorite, as you asked. Hot cakes with sausages and fried potatoes."

"Excellent," Henry said dryly.

The investigator had turned out to be a washed-up former Erie Railroad officer, who'd been ousted amidst much speculation. Some time before that, Forbes had been honored for his heroism during the war. Must be why he held onto his rank like a badge of honor.

Henry had been a Union officer, too. Assigned to repair railroads. He'd been too busy working to find an opportunity to be a hero.

Forbes could be cowardly, cross-eyed and addled, and it wouldn't matter. He'd been sent by the directors.

Henry sighed. Until he managed to get rid of their inconvenient guest, he had to keep *the Major* happy.

Which meant crow would be on the menu for breakfast.

Claire squinted at the open registration book in front of her.

"Here, these might come in handy." Henry reached over to remove the spectacles perched on her head. She had a bad habit of leaving them there. "I didn't purchase these as hair decoration."

"Oh, I keep forgetting I have them," she said, absently. She moved her spectacles to the bridge of her nose. "The Major's daughter is very attractive."

"Is she? I hadn't noticed."

Claire's expression turned wry. His youngest sister wasn't one to play matchmaker. However, she did have a maternal streak, and had pointed out that his relationships tended to be rather short-lived.

Before another uncomfortable conversation ensued, he set off in the direction of the dining room. Despite what his sister thought, he wasn't opposed to settling down. Once he found the right woman.

His last association with his boss's daughter hadn't worked out because he'd misjudged her expectations. Affection, respect and loyalty weren't enough for Kate. She'd wanted more. Apparently, she'd found it.

He didn't expect, or even want, a love match. Too much risk involved. His criteria were simpler. She needed to have a good head on her shoulders, be willing to put up with his obsessive work habits, and not require heroics from him to be happy. It wouldn't hurt for her to be beautiful.

Lucy met at least one of those criteria, a fact he'd *noticed*. What man with good eyes and healthy urges wouldn't? Not only was she lovely and refined, she possessed more grit than the majority of the male gender.

Bravery aside, leaping off a train in the middle of a gun battle could've gotten her killed. Her ignorance could be forgiven. Her father ought to know better. One more example of Easterners out of touch with daily realities in the West.

Lucy and Major Forbes had selected a table by the window. They looked to be finishing their morning meal. She lifted the china cup with a graceful motion, as if she were in a sitting room, entertaining polished gents.

Henry quickly shrugged out of his overcoat, hung it next to his hat. He made an attempt to smooth his hair. Without oil, it looked perpetually mussed. Pomades made him sneeze. In this case, he chose comfort over control.

Major Forbes spotted him first and stood. He straightened his morning coat. The old fellow must think he was in New York where business decorum called for different suits, morning and evening. Out here, men didn't change clothes multiple times a day. They had neither the time nor money. Forbes wouldn't fit in, didn't belong. He'd be leaving soon.

Sadly, his lovely daughter would go with him.

"Good Morning, Mr. Stevens."

Henry took the older man's hand in a firm grip. "It is turning out to be a good morning. The sun is shining."

Lucy twisted in her chair. Her youthful beauty struck with the force of a glorious sunrise.

"You remember my daughter?"

Forbes couldn't think he'd forgotten.

Henry made a low bow to demonstrate his good manners. He'd been an ass yesterday after that shoot-out. Bellowed at her, called her father down, had been so flustered he'd forgotten introductions. He would repair the damage today. "Miss Forbes, I hope this morning finds you well rested, and recovered."

She tilted her head in a polite nod, which moved a mass of curls gathered back in a fashion that appeared careless, yet was anything but. The color wasn't light brown, as it looked in the dim light of the depot. More a golden tone, like the honey he spread on his toast each morning. In contrast, dark lashes made her eyes striking. Green or blue? He could spend hours deciding which color was dominant.

"And you, Mr. Stevens? I hope you are recovered." Lucy assessed him head to toe.

He resisted the urge to look down to see if there was mud on his trousers. He'd cleaned up at the office as best he could. Time hadn't allowed for him to change clothes. She might think he couldn't be bothered.

"Have a seat," Forbes offered. "Join us for breakfast."

"Thank you, I will." Henry took the chair next to Lucy.

"How are our passengers?" The Major inquired smoothly.

"We took care of those who needed rooms."

"Excellent. I hope I wasn't too presumptive in offering?"

"Not at all. The idea was a good one." Henry ate his serving of crow with a smile.

Lucy sipped her coffee, ignoring him without being obvious. He puzzled over it. Last night, she'd seemed, well, somewhat taken with him.

He rarely felt inept around women. With three sisters, he

understood the fairer sex better than most men. This didn't count the first two women he'd considered for marriage. He'd been misled on both counts. Perhaps, as Shakespeare's Falstaff had declared, *good luck lies in odd numbers.*

She wore a light, pleasing fragrance, unlike the heavy perfumes some women preferred. Possibly she took offense because he reeked of horses and mud.

"Any word on those scoundrels who shot up the depot?"

Henry jerked his attention back to the Major. "Nothing yet. The sheriff has interviewed some local farmers. That lot is as closed-mouthed as clams."

"Farmers?" Forbes rubbed his chin thoughtfully. "Do you think the attack has something to do with this legal wrangling over land rights?"

Henry had his suspicions. However, voicing concerns about rising hostilities between the Katy and local sodbusters would provide fodder for a negative report. "The government is behind us on the land issue."

"Haven't the settlers appealed to Congress?"

Well, well. Forbes had done his homework. Nevertheless, no need to involve him in local politics. Given the way he'd handled those irate passengers, he might offer unhappy farmers free passes for life.

Henry leaned back with his arms crossed. "We're neighbors with the Indians to the south. It's as likely they'd attack a train."

"Why would anyone attack a train at a depot in the middle of town? That seems incredibly stupid." Lucy set down her cup. "Unless they were after someone specific."

Henry stared at her with surprise. He hadn't thought she was paying attention. In fact, she listened a little too well. "The kind of men who attack trains aren't known for their quick intelligence, Miss Forbes."

He didn't remark on the target of the attack. Until he knew who and what he had to deal with, the less said, the better.

Lucy's expression reflected disappointment. Was it something he said? He didn't dare ask what bothered her. She might pose a question he couldn't afford to answer. He found lying distasteful, even when it was necessary.

The Major set his coffee cup on the edge of the table, where a white-coated waiter filled it. "The hotcakes are delicious."

"Coffee is fine, and toast," Henry told the waiter.

"Is that all you're eating?" Lucy sounded concerned. Women worried about things men didn't think twice about. Like how much food somebody else ate.

"A large breakfast takes too much time," he explained.

Her lips softened into a smile.

Perhaps Lucy's concern went deeper than a female's nurturing tendencies. A rush of hope took him by surprise.

"Have you seen Mr. Kelly?" she asked. "How is he doing?"

Henry released a breath that was almost a laugh. Lucy hadn't singled *him* out. She was simply a caring woman. Probably the kind that adopted stray puppies. Not to mention, she would be leaving soon and taking her soft heart with her. "The bullet went through his side. It didn't strike a vital organ. He asked me to convey his gratitude."

"I do hope he'll be all right."

A worry crease marred her brow. Henry restrained the urge to smooth it with his thumb.

"The doctor says he will be. He has to stay in bed for another week."

"Another week? The poor man won't be able to work."

"You needn't worry. I'll make sure he has enough to live on."

Forbes nodded his approval. "That's a good policy, Mr. Stevens."

Policy? It wasn't the policy of the Katy to pay men for not working. He supplemented the conductor's pay out of his own pocket, as he'd done with other workers who'd been injured in the line of duty. When he became president, he'd make it a *policy*.

In the meantime, he'd not admit to anything that would draw questions about the Katy's financial viability.

"It makes good business sense," he answered.

"Yes, it does." Her father leaned forward. "I'm very eager to hear more about your policies, take a look at your operation."

Henry buttered the toast the waiter had brought. He was *eager* to know more about what the investigator had been sent to ferret out. However, launching into a business discussion in front of a lady was downright rude. "Let's not bore your daughter with the dreary details. We'll have time to talk while we tour the facilities."

Lucy folded her napkin and placed it beside her plate. "I am not bored in the least."

"Afraid I'm at fault for that." Forbes appeared proud, rather than abashed. "Lucy has heard about the railroad business since she was old enough talk. Now, I can't keep her away from it. She's become something of an expert."

Not only was the beautiful Miss Forbes courageous, she was knowledgeable about industry. With each revelation, she became more fascinating.

Henry knew only one other female interested in the business end of a railroad. Judge Parsons' daughter, Kate. That's where the resemblance ended. The eccentric railroad heiress wore bloomers and wouldn't take time to dress her hair. She had, at one time, wanted to gain control of her father's railroad to advance her causes. What was Lucy's story?

"Do you have a special interest in the railroad, Miss Forbes?"

"I'm interested in a great many things." She slid a curious glance out of the side of her eyes.

Henry wiped around his mouth, careful not to leave behind crumbs. For some reason, he felt mildly self-conscious...around a woman who looked to be barely out of short skirts. *No*, that wasn't fair. She had too much poise to be called a child. "Will you accompany your father on the tour today?"

She beamed at him. "I'd love to come along."

Perhaps he'd been too hasty with the offer. She could become a distraction. He'd hardly been able to pay attention to the investigator, a man who could upset his plans for the future.

"If the Major doesn't mind." Henry opened the door for her father to decline, which he expected.

"I don't mind. If you think it's safe."

Was this a test? He could hardly say no, which implied he couldn't provide for their safety. On the other hand, if someone tried to attack him again, it would endanger Lucy and bring on an investigation that would make the current one look like child's play.

He gave an answer that could be taken either way. "I've stationed extra guards."

"Good! That should be sufficient." Lucy scooted back her chair. "I'll go fetch my cape and bag, if you'll excuse me."

Henry took her hand to help her stand. The warm press of her fingers on his palm triggered a jolt of desire. Her eyes flashed up. Had she felt it, too?

"Thank you...Mr. Stevens."

Their hands were held together by magnets. Or so it seemed.

"Call me Henry."

Her blue-green eyes widened.

Warmth crept up the back of his neck at his blunder. He'd better have a good explanation for suggesting they become familiar after such a short acquaintance. "We aren't so formal out here."

"Oh. Then you should call me Lucy." Her dark lashes shielded her gaze as she looked down at their clasped hands.

He released her fingers before he embarrassed himself further.

As she left the room, her bustled skirt swayed with the gentle movement of her hips. His heart raced as if he'd walked too fast, when he hadn't moved a muscle. He couldn't recall having such an intense reaction to a woman he'd just met. He'd be troubled if he weren't entranced.

"Thank you for including my daughter. I know she's appreciative of your kindness."

Henry tore his attention away from her alluring form. Forbes couldn't believe *kindness* was the motive. "My pleasure."

A pleasure indeed, to share her company for a few hours. In fact, she might even turn out to be useful. Women didn't guard their words as carefully as men. Their conversations meandered through various topics, upon occasion they relayed something interesting. Lucy had special knowledge of the railroad and her father's confidences. She might let some valuable tidbit slip.

The Major checked his watch. "We can meet in the lobby. Say, half an hour?"

"See you then." Henry shook hands, still mulling over the odd remark about his *kindness*. The investigator couldn't be as trusting as he appeared. It had to be a trap.

"Oh, I almost forgot." Forbes reached inside his coat. "Here's a letter that explains what the board expects. It should clear things up, make my time here more productive."

Henry waited until Forbes had walked away to unfold the pages. He couldn't believe the old fellow had given him what he wanted. Finally, he'd learn what the directors were after.

He scanned for the important parts. *Investigate the condition of the line...* He'd expected that. *Review the books...* Tricky. He could manage.

Near the end, a line leapt out at him.

Major Forbes shall have full authority to make any and all decisions he deems necessary to improve operations. Henry reread it, first with disbelief, then outrage.

Inside his chest, a fire began to burn. Now, it was clear what the directors intended. They thought to replace him. Those dandified Easterners had *no idea* what it took to build a railroad out west. After he'd done it, and dirtied his hands in the process, they wanted him gone—and they had waited until his boss was out of the country to make their move.

He crushed the letter in his fist. By God, he'd poured *everything* into the Katy. All his energy, most of his resources. He'd even burned through his honor to achieve his dreams. *No, not dreams.* His father had dreamed, fat lot of good that'd done. *He* had planned. Meticulously. Now, this *Major* Forbes, a discard from the Erie, thought he could come out here, hand over a letter and take everything away. Snow would fall in Hell before that happened.

What about Lucy?

Henry's ears heated. God save him from scheming females. Was she as fickle as Lila, or conniving, like Kate? He hadn't been rich enough for one. The other had used him to get the man she wanted. Whatever Lucy's motives, he would not blindly walk into an ambush.

He stormed out of the dining room and took the stairs two at a time. He'd go to his room, get cleaned up. be back in the lobby on time, looking refreshed and not the least bit ruffled.

The best strategy would be to play along with the investigation, learn what he could about the Major. Every man, even so-called *honorable gentlemen*, had a weakness that could be exploited. Forbes was no different.

CHAPTER 4

"*A*re you ready, Lucy?" Her father looked up from where he sat, relaxed in an armchair, reading the newspaper while he waited on her.

"Yes, nearly ready...." She grasped the tassel that dangled from the muslin curtain to roll the shade up. Their room had a nice view of the town. It must be another advantage of her father's new position to have been given the best suite.

The sky was clear, the sun shining. Today would be warmer. She'd take her short cape. Come to think of it, she might be better off with armor, considering how easily Henry Stevens had breached her defenses. The thought nearly spoiled her good mood.

"Says here," her father read, "*the land around Parsons is rich and beautiful, with broad, fertile valleys and high undulating plains, replete with magnificent farms and happy homes.*"

"Oh, look! Covered wagons! I see a long line coming down the street."

The newspaper rustled as he turned the page.

She glanced over her shoulder. "Honestly, Papa. How can you *not* be excited? This is the wild frontier. Indian Territory isn't far. We could see natives today, vast herds of buffalo."

He folded the paper and set it aside. "For that, we'll have to leave town."

Pragmatic Bostonian.

Even if he didn't intend to kill her joy, he could show a bit more enthusiasm. He knew she'd waited a long time for this adventure. Her responsibility to him had kept her home instead of pursuing her dreams. Not that she would change a single decision. He'd needed her. Now, in his new position, he wouldn't need her as much. She could make a life for herself, out here.

He checked his pocket watch. "It's time to meet Mr. Stevens."

Her heart fluttered in anticipation. Foolish thing. It would be far easier to dislike the general manager if he looked like a villain. Much less confusing if he'd act like one.

According to the accounts she'd read about him, Henry Stevens possessed a raging ambition. He was reputed to be manipulative, demanding, and unforgiving of those who had wronged him. The man she'd met had shown great courage when he'd fended off those attackers. This morning, he had come over to greet them after it was obvious that he'd been up all night. She would've been a bear. Yet, he'd been engaging and friendly. Her heart beat faster as she recalled *how* friendly.

Lucy whirled away from the window, determined to snuff out her fascination with the Katy's general manager. This wasn't the time to get dreamy about a man. In particular, *that* man. As Eve had discovered, even serpents could be charming upon occasion.

"The railroad has provided us with a fine suite," her father remarked.

"The room is more pleasant than I expected." Its furnishings were similar to the rosewood furniture and Brussels carpets they'd sold to make ends meet. "I'm sure Mr. Stevens hopes to put you in a pleasant frame of mind, so you'll write a glowing report.

Lucy stopped in front of a full-length mirror mounted on the back of a hall tree near the door. She tried on her new bonnet—a short-brimmed Bébé style that was all the rage back home. She tied the silk ribbon to one side and eyed the effect.

Goodness, she loved hats. Wearing them. Not making them. Aunt Josephine despaired of ever teaching her how to make a proper hat. Her dear aunt had made this one for her, as well as providing her with a new traveling suit. She would repay the favor as soon she sold her stories.

Her father's reflection came into view. A faint smile teased his lips.

"What do you find so amusing?"

"You don't want to like Mr. Stevens, but you do."

She refused to admit any such thing. "I don't trust him."

Her dear *Papa* shrugged into his overcoat. "It's best not to judge a man untrustworthy until he shows himself to be. That's how I like to be treated."

"If other men had your integrity, I would agree. They don't."

Silver-tongued devils like Henry Stevens had destroyed her father's illustrious career and nearly broken his spirit. After living through that hell, she would find it difficult, if not impossible, to give her trust to an ambitious man.

She lifted her father's top hat off the brass hook, unable to ignore a twinge of worry. He'd grown thin over the past year, more apt to become ill. "You need to keep your head warm. Can't start a new job with the ague."

He combed his fingers through strands of white hair that had once been the color of wheat, then secured his top hat with a firm tap. "Nor should my daughter catch a chill. Put on your cloak."

She had plenty of layers beneath her dress, wasn't prone to chills. "My cape will be sufficient."

"As I recall, you promised to be dutiful on this trip."

"I agreed not to find trouble. There's a difference." She tucked a scarf around his neck. "Did you get the impression Mr. Stevens wished to avoid questions about those men who attacked the train?"

"He doesn't have answers yet."

"Or doesn't want to share them."

"Naturally, he's concerned about my intentions. I gave him the letter from the directors."

She looked up into her father's placid gaze. The new spectacles made his blue eyes appear larger, more trusting. "Do you think it's wise to be straightforward so soon? Now, he'll know you're here to replace him."

"I am here to conduct an investigation."

"And to put your recommendations into effect, which means—"

"Nothing."

"Nothing?" She shook her head in disbelief. "It means *everything*. I'm sure they'll soon announce your appointment to general manager."

"They already have a general manager. Henry Stevens."

"Who's angered the board with his high-handed ways—" Lucy propped her hands on her hips, becoming annoyed. "You said yourself Mr. Stevens is likely to be ousted."

"I shouldn't have told you that." Her father wagged his head, seeming to admonish himself more than her. "I'm not interested in pushing anyone out."

She'd push the angel Gabriel over a cliff, if it would save her father, so she had few qualms about giving the nudge to a mere mortal. "I know you'll do the right thing," she said demurely. "You always do."

Sadness pulled at her father's features. "That is why I intend to be honest. I have been in a similar position as Mr. Stevens."

"Similar?" She huffed in disbelief. "You didn't bribe anybody."

"Some say I did worse."

His point pricked her conscience. Her father had been ruined by rumors more than his own mistakes. "I understand what you're saying. The board's suspicions about Mr. Stevens have yet to be proved. Smoke usually means there's fire. He's ambitious, like those men who ruined you. Even if he appears to be a gentleman."

"A gentleman?" Her father's eyes gleamed. "Why, I believe you've made progress."

"This isn't funny. I'm very serious."

"Don't fear that I'm gullible, Lucy. I know what I'm doing."

"Which is?"

"Giving Mr. Stevens the opportunity to be trustworthy."

She worried her lip as she drew on her cape and fastened the frog closure. "He strikes me as a clever man. How will you know if he isn't acting honorably?"

"I suspect *you* will tell me."

The tight knot in her chest eased. At last, he was teasing her again. Over the past year, he'd found nothing amusing. In fact, during those long, dark days, it seemed he'd felt nothing at all. Grief had crushed him. First, Robbie's death, then *Maman's*, then he'd suffered that disgraceful dismissal from the railroad he'd served so faithfully and so well. The unfairness of it all ate at her. Even if her father had forgiven his betrayers, she couldn't.

Then, through his contacts with an old friend, their fortunes had improved. They'd sold the remnants of their old life, packed away their disappointments and headed West. If the station in Boston gave any indication, the whole country was on the move, aided by the ever-expanding railroads. These were, as Dickens had so aptly penned, *the best of times.*

Lucy felt certain *the worst of times* were behind them. Her father had landed a permanent position, even if he was being bull-headed about admitting it. She didn't have to put her life on hold any longer. She could start *living* adventures instead of reading about them.

She smoothed her hands over the sky-blue taffeta skirt with silk ribbons drawn up to reveal lacy petticoats beneath. Perhaps something less frivolous would've been a better choice.

With a low huff, she turned away from the mirror. She had no desire to impress Henry Stevens, didn't care to be around him, would much rather explore town for ideas she could write about. Except, she needed to make sure Henry Stevens acted honorably. How could she do that if she didn't get to know him?

"After our tour, I think I'll visit the shops." That would accomplish two objectives, doing research on her story and Mr. Stevens.

Her father opened the door. "Don't go out alone."

"I won't be alone in a town full of people."

"There was a shoot-out in the middle of a town full of people."

"It was a deserted depot before our train showed up." Lucy swept past him into the hall. "I don't imagine I'll be gunned down in the street. Parsons looks quite civilized."

He tucked her hand into the crook of his elbow. "Even if it's safe, you're a single young lady. You need a chaperone."

She patted his arm to reassure him. "I've been going out on my own for some time now. I don't need a chaperone."

His pace slowed as they approached the stairs. "Lucy, I realize these past five years have been difficult for you. I've fallen down on my duties as provider and protector. Rest assured, I won't let you down again."

"No, never!" She rushed to reassure him. "You have *not* let me down."

If anything, she had let her father down. Before, she hadn't known how to help. She'd been too young, too naïve. Now, she knew better. Just as her favorite heroine had outfoxed a wily villain, she would discover Mr. Stevens' secrets—and expose him.

THE GENERAL MANAGER waited in the lobby for them. He was turned to one side at the front window, looking out at something. Or plotting his next move. He'd changed into fresh clothes: a square-cut chocolate-brown coat, matching stovepipe trousers, well suited to his lean build. With his hands crossed behind him, shoulders squared, feet braced, he appeared as confident as a captain on the deck of his ship. *No.* Arrogant.

Lucy smiled at having landed on a perfect description. She wasn't at all attracted to arrogant men.

A hint of anger hardened Mr. Stevens' profile. As her father hailed him, he turned, smoothing his features into pleasantness.

It was an act.

She could do that, too. Present a friendly face, while remaining cautiously alert for any signs of dishonorable behavior.

"Major. Miss Forbes...Lucy," He amended, with a slight bow.

His rich bass vibrated through her. *Drat.* Apparently, he didn't even have to touch her. Simply speaking had the same effect.

"Mr. Stevens." She couldn't bring herself to use his given name. It seemed too familiar, in spite of what he'd explained about the region's informality. "You look..." She almost said *handsome.* Only a featherbrain blurted out her admiration. He flustered her because he was too polished, too smooth. Her father's enemies had been like that.

"You are prompt."

"I am prepared to meet the day." His gaze hung on her, almost as if he'd read her mind.

Perish the thought.

Her father peered out the window. "The weather looks nice enough to walk. Isn't the depot at the end of the street?"

"It is, but why trudge through the mud?" Henry replied. "I've arranged for a carriage."

Last night he hadn't been so fussy about his clothes. If he'd hired the carriage on her behalf, she wished he hadn't. Then she wouldn't have to feel bad for thinking ill of him.

He reached for her satchel.

"No, thank you. I'll keep this." She'd brought along her weapons. A notebook and pencil with which to jot down observations. Villains ultimately gave themselves away.

"Henry, wait," a female voice trilled. The dark-haired proprietor of the hotel approached him with an adoring smile on her face. Wasn't she *married*?

"Yes, Claire? What is it?" Henry's tone revealed he didn't mind the interruption.

Also, did everyone around here use given names? Or did this imply she and Henry were close? She certainly stood close to him.

"Would you mind posting this letter?" she asked.

"Not at all." Henry took the envelope. He tucked it inside his coat, returning her smile with affection. It was downright inappropriate.

Lucy caught her breath. What did she care if he knew every woman in town and told them all to call him *Henry*? She wouldn't fall for the bounder.

"Miss Forbes, do you enjoy the view from your room?" Mrs. Daines inquired.

Lucy put on her polite face. "Father and I were talking about how much we like the suite. The furnishings are beautiful."

The proprietor returned an adoring gaze to *Henry*. "My brother has excellent taste. I've asked him to pick out new furniture for our suite, as well."

Brother?

Lucy looked to Henry in astonishment. He'd said nothing last night about being related to the hotel proprietor. He also hadn't mentioned anything about giving up his lodgings. How considerate. No! How *clever* of him to put her father under obligation. She must not underestimate an ambitious man, especially one whose future was threatened.

"Yes, it is a lovely room. We don't wish to impose—"

"It doesn't matter." He cut her off before she could finish speaking.

Her father, who'd solemnly observed the proceedings, broke in. "Of course it matters. No need to put you out of your rooms."

"I'm comfortable in another room. Your daughter needs the extra space."

How much *space* did he think she required?

"We can make do with another suite," she said firmly.

"There isn't another suite with two bedrooms. Shall we go?" His curt response ended the argument. That, and his abrupt gesture toward the door.

She had no choice except to back down. This time. "Yes, well, thank you for your kindness."

"Kindness has nothing to do with it," he said under his breath, as she sailed past.

Her suspicions were confirmed, which was just as well. She didn't want his kindness. She didn't want any reason to like him.

Henry swung open the front door. He followed her outside. When he slipped his hand beneath her elbow, Lucy shivered. From fear or cold. Or nerves. She'd never played the role of a spy. It would take practice.

He assisted her into the carriage, allowed her father to slip past him, then ducked in and took the seat across from them. She arranged her skirts to make room for his long legs and ensure their feet wouldn't touch. His body gave off a surprising current.

Instead of conversing politely, he stared out the window. How very different from the charming man she'd met earlier. Did he resent her now that he knew her father's intentions?

She couldn't blame him if he did, and—blast it—couldn't help feeling bad about it. Mr. Stevens might deserve to be dismissed, but she's seen first-hand what that kind of humiliation did to a man, especially a proud one.

As the carriage lurched and started off, she turned her attention outside to occupy her mind with anything other than Henry Stevens.

Attractive false fronts adorned nearly every establishment. The buildings were lined up in rows connected by broad sidewalks. Very neat, quite organized, as if someone had planned it down to the last detail.

In contrast, the muddy street hosted chaos. Crowded in between covered wagons were cowboys on horseback, vendors pushing carts, railroaders with their tools riding to work in the back of a buckboard. Men. Everywhere. Far more than one might find in towns back east, where the civil war had taken its greatest toll on the male population. The few women visible appeared to be farmers' wives, with their calico dresses and massive sunbonnets. They hurried from store to store, rushed along by the chilly wind.

Lucy set aside her concerns for the moment to focus on enjoying the adventure. Thus far, it was more exciting than she'd imagined. This was only the beginning. Like the overture of an opera. Scenes to come promised to be even more thrilling.

She put her nose near the opening at the top of the window. Took a deep breath. The air smelled of earth and fresh-cut pine—perhaps from those boards being used to build a new structure across the street. The carriage horses' jangling harnesses accompanied the rhythmic pounding of hammers.

Parsons had a raw, vibrant energy Haverhill lacked. The small New England village had offered no prospects for work, even fewer for marriage. She had no reason to return to a place where the most exciting event was the arrival of mail from somewhere else. Her future was out here, and she couldn't wait for it to begin.

Filled with fresh vitality, she retrieved the journal from her satchel. Mr. Stevens had said nothing of interest, so she might as well use the time to capture some ideas for a new story.

"Scribbling again, Lucy?" Her father winked.

He meant no insult. Yet, he didn't take her desire to become an author seriously. In fact, he would disapprove if he knew she intended to use her earnings to supplement their income. Thus far, no one had purchased anything she'd written. Sadly, if they had to rely on her ability to support them, she would have to go back to making hats.

She replied, lighthearted. "You know me. I always have my pen and journal handy."

Henry's speculative gaze hung on her, sending skitters of awareness across her skin. Heavens, he unnerved her. The sort of reaction a fly might have to a spider.

"Where are we off to this morning?" her father asked.

Henry retrieved a small notebook from an inside pocket. He referred to it. "The roundhouse first, then the rail yard. We'll return to the depot by noon. I've instructed my assistant to have luncheon served in my office..."

While he ticked off the activities on his list, she took the opportunity to study him. One could tell quite a lot about a person by observing the small things. In order to help her father, she needed to analyze Henry Stevens, much as she would a character in a book.

The hat he'd placed beside him was one of the newer styles with a short brim and rounded crown. Called *bowlers*, they were coming into popularity, especially out West. He'd turned his collar down over a thin black cravat tied in a bow. His tawny waistcoat sported notched lapels. Overall, his style of dress indicated a modern mindset. Someone who insisted on being at the forefront of progress, if not ahead of the crowd.

He'd slid into a slouch. Otherwise his head would brush the top of the carriage. One knee bobbed. When it stopped, his fingers drummed the leather seat. Impatient. Or bursting with energy, like her brother. Robbie had nearly driven *Maman* mad. He'd never been able to sit quietly and read. Focusing for hours on paperwork would be an agony for someone like that. It must be why Mr. Stevens required an assistant.

In the daylight, his hair looked as glossy brown as a chestnut. It wasn't curly, though it had a definite mind of its own. He'd smooth it over, then several strands would spring up. Then he'd frown. Apparently, he couldn't control his hair as easily as he could his schedule.

For some reason, she found his battle touching. Probably because she understood his frustration. She'd been fighting Nature ever since it had decreed that she would be born a woman with a man's thirst for adventure. Not that there was anything wrong with being female, no more than there was anything wrong with Henry's rebellious hair.

His face had a pleasing symmetry. Broad forehead, straight nose, a strong jaw, what she could see of it. His neatly trimmed beard looked to be a shade darker than his hair, as were his eyebrows, which could lift independent of each other—as one did now, when he glanced up from his notebook.

She straightened with a casual smile. "Sounds like a full day, Mr. Stevens. I'm sure I'll be interested in seeing everything. It's been an exciting experience thus far." Lucy's cheeks heated at being caught. Heaven forbid she give him the impression she found him fascinating.

"Perhaps a bit *too* exciting," her father added.

"Keep in mind, much of Kansas is still untamed frontier." Their host shifted on the seat to draw his coat over the handle of a very large revolver tucked into a holster.

She didn't miss his point. Fair warning or scare tactics? He would certainly like to see them run home like frightened rabbits. Maybe he was the one frightened, if he felt a constant need for protection. "Do you always wear a sidearm?"

He didn't blink. "All railroad employees are armed. Our line runs through Indian Territory. The natives aren't fond of the railroad. Then, there's the rough sort that show up at every terminus, and the outlaws."

"Outlaws?" Lucy's heart beat faster. She'd like to see one. From a distance. Only if she was well-armed. "I should look into acquiring a weapon."

"That's not necessary."

Her father's objection didn't surprise her.

"It is, if she plans to travel with you along the rail line."

Henry approved of women using firearms? How progressive.

"It sounds practical to me." She made a note to look into it, settled back against the cushioned seat and held her journal in her lap.

"Don't worry, Miss Forbes. I have a firearm today, should we need it." His gaze drifted from her face downward.

Her unmentionable parts tingled. She flushed while attempting to focus on what he said, rather than the place he looked—at her bosom—or perhaps, her notebook. "Do you expect trouble from those men who attacked the depot?"

"Those cowards wouldn't dare show themselves in daylight. They prefer to sneak up on people in dark places."

The platform had been lit.

Lucy scoured her memories. Henry had been holding off the gunmen when the passengers disembarked. The waiting room had been dark, deserted. Her breath caught as she realized what it meant. "Did they sneak up on you?"

His gaze jerked up at the same time his expression went flat. She had her answer. They hadn't gunned for the train or its passengers. Henry *did* fear for his safety. He wished to hide the reason.

Wild scenarios whirled through her mind. Robbers, assassins, someone out for revenge. Questions perched on the tip of her tongue. Her father spoke up first.

"Mr. Stevens, is there something we ought to know that you're not telling us?"

CHAPTER 5

*H*enry smoothed a hand over his beard to hide a frown. Even after making a colossal blunder, he couldn't tear his attention away from the enticing curves beneath Lucy's tight-fitting jacket. This was what lust did to the male mind. Leeched the blood, destroyed its ability to reason. He'd better start using his brain for the proper purpose if he wanted to protect his job.

"There isn't much to tell. Four men were at the old depot when I arrived. I asked what they wanted. Someone cocked a gun. I didn't wait around to ask more questions."

Lucy and her father exchanged troubled glances.

Henry could only guess at what they were thinking—none of it good. He would keep his explanations short to avoid getting tangled in deceptions.

"What reason would they have to fire on you?" Forbes asked.

Henry offered the best theory he could come up with. "I suspect the attack was meant to scare me. They hit the conductor by mistake."

"You drew fire toward the train?" Lucy's disenchantment made him feel ten inches tall.

He'd never been accused of cowardice. Though, to his shame, he couldn't refute her charge. He had done as she said, however unwittingly.

The implications triggered a jolt of alarm. Good God, he couldn't have them believe he would expose them to danger. He had played up the town's wild image in a calculated move intended to worry Forbes enough to take his daughter home. The strategy had backfired, thanks to Lucy.

Henry retrenched. "Rest assured, I won't put you in harm's way."

Her frown turned doubtful. "You aren't worried for your life?"

Hell yes, he was worried. "I'm saying *you* needn't be."

"How can you tell us not to worry when someone is trying to kill you?"

She talked in circles. Or was he the one confused? Strong perfumes gave him headaches. Her faint floral fragrance didn't have the same effect, wasn't at all abrasive. It might have an adverse effect on his mental functions.

"My personal safety isn't at issue. As I said, this is still wild country. Last week, one of our crews had to fight off a robbery."

The Major's brows descended. "Your trains are regularly set upon by outlaws?"

Henry rubbed his temple. *Now* his head hurt. "A band of renegade Indians."

"Marauding savages?" Lucy exclaimed.

Henry shifted back in the seat with crossed arms. A young woman who made circular arguments and was prone to hyperbole would not best him. "A few hungry braves. On ponies."

Her father's expression turned stormy. "I can send the President a telegram, ask him to assign more troops to calm things down."

"Mr. Parsons has no power over the army," Henry reminded him, in case he'd forgotten.

"President Grant does."

The Major's connections went all the way to the top.

Henry fought a surge of panic. At one time, he'd applied the Johnson brake to stop an out-of-control train. He could certainly curtail a runaway conversation. "The situation isn't out of control. What happened yesterday is one uncommon incident."

Lucy cocked her head like a curious bird. "Didn't you say things like that happen all the time?"

Damn. Tripped on a technicality.

Henry took a firm hold on the controls. He would not be derailed. "You mistake my meaning, Miss Forbes. We aren't dealing with an Indian uprising or an outlaw army. It's a few scoundrels who want to make trouble. The sheriff has rounded up a posse to search for them. I trust he'll do his job. No need to stir up a ruckus."

"Who do you suppose would have a good reason to *stir up a ruckus*? The angry farmers you mentioned this morning at breakfast?" Her blue-green eyes were her best feature, out of a number of excellent features. When she opened them wide like that, she appeared so damned innocent. Not at all like someone plotting his downfall.

Had her father put her up to it?

Forbes leaned forward with a rapt expression. Up to now, he'd seemed content to let his daughter lead the questioning. Women weren't typically encouraged to be outspoken, although they tended to be cleverer—if not outright smarter—than men. Lucy, it appeared, topped the list.

Henry couldn't help admiring her sharp intelligence. Despite his being skewered with it. Repeatedly. "Not all farmers are angry."

He'd put a corrective plan into action. Blame it on politics. "Radical elements among the settlers have vandalized our tracks. They harass every railroad. Use any excuse to cause more trouble."

He could almost see the wheels turning as Lucy considered his answer.

"You mean the Grange Movement. I thought they were a lobbying organization. You're saying they're armed vigilantes?"

Her tendency for hyperbole could wreck his efforts to control the damage.

"A *few* radical members," he emphasized, "not the whole organization. The Grange isn't made up of gunslingers. If the newspapers start printing rumors like that, we'll have a riot on our hands. That's why we need to keep this to ourselves. Until the attackers are found and we can figure out who they are and what they want."

"That's wise," Forbes said.

Henry released a relieved sigh. Based on Lucy's preference for verbal wrangling, he'd expected to work harder to convince her father. "You agree, sir?"

"I do. Why speculate? Once we know more, we can make a full report." The Major laced his fingers in his lap in a posture of openness and acceptance.

Very suspicious.

Then, there was Lucy's sudden silence. She'd been firing faster than a repeating rifle. Now, she had nothing to say.

Henry put the same question to her. "And you, Lucy, do you agree?"

"To what? Your request that we keep silent about an attack on a railroad official?"

How was it possible? She looked like an angel, yet argued like a New England lawyer. No wonder Forbes had brought her along. She had a knack for making men—even intelligent ones—sound like blathering idiots.

"Let me clarify. Everyone already knows about the attack. Do you agree not to spread *rumors* about the gunmen being members of the Grange?"

Her brow furrowed.

Henry braced for another question.

"I don't spread rumors."

"That's good to hear." He rested back against the seat, relieved. He hadn't regained full control, but he no longer felt like he was hogtied to the engine of a runaway train.

Soon, the carriage began to sway. They'd left the main road for a rocky path leading to the rail yard. Their ride would get bumpy from here.

"You should hold the handrail—"

The carriage lurched. Lucy flew off her seat.

Henry reacted instinctively to catch her. She clutched his coat, stared up at him, flushed and open-mouthed with surprise. Her scent wafted up, delicate, enticing.

Every muscle in his body tightened.

He put her away from him before he gave himself away. She'd already accused him of being a coward. He didn't want her to decry him as a lecherous old man, too.

Her father scooted over to help her. "Lucy, dear. Are you hurt?"

"No, I-I..." Her throat worked. Nothing more came out.

Henry didn't trust his voice, either. Tense, he slid back onto the seat. Had the spill been intentional? She might intend to entrap him with a seductive lure.

Lucy busied herself with rummaging through her bag. Her hands shook as she put away the notebook she'd been scribbling in earlier. Her initial flush and the remaining high color in her cheeks couldn't be faked. Their brief contact had rattled her, too.

She kept herself busy with arranging her skirts. Slid a worried look out of the side of her eyes. Nothing coy about that. She hadn't dressed like a temptress, not with that jacket buttoned up to her chin and the cape wrapped around her, as if to ward off Arctic air.

"Thank you," she said softly. "For your kind assistance."

There was that word again. *Kind.* He couldn't think of any word to characterize him that would be further from the truth. He'd left kindness behind somewhere between starvation and poverty.

"Any gentleman would do the same." He bent over to retrieve her satchel from the floor. It looked more like a carpetbag. Heavy, too. When he set it beside her, he took care not to touch her. Best not tempt lightning.

She dragged the bag into her lap and hugged it, while regarding him with a troubled expression. Half the journey, she'd interrogated him, the other half, she'd stared at him. Not what he'd expect from a scheming female. He got the distinct impression she found him as hard to figure out.

A wry smile tugged at his lips. Hers answered in kind. They sat there staring at each other like besotted fools.

Henry's mind tripped over the obvious. He'd misread her intentions. Suspicion was to be expected, given her father's role as investigator. Lucy was a bright young woman. She was also innocent and naïve. Not hardened by life, as he was.

Forbes' stern gaze softened as it turned on his daughter. He put his hand on her arm, protectively. "Are you all right?"

Lucy gave a sharp nod. "Of course. It was only a rock."

That wasn't what her father meant based on the severe look he turned on Henry. He didn't act as if he'd encouraged his daughter to use her feminine wiles. In fact, he seemed more inclined to reach for a shotgun.

No one could blame him. Out here where men outnumbered women ten to one, even homely girls had an abundance of suitors. A beautiful woman like Lucy would be a prize that men would fight over. Steal, if they had to.

What if he stole Lucy first?

Henry restrained a smile. Pursue his rival's daughter? He had to admit, the idea tempted him. She might turn out to be the chink in the Major's armor, his weak spot. If an ambitious man wed her, he would have influence with her well-connected father.

Exploit a young woman? An attack of conscience took Henry off guard. He had never stooped so low.

Marriage wasn't exploitation or abuse. He'd honor her, pamper her, give her children and a nice home, the things women wanted. Based on her reactions, the attraction was mutual, so that didn't pose a problem.

This idea had potential. After all, he intended to wed sometime. He wouldn't easily find another woman like Lucy. Besides being an advantageous match, she had the rare combination of intelligence, beauty and spunk. If he won her affections then turned her feminine power to his advantage, he'd be unstoppable.

An inner voice counseled caution. He'd been betrayed and rejected—twice.

Those plans hadn't worked out because he'd selected mature women with hidden agendas. Young Lucy couldn't have much experience with scheming. Her only agenda appeared to be based on loyalty. He respected her for that. After they married, she'd naturally transfer her loyalty to him, and he would be loyal in return.

Henry banished his doubt. Indecision had never gotten him anywhere. He'd advanced by taking chances some considered insane. He could take a calculated risk with his future and pursue Lucy. It wasn't as if he'd be risking his heart. It remained right where he'd put it—tucked away, safe, untouchable. That was one thing he wouldn't give her.

CHAPTER 6

*T*he rumble and roar of cars being moved in the nearby rail yard greeted Lucy as she exited the carriage. Over in an open field, a massive stone structure towered several stories high. The circular building, with its arched entryways, resembled illustrations she'd seen of the Roman Coliseum. Only, this coliseum had railroad tracks leading into it.

"That's the roundhouse?" she asked.

"Awe inspiring, isn't it? Our president, Mr. Parsons, specified the design." Henry reached up to assist her off the step.

The shivers started again. She couldn't blame the cold this time. The same alarming reaction had occurred when she'd been tossed into his arms. Her body had quivered like a divining rod held close to the source of its energy. The sensation both horrified and fascinated her because she'd never experienced it before.

Henry's set features didn't give away his thoughts. However, the look in his eyes reminded her of smoldering embers about to burst into flames.

She released his hand then moved a safe distance away to wait for her father. It had to be snuffed out, this unwelcome attraction. Even if Mr. Stevens turned out to be a man she would consider as a suitor—

which he wasn't—her father had been sent out here to investigate the general manager's handling of the railroad, to ultimately replace him. To allow herself to be caught between them would be foolish. Dangerous. Her role in this threesome was to observe and learn what she could to help her father.

Henry offered her his arm.

She hesitated, recalling her reaction to their previous contact.

"The ground is uneven," he pointed out.

Sure enough, construction debris was scattered across the open field. He was being polite. She was acting like a ninny.

She curled her fingers around his forearm. His muscles tensed, which wasn't something she ought to notice. Neither was the pleasure she derived from touching him.

"Let's start with the roundhouse. It's nearly completed." Henry secured his hat. He matched his longer strides to a pace comfortable for her.

She allowed he could be considerate—as well as secretive and slippery.

Her father, who walked along on the other side, wore a thoughtful frown. Did he fear she would encourage Henry's attentions? She should've refused his offer, sought her father's arm instead. If she did that now, it would be unforgivably rude.

"What type of stone did you use for the construction?" her father asked Henry.

"Blue limestone for the walls, white limestone for the arches, same as what we used around the windows in the new depot. All of it quarried nearby. Much cheaper than brick."

"Smart decision."

"I know. I made it."

Lucy swallowed a laugh. *Overweening.* Henry's foremost character trait.

"Pride goeth before the fall," she reminded him.

Fine lines crinkled at the sides of his eyes. In the bright light of day, the color became much clearer—warm brown, the same rich tone as maple syrup and every bit as tempting.

He walked in close proximity with his leg brushing her skirt. Then his elbow rubbed against the side of her bosom. A wicked pleasure plucked at her insides. If a brief touch produced this reaction, imagine what would happen should he put his arms around her?

Her toe struck something, sent a piece of tile flying.

She stumbled. Henry caught her—again. Only his quick reaction kept her upright. Attentive, with good reflexes. She, on the other hand, had suddenly become clumsy and cotton-headed, not at all her usual self. Apparently, he brought out the worst in her, another reason not to become ensnared. As if she needed more reasons.

"Careful, Lucy," Henry said close to her ear. His warm breath sent charged currents across her skin. "We're almost done with the construction. It's still a mess."

"That's not the problem. I should've worn something more sensible than these spool heels."

"If you need boots, I can recommend a place where you can buy them."

Boots, yes, and chain mail. She must put in the order the moment she returned to town.

Henry halted beside an arched doorway. She released his arm. Drew her cloak closer to form a shield. Before she realized what he was doing, he'd shrugged out of his greatcoat and tucked it around her.

The heavy wool garment held the warmth of his body, as well as intriguing scents. Coal-fired smoke mingled with a crisp fragrance she identified as soap, and something else she could only think to call a manly scent. Wrapped in his garment was like being held in his arms.

Add *considerate* to his qualities.

She hugged the lapels. Offered him a grateful smile. "The sun was shining this morning, and the air felt warmer. I didn't think I'd need a coat."

One of his mahogany eyebrows winged upward. "The wind is

wicked out here. The weather can change in an instant. You must be prepared."

His mild rebuke shook her out of her dazed infatuation. She hadn't kept his coat because she was cold. The real reason she wouldn't admit. That bump must've dislodged her brain. This man was the scoundrel her father had been sent to investigate for fraud, not one of her imaginary heroes. Certainly not someone she ought to fantasize about, much less hug his coat and imagine his arms around her.

Irritated with herself, she swung the overcoat off her shoulders. Offered it back to him. "Thank you for reminding me. I shall be better prepared next time."

Surprise, and a touch of chagrin, flashed across Henry's face. In an instant, she regretted her uncharacteristic rudeness. She could hardly tell him it was an act of self-defense against his charms. Before she could apologize, her father took her aside.

"If you're cold, go wait in the carriage."

She flushed at his blunt reprimand. Denying the cold bothered her would only make matters worse. Later, she could speak to Henry, apologize. "Thank you, I believe I will."

Henry sent her a concerned look, which only made her feel worse.

While the two men entered the roundhouse together, she retraced her steps to the carriage. This attraction, however disturbing, didn't have to become a problem if she ignored it. She wasn't so inexperienced she didn't know how to tactfully turn away unwanted attention. She would take Henry's advice to "be prepared" the next time.

Lucy retrieved her bag, which contained a few of her favorite novels, along with her notebook. She was mindful of her father's wishes. However, she wouldn't sit in a carriage to wait like a well-trained dog. Submissiveness had never come naturally—another one of her *flaws*, according to her aunt. Her mother hadn't seen it that way. She'd encouraged Lucy to be bold and confident. That's what she would advise now.

It would be a while before her father and Henry returned. She would take the time to discover what she could, perhaps find some workers to interview.

The wind nipped at Lucy's cape on her way to the graveled edge of the noisy rail yard, where trains were being switched onto different tracks.

On the far side of all those tracks, a burly man wearing a short-billed striped hat stood next to a locomotive. He was engaged in conversation with an engineer who leaned out the open window.

Closer to her, another engine puffed, as it backed a line of freight cars towards a caboose. A switchman waited, prepared to couple the cars together. This dangerous task involved placing iron spikes or "pins" into links as they were guided into slotted drawbars, which locked the cars together. Men often lost fingers in the process. Some lost their lives if they were struck by a moving car or caught between them.

Lucy held her breath.

A boy appeared on a nearby track, seemingly out of nowhere. He didn't look to be more than ten, at most twelve. He pulled a railroad cap down to his ears. He also wore a man-sized coat over his denim bibs. The hems had been rolled up above his bare feet.

Factories in the East employed children. Did the railroad? If so, she would have a talk with Henry. A child shouldn't be forced to labor for hours in any environment. A switchyard was far too treacherous a place for one to be working or playing, or whatever the boy was doing.

The lad glanced her way, then took off in the direction of the moving cars.

Lucy's heart tripped. *"Mon Dieu.* Stop, boy! Get away from there!"

He didn't look back. With all the noise, he probably didn't hear her.

She darted an anxious glance back at the roundhouse. Henry and her father were still inside. Regardless, they were too far away to reach the child before he got to the tracks where the cars were being coupled.

Lucy waved at the switchman. He wasn't watching.

No one was watching—except for her.

She picked up her skirts to run to the child's rescue.

HENRY LED the Major on a tour at a brisk clip. He had no need to explain what the railroad man already knew, the workings of a roundhouse. Warm sunshine shone through an opening in the partially finished roof of the railroad's new stable for its herd of steam engines.

The cold wind whistling through the arched entries cut through his wool overcoat. That short cape Lucy had brought wouldn't do her much good. Thankfully, she was tucked in the carriage.

She might be upset, though. He'd offended her. Again. Only, this time he didn't understand why. All he'd done was offer his coat and tell her about the changeable weather.

Even so, her tart reaction didn't irritate him as much as the Major's response. Forbes had dismissed her as one might chide a disobedient child. Lucy was a woman, fully grown. Clearly, her father hadn't accepted this. Another reason marriage would be good for her.

"How much will all this cost?" Forbes gestured to the inside of the building.

The board had financial information that would've answered the Major's question, which meant he must doubt the official report. He was fishing.

Henry's instincts went on alert. "The directors approved construction. Mr. Parsons signed off on it. I assume they didn't send you out here to collect facts they already possess."

The noontime sun shining through the open roof glinted off the Major's spectacles, making it difficult to see his eyes and what was behind them. "I'm not privy to their plans about how the remainder of the work will be financed. I've been asked to review the operations, make sure we're spending wisely. Find ways to increase our revenues."

The directors wanted their man to find more money. That was rich. There wasn't an extra penny. Henry had pinched every one. Lately, he'd been digging into his own pockets, trying to hold on until his boss returned from Europe with an infusion of foreign capital.

He had no doubt Mr. Parsons would reimburse him once he explained his reasoning. Regardless of motive, falsifying reports would get him fired. He had to prevent Forbes from discovering his juggling act.

"Tell me your suggestions," Henry stated.

"I don't have any, yet. Thought we might come up with them together."

Together? Forbes couldn't be serious. Or was he? He wasn't only out to abscond with the top job. The presumptive ass wanted to steal ideas, as well. *His* ideas.

"Are we writing your report *together*?" Henry said dryly.

Forbes' shoulders stiffened. The barb had found its target. "Mr. Stevens, contrary to what you believe, it is not my intention to undermine you. If we work together, we will both win."

Henry struggled to contain his anger. The directors had sent an imbecile. Or they thought he was one. Their man was good at the sincerity act. He wasn't fooled. He'd met all types of pretenders, had learned how to best them at their own game.

"Together, eh? It's not how I normally work." Henry put out his hand. "Let's give it a try. You'll have my cooperation."

The Major's stern frown softened into a pleased expression. He took Henry's hand in a firm shake. "Very good."

That took care of one problem, putting Forbes at ease, which would make him easier to manipulate.

Henry cast a worried glance at the arched exit. "We should go check on Lucy. I offended her without intending to, then you were rough on her."

The point needed to be made, and would eventually lead to a discussion about turning responsibility for Lucy over to her husband.

"Rough?" Forbes rubbed his chin. "Perhaps I was."

"She isn't a child."

The older man looked startled. Then he breathed out what sounded like a chuckle. "No, no she's not. Thank you for reminding me."

The Major wandered over to the massive turntable. "Why don't you go ahead, speak with her. I'd like to look around for a few minutes."

Henry hadn't expected Lucy's father to give him permission to speak with Lucy in private. Maybe the Major's change of heart had been brought about by the promise of cooperation. All the same, it offered a splendid opportunity.

He hurried out to the carriage.

Lucy wasn't there.

The driver reported he hadn't seen her. Neither had a guard posted at the rail yard. How could they? The two loafers were seated on a low stone fence, smoking, absorbed in a game of cards. Wild Indians could've ridden in and taken Lucy away and they wouldn't have noticed.

Worried, Henry strode off to check the surrounding buildings. Given her curiosity, she might be exploring the new machine shop or the foundry. A construction site was too dangerous a place for her to be wandering around. Not to mention, those men who'd tried to kill him were still on the loose.

He swore under his breath. If he hadn't been so preoccupied with her father, he might've done a better job of ensuring her safety.

A shrill whistle came from behind. A warning.

He whirled around. His gaze swept the busy rail yard. His heart slammed to a stop.

Lucy! Chasing a ragged youth who'd sprinted across the tracks. Behind a *backing* train. Good God, they could be killed!

Henry dashed to close the distance. Gravel crunched beneath his shoes as he vaulted over multiple sets of tracks. "Stop! Brake!" He waved at the brakeman atop the line of moving cars, motioning for him to bring the train to a halt.

A moment later, came a loud squeal. Steam hissed from the engine's stack as the slow moving cars rolled to a shuddering stop.

"Lucy!" Henry yelled.

She darted behind a stationary boxcar a few yards away. Could she not hear him? He'd gotten the attention of everyone else in the rail yard. He caught up with her as she climbed inside the open door on the side of the car.

Henry grasped a stocking-covered ankle. "What the devil are you—"

"Unhand me!"

Something heavy whacked him on the side of the head. The force of the blow sent him staggering to one side. That heavy satchel, she'd wielded it like a mace.

She twisted around with an angry expression that quickly shifted to dismay. "Oh, I didn't realize..."

The boy she'd been chasing hurtled out of the opening, hit the gravel with both feet then took off running.

She pointed excitedly. "Stop him, Henry. It's not safe out here."

"Really?" he drawled. She'd scared ten years off his life. Then she'd laid into him with that satchel. Now, she was issuing orders. He'd deal with the disobedient child later. At the moment, he had his hands full with Lucy.

Her legs were a fraction too short to reach the ground. Henry let her dangle. Served her right for getting into this predicament. Problem was, he couldn't tear his gaze away from her bustled backside. He'd give up another year of his life if he could see what was beneath those layers of petticoats.

She searched for the ground with her the toe of her shoe. "Will you kindly assist me?"

"If you don't brain me with that bag again. What do you carry in there, bricks?"

"Books. I didn't realize it was you who'd come up behind me."

Somehow, he didn't think that would've mattered.

He circled his hands around her tiny waist. Anger, and a host of other feelings he dared not name, heated his blood. Quick as he could, he set her on the ground.

She started off in the direction the child had fled without so much as a *thank you*.

"Not that way. Those other cars are still moving." He took her arm with a firm grip. Would drag her out of danger, if necessary. After they'd left the rail yard, he gave a wave to let the men know they could resume their work.

Lucy tugged at his grasp. "Release me, sir."

He caught her bag before she could swing it at him again. Although she seemed bright, she might also be a tad crazy. After all, normal women didn't haul around a library in their satchels or chase urchins around busy switchyards.

"Mr. Stevens..." She twisted her arm, winced. "Henry, please. You're hurting me."

He instantly relaxed his hold. His insides, already knotted with worry, tightened with regret. "That was not my intention."

She held her arm protectively against her chest. "Why did you grab me?"

"Why?" He echoed, incredulous. What kind of stupid question was that? "Unless you're deaf, you must've heard the squealing brakes. Noticed that train bearing down on you. Do you always behave recklessly?"

Hurt flickered across her face, soon replaced with a mulish expression. "Do you always snatch women's bags?"

He dropped the heavy satchel next to her. It landed with a thud.

Lucy picked it up, brushed it off, then hung the strap over her shoulder without blinking at the weight. She might not need a gun, after all. "I was not being reckless. At every moment, I knew where the cars were. They weren't moving fast."

"Ah, that's why they had to stop suddenly," he replied dryly.

"As a precaution, I suppose." She lifted her chin, not a bit repentant. "If that boy hadn't run out in front—"

"Why did you chase the little wildcat?"

"Why did he run away?"

"Kindly stop replying to my questions with more questions."

Lucy threw an anxious glance over her shoulder. "I'm worried about him. He shouldn't be out here. He's too young to be working."

Not only did she adopt stray dogs. She went after stray children, as well. That wouldn't work with Billy, who had the instincts of a feral cat. No doubt, he'd found this chase amusing and invigorating.

Henry's heart still pounded from the fright Lucy had given him. "You nearly got yourself killed for no reason."

"No reason?" With a frown, she pointed in the direction Billy had run. "That's a *child*, Henry. A child, wandering about in a rail yard. If you are worried about me, I can't believe you aren't concerned about him."

"That *child* knows this rail yard as well as I do." Henry removed his hat to wipe his damp forehead. Annoyingly enough, Lucy didn't appear to have broken a sweat. "I've told him to stay away. He's a poor listener. Like someone else I know who was supposed to be in the carriage."

She ignored the jab. As well, she'd ignored his questions and his commands. She tried his patience worse than the boy. "Does Billy have a home?"

"Last time I checked, he did. I'll deal with him later—"

"You're not sure?"

Henry threaded his fingers through his hair. He'd be pulling it out before long if she didn't start listening. He replaced the bowler. Put a cap on his anger. "This isn't about Billy. I want your promise that you'll not wander off alone. Or I won't allow you to accompany us when we go out to inspect the line."

"*You* won't *allow*? Her eyes flashed in open rebellion. "You have no authority over me."

Her response flipped a switch inside him. By God, he had every right to see to her safety. He'd have even more rights when he was her husband.

He grasped her shoulders. If she were a child, he'd turn her over his knee. As he'd pointed out to Forbes, she wasn't a child. Not to mention, he ought not even contemplate spanking her. That brought up a whole host of images that shouldn't be in his head. "My authority extends to anyone on railroad property," he ground out. "That includes you."

Her throat worked convulsively as she swallowed. A romp around the rail yard hadn't frightened her. Apparently, he'd succeeded in doing so.

His anger drained about the time his conscience started putting up a fuss. She wasn't one of his workers to be ordered around. She was a gently bred young lady who required a gentler hand.

He softened both his tone and his grip. "Lucy, look at me."

Her gaze shifted in the direction of the rail yard. Her color warmed to a pink, healthy glow. Another act of rebellion brought about by another order.

He really needed to worked on his finesse, which seemed to have deserted him about the time he'd climbed into the carriage with her.

"You have a smudge," he observed. With his thumb, he rubbed the soft skin on her chin. His heart thumped with something much different than fear or anger.

He slid his hands down her shoulders. Maybe her recklessness drew out his protective nature. Or was that a convenient excuse to put his arms around her? "I want to keep you safe. That's why I must insist you stay close."

At last, she gave him her attention. The tint in her cheeks deepened to a rosy blush. "I'm no longer in danger."

His gaze fastened on her lips. Full, pink, and just begging to be kissed. She was such an innocent. Brave, as well as naïve. "You're in danger now, and you don't even know it."

BEFORE LUCY'S mind could whir into motion to tell her feet to move, Henry bent his head and took her mouth in a burning kiss. She froze beneath the unexpected assault. Her heart fluttered like a frantic bird trapped in a greenhouse.

He cradled her jaw with his hand to turn her face upward. Was that so he'd have a better angle to ravish her? She'd never been ravished before. It wasn't cruel or hurtful or anything like what was hinted at in the novels she'd read.

His kiss softened to a gentle persistence. She hardly realized when her lips parted.

What came next proved to be more surprising. The lush pressure of his mouth, the seductive way he teased her lips with promises of immoral pleasures.

Who knew ravishment could be such a wondrous thing?

In the midst of rapture, she barely heard the warning.

Escape.

Or at least try not to give in so easily.

As if he sensed her indecision, he coiled an arm around her waist and brought her fully up against his solid form. He then plundered her mouth as thoroughly as a pirate might loot a captured vessel.

Pleasure bound her. A delicious fire melted her bones. She had no desire to fight.

Where was the fun in simply being his victim? A heroine worth her salt would turn the tables on a villain.

As he ravished her mouth, Lucy ran her hands over her attacker's broad shoulders. This didn't feel like an assault, although she hadn't given him permission. She couldn't resist rubbing her palms over the smooth wool of his coat. Underneath, he was all lean muscle, with a powerful form delightfully different from hers.

The hoyden in possession of her mind issued more orders. She moved her hands to his chest to explore an unfamiliar landscape, roam the steely strength of his arms.

Such power, under tight control. What would happen if he unleashed it?

Fear flickered, at once eclipsed by a stronger emotion. *Desire.* In her most intimate dreams, she'd imagined how it might feel. Those secret longings hadn't prepared her for this urgent hunger, this intense longing to touch and be touched.

She reached up to caress his beard. Soft. As she slid her fingers over his ears, she discovered the hair on his head was softer. She couldn't resist fondling it.

His chest rose and fell. Her breathing quickened. The pounding of his heart echoed inside her chest. Lucy sensed they were both close to losing control. Strangely enough, the realization didn't frighten her, yet she had enough sense left to step away from the cliff.

She arched away from him to break off the kiss. In his searching gaze, she saw her own bewilderment reflected. Lingering sensations left her confused, aching for something she hadn't thought she wanted.

He moved his hands to her arms, then, with seeming reluctance, released her. "Don't run off again."

Was that all he had to say? Hadn't he felt the earth tilt sideways or was that in her imagination? His touch muddled her thinking, did strange things to her insides. She'd felt that kiss all the way to her toes, which had curled with pleasure. Her lips still tingled. She'd been so caught up in a passionate fantasy she'd ignored every warning sign along the way.

Reality sent her plummeting to earth. God knows why he'd kissed her—to make some absurd point, perhaps. And she was supposed to *observe* him, not *embrace* him.

Desperate to escape before she did something foolish like cry, she scooped up her bag then struck out, away from the rail yard.

"Lucy."

Her skin quivered in response to his harsh call. She hugged her cloak, quickened her pace. Try as she might, she couldn't outrun desire. Not when it coursed hot as fire through her veins.

He caught up to her with his longer strides. "Lucy, wait." His voice came out softer, almost pleading.

A flood of tears threatened. She swallowed the surge. "I don't recall giving you leave to be familiar, Mr. Stevens."

"That wasn't my intention, I meant to—"

She turned on him, unleashing outrage, her only defense. "That is the *second* time you've made that excuse. Your intentions don't matter. You've made your point. It's not safe out here."

Hot with shame, she made a beeline for the roundhouse.

Her father stood near one of the arched entryways. Another man stood next to him.

Panic caught in her throat. Had they seen Henry kiss her?

"Slow down." Henry's fingers locked around her arm. His powerful grip halted her forward motion. "Don't make it look as though you're running from me."

Mortified, she jerked out of his grasp. "If you'd stop following me, I wouldn't have to run."

He stayed at her heels like a watchdog. Try as she might, she couldn't leave her tormenter behind. To get away, she would have to go back to town. Given his earlier warning to *stay close*, she wondered what his reaction would be. To kiss her again?

God forbid.

Her father met her halfway with a frown that sent a frisson of alarm up her spine.

The man who accompanied him was clothed in solid black. An undertaker? How convenient. Someone would be here to take her body away after she expired from humiliation.

"Is there a problem?" her father asked.

She tried to catch her breath, still winded from walking at a brisk pace in a tight corset. "H-Henry..." she started. *No, don't use his given name. That's too familiar.* "Mr. Stevens was warning me of the dangers of...of the rail yard."

Actually, she'd only been in danger after Henry started kissing her. Before that, she was perfectly fine, despite what he thought.

Her father's eyes narrowed. "You were in danger?"

The answer lodged in her throat. If she said *no*, he'd catch the contradiction. If she said, *yes*, he'd put her on the first train home.

Henry appeared at her side, disgustingly calm. "Miss Forbes had something in her eye. A cinder, I think. I helped her remove it."

He sounded so convincing even *she* believed him. Before she could support his claim, he held his hand out to the black-garbed stranger. "Good morning, Milt."

"Stevens." The man pumped Henry's hand while he eyed Lucy with curiosity. "I've made Major Forbes's acquaintance, so this must be—"

"The Major's daughter." Henry turned to Lucy with a warning in his eyes. "Miss Forbes, this is Milt Reynolds, editor of the *Parsons Sun*."

Not an undertaker. Worse. A newspaperman.

Lucy felt faint. Her shame might be tomorrow's headline. She drew in a fortifying breath. "Mr. Reynolds. I'm very pleased to meet you."

The editor doffed his top hat. "The pleasure is mine, Miss Forbes. I see that Parsons stands to gain another rose to grace our growing garden of young ladies."

She acknowledged the overused metaphor with a polite nod. No more conversing about roses and gardens. Most especially, not about her. "Are you here to see the roundhouse?"

Disappointment flickered over the editor's face. He might've hoped she would give him more fodder for a salacious story.

"A photographer is on his way over to take pictures. Although..." He sent Henry a questioning look. "I'm more interested in hearing about those men who attacked the train."

Lucy released a relieved breath. The winds had shifted in her favor. In Henry's direction.

If he was displeased, she couldn't see it in his unruffled demeanor. What a master at hiding his emotions. Another note she must make, once her hands weren't shaking.

"Nothing's changed since we spoke last night," he said to the editor.

Mr. Reynolds reached into his coat. He withdrew something cut from a newspaper. "Have you seen this letter printed on the front page of the *Thayer Headlight*?"

Before Henry could answer, Reynolds unfurled it and began to read:

The Honorable Mr. Stevens says his land office will make a fair settlement on portions of the Osage Cede Lands for settlers willing to sign contracts. We know the railroad has no just claim to these lands. If Mr. Stevens had the brains of an oyster, he would know it too. His banditry will soon come to an end. A friend of the settlers told us on very good authority that justice shall be meted out.

The barely veiled threat made goose bumps pop up on Lucy's arms.

Henry appeared nonplussed. "Rich is a blowhard. He loves to stir the pot."

"Or he may still hold a grudge for being duped into selling his land," Mr. Reynolds countered.

Henry folded his arms over this chest. "What's your point, Milt?"

Lucy gaped in surprise. Mr. Reynolds had all but called Henry a cheat. Men dueled over lesser insults. Henry didn't even refute it. However, the tips of his ears had turned red. Offended...or guilty.

Her father's attention remained on the editor. He might not have noticed Henry's uncontrollable reaction. "Who wrote that letter?"

"One of the local Grange leaders." Reynolds returned the clipping to his pocket. "He is, as Henry points out, *a blowhard*. Still, the railroad can't afford to ignore what's happened around here. The Grange has held protests, barricaded trains, shot up the depot—"

"Don't print that," Henry interjected. "We don't know who those attackers were."

The editor proceeded, undaunted. "Could be in retaliation for the murder of those two farmers who disappeared near Cherryvale."

Henry's neck turned crimson.

Lucy lifted trembling fingers to her lips. She'd kissed a *murderer*?

"Those disappearances have *nothing* to do with the railroad." Henry spoke firmly. He didn't release eye contact with the editor or show other signs of lying. Except for his flush, which seemed to indicate anger.

"You'll admit the men were troublemakers."

"You're fishing in a dried-up pond, Milt."

"Oh, I don't know," the editor smiled with satisfaction. "Looks like the fish have started to bite."

Her father's frown conveyed his displeasure with the editor's pushy ways.

Clearly, Mr. Reynolds had baited Henry. She'd seen her father ensnared with similar tactics regularly practiced by reporters back east. In this case, could there be a thread of truth in the editor's implications? Henry had as much as admitted to conflict with The Grange, *and* he wanted to keep it quiet.

His gaze met hers, daring her to doubt him. She didn't know what to believe. Her instincts warned he had something to hide.

"Major, Miss Forbes, have you seen much of Parsons yet?"

Lucy swiveled her attention to the editor. She'd hoped he wouldn't notice she was still there.

"I'm afraid we haven't had the opportunity," her father answered.

The editor executed a slight bow in her direction. "If your father can do without your company, perhaps you'll allow me to give you a tour."

Much as she'd love to explore Parsons, she wasn't interested in having the sly Mr. Reynolds as her guide.

"She doesn't need a tour." Henry's presumptive response poured fuel onto her suspicions.

If she went with Mr. Reynolds, she could return to town without disrupting her father's plans. Plus, she'd have a chance to ask questions about things Henry didn't want her to find out.

"Actually, it's a perfect idea," she replied to the editor. "You don't mind, do you Father?"

"Not if that's what you'd like to do." Her father's tone implied he wasn't keen on the idea.

He wouldn't stop her from going.

Henry's impassive mask cracked into a frown. *Oh my.* He was *not* happy. If he made a scene, the newspaperman might read too much into it and link them together.

With an apologetic smile, she took a step back. "I've been enough of a bother for one day."

"You're not a bother," Henry stated.

Now *that* was a lie. He appeared very bothered. Worse, he bothered her a great deal. For an insane moment, she'd let attraction overcome common sense. It wouldn't happen again. No matter how exciting his kisses might be.

"Shall we go?" Lucy took the editor's arm. For the first time in her life, she walked away from adventure.

CHAPTER 7

*L*ucy retied the ribbons beneath her chin as she trekked across the open field to the editor's waiting buggy. At some point while in Henry's clutches, her bonnet had been knocked askew. Her insides were knotted so tight there would be no untangling them.

Thank goodness Henry hadn't caused a scene, despite his furious gaze. What could he do? Tell her father to lock her up? She could manage her father. She would have less success with managing Henry.

"Where shall we start our tour?" she asked her guide. Eager as she was to see Parsons, she didn't really care where they started, so long as it wasn't anywhere near Mr. Stevens.

"The newspaper office, then our new school. There's a fine bakery in town where we can pick up something to eat. We'll be back in time for the inauguration ceremony at the depot."

"Very good." If she had to deal with Henry again today, it would be in a crowd.

In the meantime, she could talk to other people, find out what they thought about the enigmatic general manager, piece together the puzzle that was Henry Stevens. For her father's sake. Not because she was attracted to him.

In some perverse twist of fate, she'd apparently developed a passion for the one man who could ruin her life. Henry was under investigation for fraud, and—if the editor were to be believed—might also be a murderer. Her taste in men generally tended toward the heroic type.

Mr. Reynolds assisted her into the one-horse buggy. He tossed a heavy cover over her lap. Henry's face had turned this exact shade of burgundy when she'd accepted Mr. Reynolds' offer.

He couldn't be jealous of the much older man. He was angry because he feared what she might discover about him. All the more reason to snoop.

The editor climbed in, secured his top hat and flicked back the tails of a fitted black coat that had been years out of style when she was still in pinafores. He grasped the reins. His black horse, as bony and unbecoming as its master, shook its head then set off at a dutiful plod.

Ahead of them stretched a treeless plateau. To the west, beyond the rail yard, the ochre grassland stretched out, seemingly forever. No farms were visible, though she knew they were out there. The soil was reported to be as rich as Eden, which was why thousands of settlers had swarmed into Kansas after the war, in search of a better life.

She longed for a better life, too. Only, she dreamed of adventure, independence, and, yes, eventually romance. Love would be wonderful with the right man. One who wasn't an ambitious, arrogant scoundrel.

Her conscience pricked. She had yet to confirm that Henry was a bona fide scoundrel.

"Mr. Reynolds, why did the man who wrote that editorial believe he was cheated?"

The editor guided the horse around a rut in the road. "Stevens posted notices in the newspaper that stated the Katy would locate its headquarters fifty miles from here. That convinced Rich to sell the land he'd purchased around Parsons for dirt cheap."

"Were the notices false?"

"Best as I can tell, the Katy never intended to build anywhere except here."

This was disappointing news, to say the least.

"Would you say he acted dishonorably?"

"Some say he did. The way Henry tells it, Rich used confidential information to nab land intended to be a town site. Then he wouldn't take what the railroad offered him. Thought if he held out, he could get rich. When he read those notices, he couldn't get rid of that land fast enough." The editor chuckled, as if it amused him.

She could admit to respecting Henry's cleverness. However, what he'd done was wrong, despite the other man's intentions. Her father wouldn't have handled it that way. "Do you believe the attack on Mr. Stevens was motivated by a desire for revenge?"

"If Rich intended to shoot Henry for getting the best of him, he would've done it by now. He's had more than two years."

"It's possible he carries a grudge..." She had hauled one around almost that long, to the point of imagining in some detail the kind of violent end that should befall her father's betrayers. "If he believes he was treated unjustly."

"Ah. To be treated unjustly, one would have to be just."

Was that supposed to be a joke? The editor hadn't taken her seriously.

"Is that your version of the Golden Rule? As I recall, we're to treat people how we'd like to be treated. Not based on whether or not they deserve it."

Mr. Reynolds' smile faded. "Miss Forbes, you are taking too much from my words. I meant to provoke Mr. Stevens, not indict him."

She leapt upon the inconsistency. "It certainly sounded that way. You accused him of cheating, implied murder. Are those assumptions?"

Reynolds lifted a hand, as if to ward off her attack. "*I* didn't accuse him of cheating. Rich did. As for the other..." The editor's visage turned somber. "Those two settlers aren't the only ones who've gone missing. Eight people have disappeared over the past two years. Most of them were last seen near a trail that crosses the railroad line between here and Fort Scott. Those are facts, not assumptions."

Lucy resisted the temptation to jump to conclusions. "How do you know Henry Stevens had anything to do with this?"

"I don't."

"You implied he did." Lucy pondered the motivation. "Is there some reason you don't like Mr. Stevens?"

The editor frowned at her question. "I don't *dis*like Henry. He's always been supportive of the newspaper. Well, until we opposed him on the land dispute. We locked horns over that."

"Do you think he's capable of..." she could hardly say the word. "Murder?"

"A man's capable of anything if he's got the motive. Out here, Stevens rules the railroad. He makes all the decisions about operations, legal problems, land disputes..." Reynolds let the implication hang from the end of the sentence like a noose.

The scales weren't tilted in Henry's favor. On the other hand, the evidence had looked bad for her father and he hadn't been guilty.

"Are you telling me this to make me doubt Mr. Stevens, or to find out what I know?"

The editor gave her a sharp look. "I'm telling you because you ought to be careful."

Fear zinged through her. "Me or my father?"

"Both, I'd say."

Lucy shivered at a sudden chill. She peered up at leaden clouds, certain the temperature of the air had dropped, and drew up the blanket. How much warmer and more secure Henry's coat had felt, and his arms.

Absurd. She hardly knew him. She had to stop behaving like one of those silly, tragic heroines who succumbed to the villain, despite having every opportunity to observe his corrupt nature. The board viewed Henry as a maverick. The settlers had revolted against his policies. Someone hated him enough to try to kill him. Even if he wasn't a murderer, what more proof did she need that he was a scoundrel?

Near the edge of town, she spotted a two-story white frame building with *The Parsons Sun* painted in large block letters on the side. "Oh, there's the newspaper office."

"Our first stop." Mr. Reynolds shook the reins. The horse picked up the pace as tiny snowflakes began to fall.

Incredible. The day had gone from sunny to snowy in a matter of hours.

Lucy pulled the thick woolen cover to her chin. The half roof provided minimal protection in the open buggy. That carriage had been a good choice. "Mr. Stevens was right about the changeable Kansas weather. I will be better prepared the next time we go out."

The editor's lips stretched into a grim smile. "You should be prepared for more than bad weather, if Mr. Stevens accompanies you."

CHAPTER 8

*G*ravel crunched. Someone trying to sneak up. Billy peeked out from the shadows underneath an idle boxcar. The old gentleman in the top hat still waited by the carriage. The lady who'd chased him had gone off with the newspaperman. That left...

"Get out here. Now."

The knot in Billy's throat got as big as the one in his stomach. For a frantic moment, he considered rolling to the other side of the track to escape.

The Chief wasn't weighed down with heavy skirts. He could run faster than a woman. Not only that, he'd be madder than a wet cat if he had to give chase.

Resigned, Billy crawled out of his hiding place. He brushed the loose dirt and cinders off his clothes. With as much courage as he could muster, he looked up at a towering figure that blocked the sun. The only person in the world he held in absolute awe.

"Well? What've you got to say for yourself?" the Chief asked him.

Billy responded as he always did when confronted with wrongdoing. He professed his innocence. "I didn't do nothin' wrong."

"Nothing?" The Chief's curt response made Billy's knees quake.

"That young woman you led on a merry chase could've been killed. I'd say that's something."

Billy chewed the inside of his lip. He hadn't been trying to get anybody killed. He ran so he wouldn't get caught somewhere he shouldn't be. How was he to know that lady would come after him? "Didn't mean no harm."

"No, I don't believe you did. But you didn't think. And not thinking can get people killed out here." The hand placed on Billy's shoulder felt friendly, not tight or painful. The Chief's expression didn't look so angry anymore either. "Anything hurt?"

Billy shook his head, perplexed by the sudden show of concern. "N-no sir."

"It will when I'm through with you." The Chief took him by the wrist.

Now he was going to get it.

Billy darted a fearful look around. The switchman ignored them. The brakie didn't come down off the top of the train. The hogger at the engine's controls didn't even look over. None of the men in the rail yard would challenge their boss.

The Chief was the law on the Katy. Those that worked for him said he didn't have no softness, not even a spoonful of pity. Couldn't abide a slacker, though he paid well for a hard day's work. Billy couldn't recall if any of the railroaders mentioned getting thrashed.

"You gonna beat me?" He couldn't keep a quiver out of his voice. He wouldn't cry, though. Never had done him any good with them others who'd beat him.

The Chief's long strides slowed. "I've got a job for you."

"A job?" Billy's spirits soared. That's what he'd dreamed of, to go to work on the railroad. "That ain't worse than a whipping."

"We'll see if you think so after you're finished."

They crossed the yard and didn't stop until they'd reached one of the big steam engines. Excitement made Billy tremble like a leaf in a high wind.

"Mr. Tobias," hollered the Chief.

The hogger leaned out the window. "Yes sir?"

"This is Billy. Put him to work wiping the engine. Don't let him stop until it's clean enough to serve food on."

The engineer took off his cap, scratched his head. "He ain't much to look at."

"Neither was I when I was his age, and I could do a day's work."

Billy couldn't imagine the Chief being his age, much less small.

The Chief squatted down, eye-to-eye. He looked awful stern. Except there wasn't cruelness in his gaze or in his grip. "After you're finished here, you have to go back to the farm."

"But..." the protest died on Billy's lips. He'd tried arguing with the Chief before. It did no good. Even if Mr. Zeller worked him from sunup to sundown, then thrashed him when he complained, he'd still be able to sneak away and come back. Do whatever odd jobs the railroaders might have for him. Show them he was stronger than he looked.

The general manager frowned like he'd read Billy's mind. "Don't come out here again. Stay on the farm, work hard, go to school. When you're eighteen, if you still want a job with the railroad, we'll talk."

Billy's heart dropped faster than a stone in a creek. *Eighteen?* He couldn't stand being a farmer for that long.

CHAPTER 9

The editor left Lucy at the hotel. She'd told him she needed to drop off her books before returning to the depot for the inauguration ceremony. In fact, she wanted to do some snooping around on her own beforehand.

She didn't know what to believe about Henry's involvement in those disappearances. Mr. Reynolds had been careful not to outright accuse the general manager, then he'd delivered a clear warning. It wouldn't hurt to find out what others thought.

Next to the hotel stood a billiards hall. Interesting. Not the sort of place she should visit. Across the street were a variety of shops, including a dressmaker and milliner. She could easily continue her snooping among gabby women without drawing undue attention.

She carefully lifted her hems to step around a deep rut cut by wagon wheels, then dodged a buckboard loaded with building materials, ducked around a prancing horse. She slipped between two wagons at a hitching post, finally made it to the other side. Who knew crossing the street could be an adventure?

Next, she had to contend with the sidewalk, weaving through the tight-packed crowd like a minnow amidst a large school of fish. Except, everyone swam in different directions.

She halted at a window display with hats. Her aunt knew every woman in Haverhill and their families. The proprietor of this millinery shop would be well informed.

Lucy entered, jingling the bell. The familiar sights and soft feminine scents soothed her agitated nerves. Several customers hovered over glassed cases where fans, gloves, handkerchiefs and undergarments were displayed. Straw hats and feathered bonnets lined the shelves in an admirable, if a bit outdated, assortment.

A gray-haired woman with a crisp white apron approached. "What can I show you, miss?"

Lucy couldn't admit she wasn't here to buy anything. At the same time, it would be rude to launch into questions without making polite conversation. A sincere compliment was always a good way to start. "I was admiring all your hats. My aunt owns a millinery shop near Boston. I don't believe she has as wide a selection."

The woman beamed. "Why, thank you. I'm the owner, Mrs. Bannerman.

"Lucy Forbes." She dipped in a polite curtsy.

"Pleasure to meet you, Miss Forbes." The owner's eyes shone with interest. "Is that bonnet you're wearing from your aunt's shop?"

Lucy touched the frilled edge. "Yes, it's a new style. They call it a Bébé."

She spent several minutes chatting about hats, and found out Mrs. Bannerman knew all the *important* ladies in town, as well most of the families in the area.

A thought nudged at the back of Lucy's mind. "I saw a boy out wandering around near the rail yard. When I tried to talk to him, he ran away. Someone said his name was Billy. Would you know him?"

"I know several boys named Billy. Don't reckon they'd be loitering in rail yards."

"This boy comes up to about my chin. Sandy hair. Slight build. He wears castoff clothing, railroad coveralls and a brown cap."

Mrs. Bannerman's lips pursed with disapproval. "Sounds like a vagrant. I wouldn't worry about him. That kind always finds what they need. If they can't, they steal it."

Lucy was tempted to point out that abandoned children rarely found what they needed. If they did steal, it was out of desperation. Unfortunately, a great many people shared Mrs. Bannerman's attitude, which was why so little had been done for children who wandered the streets in eastern cities. How disappointing to find out things were no different out here.

She resolved to get some answers from Henry after the inauguration ceremony. "I don't suppose you know Mr. Stevens?"

"Mr. *Henry* Stevens? Of course I know him. Everyone around here does. He's the general manager of the Katy. Him and his partner run the land company that owns half the town, along with most of the land around it."

Not only powerful, rich, as well. Nothing wrong with that. Unless he'd earned his money by defrauding the railroad.

"An influential man. I'd like to get to know him."

Mrs. Bannerman gave Lucy a quick once-over. "You will, I'm sure."

Her response implied Henry had a reputation with the ladies. Given how free he was with his favors, this wasn't a revelation. A disappointment, perhaps.

Lucy lowered her voice. "Does he seek out every new woman who moves to town?"

"Seek out?" The older woman seemed to consider how to answer. "No, I wouldn't say that. He's a good catch, though not eager to be caught."

Mrs. Bannerman was getting the wrong idea. Henry's eligibility wasn't of concern.

"Who said anything about catching him? He's an older gentleman, isn't he? I heard he founded the town."

"He did—and named it after his boss."

"Smart man," Lucy acknowledged. Stroking the railroad president's ego sounded like something Henry would do. Opportunistic would join the list of character traits.

From behind Lucy came a soft voice. "If you want to know about Mr. Stevens, you should talk to the men who work for the Katy."

Lucy acknowledged a woman dressed entirely in black. "Do you know him, too?"

"Yes, miss. My husband helped build the railroad. He was a switchman." A shadow passed over the woman's long face. "Until he was killed in an accident."

"I'm so sorry." Lucy's heart went out to the widow. She understood the pain of losing loved ones, compounded by financial distress. "How are you getting along?"

"That's what I wanted to tell you." The switchman's widow leaned in. "Mr. Stevens has been good to us. He made sure my children don't go hungry. He writes us a check every month."

"On the railroad's account?"

"On no, miss, his own. The railroad doesn't have a pension for widows and orphans."

This surprising glimpse into a softer, gentler side of the ambitious general manager pleased Lucy. She recalled Henry's comment about giving the conductor cash to get by. He'd meant his own money. Ambitious men were rarely that generous. A killer wouldn't care.

Someone standing behind her cleared her throat. Lucy turned, realizing the woman had inched closer to listen to the conversation. Frizzy blonde curls peeked out from beneath a massive sunbonnet. Her muslin dress had faded from too many washings. If she were poor, she wouldn't be shopping in this fine millinery. She must be frugal.

"That Mr. Stevens, he's not so worried about the *farmers'* children," she confided to Lucy. "He wants my husband to pay him ten times what our land is worth."

The switchman's widow sidled closer. "They're squatting on *railroad* land that's *worth* ten times what they're asking because they built the line through it."

The farmer's wife propped her hands on her generous hips. "Worth more since *we* improved it, you mean. That Mr. Stevens is greedy."

"He donated land for the school and two churches, which is more than any farmer has done," the widow flung back. "If not for him and the railroad, this town wouldn't exist."

Lucy glanced around, worried. Nervous customers had started to slip away. The owner might blame her. "Ladies, I didn't mean to cause trouble. What I really want to know is what happened to those men who've gone missing."

Silence fell over the store. Thick. Suffocating.

Mrs. Bannerman was the first to take a breath. "I'm not sure what you've heard. I can't believe Mr. Stevens would have anything to do with *that*."

"I'd believe it." The farmer's wife nodded. "Word is, he got rid of them because they caused trouble for the railroad."

The widow huffed. "That's gossip. If he got rid of every farmer who caused trouble, the entire county would be depopulated."

Things were getting uglier. Lucy still didn't have definitive answers.

She stepped between the two bickering women. "I suppose the newspaper will report on anything new."

"Everybody's got theories about what happened. Precious few facts," Mrs. Bannerman added. She showed the diplomacy required of a successful shopkeeper.

The railroad widow leaned in, lowered her voice. "I hear that fortuneteller up near Cherryvale is holding a séance. To help find the missing men."

Séance? That sounded interesting. Communicating with ghosts was nonsense, of course, practiced by charlatans. The people who showed up might have theories about what had happened to the missing men.

"Where did you say this was?" Lucy asked the widow.

"Out at the Bender place. An old Dutchman and his wife have a grocery and serve meals. Call themselves Spiritualists. His daughter advertises her services all over town. She claims to be able to talk to the dead."

Lucy felt a tug on her arm. The farmer's wife pulled her aside, shook a finger in her face. "Miss, you don't want to go there. That fortuneteller, she's doing the devil's work."

~

HENRY'S OFFICE on the second floor of the new depot overlooked Parsons. From his vantage point he could see every place Lucy might visit, as well as those she ought not visit. He searched the damp sidewalks. People had ventured out after that brief spate of snow. No sign of Lucy.

Granted, he'd blundered, which explained why she had run off with the editor.

He wouldn't apologize for kissing her. It had been worth the risk. He'd do it again, given half the chance. Her response, that of an innocent, yet with so much passion. God above, he'd nearly lost control. The lapse had shaken him, as did the realization of how much power she could wield over him. That wasn't part of the plan.

"Do you see her out there?" her father asked. "I thought she would be back by now."

If Forbes was worried, why hadn't he stopped her from leaving?

Henry scowled at his reflection in the glass. He'd resolved the problem of one errant waif. Lucy wouldn't be so easy to restrain. No telling what she'd gotten into with three whole hours to wreak havoc. It'd taken her only a few minutes to start climbing into freight cars.

"She's being given a very thorough tour, I'm sure," he said, without clenching his teeth. Irrational jealousy wasn't a valid reason to strangle the editor. Besides, Lucy wouldn't be interested in a married man twice her age.

The thought brought Henry up short. For all he knew, *he* could be twice her age.

He turned away from the window, annoyed. "She should've stayed with us."

The Major set aside the reports, including expense records—the ones Henry would allow him to see. Thus far, Forbes hadn't questioned anything.

"Do you trust Mr. Reynolds?" Forbes' guarded reaction to the editor could be due to his tainted past. However, this question had to do with Lucy. The Major wanted to know if her reputation would be safe.

Henry pushed a newspaper away from the edge of his desk to prop his hip on the corner. She was safer with Reynolds than with him. "There's no need to rush out to look for her. Milt won't let her come to harm."

Her father didn't appear convinced. "You don't appear to be fond of him."

"I'm not fond of newspapermen, in general. Milt Reynolds is a decent man. He's married, has two daughters, one close to Lucy's age. The eldest is nineteen." Henry added the last tidbit to prod information out of his guest.

Forbes leaned back in his seat. He laced his fingers across his middle and held Henry's gaze. "Lucy isn't that young. She's twenty-two. The same age her mother was when I married her. I was about your age. Thirty."

"I'm thirty-five," Henry stated. Not a secret, nor was it important. He'd decided to marry Lucy, and marry her he would. After he convinced her to talk to him again.

"If that editor wants a story, Lucy can give him one," Forbes said smoothly.

Henry swallowed, hard. She wouldn't let on about the kiss. It would make both of them look bad. "What kind of story?"

"Oh, one of those sentimental types she enjoys reading. She can recite whole passages written by Mrs. Southworth." Her father's mouth kicked up in a half smile. "You've probably noticed that bag of books she carries around."

Henry rubbed the side of his head. "Yes, I've noticed."

So, Lucy used her bag for something besides a weapon. Somehow, hearing she was a bookworm made her quirkiness even more charming.

"Mrs. Southworth, eh? My sister has mentioned her novels. I haven't read one."

"That doesn't surprise me," Forbes said with a chuckle. "Her books are a bit fanciful, like Lucy. Wouldn't appeal to a man who's concerned with practical things, such as running a railroad."

Henry considered the Major's assessment. True, he wouldn't care for those novels. As for Lucy, he found her sentimentalism rather endearing. "There's nothing wrong with a woman having a romantic nature. As long as she understands the difference between fantasy and the real world."

All humor faded from the older man's face. "Lucy understands the difference. Though she doesn't look at things the way you and I do. To her, life isn't a race to be won or a burden to be borne. She lives each day with fresh hope and dreams for the future."

Dreams, another thing Henry didn't believe in, though he wouldn't begrudge Lucy having them. "She's young and hopeful. That's good, isn't it?"

"It is..." Her father paused noticeably. "As long as her hopes aren't crushed."

Henry knew when he'd been challenged. He'd built his reputation from crushing the competition, not women. "That's the last thing I'd want to see."

"You agree, then. She needs someone who will deal with her gently. Be patient and kind."

"Of course." Henry vowed he would be more patient the next time.

Her father's gaze sharpened. "Someone who realizes how special she is. How valuable. Like the pearl of great price."

In that parable, as Henry recalled, a man had sold his land to buy an expensive gem. The implication being, Lucy would cost him something. Well, he didn't think he'd get her for free. He could afford whatever bribe Forbes set up.

"Yes, Lucy is unique." He meant it. She had a rare kindness, boundless courage, and an adorable inquisitiveness. Her reckless streak would need to be addressed. The more he learned about her, the more fascinated he became.

Forbes rested his arms on the table, ignoring the papers in front of him.

Henry sensed he'd missed something. He couldn't read minds. He'd made his interest in Lucy clear enough. "Is there something about me, in particular, that troubles you?"

"That which you prize above all else. Your ambition."

Ah, now it was clear where this was leading. Forbes wanted him to step down from his position with the railroad. In return, he'd get the Major's blessing to wed his daughter. Rather mercenary. Nevertheless, using Lucy as a bargaining chip was a brilliant move. If an agreement could be reached, Forbes would win without a fight.

Henry conceded grudging respect. Not that he had any intention of giving up his mistress, the Katy, for his wife, Lucy, though he had to admit he was tempted. Why trade off one when he could have both?

The trick would be getting Lucy alone to woo her without her father's interference. If that kiss gave any indication, it would take a week, maybe two, to coax her to his bed. How could he distract Forbes in the meantime? Having defeated the smartest, most powerful barons in the industry, he could come up with a plan to outfox one old man.

Henry stared at a railroad map affixed to the opposite wall. The Katy's lines spread out over parts of Missouri, Kansas and Indian Territory. The black marks ended six miles over the Texas border. Excitement thrummed through him as an idea formed for how he might get Forbes out of the way and give him enough rope to hang himself—figuratively, of course.

"You make a good point, Major Forbes. My work consumes me. I have no one else to depend on. For instance, now. I need to be in two places at once to deal with problems here and in Texas."

Forbes eyed the map. "What's your problem in Texas?"

Glad you asked.

Henry hopped off the desk. He pointed to the Red River. "As soon as we crossed the border, a Texas judge slapped an injunction on us for not having a charter to operate there. We don't have a charter because the state won't grant us one."

"Why not?"

"Politics. The Texas Central wants the interchange between our lines located in Red River City. We established it in Denison. The Texans won't budge."

"You can't get the injunction overruled?"

"To drag it through the courts could take months. A year. Any amount of time is too long. We need to be operating in Texas *now*." Henry smacked his fist in his palm for emphasis.

Forbes nodded. "You've held talks?"

"Multiple times. They know we're in a tough spot. Spring is when we make most of our money from cattle shipments headed north. If that injunction holds, we'll lose business to the A&P, our biggest competitor." Henry couldn't make it plainer. Unless he pointed out that the Katy teetered on the edge of bankruptcy, which he wouldn't. He preferred to keep his job.

The Major shifted forward. "You want me to negotiate a deal with the Texas Central?"

Henry turned to study the map, as if the decision was a difficult one. It wasn't. He'd prefer being tossed into a rattlesnake pit than deal with those Texans again. Little chance the Major would fare better. Why not let him try? Might change his mind about wanting this job.

"If you're willing," Henry said, at last.

"Why wouldn't I be?"

Here was the crux, which was central to the plan. The Major would have to choose between duty and his daughter. Seemed only fair, considering he wanted to put a potential son-in-law in the same predicament.

"You'll have to go down there and lock horns with those hardheaded Texans. They won't come up here."

Forbes seemed surprised at the answer. "Can't think of any reason I couldn't do that."

Henry could come up with one. "Lucy. She can't go with you."

CHAPTER 10

an't go? Lucy couldn't believe what she'd heard Henry say. She had come back to the office in time for the inauguration ceremony, only to find him at it again, issuing orders. Only this time, he bossed her father around and told him he couldn't take her along.

"*Where* can't I go?"

Henry, who stood facing a large railroad map, turned sharply at her question. For an instant, his unguarded expression revealed his reaction—surprise, followed by consternation.

She'd interrupted a conversation he didn't want her to hear.

Her father twisted in his chair. "Lucy, my dear." He came to his feet, appearing uncomfortable, like a co-conspirator. "We were worried."

"Mr. Reynolds and I took shelter from the weather." She opted for the easiest explanation. She wouldn't let on that she'd been snooping around. Her warm feelings toward Henry, inspired by the widow's story, had cooled rapidly.

"Come in." Her father pulled a leather armchair over next to his.

Before she took the seat, Lucy surveyed Henry's office. The majestic mahogany desk, bookcases, sumptuous leather chairs and tables to match—an office fit for a railroad monarch. Henry's ultimate goal, no doubt.

"Very nice furnishings," she conceded without acting impressed.

"A gift from Mr. Parsons," Henry replied. "We were talking about—"

"Me." She sat, smoothing her skirts. "I heard."

His dark gaze moved over her, sending her nerves into a wild dervish. She couldn't stop thinking about their kiss—the one that had melted her insides—despite her fear that it hadn't meant anything to him. Dwelling on Henry's kisses would not help her father. She had to assume the role of calm observer and ferret out his true intentions.

She gestured, casually. "Please, Mr. Stevens, finish what you wanted to say."

Henry smoothed his hand over his beard. Whenever he did that, she got the distinct impression he was hiding something. "An injunction in Texas prevents us from providing service there. Your father has agreed to go down to negotiate a settlement. You can't go with him."

She gripped the arms of the chair. It was that, or leap up, get into his face to tell him *precisely* what she thought of his presumptive attitude. He might be Lord of the railroad, but he wasn't, and would never be, Lord over her life. "I don't believe that's your decision to make."

Her father's voice rumbled next to her ear. "Give Mr. Stevens an opportunity to explain."

Unbelievable. Her father had switched sides in the time she was out. How Henry had accomplished this, she couldn't imagine. Panic mingled with outrage. "There is no explanation, other than his puffed up sense of self-importance."

Her father rebuked her with a look.

Lucy folded her hands in her lap, simmering.

"Denison is no place for a lady." Henry's impassive delivery irritated her more than his explanation, which was bad enough.

"I've heard that one before. *No place for a lady* is a tired excuse men use for going somewhere they shouldn't."

He didn't blink at her challenge. "It sits across the river from Indian Territory. Being a terminus point, it attracts every kind of low life you can imagine. It isn't a town as much as a collection of saloons and other unsavory establishments."

"That doesn't sound like a safe place to meet." Her father, at least, remained rational.

Henry appeared undaunted. "The town isn't civilized—yet. It will be soon, after we establish Denison as our permanent interchange. If we hold settlement talks there, it gets the point across."

Her father's expression turned thoughtful. "Makes sense."

Henry had missed his calling. He ought to be selling snake oil. He couldn't expect her to believe that nonsense about needing help. His pride wouldn't allow him to share the glory.

She asked the obvious question. "Why don't *you* go down there?"

He gazed down from a superior elevation with his arms folded over his chest. "The Texans don't like me."

No wonder.

"What you mean to say is, you tried and failed."

His nostrils flared. "Failed is not a word I use."

"Who could doubt it?" Her father said. He had to be wise to Henry, yet his tone implied he hadn't made up his mind about Henry's intentions. Worse, he loved nothing better than to be given a problem to solve.

"If I succeed..." he started.

Henry finished the thought. "You would avert a financial crisis."

In other words, he would be a hero.

Lucy's stomach churned with frustration. How smoothly Henry led her father to an agreement, one that required him to leave her behind. For what purpose, she had yet to figure out. Instinctively, she knew Henry was up to no good. However, further argument at this point would be counterproductive.

She would reverse direction. Remain in Parsons and continue her investigation. Henry couldn't prevent her from talking to people.

Her father laid his hand over hers. "Lucy, while I'm gone you must—

"I'll remain here," she said, in her most dutiful tone.

"No. It's not proper for you to be here alone. You'll go home. Stay with your aunt."

Her heart leapt in panic. Go back to Haverhill? No, she couldn't. She *wouldn't*. He needed her here to protect him from snakes like Henry. If he failed to secure this position, they would be in dire straits. He'd be jobless. She would have to return to working in the hat shop. No time for adventures. No time for writing. She'd shrivel up and die.

She clutched her father's arm, tried to keep the panic out of her voice by adopting a lighthearted approach. "You know I'm useless there. Aunt Josephine only put up with me because *Maman* insisted on it. I have no talent for making hats. My home is here now—"

"You won't have to wait for long." Her father patted her hand. When had that gesture ever comforted anyone? "Once I'm finished, I'll send for you."

"That sounds like a plan."

Henry's dismissive remark struck with more force than a slap. She shot him a look that would've killed, had it come from a gun. Not only did he want her father gone, Henry wanted her gone, as well. Why?

Her heart constricted from the pain of both rejections. He must think because he'd kissed her, she would demand marriage to salvage her reputation, and this was his way of squirming out of it. Why, she wouldn't take him if he begged on both knees.

He rounded his desk to search under some papers. "Here's a file with helpful background. There's a meeting tomorrow with Mr. Munson. I've devised a strategy for the negotiations. You can take my place..."

"I'll pack tonight." Her father was back to being practical. "And purchase a good firearm."

He wouldn't tote a gun unless he believed he was in danger.

Lucy's breath caught as the puzzle pieces fell into place. Outraged, she came out of the chair, stalking Henry, who still bent over his desk. "Why you...you *skunk*. I know what you're up to. You're sending my father to that violent place so he'll conveniently disappear, like those missing farmers."

Henry jerked upright, spun around to face her. Shock registered on his face before he schooled his features. "Is that what you think?"

She fisted her hands at her sides. In less than a day, Henry had toyed with her affections, all the while plotting her father's demise, and she had almost fallen for him. She'd been all over town to seek evidence. Not of his guilt. His *innocence*. She'd chased any scrap of gossip that might show him in a more favorable light. Oh God, what a fool she'd been. "What else am I to think, you evil man?"

His mask slipped, revealing hurt and confusion. It wasn't real. His concern wasn't, either. He was a master manipulator. He'd convinced her father to send her away without actually suggesting it. "You might think I care for your safety," he said, with utter sincerity.

Her fury redoubled. "Care for *my* safety? You don't care about anything except your precious position."

Her father appeared at her side. He took a grip on her elbow. "You're overwrought, Lucy. I'll escort you back to the hotel."

She stiffened at the rebuke. Her father rarely raised his voice. He hadn't scolded her since she was a child. Now he'd done it twice in one day. Couldn't he see Henry had pitted them against each other and schemed to betray him? Based on his stern expression, pointing that out would only make him more intractable. She would have to wait until he was out from under Henry's influence.

"Just a moment. I'd like to hear what she thinks I've done." Henry rested his hip on the corner of the desk. He crossed his arms over his chest. That gesture again. Maybe it was more defensive than confident. A way of shielding himself from her.

How laughable. She had no weapons, save her sharp tongue— and her pen. With that, she could destroy him, should he bring harm to her father. "I've told you what I think. There's nothing more to tell."

A knock sounded at the open door. Mr. Caldwell. He'd been

downstairs in the ticket office when she'd arrived. He dressed like his boss, right down to the Congress shoes. Even sported facial hair, though sparser and trimmed into a goatee. Did he aspire to become like Henry? She might warn him the Devil would require his soul.

He gave her a friendly smile before turning his attention back to his boss. "Beg pardon for interrupting. The mayor is waiting. It's nearly time for the ceremony."

The depot's inauguration. She'd forgotten about it in the heat of the moment.

Henry dipped into his waistcoat pocket. Checked his watch. His voice remained as flat as his expression. "Thank you, George. We'll be down shortly."

Still frowning, her father offered his arm.

Lucy ignored it. She refused to be banished to her room for speaking her mind. "Please, go on with Mr. Stevens. You don't want to miss any of the ceremony." She approached Henry's assistant with a smile. "I'm sure Mr. Caldwell won't mind escorting me to a seat."

HENRY SUFFERED through the inauguration ceremony, which was held on a makeshift platform in the stiff March wind. Afterwards, he invited the crowd into the new depot for coffee and doughnuts. The speeches had been short, with the cold preventing anyone from rambling too long. He'd been too distracted to remember his speech, had ended up reading it.

He couldn't believe Lucy actually thought he'd have her father assassinated. *Evil man,* she'd called him. And the way she'd looked at him, as if she wanted to stab that pencil into his chest.

That fool Reynolds must've put those foolish notions into her head. By God, he could shut down the *Sun* in the space of a week by suggesting to railroad-dependent merchants they shouldn't advertise with a gossipmonger.

Inside the spacious lobby, he stretched to his full height to peer over the heads of the guests. He had to find Lucy, ease her fears before things got out of hand.

He spotted her father engaged in conversation with the mayor and a group of businessmen. Forbes cast a worried glance across the room. Henry followed it.

Ah, there she was, drifting along a far wall, examining a series of framed photographs while Caldwell, the impertinent pup, hung on her heels like a lovesick swain.

Henry bit back a curse. Strong emotions interfered with a man's control and clouded his thinking. Like now, for instance. Jealousy would have him believe that his assistant would be considered a desirable catch with his pretty face and perfect pedigree. That's why Lucy had boldly asked him to escort her. A calmer mind would know she'd done it to make a point. That she would not be bullied or controlled by a more powerful man.

Manipulation, pure and simple. For instance, he'd acted as if he wanted her gone when the opposite was true. He had expected her father to try to send her away and had had already come up with an idea about how to prevent it. He hadn't figured in Lucy's suspicions.

Murder. That nasty punch to the gut had caught him by surprise.

He made his way through the crowded lobby, greeting visitors, picking up snatches of conversations about the marble floors, the boring speeches, complaints about the weather. He approached his assistant. Tapped him on the shoulder. "Mr. Caldwell. Thank you for taking good care of our guest."

The younger man, being bright enough to get the message, took his leave.

Lucy threw a bland look over her shoulder, then went right back to studying the photographs.

Henry's face got hot. She could *try* to ignore him.

He clamped down his ire. The situation required diplomacy, which meant he couldn't begin with a volatile question, such as, *What the hell makes you think I'm a murderer?* No. The conversation should start off casual, wind around to what she'd heard, and then he could dispel the myths.

"What do you think of our new depot?" He kept his tone pleasant.

"Impressive," she murmured.

"Are you enjoying the photographs?"

"Yes."

"If we're to have a conversation, you'll need to do better than one-word answers."

"Are we having a conversation? I hadn't noticed."

Henry took a deep breath. He'd dearly love to shatter that icy façade the way his men blasted through sheer rock—with dynamite. Then, after he exploded in anger, he'd have a pile of rubble. Better to melt the ice. Find something he could use to get her talking.

She leaned in to get a closer look at a picture of sweaty tracklayers who'd been in the midst of pounding down rails. A moment later, she moved to the next image. Tiny figures atop a nearly completed span across the Verdigris.

Henry's chest tightened, as it always did when he looked at this particular photograph.

Why this one? She could've stopped at any other picture. An explanation would no doubt detract from her thoughts about him being a murderer. Or maybe not.

"That's in Indian Territory, over a confluence of three rivers. The longest bridge we ever built. We lost ten men when the center span gave way. Fell two hundred feet into the river."

She swiveled her head to look at him. Horror filled her eyes. "How awful..."

Awful didn't begin to describe it. When he'd reported the disaster to his boss, his voice breaking, Parsons had coldly pronounced, *Success isn't for the faint of heart, Henry, or for those with a squeamish conscience.*

"Another fifteen men died from cholera that summer. Hundreds more succumbed to swamp sickness. Most recovered. Many still suffer from the effects. They kept working, though. Good men. Brave men." Henry swallowed to clear the lump obstructing his throat.

The crews had obeyed his orders. *Work faster. Work harder.* How many men had died because he wouldn't quit?

He hadn't spoken to anyone else about what had happened. For some reason, he felt compelled to tell Lucy. Why, he wasn't sure. It wouldn't likely make her warm to him.

She searched his gaze. "Is that why you have their pictures here? To honor them?"

How quickly she'd picked up on that. Strange, how she saw things so clearly that others didn't. "It seemed proper."

"I agree. A much better choice than pictures of rich old men."

She meant the images of the railroad elite that graced most depots.

"You can find Mr. Parsons' portrait by the front door." Henry gestured at the painting he'd given a place of honor.

"And yours?"

"I haven't had my portrait painted." And he never would.

Her lips tipped up. "Because you're not old enough?"

The tightness across his shoulders eased. She poked gentle fun, which gave him a way out of an emotional minefield. She had sensitivity he lacked.

"Deeds should be remembered, not faces."

"I agree," she said.

He directed her to the next picture. "That's the bridge over the Red River. You can see Colbert's ferry in the water. He complains about how much business he'll lose because of the railroad. He's already made a fortune with what he charges folks to cross."

Lucy turned to look at the photograph. Henry's attention wandered to the tender skin behind her ear. He longed to put his lips there, explore that sensitive spot, find others that would make her gasp with pleasure. Passion, lust, whatever one called it, could be a fierce beast. Recently, it had grown to enormous proportions.

"How much more do customers pay to use the railroad?" Her casual tone indicated she was unaware of the battle he waged.

"Half what it costs to use the ferry, and we take them farther." He redirected his eyes to the photograph so he wouldn't be tempted to give up the fight and drop a kiss on her neck. Instead of gasping with pleasure, she'd probably beat him senseless with that bag of books.

"That's the first train to cross into Texas. See the engineer leaning out the window? He had the whistle wide open when he came across the bridge."

"Is this you, celebrating?"

Henry stared at his unsmiling image. He recalled standing in front of the brightly festooned locomotive, wearing a brand new suit. He'd expected to be promoted that day. Optimistic, or deluded, as it turned out. A year later, he was still waiting. Mr. Parsons had to retire sometime. When he did, he would keep his promise.

"We entered Texas, a year ago Christmas Day. Best present I ever got."

"You don't look very happy about your present."

Henry smoothed his hand over his beard. He'd been worried what might show through in a photograph, that the camera's eye would somehow see through his heavy beard and capture his true image. "The sun was in my eyes."

"It looks like you're standing in the shadow."

"I don't like having my picture taken." He didn't like mirrors either.

"You're a prominent figure. I would think you'd be used to it by now." Lucy's keen appraisal made him nervous. For a moment, he feared she saw through his disguise.

"Who was the photographer?" she asked.

He released a relieved breath. "Adella McGrady, our foreman's wife. They were married a week after we crossed the border into Indian Territory and whipped our competition."

"The race with the Border Tier?" Lucy's brow furrowed. "I read about that. One of the stories said you tricked the other crew into laying track to the wrong marker."

"They got their directions from some Indians." He didn't add that the *Indians* happened to be Irish. She might confuse his cleverness with deceit. He could list far more crimes committed by his competitor.

She leaned forward to peer at the image of a couple in front of a canvas building with a painted wooden sign overhead. "Who are these people?"

"Mr. and Mrs. McGrady."

"They're standing in front of a saloon."

"One of McGrady's men owns the place. Adella thinks nothing of going into saloons, or anywhere else, for that matter."

"Adella?" When Lucy she met his eyes, he couldn't look away. It was damned disconcerting. "You admire her."

Henry shrugged to hide his discomfort. Admire was one way to put it. He'd certainly stopped *admiring* her when her shenanigans had nearly cost him the race. "Hard not to respect Mrs. McGrady. She stuck by her husband no matter how bad things got. Even helped nurse the men when they were sick."

"She followed the construction?"

"All the way to Texas."

Lucy's narrowed eyes telegraphed trouble. "So, she can follow the railroad, but I can't go to Texas?"

He had to remember how quickly her mind worked. He would turn what she perceived to be an insult into a compliment. "You're a gently bred lady."

"Mrs. McGrady looks like a lady."

"Don't her looks fool you. She's tough. She served as a spy during the war." Afterwards, for a dirty politician. No need to go into that convoluted story. "You aren't used to being on your own."

Most women liked to be coddled. Lucy's frown indicated she wasn't counted among them. "I'm not as inexperienced as you think, certainly not a piece of china. Why don't you admit you don't want me around because I might get in the way of whatever plot you're hatching?"

"I plan, I don't plot. And I have never *hatched* anything."

"Then why do you want me to leave?"

It was time he began correcting at least one of her misconceptions. He lowered his voice to a conciliatory tone. "Lucy, I don't wish for you to leave."

"You said it was a good idea."

He'd said that to conceal his real purpose from her father. However, he'd done enough confessing for one night. "That's because I want you to be safe."

"Safe from who—you?"

Heat streaked up his neck to the tips of his ears. "Look here," he whispered harshly. "I don't know what Milt Reynolds told you, but you might give me a chance to explain before you convict me."

Something akin to doubt crossed her face before she buttoned it up behind a starched expression. "You'll deny it.

"Deny what?"

"That you had something to do with those men's disappearance."

"Of course I'd deny it. I had nothing to do with it." He searched her eyes, could tell she wanted to believe him. She remained fearful for some reason.

"Why should I trust you?"

It was on the tip of his tongue to tell her not to trust anyone. It wouldn't help him, even if it was the best advice. "Why do you *dis*trust me? Because I kissed you?"

Hurt clouded her eyes. She blinked rapidly like she was about to cry.

Desperation gripped him. He could manage rowdy railroad workers and rioting settlers. He was at a loss when dealing with a woman's tears. It triggered disturbing memories. His mother's quiet weeping after his father had invested the last of their money in a foolish scheme. His sisters' frightened wails when they'd learned they were orphaned. He hadn't been able to comfort them. He couldn't comfort Lucy, either.

Henry whipped out his handkerchief and stuffed it into Lucy's hand. He had no better idea how stop the flow once it started. He glanced around, uneasy. If she burst into tears that would compound the problem by drawing attention. He could walk away. Yet, he sensed he was close, so close to breaking through her distrust. Instead of retreating, he would advance. Bare his soul. Or part of his soul—the good part.

"Follow me out back. We'll have more privacy. I have something to tell you."

Lucy didn't follow when Henry walked off without a backward glance. She opened the crisp white handkerchief he'd given her, which had been stitched with bold initials. He'd feared she would cry. What did he expect her response would be after he threw her indiscretion in her face? It would serve him right if she went directly to the sheriff to report what she suspected. Except, a lawman wouldn't act on gossip, and she had to admit to having doubts about her own assumptions.

That heartbreaking story Henry had shared about those workers who'd died and his desire to honor them had given her another glimpse into the soul of a truly admirable man. She'd seen his other nature, too, as smoothly cunning as the serpent that coerced Eve to eat the apple.

Would he offer her forbidden fruit? Her foolish heart leapt in anticipation.

If he desired another kiss, he wouldn't try to get rid of her. Whatever it was he wanted, she wouldn't find out standing here.

LUCY WENT OUTSIDE to satisfy her curiosity. Only Henry would brave the cold. No one else had. Not even to admire the shiny black locomotive parked beside the platform. On the tender box, the gilded letters MK&T were emblazoned on a red shield. Lord Henry must've come up with the heraldic design. She'd bet he had royal ancestors, with the way he issued orders and expected everyone to jump.

An arctic wind whipped around the corner of the building. Before she could draw her cape closer, Henry had taken off his overcoat to drape it over her shoulders. The second time today he'd made the courtly gesture.

She hugged the lapels, unable to resist the coat's warmth, its tantalizing scents. "You needn't give me your overcoat."

"I won't—when you remember to wear a warmer wrap." He drew

her next to the brick wall, positioning his back to the biting wind to further shield her from the cold. "Better?"

"Much," she admitted. He played the part of a gentleman exceedingly well. She'd give him that. "I hope you didn't bring me out here to scold me about my wrap, or..." She trembled from nervous excitement. "Teach me a lesson."

He gazed at her intently. "Neither. You have several misconceptions I intend to clear up. The first being, why I kissed you. I didn't do it to teach you a lesson or to punish you."

Why did you kiss me? She almost asked the question. His answer wouldn't be what a woman wanted to hear. It wouldn't involve his heart. He was a man, after all. Men had urges. He must be trying to apologize for acting on one. Although he made it sound like *she* was the problem.

She blinked up at him, bemused. "Is that the best you can do?"

"Would a whip suffice?"

Her startled laugh came out as a cough. "That's not...not what I meant."

He didn't smile. "Do you understand what I'm saying?"

"You're sorry?"

"Yes, and I'd like to make it up to you."

Lucy hated how eagerly she looked forward to that. She was weak where he was concerned. Worse, he knew it. He shouldn't expect her pardon would come easy, yet he'd surmised correctly. Her inclination was to forgive. Still, she wouldn't go so far as to trust him.

"How do I know you're not doing this to get me to agree to something I shouldn't?"

He arched an eyebrow in question. "Such as?"

"Talk my father out of going to Denison." She watched for his reaction, expecting a flush of anger. Instead, the look he gave her was one of disappointment.

"Why would you do that? The directors want improved earnings. That will only happen after this injunction is lifted. The Texans won't deal with me. Your father is more agreeable in nature. Clever enough not to give away the advantage. He's perfect for the job and he knows it."

Henry made it sound so reasonable. She wasn't convinced. He had some other purpose in mind that he wouldn't admit. She had to find out, in spite of her father's insistence that she leave. Without her own funds, she couldn't remain, unless...

She peeked at Henry from beneath her lashes. His burning gaze made her shiver. He'd brought her out here to apologize, yet he was standing close. So close her body hummed with awareness.

He felt this attraction, too. She could use that to her advantage.

Her breath caught at the disgraceful thought. Still, didn't he deserve a dose of his own medicine? He'd manipulated her and her father. In fact, his apology might only be intended to soften her up so she wouldn't disrupt his schemes. "You said earlier you didn't want me to leave."

He leaned his shoulder against the side of the building, which created a greater sense of intimacy and made his interest in her unmistakable. "Could your father be persuaded to allow you to remain in Parsons?"

Lucy hid her hands inside the coat to hide her trembling. She'd entered unknown territory, having never used her feminine wiles to charm a man, much less a snake. "He might reconsider, if I had a companion. Someone who would be willing to stay at the hotel with me. Do you know of anyone?"

Henry's slow smile made her insides jump.

"Someone my father would approve," she added quickly. "A matron or widow."

He heaved an exaggerated sigh. "Sadly, I don't meet the requirements."

Lucy's face turned warm, and afterwards her entire body. The idea of sharing quarters with Henry should be frightening, not thrilling. "A woman of good character. He'll ask for references."

Henry straightened, becoming serious, businesslike. "Yes, I know of someone. She has excellent credentials. I'll have an answer for you in the morning."

"That quickly?" Lucy couldn't believe it would be that simple. However, if Mrs. Bannerman were to be believed, Henry knew everyone in town. "Thank you."

He acknowledged her gratitude with a polite nod. "The least I can do, considering. I'm the one who created your dilemma."

A proper companion would put her father's concerns to rest. While he was gone, she must start the process of emancipation, in order to have the freedom to make her own decisions. That required a job. The very thought of working in a store like her aunt's hat shop was enough to depress her. She wanted to write. Who would buy her stories? She hadn't worked up the nerve to offer them to anyone. Not even the newspaper editor.

Henry could help. He had influence. Every business in town depended on the railroad.

She tried batting her eyelashes. "I hope I'm not too bold in asking one more favor."

He relaxed his arm against the wall and leaned in. "Not at all. What else can I do?"

So far, so good. Though, if he was like most men, he wouldn't approve of what she was about to ask. "I don't wish to be a burden on my father," she started, by way of explanation.

Henry actually looked pleased by her desire for independence. "No, of course not. Nor do you have to be."

She released a relieved breath. "I'm glad you understand. Perhaps you'd be willing to speak with Mr. Reynolds about allowing me to write stories for the newspaper?"

"The newspaper?" He drew back with surprise. Perhaps she'd misread his earlier reaction.

"Do you believe it's wrong for a woman to aspire to a career?"

"You want a *career*?" His bemused tone disappointed her.

"Some of the most popular writers today are women. You might not know of them, being older and more conventional, like my father."

He straightened, his features stiffening. "How old do you think I am?"

She'd offended him. Not a very effective strategy for gaining his assistance. "It doesn't matter—"

"Thirty-five. Your father has to be close to sixty."

"Yes, well, my point wasn't about your age. I was remarking on your mindset. A man who isn't hemmed in by conventional thinking wouldn't object to a woman pursuing an occupation."

Henry regarded her intently. "That's what you're looking for? An unconventional man?"

Lucy nearly lost her nerve. Drawing close to fire without getting burned required cleverness and courage. She needed both to have the future she envisioned. "I'm not on a manhunt. I need a job," she said firmly. "You said you wished to make amends for your earlier offense. I should consider it an adequate repayment if you would approach Mr. Reynolds on my behalf."

CHAPTER 11

*H*enry suspected Lucy would try to stay in Parsons. He hadn't expected her to ask for his assistance. An unexpected boon of which he planned to take to full advantage.

The next morning, he tracked down Claire in the hotel's kitchen pantry. She wouldn't refuse his request. After all, he'd come to her aid when her husband hadn't been able to work to support them.

His petite sister stood on a ladder in front of floor-to-ceiling shelves, which contained sacks of flour and sugar, along with an array of cans and jars containing meat, fruits and vegetables. They had both come a long way from their childhood, spent in a cold hovel without enough to eat. With only each other to count on.

Not one to waste time, Henry plunged in. "I need a favor."

Claire turned her attention from the shelves to a ledger in her hand. She spoke while writing. "What sort of favor?"

"Major Forbes needs to go to Denison on business. His daughter wishes to remain here. He's concerned for her safety. I'd like to tell them you are willing to act as a chaperone."

Claire twisted around so sharply she almost lost her balance. Henry moved to catch her if she fell. She grabbed the side of the ladder and righted herself. "You want me to do *what?*"

Her horrified expression told him what she thought of his plan. "Chaperone."

"Where did you get the idea that I have time to chaperone a girl?"

Her misconception about Lucy's maturity annoyed him. "She isn't a girl. She's a young woman of twenty-two."

"I don't care how old she is."

Lucy had said as much about his age.

"Why aren't women concerned with exactness when discussing matters involving numbers?"

"Oh, good grief, Henry." Claire turned back to her task, muttering. "I don't have time to delve into philosophical questions."

"This is not a philosophical discussion. You live here. Lucy wants to stay here. Being her chaperone seems an easy enough assignment."

"Easy?" Claire harrumphed. "That's because you have no idea what I do."

He frowned up at her, annoyed. "I know exactly how much is involved in running a business. All I'm asking is for you to keep an eye on her."

Claire sought a lower step with one booted foot, found it, then reached with the other. Henry held the ladder in place until she made it safely to the floor. She slipped her notebook into one of two large apron pockets. She'd no doubt selected that plain brown dress for practicality. She could benefit from a dose of Lucy's natural sense of style. "I'm sorry Henry. I'd like to help, truly. I simply don't have time to play nursemaid."

"Not nursemaid. Companion. She'll be with me mostly. You won't have much to do. Say you're willing."

His sister heaved an exasperated sigh. "Why me?"

"It has to be an older woman. A widow or a matron."

"*Matron?*" Claire's face reddened. "Henry Stevens, I am eight years younger than you. If I'm a matron, then you're an old codger."

Her cutting remark bounced off because he knew she didn't mean it.

"Your hearing appears to be going before mine. I didn't say *you* were matronly. You're older than Lucy, married, a respected member of the community. You live right here. It makes perfect sense to me."

Claire rolled her eyes, an irritating habit she'd picked up from older twin sisters, who also rolled their eyes that very same way when they thought whatever had been said was ridiculous. Henry recalled his mother had done it, as well. Had to be a trait handed down through generations of women.

Once again, Claire muttered to herself as she turned to an arrangement of cans on different shelves. He couldn't see the usefulness of her pattern. He wasn't here to discuss her organizational habits. He needed her agreement to a small favor.

"Well?"

"What's your interest in this girl, Henry?"

"Stop calling her a *girl*. She's a woman."

Claire laughed softly. "She's easily fifteen years younger than you, brother."

She stacked the vegetable cans into a pyramid, with the fruit next to them. His sister's arrangement began to make sense even if her concerns didn't.

Henry moved behind her, talking over her right shoulder. "So, you do care about numbers. Your estimate is wrong, though. I'm thirteen years older. That doesn't make her a child."

"Then why ask me to look out for her?"

He answered as honestly as he could without going into details. His sister didn't need to be privy to all his plans. "You were the first person I thought of when she asked me if I knew a woman of good character."

Claire stopped her activity. She turned to Henry with a can in each hand. "You're moving chess pieces around again."

Those looked like cans, and *she* was moving them.

"Chess pieces?"

"People." She set the two cans on an empty shelf side by side, with the labels turned out. "You like to direct people's movements, make them do what you want."

The remark stung, even if it was true. He reached over her head to place a can on a shelf too high for her to reach. "Is that what you think I'm doing to you?"

She fussed with the arrangement she'd created without looking at him. "You've been very good to me, Henry. I could never repay you for everything you've done."

"Repay me?" That remark annoyed him more than the one about the chess pieces. "You're my sister. I don't expect repayment."

Finally, she turned. Her brown eyes—their only inheritance from their father—filled with warmth. Also, a hint of sadness. "Yes, you do. Not money. You want something more valuable. But you don't have to buy it. You have my love and loyalty, regardless."

Something twisted painfully inside Henry's chest. He forced out a laugh. "Don't be ridiculous. I provide for you because it's my responsibility."

That was the wrong thing to say.

His sister's features tightened with offense. "As a married woman, I am no longer your responsibility. Hannah and Bridget have their own business. You don't have to take care of us any longer."

The air in the pantry grew thin. Henry drew in a deep breath to dispel the sense of suffocation. Claire was wrong. They did need him. And he wouldn't let them down, not like his father had done.

She brushed loose strands of hair out of her face. When had that worry line across her brow and the dark circles under her eyes become permanent? He should've noticed earlier how weary she looked.

The mantle he wore as elder brother grew heavier. He'd hoped to make Claire's life easier by bringing her and her invalid husband out here, arranging for them to have the hotel. Clearly, she felt obligated. If she refused to help, it meant she was overwhelmed.

"Claire, you are not obliged to do anything you don't wish to do. I'm sorry if I've given you that impression."

The brackets around her mouth eased. Her eyes softened. "I suppose since Miss Forbes is staying here in the hotel, I could look in on her. Take her shopping when I go out. Introduce her to some of our friends."

He'd won. So why did it feel like he'd lost?

Before she could change her mind, he sidled toward the pantry door. "You won't have to do much. She's asked me to find her a job."

"A job? Then why on earth does she need me to...?" Claire shook her head and waved a hand in the air. "Oh, never mind. I'm too tired to figure out whatever it is you're up to."

"What makes you think I'm up to something?"

His sister leveled a knowing look. "Henry, you are *always* up to something."

AN HOUR LATER, Henry arrived at the newspaper office to present his demand.

"You want me to employ Miss Forbes as a reporter?" Milt Reynolds stood and braced his hands over the scattered papers cluttering his desk. His eyebrows formed a single bushy line, surprisingly thick, in contrast to the sparse hair on his head. "It is not my policy to employ women."

Henry leaned back in the chair to stretch out his legs, sending the clear message that he didn't give a damn. "Didn't ask if it was your policy. I asked you to do me a favor."

"You haven't done me any favors lately. In fact, you cancelled the railroad's advertising when I printed that editorial on the land dispute. I presented both sides of the issue."

"Your bread isn't buttered on both sides."

The editor, who also happened to be the publisher, dropped back into his seat. "*The Sun* is not your personal mouthpiece, Mr. Stevens. We're here to serve the public good, not give the railroad preferential treatment."

"Then you won't mind if the railroad doesn't grant you free passes. Or doesn't pay twice the price for advertisements we don't need. Or doesn't make contributions to your campaign when you run for state senate."

Reynolds glowered. "Curse you, Stevens."

"Already taken care of, thank you." Henry laced his fingers behind his head. He knew he'd get what he came for, as soon as the pompous ass let go of the notion that he was morally superior. Milt Reynolds was no better than any other man. Each one had his price.

"You don't have to buy it." Claire's words popped into Henry's head.

This wasn't at all the same, he argued back. Of course, he didn't have to buy his sisters' loyalty. Everyone else sold theirs to the highest bidder.

Henry shifted forward with his hands on his knees and met the editor's glare. "Don't waste that high-and-mighty 'we're here for the public good' claptrap on me. I know what you want. I'm willing to give it to you—*if* you do as I ask. God knows you *owe* me after telling Lucy that I'm a murderer."

Reynolds' face darkened. "I didn't tell her that. She misunderstood."

"You're responsible for her misunderstanding."

The editor made a steeple with his fingers, trying to look important. "What makes you think she'll be a good reporter? For all I know, she can't write anything but recipes."

"It doesn't matter whether she can write. You're an editor. Fix her copy."

Horror flashed across the other man's face. "You can't expect me to print it."

"Print it, and give her full credit."

"Print it?" Reynolds sputtered. "Why? Miss Forbes is a genteel young lady, supported by her father. Surely, she doesn't need the employment."

"She doesn't need it, she wants it. I intend to see that she gets what she wants."

Awareness dawned in the editor's eyes. He leaned back and rubbed his chin thoughtfully. "I think I'm beginning to understand. Well, well...never thought I'd see the day Henry Stevens let a young chit lead him around by the nose."

Henry smiled without humor. "I'm content to be led, for the time being."

Of course, Lucy was using him. She was so obvious. Transparent even. He hadn't realized she wanted a career, much less with a newspaper. He'd quickly figured out how he could turn her request to his advantage.

Reynolds picked up a pencil. He rolled it between his fingers. "She may not be as easy to corral as you think."

"I would be disappointed if she were." Henry came to his feet. He crossed the office to look out the window.

The street teemed with activity. Riders, buggies, wagons loaded with building materials and supplies for farms. Parsons had grown fast, and the Katy was growing with it. After his boss reimbursed him for his expenditures on behalf of the railroad, he'd start construction on a house. Lucy could put her touch on the design and decorations. He'd take her East on a shopping spree to purchase furnishings. That ought to please her.

His pulse quickened as he imagined how his new bride might show her gratitude. He'd only gotten a small taste of her passion, yet enough to know she would be an eager lover. He would exercise patience, coax her to his hand, as he'd seen the Indians do with a spirited horse.

"One more thing," he said over his shoulder. "Assign her to cover the railroad."

"The railroad?" Reynolds blurted. "What the devil are you thinking? A woman can't go traipsing all over creation, covering the railroad."

"I'll take responsibility. She can travel with me."

At the other man's silence, he turned.

The editor regarded him with distaste. "She's an unmarried young lady, Henry. If she travels with you, her reputation will be ruined."

"It won't be if she's my wife."

CHAPTER 12

The next morning dawned bright and sunny. Lucy recalled Henry's warning about the fickle Kansas weather. She wore a heavier cloak.

It was a short walk from the hotel to the depot, where her father would catch the morning train to Texas. They went together, in silence. She still harbored reservations about his decision to go to Texas. He still wore a thunderous frown, which had descended when she'd told him about her plans to stay in Parsons.

The knots in her stomach twisted tighter. She'd done the right thing. Her father needed her here, where she could help him most, not in Haverhill in her aunt's hat shop where she'd be of no use to anyone.

He escorted her to a bench beneath a chalkboard marked with the day's train schedules, then set his case on the ground. Other passengers streamed past them. "You have not yet convinced me you should remain here."

She thought he might say that.

Instead of losing her temper, she took a logical approach, as she'd seen Henry do. "Mrs. Daines is a respectable married woman. She lives in the hotel, and has agreed to act as a chaperone when I need one."

Henry hadn't wasted a moment putting those wheels into motion. The offer of his sister as a chaperone had been very clever. That would make it easier for him to be alone with her. Was his plan to ruin her or get information from her? Either way, she could be clever, too. She would use this opportunity to befriend Claire and learn more about Henry.

"It's all very proper, Father."

"This arrangement you've made with the newspaper isn't."

The arrangements weren't final. Yet. Henry was supposed to talk to Mr. Reynolds. After that, she assumed the editor would ask to see samples of her writing. The process might take a few days. She didn't say so because she didn't want her father's interference.

He didn't have to tell her that her reputation was at stake. Other women had sacrificed to realize their dreams. She would, as well. Only, not in the way Henry had in mind. "I don't see how writing stories for the newspaper can be construed as inappropriate. Mrs. Southworth got her start that way."

Her father's glower remained. "Mrs. Southworth is a middle-aged widow. You are an unwed young lady. You have no business wandering about, collecting stories."

"Most of the time I'll be in the newspaper office, or in my room, writing." Lucy hugged his neck so he wouldn't see the lie on her face. She couldn't remain inside and accomplish what she intended. "Please, let's not be cross with each other right before you get on the train."

He searched her face anxiously. "If this matter can't be resolved quickly, I'm coming back. I won't leave you here alone for more than a week."

She understood his fears, having faced her own demons. They had only each other left. It terrified her to let him go. At the same time, she felt trapped. Somehow, she had to find the right balance. A first step would be this brief separation.

"I'll be *fine*. You must take the time you need to negotiate with the

Texas Central. Get the injunction removed. I don't think Mr. Stevens believes you can do it. That's why he's asked you to go in his place. His arrogance will be his undoing."

Her father's gruff expression melted into sadness. "You may be right."

Lucy's heart stumbled. That was as close as he'd come to declaring Henry an ambitious schemer. "I know you hoped he would turn out to be more like you."

Her father shook his head slowly. "I hoped he would turn out to be better."

What had made him think such a thing? The two men couldn't be more different. Her father's rock-hard integrity had cost him his job. Henry, it seemed, would do anything to hold onto his position.

She lovingly touched her father's cheek. "No man could be better than you."

He captured her hand. "Lucy, my dearest girl, you are more precious to me than anything. If something should happen to you...."

"Nothing is going to happen." She swallowed the urge to cry. He would reduce her to tears, talking like this.

Smoke spewed from the engine's stack, clouding the air, stinging Lucy's nose and eyes. A brief flash of panic swept through her. For another moment, she clung to his arm.

"All aboard," the conductor called.

Her father picked up his case. She walked beside him in the direction of the parlor car. As a railroad executive, he'd travel in comfort. All around them, passengers said their goodbyes to loved ones. If she tried to explain her fears and hold onto him, she'd embarrass him.

"Keep that pistol you purchased handy," she reminded him. "If the town is as rough as they say, you may need it." She rose up on her toes to kiss his cheek, determined not to cry. *Bon voyage, Papa*. I shall pray for your success and swift return."

After the train had rumbled out of the station, as the smoke cleared, Lucy remained at the edge of the platform. She continued to stare down the long set of tracks after everyone else had left. What if she'd been wrong to let go? If something happened to her father, she would never forgive herself...or Henry.

"He'll be back soon."

She whirled around at the familiar voice. Her traitorous heart bounced inside her chest.

Henry stood close enough that she could touch the gold watch fob that dangled from the pocket of his forest green waistcoat. His suit had threads of the same color woven through the brown wool. The man certainly knew how to make a statement.

His eyes gleamed, as if he'd noticed her admiration. He tipped his hat. "Good morning, Miss Forbes."

Heavens, she hated to admit her gladness at seeing him. Because of the job. That was the only reason she would allow. "You surprised me..." Their arranged meeting wasn't for another two hours. His eagerness flattered her. "I didn't expect you until later."

"My office is up there." He pointed to a window on the second floor. "I saw you down here. Thought we'd waste less time if I came out."

The air went out of her pride. He hadn't been in a hurry to greet her. He'd seen it as a chance to save time. "I see. You must maintain a tight schedule. Like those trains," she gestured at the chalkboard mounted on the depot wall.

"Schedules can be altered when necessary." He reached inside his coat pocket, retrieved his diary, opened it to show her. "See? I've cleared the whole day to be an attentive host."

She stared at the page with a pencil mark through it and her name written in his bold hand. Excitement shimmered through her, followed by a burst of alarm. Even if his intentions were honorable, which she doubted, spending an entire day with him would send the wrong message.

"That's very kind of you. Don't disrupt your schedule on my account. I've already asked your sister to go shopping today."

The notebook went back into his pocket. He regarded her with puzzlement. "Didn't you say you wanted to write for the newspaper?"

She caught her breath in surprise. "You've had a chance to speak with Mr. Reynolds?"

"I did. He's agreed to take you on—as a reporter."

"A reporter?" Her joy came out in a gleeful laugh. She'd thought she would be lucky to get a few stories published. Why, this was beyond what she'd asked. More than she'd dreamed possible. She could make a living, while continuing to write fiction. The newspaper might even publish one of her books in serial form. She could become independent sooner than expected. And she had Henry to thank for it.

"Henry, thank you." She threw her arms around his neck and gave him a hug. "Thank you so much."

He went still for an instant before his arms went around her in a tight embrace.

Lucy came to her senses with a start. She scrambled backwards to free herself.

He snagged her elbow. "Look behind you."

She twisted to peer over her shoulder. Her heart slammed to a stop. Her heel touched the edge of the platform. The tracks lay several feet below. With another half step, she would've had a nasty fall. *"Bonté divine!"*

He gently drew her away from the edge. "Why do you do that?"

"What?" She released a nervous laugh. "Hug strangers or fall off the edge of platforms?"

"That wasn't English you were speaking."

She withdrew her arm from his grasp. His touch rattled her more than the potential fall. "My mother spoke French. Her expressions come out sometimes, when I'm startled."

He regarded her solemnly. "What did you find more startling? Hugging me or almost falling off the platform?"

"Oui."

Her coy response coaxed a genuine smile out of him, one that showed his teeth—white and healthy, the front ones slightly overlapped. Strangely enough, the small flaw made him more attractive, not less. She'd swear he had a dimple in his cheek. With the beard, it was hard to tell.

Lucy brushed bits of ash from her sleeve to distract herself. However handsome, Henry was not to be trusted. She wouldn't forget herself again. No more hugs. No more touching. No being alone with him either. "When do I start work?"

"Today." His voice carried a hint of amusement.

She looked up to see what he found so funny. "Did Mr. Reynolds mention what he wants me to write about? I suppose he'll assign me to church dinners and social events."

Henry shook his head.

For the life of her, she couldn't figure out why he looked proud of himself.

"He has something more important in mind. You will report on the railroad."

"The railroad?" She couldn't imagine an editor would give a green reporter such an important assignment, certainly not without knowing the least thing about her. Being the railroad correspondent would mean travel, and daily contact with...

Henry.

She flushed as his ploy became clear. He'd found a perfect way to control her. Ruin her, more like. Such an assignment wouldn't *taint* her reputation, it would *shred* it.

Lucy held her tongue to keep from lashing him with it. After all, she couldn't scold him for essentially doing what she'd asked. "How did you manage to talk Mr. Reynolds into making me a railroad correspondent? That seems unlikely, considering my gender and inexperience."

"He trusts my judgment."

She gave him a doubtful eye.

"And he relies on my good will."

He'd bribed the editor or threatened to undermine the newspaper. Either way, he'd acted dishonorably to fulfill her request. Disappointment sluiced through her, surprisingly painful.

She sighed. "Don't you mean *money*?"

He arched an eyebrow imperiously. "Given your father's experience, you should know that wielding influence requires money and power. Fortunate for you, I have both."

"Yes, very fortunate." She couldn't muster much conviction.

"Is this not what you wanted?"

Curse him, he knew very well it was more than she could hope to accomplish on her own. He'd offered her the chance of a lifetime. She couldn't turn it down. On the other hand, she wasn't so naïve as to think he didn't expect something in return.

"I fear I will be in your debt."

"Not at all." He offered his arm. "It's my pleasure to be of service."

"Indeed?" If she knew one thing, she knew that Henry was a businessman, first and foremost. He viewed things from the standpoint of what could be bought or sold. Relationships were reduced to figures, calculated for their value. As such, he would expect to gain from this transaction.

She had only one thing he could possibly want. Sadly, she couldn't deny her attraction to him or her curiosity about what it might lead to. While such a relationship might give them both a great deal of *pleasure*, the cost she would pay was far too high.

HENRY ESCORTED Lucy to the offices of the *Parsons Sun*. He waited while she spoke with the editor about her assignment. Afterwards, he accompanied her to the depot. He might've arranged the job for her. That didn't mean he'd let her wander around alone. She'd be too tempting a morsel for some unscrupulous ruffian.

As they strolled down the sidewalk, he laid his hand over her smaller one, which he'd tucked into the crook of his elbow. Older women gave them curious stares, while the younger ones threw envious glances. Men, regardless of age, went bug-eyed with interest. They grinned like idiots when Lucy responded to their greetings. Every time a man looked at her, something sharp and hot speared through Henry.

Absurd. He couldn't go around throttling men for admiring her. Who wouldn't?

Lucy looked positively enticing, as fresh as those pink rosebuds that dotted her dress. Her bonnet, which she'd tied with a cheeky bow, did little to shield the sun's bright rays. Its sole purpose appeared to be to frame her face and draw attention to the honeyed curls escaping from the back. Some sort of feathery bird's nest adorned one side.

He'd never understand why women paid exorbitant prices for ornamentation they could retrieve out of a tree.

She reached up, touched the stuffed bird.

"Checking to see if it's flown?"

"Are you making fun of my hat?"

"Never. I'll buy you dozens like it, should that please you." He'd buy her anything she wanted if it elicited another hug.

Henry couldn't recall the last time a woman had spontaneously thrown her arms around his neck with genuine gratitude, much less fondness. He'd wanted to hold her, enjoy the rare moment. She'd leapt out of his arms, startled, he supposed, by her unorthodox behavior. If he did something else nice, perhaps she'd forget herself again. "I've noticed you like hats..."

She sighed, as if he had discovered a great secret. "A weakness of mine, I'm afraid. Ever since I was a little girl. My mother took me to my aunt's hat shop and let me try them on. Aunt Josephine said I was much better at modeling hats than making them."

Henry could imagine Lucy in front of a mirror, trying on hats. He could also imagine her modeling a variety of underclothing, a thought he shouldn't entertain. He needed to be on his best behavior, at least for a day. Otherwise, his bird might fly. "What else do you like? I mean, besides hats?"

Her gaze turned speculative. "Aren't *I* supposed to be the one asking questions?"

"You seem less enthused by the prospect." He hadn't received a hug for that.

"Oh, I am. Looking forward to being a reporter that is. As for following you around..."

He drew his own conclusion from her wary tone. Her concern wasn't surprising. After all, she was a lady. He'd taken liberties. She still hadn't forgiven him, despite what she said. "You have nothing to worry about. I've arranged everything."

"That's what I fear."

A bad case of nerves wasn't what he wanted to inspire. Somehow, he had to put her at ease. He had no intention to harm her. He might not even need to seduce her if she responded well to kisses and agreed quickly to marriage. Either way, he'd ensure her standing as a respected lady.

He guided her through the crowded station to a waiting train. As instructed, the crew had attached his private car behind the engine. "We'll start with a tour of the line. It's what I usually do for railroad correspondents."

A tour of the southern branch would take the entire day. He could use the time to get to know her better. He'd even arranged for an intimate dinner—*not* something he usually did with reporters. He wouldn't mention that quite yet. "Ready to get started?"

"Certainly." Her brightness seemed a little forced.

Lucy knew the risks, yet she faced her uncertainty as bravely as any soldier.

Henry experienced a moment of regret. If she took her job seriously and went along with him, her reputation would be sullied. Then he'd fix everything by marrying her. No one would dare spurn the wife of the most powerful man in town.

"Mr. Reynolds was kind enough to explain the details of my assignment."

What had she been told? Didn't matter. He'd guide her to the subjects he wanted her to cover. "Does Milt expect a daily report on our construction?"

She shot him a questioning look.

"We've sent tracklayers north to start work on the Sedalia

extension," he explained. "By the end of March, we'll have the bridge finished. That will connect our lines through to Chicago."

Her eyes widened. "In less than a month? Amazing."

Amazing was one word for it. *Impossible* was another. They'd be lucky to have a bridge over the Missouri River done by the end of May. However, he wanted competitors to believe the Katy would soon bypass St. Louis. He knew how to play the game. Newspapers thrived on falsehoods and exaggeration. He gave them what they wanted.

Only now, he faced a conundrum. Lucy would soon be his wife. He didn't want to start out with lies. On the other hand, he didn't see how he could be honest, given her role as a reporter. This would be trickier than he'd anticipated.

"On second thought, your readers might enjoy something more interesting than a report on our construction progress."

"Actually, Mr. Reynolds wants me to write a special article. A profile piece. On you."

"Me?" Henry's instincts ignited. Reynolds had some ulterior motive. Actually, everyone had ulterior motives. Some were better than others at concealing them. In Reynolds' case, it was clearly an act of spite for forcing his hand. "What about our progress on opening up the Indian Territory? Or the proposed route through Texas?"

"Oh, I can include some of that..." She gave a casual wave, as if those historic milestones were of little importance. "He wants a personal story. He said since you're willing to have me tag along, I might as well write a feature about you. Your responsibilities, the kinds of problems you encounter, decisions you make, that sort of thing."

Henry wasn't sure he liked the idea of an article focused primarily on him, especially if he wished to be honest with her. The truth wasn't always flattering. Actually, it was rarely flattering. "I doubt you'll find me interesting enough to devote an entire article to the topic."

She gave him a side eye. "Oh, I'm inclined to believe I could write an entire book about you, Mr. Stevens."

Her teasing smile proved irresistible. "Very well, I'll submit to an interview. First, let me introduce you to one of our engineers."

He guided her past the tender box to the open cab of their newest engine. She'd have a hard time climbing up there in her dress. If she slipped, she'd fall down between the train and the platform. "If you'll allow me."

She eyed the distance between the platform and cab, then hefted her bag over one shoulder and reached for the handrail. "I can manage."

"Whether you can manage or not, I intend to assist you." Without waiting for her answer, he grasped her around the waist then hoisted her into the cab. He swung up behind her.

The engineer at the controls nudged a short-billed cap to his hairline and wrinkled his forehead in confusion. No wonder. It wasn't often ladies visited this part of the train.

"Lucy, this is Mr. Tobias, one of our most experienced engineers," Henry made the proper introductions. "Miss Lucy Forbes works for the newspaper. She'll do reports on the railroad."

"Not only the railroad," she interjected. "A feature on Mr. Stevens."

The engineer grinned. "A story about the Chief, eh? That oughta be a good one."

"The Chief?" Lucy turned a curious look on Henry.

"It's what the men call me." He shrugged, as if it meant nothing. Actually, he was exceedingly proud of it. These men were his tribe in every sense of the word. He not only led them. He took responsibility for their wellbeing.

Lucy reached into her bag, retrieved her notebook and a pencil. "What do your *competitors* call you?"

The Irishman at the controls hooted.

Henry smiled, more constrained. "It's not something you could put in the newspaper."

The engineer wrapped a gloved hand around the throttle. Nearby, indicators monitored steam pressure and speed. "How about we show Miss Forbes how fast our new hog can run, Chief? Thirty miles an hour, easy as pie."

He'd bet this new coal-burning engine could do better than that. "Take her full steam. Not for long. Don't want to burn up all our profit." Once they actually had money left over after expenses were covered. It made his head hurt to think about the railroad's financial situation.

"Mr. Stevens!" The call came from outside the cab. On the platform, Caldwell looked up, shading his eyes with his hand. "Sir, there's a message for you."

If a message had sent Caldwell out here without his hat, it must be important.

"Excuse me a moment," Henry said to Lucy before he hopped down.

Rather than staying put, she followed, landing on the platform with a thud.

He took her arm and bent down so only she could hear him. "Next time, you must allow me to assist you. If your dress caught, you'd take a nasty fall."

She glanced at the frothy skirt. "Hm. You're right. I should don more appropriate clothing to go along on these excursions. I hadn't thought about that."

He hadn't chided her because of her clothing. "Your dress is fine. Don't leap off trains."

"I didn't leap. I took a big step."

Henry bit back a reply. Once they were wed, they would come to an understanding about the extent of her independence. He drew the line at safety, even if she didn't.

Caldwell's gaze hung on Lucy. Presumably, he hadn't come out here to ogle her.

"What is it?" Henry demanded.

His assistant jerked pencil straight. "One of our trains got stopped by a posse, up near Paola. Had a county judge with them. They chained the engine to the tracks."

"They *what?*"

"Took possession of our property, sir. Said they'd release it after we finish laying track through the town, according to our agreement."

"Our *agreement?*" Henry longed to wring that judge's neck, and the necks of every other member of the so-called posse. Bunch of con artists and extortionists. "They haven't paid the bond money they owe us. We aren't completing that track until they do."

"Yes, sir. I already sent the message, assuming you'd say that." Caldwell darted a nervous glance at Lucy before he continued. "Sir, you'll recall we haven't paid county taxes. The judge ruled they could confiscate our equipment to cover the amount we owe."

Henry's face got hot. His money-saving decision to withhold tax payments had backfired in an unexpected, altogether unacceptable way. "That...that's blackmail."

"It appears they have you over a barrel. Or shackled to the tracks, as the case may be." Lucy's eyes gleamed with mirth. She seemed not to grasp the seriousness of the situation.

"Get McGrady." Henry barked instructions. "Tell him we'll be leaving for Paola before dawn. I want a crew of his fastest men. Have them load the big iron. We'll lay that track tomorrow."

His assistant hesitated. "Tomorrow's Sunday, sir."

"I don't care if it's the Second Coming. We'll finish that line and get our engine."

Caldwell sped away to do his boss's bidding.

"How much do you owe in taxes?" Lucy's question came from behind.

Henry spun to face her. The railroad's tax delinquency wasn't a story he planned to give her. "Doesn't matter. Our track isn't complete yet, and they haven't delivered our bond money."

"So...what you're saying is, you've been holding them hostage until they do what you want. Now, they're doing the same to you."

He'd forgotten he was dealing with Lucy the Intrepid. She'd plunged head first into this reporter role. While he admired her gumption, he wouldn't let her get away with making him the villain in a sideshow.

"You make an interesting point, Madam Reporter. However, you're incorrect. We've acted in accordance to a contract that calls for the delivery of funds *before* the line is completed. They, on the other hand, have taken possession of our property without our permission. That's called stealing, in case you've forgotten the meaning of the word."

She appeared nonplussed. "If that's true, why did the judge side with them?"

"Someone with *influence* convinced him, I presume."

Disappointment leaked out onto her face. He wasn't sure if it was directed at the crooked judge or at him, for reminding her about how things operated in the real world.

"If you believe that, why would you bow to their demands?" she countered. "Challenge the ruling."

He could find a friendly judge to overrule it. However, if he put up a fuss it would draw attention to the dispute and the railroad's true financial situation might come to light. He'd be fired before he could pack his bags. "We need that engine now. Not when some judge gets around to considering the matter. We'll finish the line. They'll pay the money they owe us. You'd agree that's fair?"

She gave a slow nod. "Sounds fair."

"*More* than fair. I'll have to divert workers and supplies we need elsewhere." His frustration boiled over. "If they don't pay us that bond money the day the track is completed, they won't see another train until they do."

Her pencil moved across the page. She'd seemed to be writing more than what he'd said.

His gut tightened. He'd better guard his tongue. Lucy wasn't his wife, yet. Even afterwards, he shouldn't rely on her as a confidante. He'd learned the hard way to rely on no one except himself.

He checked his watch, out of habit more than a need to know the time. They were running out of that precious commodity.

Lucy's gaze moved from the watch to his face. "I don't suppose you'll be able to work with me on that article I'm writing."

He tucked the timepiece into his pocket, still fuming. Not only had this caper cost him time and materials, it interfered with his other plans. The ones involving Lucy. "Not today. Maybe tomorrow we'll have a few hours together."

"You want me to come with you?"

She'd be in the way.

What did he care? He had to squeeze in every spare minute to woo her. He couldn't do that if she wasn't with him.

"You're the railroad correspondent. I assume you'll want to accompany us." He gestured to his car, with *Prairie Queen* painted in gold across a red banner. The moniker fit better with Lucy riding inside. "We can make the trip in relative comfort."

She looked in the direction he indicated. "In your private car?" Her throat convulsed, as if she'd swallowed a mouthful of nerves. "I believe I'd be more comfortable riding with the workers."

Henry huffed. She couldn't be serious. "You can't ride in the workers' car."

"Why not?"

"For one, it's crowded and noisy, and..." He considered how to explain the dangers without offending her. "Construction crews aren't hired for their good manners. I won't risk your safety."

She eyed him askance. "You're saying I'm safer with you?"

"I can promise I have better manners."

CHAPTER 13

*T*he train left for Paola the next morning while it was still dark. Henry made good on his promise. He didn't make advances or do anything impolite. In fact, he played a delightful host, and the time passed much too quickly. Lucy had to remind herself she wasn't along to enjoy his company. She had a job to do.

Before the train had squealed to a halt, a construction crew made up of broad-shouldered Irishmen leapt off. They began unloading the flatbed cars. Mules were hitched to haul ties and iron rails to a graded bed, which had been prepared for the last two miles of track.

Lucy pulled a shawl over her shoulders. She'd picked out a simple striped shirt, a serviceable Navy serge skirt, and boots. Henry shouldn't feel compelled to lift her into railcars today.

As she exited his parlor car, he reached up from the ground to take her hand. This much she allowed. He seemed determined to make up for past offenses, and he was being a perfect gentleman. It wasn't in her nature to hold a grudge.

They'd reached the outskirts of town as dawn unveiled the prairie. To the west, grassy plains stretched out as far she could see. Overhead, clouds with fat, gray underbellies scudded across a smoky sky becoming lighter by the second.

She drew strands of hair whipped by the ever-present wind away from her face. "It's beautiful."

"I agree." Henry hadn't taken his eyes off her.

She blushed at the compliment. "Thank you for inviting me along."

"Are you disappointed I won't be your guide for the day?" He looked sad, which made her ridiculously happy.

"Don't worry about me. I'm here to observe."

"No more questions?"

"Not at the moment." Lucy tucked her notebook into her bag. On the trip up, he'd talked mostly about the railroad and had dodged personal questions. She hadn't pressed, even though she was curious. If she acted too interested in Henry, the man, he might misinterpret her motives. Besides, she was here to report on the railroad's progress, and, in doing so, tease out whatever secrets Henry might be hiding.

All around them, the workers continued to unload supplies. Some went to work laying track. Others stacked ties. Everyone knew their job and did it without hesitation or complaint.

Her boots crunched on the dead grass as she walked beside Henry. They passed by the train then continued on to where a lone engine was shackled to a spot where the tracks ended. "Do you suppose they thought it would be funny?"

"Someone did." Henry's voice conveyed no emotion. Neither did his expression. Only the dull red stain creeping up his neck revealed how he really felt about the joke.

As good as he was at hiding his emotions, he couldn't control his physical reactions. When he became angry or embarrassed, his neck turned red. His nostrils flared when he was annoyed. When aroused, his eyes grew dark and high color flushed into his face. His beard hid most of it. Except for the faint stains beneath his cheekbones.

Lucy watched him carefully. The more she learned about him the better. She wouldn't fool herself into believing she could understand Henry. He was frighteningly complex, devilishly clever, and extremely dangerous. In short, fascinating.

"Why don't you sit over here?" He directed her to the cab of the shackled engine. "It's not going anywhere."

She smiled at his dry wit. Before he could take hold of her waist, she hoisted herself onto the edge. "I'm dressed more appropriately today."

"Yes, I see that." Was that a twinge of disappointment in his voice?

He shed his suit coat and tossed it beside her. "Keep an eye on this for me."

"Are you leaving me in charge of it so I won't wander off?"

As he rolled up his shirtsleeves, he gave a nod to the chains wrapped around the engine's iron wheels. "Are you suggesting I might need those?"

"Whatever for?" she asked, innocently. "You absolved my debt, remember?"

"Did I?" He gave her a slow smile that made her insides quiver.

When he walked off to join the other workers, she remained on her perch. Not because Henry had told her to stay put. She wanted to observe him. This seat offered the best view.

Rail by rail, the tracklayers advanced toward the town. The clang-clang of their hammers rang out in a steady rhythm. Between that, the braying mules, and shouted orders, they made an awful racket. If the residents had been asleep when the train arrived, they weren't sleeping any longer. Lucy suspected Henry knew this and it pleased him.

His white cambric shirt stretched across his broad shoulders when he swung a long-handled hammer in a smooth motion. It came down on the spike with a resounding ring.

As the sun climbed higher in the sky, her respect for him increased. Laying track wasn't something the general manager of a railroad typically did. Henry handled the tools like an old hand. The way he'd jumped in to help showed he didn't consider himself above hard work.

The sweat-dampened shirt clung to his lean, athletic form. By contrast, the tracklayers working next to him were thickly muscled.

Based on the way Henry swung that hammer, he was plenty strong. She'd felt his strength when he had embraced her.

Tingles raced across her skin, the same reaction she'd experienced when he'd kissed her. Only now, the shivery feelings were accompanied by an urge to run her hands over his long back. Acting on her fantasy was out of the question. That didn't mean she could erase it from her mind.

She picked up her notebook, used it to fan her face. What would Henry do if he could read her sinful thoughts? Use it to his advantage, of course. He used every opportunity to his advantage.

Wasn't she doing the same? What she'd told him about Mr. Reynolds assigning her to do an article on him wasn't quite truthful. The editor had requested she give him reports about what she observed and he would put the story together. Disappointing, though not surprising, to realize he didn't take her seriously. Nevertheless, she'd do as he asked, while taking her own notes on Henry to help her father with his investigation.

Thus far, Henry hadn't turned out to be the scoundrel she'd expected. Ulterior motives aside, he'd gone out of his way to help her remain in Parsons. He showed respect for her intelligence, answering endless questions without treating her curiosity like an illness that needed to be cured. She was beginning to truly *like* Henry, although she knew better than to trust him.

Mid-morning, pealing bells from a church steeple in the center of town called congregants to worship. A short time later, a group of residents in their Sunday best appeared on the dusty road alongside the railroad tracks.

The portly man in the lead, who advanced on bowed legs with his arms swinging, reminded her of an angry bulldog. His pack consisted mostly of women, dressed in dark colors. The only clue to their identity—Bibles clutched to their breasts. If these people were from the church, the unhappy leader was likely the preacher. He made a beeline for the railroad workers with the tails of his black frock coat flapping behind him.

A few fluffy clouds marred an endless blue sky. Nevertheless, Lucy sensed the storm a-brewing.

She hopped down, then hesitated. As a reporter, she ought to investigate. As a woman, she knew how it would look, with her being the only female amongst an army of men. In spite of her unease, she started over. She hadn't accepted this job to be a bystander.

By the time she reached the workers, the reverend had found Henry, pulled him aside, and was in the midst of giving him an earful about his *heathen ways*.

"This is the Sabbath," the preacher declared. "In the name of the Lord, I beseech you and your men to put down your tools. Come with us into worship."

The women bobbed their heads in agreement.

Not a single man put down a tool or stopped what they were doing.

Henry acknowledged the reverend's request with a polite smile. "We appreciate your kind invitation, Reverend. I'm afraid we'll have to worship out here. His honor, Judge Judah—he's a member of your church, I believe—told us to complete this track or relinquish our property. We aren't keen on giving up a brand new engine, so..." he gestured to the workers. "The line will be completed post-haste. As ordered."

The reverend's expression hardened. "Sir, you are under higher orders to observe this day of rest. The railroad shouldn't even run trains on Sundays, much less construct track."

Sabbath trains remained a hot issue in the east, as well.

Henry leaned on the long-handled hammer. "The Lord will understand. He did some work on his day off, as I recall."

"You aren't the Lord," the preacher snapped.

"Won't argue that. We're all sinful men, as the Good Book says. Remember us in your prayers." Henry doffed his hat, then went back to work.

The reverend turned to Lucy with a disapproving scowl. "What are *you* doing out here, young lady?"

She steeled her nerves. "I am a reporter. For the *Parsons Sun*."

His congregants eyed her with disapproval. The women whispered among themselves. Lucy didn't need to hear the words to understand their meaning.

"You should be in church." The reverend emphasized the point with his forefinger.

"She's here to bear witness to our work," Henry called out. "And to pray over us."

Lucy nearly swallowed her tongue. She'd never spoken so flippantly to a man of the cloth. Warily, she eyed the cerulean sky, half-expecting to see a ball of lightning streak down to consume Henry and his men in flames.

"This is the Lord's Day. We shall be glad and rejoice." The reverend turned to the women. He shooed them into a line alongside the graded bed. A moment later, they began to sing.

"Rescue the perishing, care for the dying, snatch them in pity from sin and the grave; weep o'er the erring one, lift up the fallen, tell them of Jesus, the mighty to save." The women raised their voices in the familiar chorus: *"Rescue the perishing, care for the dying..."*

Henry kept hammering. He started singing a different hymn. *"Work, for the night is coming. Work through the morning hours. Work while the dew is sparkling, work 'mid springing flowers. Work when the day grows brighter, work in the glowing sun. Work, for the night is coming, when man's work is done."*

As he continued the sacred chorus in his fine bass voice, several of the men joined him. Soon, their voices vied with those of the ladies, who frowned and sang louder.

"Though they are slighting him, still he is waiting, waiting the penitent child to receive; plead with them earnestly, plead with them gently; he will forgive if they only believe."

A laugh erupted in Lucy's throat. She clapped a hand over her mouth to keep it from bursting out. Likely, she'd burn up with him if she giggled at Henry's deviltry.

The songs continued. For every one the women sang, Henry led the men in a counterpart. *Irreverent scamp.* However, no one could call a man that well-versed in hymns a *heathen.*

After several songs, the reverend and his choir turned away. Their shoulders sagged as they departed, wagging their heads, pronouncing Henry and his men "beyond redemption."

The railroaders went on singing, moving from hymns to a love song, *Little Maggie May*. Then on to a silly song, one about a girl with lobster-claw hands who played on nine pianos.

Lucy enjoyed the show immensely. She couldn't keep her eyes off the ringleader. She really shouldn't be so amused...or fascinated...or attracted. In fact, she was supposed to be spying. She could stay here and watch Henry work—not an unpleasant idea—or go back to the rail car and snoop around.

When he turned his back, she slipped away.

HENRY'S OFFICE on wheels served as a combination sitting room and study, complete with wood paneling and a stove for heat. More practical than stylish. Lucy went behind the desk to a bookcase, mounted to a partial wall. Earlier, she'd noticed some interesting-looking volumes. Perhaps his secrets would be revealed in one.

She flipped through several leather-bound journals. Correspondence concerning railroad construction, requests for land allotments, nothing diabolical about that. After she'd returned the books, she turned her attention to the desk. The drawers contained files, which were as dry as the journals.

In one of her favorite novels, the heroine found a hidden compartment underneath the secretary. She crawled into the space beneath the desk and ran her hands over the bottom. No secret levers or pulleys. Being rather new to espionage, she might be missing something.

Where else might he stash personal papers?

Lucy ventured behind the partial wall to the sleeping quarters, a compartment barely large enough for a pine bed, washstand and short wardrobe. Inside hung shirts, trousers and underclothes. All neatly folded and stacked. Under the bed, only a pair of boots.

Nothing hidden in here, unless...

She sank her hands into the soft feather mattress. Next, she picked up the pillow. Without thinking, she held it to her face. The case smelled like Henry. Her body tingled in response. Startled, she threw the pillow onto the bed. She was supposed to be on a search for evidence, not sniffing his bedding.

From the other room came the sound of the door opening.

Her heart flapped wildly in her chest. *Mon Dieu!* What excuse could she use for being in his sleeping quarters?

The floor creaked. Someone walked slowly, cautiously.

A moment later, Henry appeared with a revolver in his hand. Appearing relieved, he holstered the gun. "When I didn't see you, I thought something might've happened."

Her stomach knotted with guilt. He'd come to search for her, not because he thought she was a spy. He'd become concerned about her safety. To her mortal shame, she had to lie. "I felt a bit lightheaded. Thought I might rest awhile."

"Are you ill?" He sounded worried, which made her regret suspecting him in the first place. She'd feel better if his concern was an act.

"No, not ill. It's the sun or maybe the excitement." Lucy swallowed the rest of that falsehood. She'd *never* become faint from excitement, nor had she swooned from anxiety or alarm. She had the constitution of a workhorse.

Henry's fine white shirt and wool trousers were smeared with grime. Somewhere along the way, he'd shed his waistcoat, probably to prevent it from being ruined. He halted directly in front of her and removed his hat. His hair, damp with perspiration, stuck to his head. A tangy scent triggered some deep, primitive urge that sent her heart racing.

Who knew a sweaty man could be so arousing?

He lifted his hand to her cheek, perhaps to check for fever. Heat and roughness grazed her skin. Surprised, she grasped his wrist, turned his palm upward. Around existing calluses were reddened areas, blisters. Seeing the injury, her heart ached.

She smoothed his fingers open, unable to resist stroking them tenderly.

He went perfectly still.

Suddenly aware of what she was doing, she dropped his hand.

Oops. Shouldn't have touched him.

"Lucy..." The way he said her name, rough, almost pleading, touched off a wave of longing. Before she could step away, he captured her waist and his mouth came down on hers, cutting off her gasp.

All the promises she'd made to herself, her determination not to succumb, flew away like dandelion fluff in a strong wind.

The room spun. Her knees grew wobbly. *Now* she knew what it felt like to swoon.

She flung her arms around his neck before she collapsed at his feet.

He held her tightly against a wall of muscle as he slanted his head to fit their lips together more perfectly. His kiss—alternately soft and tender, wicked and tormenting—sent a torrent of heat coursing through her.

Had God hurled a ball of lightning, after all?

Desire warred with the small fragment of reason that remained. She couldn't give in to these overpowering feelings. It was wrong, sinful. Even if it felt right and wonderful.

With a shudder, she arched away.

Rather than release her, he sought her neck, placing half-open kisses on her exposed flesh. His lips tracked her fluttering pulse to a spot beneath her jaw. He cradled her nape while he traced her ear with the tip of his tongue.

She hadn't thought of that spot as particularly sensitive. His tantalizing touch released a flood of sensations. Her skin quivered, her breasts swelled, the tips stiffening into hard buds. Dampness flooded her most intimate parts.

She forgot reason. She forgot caution. She forgot everything except her hunger for another one of his kisses. Desperate, she sought his lips. He met her, open-mouthed. Their tongues touched, twined, engaged in an intimate, provocative dance. She shivered, aching with desire.

More than a lesson in how to kiss, he invited her on a journey into uncharted territory. A vast, erotic terrain stretched out before them. One she longed to explore. A persuasive voice in her head—the one that nearly always got her into trouble—whispered. *Follow.*

HENRY SENSED the moment Lucy gave in to passion. His mind filled with the lurid image of pressing her down into the soft mattress, sinking deep inside her, as he feasted on her smooth ivory skin while her soft sighs curled into his ear.

His hand shook when he lifted it to unbutton her shirt. Beneath, she wore a camisole and a corset, which supported her delightful treasures. He eagerly sought her breast—a perfect handful—and couldn't suppress a moan. Beneath a thin layer, he located the hard nipple and rolled it between his fingers. Her sharp breath drew air from his lungs into hers.

His body, already burning up, grew hotter. His need so intense it threatened to incinerate him. "Oh God, Lucy..." he murmured against her mouth.

She answered by tightening her arms around his neck. The movement pressed her breast into his hand. Without words, she gave him permission.

Satisfaction surged through him. He'd gotten what he wanted—Lucy in his bed and wed soon after. What choice would she have?

Another, less gratifying emotion encroached on his celebration. She'd resent him once she realized he'd seduced her to press his advantage. Any affection that might be growing would shrivel up and die. If he wanted to own more than her body, he couldn't claim her like he'd stake out a parcel of land.

Henry fought to gain control of his raging lust. He'd never been so close to losing the battle. The way she kissed him, with an alluring mixture of awkward innocence and soul-deep hunger, stole his reason. Using every ounce of willpower, he forced desire to bend the knee. After savoring her lips for one final moment, he drew back.

Lucy blinked up at him with a soft, dreamy gaze, her lips damp and swollen from his kisses. She toyed with the hair above his collar. He longed for her to drag her nails over his scalp, tug handfuls of his hair as he wrung pleasure from her body.

He banished the thought and placed a chaste kiss on her parted lips. "Lucy, sweetheart." He didn't have to practice the endearment. It came naturally. "We should wait."

A flush swept across her face with the swiftness of a prairie fire. She withdrew her arms and pushed him away, as the dazed expression transformed to stark humiliation. She opened her mouth as if she might speak, probably to curse him for taking advantage. Then she turned away, her shoulders slumped, conveying without words her defeat.

His conquest, if that's what it was, left him feeling empty.

Gently, he turned her around to enfold her in his arms. She didn't struggle. Instead, she burrowed into his chest, seeking comfort.

He couldn't remember the last time anyone had turned to him for comfort, let alone wanting him to offer it. Lucy called to some part of him that he'd lost. The best part.

Slowly, the wild blaze that licked at his body retreated into a warm fire. Still, he continued to hold her. If she'd let him, he would keep her in the protective circle of his arms forever.

"Marry me." The words rushed out like he'd been holding them in and couldn't contain them any longer.

She wriggled out of his arms. "*Marry* you?"

The way she said it made his proposal sound loathsome.

She scrambled off the bed, then seemed to realize she'd backed herself in to a corner. An irony he didn't miss. She must know he could have her in that bed in less than a minute. He doubted she'd praise him for his self-control.

"You're surprised." He was. Hadn't planned to blurt it out quite so soon.

"I'm *shocked*." She looked it. "You hardly know me."

Henry flexed his fingers. He resisted putting his hands on her to show her how well he knew her. Now that he'd let the cat out of the bag, there was no point in trying to put it back in. He had to forge ahead, convince her. "I know enough to deduce we'd be well suited."

She turned her face away with a grimace. Did the idea of marriage to him upset her stomach? Her reaction stung his pride. He wasn't poor or uncouth, had never had a problem finding females eager for his company. Rich, attractive women, who weren't nearly as much trouble.

He bit back the sarcastic remark, which even *he* realized would put a quick end to his hopes. "You're attracted to me. I feel the same for you."

In fact, he'd never been this besotted, not even with his first love. He wasn't about to give Lucy the upper hand in this relationship by admitting as much.

She shook her head. "That doesn't mean we ought to marry."

If he'd bedded her first, she wouldn't be saying that.

Henry kept a tight hold on his frustration. Young, innocent Lucy, understandably scared, confused. With patience, he could win her. Despite her objections, he sensed she wanted to be wooed. He tugged his lips into a wry smile. "I could kiss you again. That might change your mind."

Her eyes rounded with alarm.

"I won't," he added, regretfully. "Out of respect."

Her brow knitted with confusion. Or was that disappointment? Even better.

"Don't answer yet. Think about it."

She jerked her chin up, signaling her intent to be bullheaded. "There's nothing to think about."

"That kiss. I'd say that's worth thinking about."

Her cheeks flamed. She scooted to one side, apparently intending to leave the small sleeping area. She couldn't as long as he remained in the doorway. Her face reflected consternation. "I know how this must look, finding me here. I won't deny, I-I find you attractive, but I can't."

Her stammering could be attributed to nerves. He suspected it was more than that. She was aroused, unsettled, confused. By God, she wasn't indifferent. That gave him a toehold in the mountain he had to climb. He reached for the next outcropping.

"Think about it, Lucy. That's all I ask." For now.

Soon, he'd ask for much more. By then, he'd make certain she would be willing to give it to him.

CHAPTER 14

The clock on the mantle chimed once, twice, three times. Lucy looked up from the desk where she sat in the hotel suite, attempting to write. This day had dragged like the day before, and the day before that. The last exciting day had been Sunday, when Henry had almost succeeded in seducing her.

She trembled. Not with fear, even if it should be. When she dwelled on thoughts of Henry, her head filled with all manner of sensual imagery that hadn't been there before. Worse, her body quivered in anticipation of the next encounter.

There couldn't be a next encounter. It shamed her to think how ready—no, how *eager*—she'd been to let him compromise her. If he hadn't stopped...

Why had he stopped? Decency? He seemed determined to prove he was a gentleman. Perhaps he hoped to impress her so she wouldn't write something scathing about him.

As for his unexpected proposal, she hadn't been able to figure that out, despite thinking about it until her head hurt. Her father didn't have money. Her lineage wasn't particularly impressive. Given Henry's burning ambition, she'd bring him nothing of real value. A marriage between them made little sense, which deepened her distrust.

She dipped her pen in the inkwell, determined to focus on her writing. While she'd been hiding in her room like a coward, she'd drafted a story for the newspaper. An amusing account about the fastest tracklayers in the West and their musical feud with a local choir.

Mr. Reynolds had come by to congratulate her on it. He acted pleased to discover she could actually pen something worth printing. He'd asked her to submit another story. Why not try her hand at that profile she'd told Henry she was working on?

After reading what she'd written, she scratched it out. She couldn't come up with the right words to describe him. Charming and brave, yet ruthlessly ambitious. Gracious one moment and impertinent the next. He could turn his attention on her with breathtaking intensity while she sensed his mind remained occupied with multiple schemes at the same time.

He had so many facets she feared it would be impossible to discover the real man. Unfortunately, that didn't stop her from wanting to try, which was why she'd avoided him for the past three days. She couldn't accept his proposal, yet couldn't bring herself to refuse.

With a restless sigh, she got up from her seat and raised the window. She needed fresh air, and something to distract her from dwelling on the enigmatic Mr. Stevens.

Sounds drifted up from the street below. Shouts from men on horseback who led a caravan of wagons. The wheels creaked. An ox lowed.

Lucy swung her gaze in the direction of the depot. Why she kept looking for Henry, she didn't know. She'd replied to his messages with the excuse she was "indisposed." That word could mean any number of things, most of them perplexing to men. Not Henry. She'd half expected him to storm up the stairs, break down her door. Instead, he'd complied with her wishes and maintained a polite distance. How unlike him.

A knock sounded.

She spun around, her heart taking off faster than a breaking horse. "Yes? Who's there?"

"It's me, Claire. I have some tea and sandwiches for you."

Lucy sloughed off disappointment. She shouldn't long to see Henry, and she certainly wouldn't invite him into her room. His sister, on the other hand, provided a welcome distraction.

She smiled as she opened the door. "Please, come in..."

Claire swept into the room, balancing a tray with a teapot and a plate of sandwiches. "I noticed you missed the noon meal. You must be starving."

She set the items out on a small table between two stuffed chairs. Somehow, Henry's sister found the enough time to wait on guests, run the hotel, take care of her *invalid* husband.

Reportedly, Mr. Daines suffered from war injuries and couldn't get around. However, the previous evening, around midnight, Lucy had heard a noise in the hallway. She'd cracked open her door, seen a disheveled man in his dressing robe on his way down the hall. Claire, hugging her wrapper, ran after him.

Her husband, Lucy presumed. The poor man appeared well enough to walk, yet it was clear that something was wrong with him. He'd held his hands over his ears, mumbling and crying. His words made no sense, something about noise and blood. Claire spoke too softly to be understood. Her tone sounded soothing. He'd cursed her, then muttered unintelligibly. At last, he'd allowed her close enough to lead him back in the direction of their rooms.

Lucy crossed to where her hostess had arranged the repast. "Thank you for thinking of me. I get busy writing and forget to eat."

"It isn't good to skip meals. You won't have enough strength to lift a pen." Claire's eyes gleamed with amusement. Witty, like her brother.

"That pen was getting heavy," Lucy quipped.

Claire set out two cups, an obvious hint. This was the first time she'd indicated an interest in visiting. Perhaps she needed someone to talk to, or she might've come at Henry's urging. Although it seemed unlikely that she'd have time to be a spy, on top of her other responsibilities.

Lucy gestured to a chair. "Why don't you join me?"

"Thank you, I believe I will." Claire sank into one of the two cushioned chairs then arranged her serviceable skirts. She had the same warm coloring as Henry, but not his sense of style. The cool grays didn't compliment her coffee-colored hair, golden-brown eyes and creamy skin. She might not be aware. Or she might've chosen dowdy attire on purpose, to put off male guests. Whatever the reason, she kept her secrets to herself. A trait she also shared with her brother.

"Have something to eat," Claire urged. She poured tea into two cups, while Lucy selected a sandwich.

She took a bite. "Mmm. Smoked ham."

"There's butter and jam, too. I made blackberry preserves last summer."

Lucy took a sandwich to sample it. "Delicious," she declared. "I can't imagine how you have time to make jams in between running the hotel and tending to your husband."

Claire's pleasant expression faded.

Too late, Lucy realized her blunder. Her hostess clearly didn't want to talk about her husband's late night foray. He could've been in the throes of a nightmare, or drunk, or...several men from Haverhill had returned from the war with their minds more broken than their bodies. Whatever the case, Claire's obvious devotion, and the tenderness she exhibited in dealing with a heartbreaking situation, touched Lucy deeply. She wished she knew what to say to convey her admiration without embarrassing Claire.

"Do you take sugar and cream in your tea?" Claire deftly sidestepped the issue.

Honoring her wishes, Lucy let it drop. "Yes, please. Two sugars."

"Some friends of ours are having dinner party tonight," Claire said while she doctored the tea. "I thought you might like to come with me."

"That sounds like fun. Much better than staying cooped up. I'd love to meet your friends." Lucy regarded her hostess with curiosity. This was the first time Claire had suggested an outing. She had to be aware of Henry's interest. "Will your brother be there?"

Claire's eyes flashed up, yet her expression remained unreadable. She had her brother's talent for concealing her reactions. "Yes. He and Matthew are business partners."

That answered Lucy's question. Henry had no doubt suggested it as a way to lure her out. She'd go. Not because she wanted to see him. Because she had to stop hiding.

If she would consider Henry—and that was a big *if*—she needed to know more about him. Meeting his friends would be one way to learn. So would asking questions of his sister, who up until now had seemed reluctant to talk about him.

Lucy wiped her fingers on a napkin, laid it on the table. "Have you seen Henry today?"

"I see him every day." Claire took a sip of her tea.

"Well, yes, of course you do." Lucy glanced around at the expensive furnishings. It seemed odd that he lived in a hotel. Surely, he had enough money to build a house. "How long has he rented these rooms?"

Claire cradled her teacup, seeming to consider how to answer. "Henry built this hotel for us. I wouldn't charge him for a room."

He'd given his sister a *hotel?* Surprising, though not as much as it might've been, had Lucy heard about it before discovering Henry's benevolence to his employees.

"He's very generous," Lucy acknowledged.

"Yes, he's done a great deal for me and my sisters, and...he rarely asks for anything."

Except for his sister to act as a chaperone.

Lucy's face warmed as Claire's underlying meaning became clear. "It's on my account Henry approached you. You've accommodated me, despite the inconvenience. I'm terribly sorry to have put you out."

"Oh no, that's not at all what I meant." Claire's eye's widened with chagrin. "Please don't apologize. I've enjoyed getting to know you. I should've explained. Henry is the eldest. He's always been very responsible. He supported me and my two sisters after our parents died. Over the years, he's been more than generous. We don't wish to be a burden."

Lucy set her teacup on the table, pondering Claire's remark. Henry's liberality to his family and his employees suggested he was a man of honor with a big heart. Not the kind of person who would pilfer company funds. Possibly, he'd run into financial difficulty, yet still wanted to be supportive. "Has he ever said anything to give you the idea that you're a burden to him?"

"No, never." Claire's eyes were downcast, her voice melancholy.

Lucy toyed with a button on her jacket. Her aunt came to mind. She didn't know how to express love except by giving things. Hats. Gloves. Clothes. "Being lavish with gifts is his way of showing love, perhaps."

"Yes, I think you're right. He doesn't seem to know how to show affection any other way. I know he loves us, but I don't recall him ever saying it. I do worry about him because..." Claire hesitated. "He's very driven."

Another piece of the puzzle. Lucy fitted into a picture that was emerging. Henry's magnanimity could be due to a strong sense of responsibility, as well as his need to show affection without knowing how. It could also be his way to control people. She hadn't heard any of his men speak ill of him. They admired him. But they might also feel obligated. Worse case, they viewed his gifts as bribes.

Had he given Claire the hotel to keep her quiet? She was talking now. Perhaps she was uncomfortable with keeping his secrets.

"Henry does appear to be ambitious. Men who are focused on success are sometimes driven to do things they might otherwise not do." Lucy left the door open, waiting for his sister's response.

Claire shook her head, slowly. "He didn't used to be like that."

"Are you saying he's changed? How?"

"If you'd known him when he was younger, you'd understand what I mean..." A smile played around Claire's lips. "There was a time, when he was at an age when most boys don't pay attention to little girls, he let us talk him into playing with us. My sisters and I took turns being Snow White and Rose Red. Henry acted the part of the bear who turned into a prince."

Lucy breathed out a surprised laugh. She hadn't expected a fairy tale, especially one with Henry playing the part of a prince. "My brother would never have done that. He got annoyed when I wanted to tag along."

"It took some convincing, I'll admit. He thought he was much too old for games." Claire took a sip of her tea. "There are six years between him and the twins, and he's eight years my senior. But we could talk him into it if we begged long enough."

"You're saying he was soft-hearted."

A slow, sweet smile broke out on Claire's face. "Very..."

Henry, a softhearted hero. Few would believe it, based on the man he'd become.

The bear had taken over.

This wasn't at all the revelation Lucy had expected. Claire wasn't confiding Henry's secrets...or maybe she was. "What happened? What changed him?"

Claire stared into her empty teacup, seeming to become lost in her thoughts. "Our mother died during a terrible smallpox epidemic. We all took it hard. Henry was devastated. Then, my father went very suddenly. We were orphaned, without a place to stay, poor. Henry, who was the oldest at fourteen, took us to live with relations. He went to work for the railroad to support us."

Lucy's heart lurched. Henry had started out with nothing, save responsibilities, and had succeeded against all odds. He'd even reached a position that would seem unattainable for a poor boy with no privileges. "That means he didn't finish formal schooling. He seems well educated."

"Mostly self-taught. We attended school when we lived near one, but Henry read everything he could get his hands on. He's very clever with machines." Claire's pride in her brother was evident. "He worked hard and moved up the ranks in the railroad. He made sure we had whatever we needed."

Henry had been little more than a boy when he'd been forced to shoulder a man's burden. Only the most dedicated, determined, driven person could have accomplished what he'd done. This also explained a great deal about his protective nature, his sense of responsibility, even his generosity with those who had less.

More importantly, Claire hadn't implied her brother's involvement in wrongdoing. She no doubt worried about his job. She had to see the investigator's daughter as a threat to Henry.

Lucy's conscience cringed. *Guilty as charged*. She had been fishing for evidence to indict him, using the job he'd arranged for her to spy on him. What kind of person did that make her? "I can't imagine what you must think of me. Did you tell me this to warn me away?"

Claire raised her head, her eyes bright with tears, her expression, bemused. "No...not at all. Henry can be a difficult man to understand, but I believe he cares for you. I want you to know who he really is, underneath. He's forgotten. He needs someone who can remind him. I think you might be that someone."

CHAPTER 15

*S*hadows slashed across the road as the sun vanished behind the depot tower. Railroad workers finished for the day trudged into the saloon and billiards hall across the street from the sheriff's office. Henry stared out the window, more interested in what might be happening inside the neighboring Belmont Hotel, where Lucy had holed up.

Whether she wished to avoid him or postpone the inevitable, she would have to talk to him tonight at the dinner party. This wooing process would move along much faster if she would cooperate. In the meantime, another important matter needed his attention.

"Have you made an arrest?" Henry suspected that was why Frank Garrity sent for him. The sheriff had been investigating the attack at the old depot.

"Not yet," came the drawled reply.

Henry threw an irritated glance over his shoulder. "If you don't have new information, why did you ask me to come over here?"

The sheriff tilted back his chair to prop his dusty boots on the desk. His apparent lack of urgency rubbed Henry the wrong way. "Didn't say there was no new information."

Damn him for being coy. Or was he making excuses for not doing anything?

After hearing about Franklin Garrity's daring exploits during the war and as an army scout, Henry had expected a man of action. That must've been before Garrity crawled into a bottle after a bullet intended for him had struck his wife instead. Seeking solace in whiskey could've fermented his brain, which would explain the slowness—and his slovenly appearance.

Lion-colored hair streaked with gray hung past his shoulders, and that drooping mustache hadn't been trimmed in months. He had on the same worn jean trousers and buckskin coat he'd worn when he first arrived two years ago. Didn't look like either had been cleaned. The town paid their sheriff well. Being on the hiring committee, Henry had made sure of it. Men who earned a good salary generally spent their money. What did Garrity do with it? He didn't purchase haircuts or buy new clothes.

"Do you plan to share this new information before we grow old?"

The lanky sheriff tipped his chair forward, crossed his arms on the desk. "The owner of the livery said he saw four men ride out of town. He thinks he recognized one of them."

The chair creaked as the sheriff unfolded his oversized frame with the same slow deliberation he'd shown when he sat down. They were the same age, though Garrity looked older, and as worn out as his boots.

He took down one of the *Wanted* posters tacked to the wall. "Jasper Byrne."

"Byrne?" The name sounded familiar. The image wasn't.

Henry studied the poorly printed photograph of a dark-haired youth seated with a carbine in one hand and pistol in the other. He had the stub of a cigar clamped between his teeth and his chest puffed out like a banty rooster. A boy posturing as a man.

"He's a kid," Henry exclaimed, surprised.

"That's an old photograph. Taken during the war. He was probably fifteen or thereabouts. He's ten years older, ten times as mean. He leads a gang of thieves down near the border. They hide out in the Territory."

The worst sort of low life took sanctuary in that godforsaken stretch of Indian land.

Cold swirled in the pit of Henry's stomach. "Why would this outlaw come after me?"

"Somebody paid him."

Henry feared as much. Hearing it confirmed worsened his sense of dread. "What do you plan to do about it?"

The sheriff better have a plan or Henry would come up with one.

Garrity returned to his chair. "I sent word to the federal marshal. He's got men who'll go into Indian Territory to bring back outlaws like Byrne."

The killer in the poster seemed to grin maliciously at Henry.

"Who do you reckon hired him?" Garrity asked.

Henry shook his head. "I have no idea." A competitor? Angry farmers? There were plenty of enemies to choose from. Fear leapt like flames in his gut. If an assassin was after him, that meant Lucy was in danger, as well.

Good God, he couldn't allow her to continue to accompany him. Maybe Milt could find something else to keep her occupied. Assign her to those church events, like she'd originally assumed. It would slow the process of wooing her. At least she'd be out of harm's way.

"There's something else you need to know."

The sheriff's grim expression told Henry he wasn't going to like what came next.

"Another fellow has turned up missing. A doctor. William York. You may have heard of his brothers, Ed and Alexander."

"Hell yes, I've heard of them." The York family was wealthy. Well-connected. Alexander was a Kansas senator. Ironically, he'd made a name for himself from accusations about bribery. Specifically, railroad bribes to Congressmen.

Henry narrowed his eyes. If the sheriff implied that *he* had anything to do with this doctor's disappearance... "I don't know Senator York's brother, the doctor."

147

"I'm not saying you do. Two of the missing men were vocal about opposing the railroad. There's some who think you had a hand in—"

"That's nonsense and you know it."

"Doesn't matter what I think." Garrity opened a dog-eared notebook on the desk. Inside were scrawled notes. "According to my records, this makes nine men who've vanished over the past two years. Most were last seen in the same general vicinity, close to where the Osage trail crosses your railroad line. It's got folks scared. They're looking for somebody to blame."

Henry threw his arm out, gesturing at the plethora of *Wanted* posters. "Hell, Frank. You know we've got outlaws all over this state. Scoundrels at every stop between here and Texas. They target travelers all the time."

"Bandits don't generally hide corpses."

"Maybe these bandits don't want to leave a trail of dead bodies."

"Yeah, maybe..." Garrity stroked his mustache in a thoughtful manner. He leaned back with his arms crossed casually over this chest. "I've deputized a special posse to help with the search. The senator is on his way to join us."

"Senator York? Coming here?" Alarm shot through Henry. That was the last thing they needed, an unfriendly politician nosing around. It would only complicate matters, especially once York got wind of the gossip being spread around by resentful settlers.

The sheriff's jaw muscle tensed. He didn't appear much happier with the news. "York thinks we're not doing enough to find his brother."

We? Henry picked up on that. Since when had the disappearances become *his* problem? The sheriff should've acted quicker to find those men. He could've asked for extra manpower.

Henry held back a rebuke. Wrangling over past decisions wouldn't accomplish anything. He had to act. "I'll assign a crew to work with you, alert the guards on our trains and in the depots. They can help with the search."

"That's a start..."

The sheriff was right. Henry knew he needed to do more. If for no other reason than to convince the senator that the railroad was one hundred percent committed to finding those missing people.

He paced the width of the small office. "Post a reward. Two thousand dollars to anyone who comes forward with information that helps us locate these missing persons or find out what happened to them."

Garrity picked up his pencil. He licked the end and wrote in his notebook. "The railroad offering a reward, that'll help."

The reward wouldn't come from the Katy's coffers. As it was, they were barely making payroll. It would have to come out of Henry's pocket. As general manager and future president of the Katy, he had a responsibility. To ensure the railroad acted in the public interest. He'd put this down as another investment in his future.

What of Lucy's future? She couldn't continue to roam around as a newspaper reporter, regardless of the assignment. Her recklessness would be her downfall. No women had gone missing. Still, he wouldn't take a chance on her life.

He returned to the window and stared across the street. He could persuade her father to take her east. If he spelled out the dangers, it would require giving away information that could be used to convince the board to replace him. He'd ask Lucy to quit. She'd demand a detailed explanation. Even then, she would try to find a way around it. Considering how important that job was to her, she wouldn't resign.

His options narrowed to one. It made his heart ache with regret. He had to ask Milt to fire her.

CHAPTER 16

The dinner party was held at the lavish home of one of Henry's business partners, Matthew Angel. Besides Lucy, there were only a handful of other guests: Henry's sister, and the bank president, another one of Henry's friends.

As soon as Lucy arrived, she was paired with Henry. She'd expected it. Frankly, she looked forward to it. So much so, she'd spent two hours fussing with her hair and picking out an evening gown. A burgundy silk decorated with cream lace and seed pearls, which complemented her coloring and showed off her figure. She deemed her efforts worth it when Henry's eyes warmed with approval.

After the meal, they retired to the parlor to play memory games.

Henry won every time. Except for when he let her win.

He sat next to her on the brocade sofa, his ankle crossed over his knee, dressed in formal black, heartbreakingly handsome, more relaxed than she'd ever seen him. He must be confident because she'd delayed in refusing him.

Admittedly, her heart had softened, especially after Claire's revelations. She'd seen him in a new light, which had increased her respect and admiration. She already liked him. Being honest, she more than liked him. Even given all that, she could see no future with a man bent on defeating her father. Henry had fought tooth and nail to attain success. He wouldn't give up his position without a fight. She could see no way around it. Later this evening she would tell him she couldn't marry him.

For a few hours, though, she wanted to enjoy pretending they were a couple.

From across the room, Jeannie Angel, an ethereal blonde beauty, smiled at Lucy. "I wanted to tell you how much I enjoyed your story in the newspaper about the musical competition between the choir and the tracklayers. Will you be writing more articles about the railroad?"

Lucy drank in the praise. "Oh yes, I do plan to write more—"

"Only if I promise to sing again," Henry quipped.

Laughter rippled around the room.

Lucy stared at him, stunned. She'd been about to explain that she was the new railroad correspondent when he'd interrupted.

Amusement danced in his brown eyes, along with something that looked surprisingly like a warning. She got the oddest sense he didn't want her to talk about her new job. Perhaps his friends weren't open-minded about women working in male-dominated occupations. She couldn't imagine why it mattered to him. It was *her* reputation. Unless he feared it would somehow reflect poorly on him because he'd asked her to be his wife.

How disappointing. Perhaps he'd only arranged the job so she would be grateful and more willing to consider him. She couldn't marry a man who wasn't proud of her accomplishments.

"Do you have any requests?" he asked.

"Requests?"

"Something you want me to sing?"

Oh. He was still on that. Her mind kept drifting forward to the moment when she would have to refuse him. She dreaded it. "Do you know any songs from operas?"

"Operas?" Henry released a deep laugh. "Not a line. Do you?"

"I know quite a few. My mother sang in the Grand Opera in Paris before she married my father. When she was eighteen, she starred in the role of *Valentine* in *Les Huguenots*. She sang several concerts for *Monsieur Berlioz*."

The room had fallen silent. All eyes were on her. Had she sounded snobbish? She rarely spoke of her mother because when she did reminisce her father became morose. Not talking about *Maman* made it seem like she hadn't existed, and she'd been such a wonderful person.

Henry leaned in to whisper, although loud enough for the others to hear. "You never told me your mother was a famous opera singer."

"You never asked."

His mouth hitched up on one side. "Do you have other secrets I should know about?"

Secrets? She wasn't the one who hiding things, at least nothing of consequence. "Not as many as you, I'm sure."

A soft guffaw came from across the room. "She has a point, Henry," said Mr. Claymore, the owner of the bank. "Any secrets you'd like to share?"

Claire, who occupied the chair next to the banker, ducked her head, smiling. The two Angels exchanged amused glances.

Henry's eyes crinkled at the corners as he leaned back, though, he didn't look as amused as everyone else. "Imagine that. The daughter of a famous opera singer, right here in Parsons."

The ball sailed over the net, back into her court. She must remember not to engage him in a public volley.

"Would you be so kind as to sing for us, Miss Forbes?" Jennifer Angel smiled at her expectantly.

Lucy's throat grew tight. In hindsight, she shouldn't have mentioned her mother's brief career. When people found out, they assumed her daughter had the same talent. To her great disappointment, she couldn't carry a tune. She and her father often joked about it. She wasn't laughing now. Her face grew warm as the guests waited for her answer.

Henry shifted forward, putting both feet on the floor. He slapped his hands on his knees. "As much as I'm sure Miss Forbes would love to oblige, it's getting late. We'll have to put off the concert until another time."

Lucy's breath left in a relieved gust. She could've kissed Henry Stevens right then and there. Again, he'd saved her. This time, from acute embarrassment.

After they'd thanked their hosts and dispensed polite farewells, she let Henry help her with her wrap. They were soon on their way out the door. It wasn't until after she'd descended the front steps and exited the gate that she realized his sister wasn't with them.

She turned to Henry. "Aren't we waiting for Claire?"

"Mr. Claymore will escort her home." Henry tucked Lucy's hand in the crook of his elbow and started down the sidewalk.

"Thank you for getting me out of an awkward situation." It was time to confess what she suspected he knew already. "I can't sing."

"And I can't write amusing stories." His lighthearted dismissal erased the last of her embarrassment, and made her even more reluctant to give him the glove. "Besides, I wanted to have some time alone."

The flutters infesting her stomach earlier returned. At some point in their walk back to the hotel, he would bring up the subject of marriage. She owed him an answer. If the heated looks he'd been giving her were any indication, he wouldn't wait much longer. She had to stop examining why she was reluctant to end their brief courtship and end it.

The sky formed a canvas for a brilliant full moon. Beyond its halo, glittering stars were too numerous to count. She could pick out a few familiar constellations, others were strangers. The sky over the prairie seemed bigger than the sky over Haverhill. Other skies out there, she longed to see those too. If she married, she might never have the opportunity. Another reason to refuse.

She tightened her hold on his arm to enjoy the last few moments of close contact. My, she would miss these intimate walks with Henry. Even if she believed in something as unlikely as love at first sight, there were too many barriers to their happiness.

Their steps echoed in the quiet evening. The clock tower, lit by gas lamps, rose over the homes built on the outskirts of town. "Look, you can see the depot from here."

"You can see it from anywhere in Parsons."

"I suppose you had a say in that," she teased him.

"Hard not to when I planned the town."

She laughed softly. Of course. "A hidden talent you never told me about."

"You never asked." He referred to her earlier response to his same comment. Another thing she would miss, his quick wit.

She had to stop counting all the reasons she admired him or she would sink into melancholy. "How many other towns have you laid out?"

"Four along the rail line. Parsons is my biggest project to date. Soon, I'll start another." He took her by the shoulders, turned her to face an empty field. "A house."

Lucy stared at the moonlight-drenched expanse of dead grass and weeds and tried to imagine the kingly home Henry would build on it. "I wonder what it will look like."

He slid his hands down the sides of her arms, leaned over to put his lips by her ear. "Say the word and you can help me design it. Fill it with furniture...and children."

A delightful tremor went through her. For a guilty moment, she let her eyes drift shut. She imagined herself in a rocker on a wide porch, cradling a brown-eyed baby. Her yearning surprised her. She hadn't thought she wanted children, certainly not for some time.

"All you have to say is *yes*." Henry's breath caressed her ear, eliciting another shiver.

At her hesitation, he turned her to face him. "If you could have any wish granted, what would it be?"

He wanted her to say she longed for a home and family. As a woman who valued her freedom, she hadn't put marriage at the top of her list. Not until she'd met Henry.

"I've always wished for adventure."

"You haven't had enough since you arrived?" he replied in a wry tone.

"It only whetted my appetite for more."

She strained to see his reaction to her unconventional answer. His face remained in shadows. As he'd pointed out earlier, he didn't know much about her or what her life had been like. She wanted to explain, so he would understand.

"My mother fell ill shortly before my thirteenth birthday. My father was busy with work. He traveled all the time, there wasn't anyone else who could take care of her. Robbie was gone by then. Killed in the war. The responsibility fell to me. After she passed, I had to look after the house, and...my father." She didn't elaborate on his difficulties. That wasn't something she would share with his enemy. "I didn't have time for adventure."

Henry nodded. "Now it's your turn."

She couldn't have said it better. "That sounds selfish, doesn't it?"

"Not at all. You deserve to enjoy life."

He rubbed his hands over her shoulders. She shouldn't allow the touch, much less enjoy it. If he noticed her consternation, he didn't let on. "If you want adventures, we can have them. After we get married, we'll travel the West together."

A tempting offer, her very own travel guide with extra benefits. She sighed with longing, her breathing quickened. His ardent pursuit would suggest she meant a great deal to him. Before she refused, she had to know if his heart was involved.

"Why?" The question came out on a rush of breath. "Why do you want to marry me?"

He released a soft laugh, a sound of disbelief. "You're beautiful, intelligent, gifted...a woman of many secrets. I want to uncover those mysteries. Delve into that intriguing mind of yours. Explore every facet of your lovely body."

Pretty compliments. Not a word about love. Without love, none of the rest mattered. She bade reluctance adieu, prepared to refuse him.

Before she could speak, his lips brushed hers.

Lucy's heart accelerated. Henry's kisses, like the wine they'd had a dinner, made her head swim. She shouldn't partake. This would be the last kiss they shared. The last one she would remember.

She circled her arms around his neck, drew him closer. Their lips merged. Charged energy coursed through her, detonating an explosive display behind her eyelids. She'd never been able to resist fireworks.

He splayed his fingers around her waist to hold her tightly. This time, however, he allowed her to the lead in the sensuous exploration.

Emboldened, she captured his face in her hands. With her thumbs, she stroked the soft hair on his cheeks while she explored the contrasting smoothness of his lips. Initiating such an intimate kiss had to be the wickedest thing she'd ever done—and the most exciting.

HENRY HAD EXPECTED A PECK, at best, a close-lipped kiss. Lucy did nothing by halves, kissing no exception. For an innocent, she learned fast. He wouldn't complain.

With a groan, he grasped handfuls of her bustled skirt and hauled her against him, holding her as close as he could, given the multitude of layers between them. He longed to scoop her into his arms, carry her off to some quiet place and initiate her to lovemaking. Based on how fast she picked up kissing, she would become an expert at other matters in no time.

The clop of hooves alerted him to the approach of a buggy.

He broke off the kiss, pressed her face against his chest and turned her away from the street. Despite her eager response, she wasn't a trollop. He was still enough of a gentleman not to treat her like one.

"Let me go."

He detected anxiety in her muffled voice. He kept her face hidden until the rumbling wheels faded into the distance. Then he loosened his hold. "No one saw you. It's all right."

She took an abrupt step back. "No, it's *not* all right. I shouldn't have done that."

Henry didn't experience as much as a twinge of guilt. However, Lucy was obviously stricken with the useless emotion. He would absolve her. "A kiss is permitted if you're my betrothed."

She squirmed out of his arms. The silvery moonlight on her face revealed panic. "You know I can't marry you."

Her vehement denial punctured the happy bubble, which had surrounded him the entire evening. She had dressed to please him, peered at him out the sides of her eyes when she thought he wasn't looking, openly flirted with him. What did that signify, if not interest? Her sudden retreat confused and annoyed him.

"What I *know* is you like kissing me."

Even in the moonlight he could see her blush.

"That doesn't matter."

His temper flared. By God, she couldn't kiss him like that then say it didn't matter. It was a matter of grave importance. In fact, her feelings for him might be the only thing that mattered.

"Why not?" he demanded, capturing her arms.

She didn't attempt escape. Rather, she stood there, looking up at him, stoic. "If we married, I'd be forced to choose between you and my father. I would never choose you."

Her declaration sliced through him. Startled at the pain, he released her. He had expected she'd feel torn. At the same time, he had hoped she might experience some small tug of loyalty in his direction.

Wishful thinking. He hadn't engaged in such foolishness since before his father's death. He had to get back to approaching this marriage without sentimentality. Oh, he could care for Lucy. If he were honest with himself, he could admit he did care for her, a great deal. Nevertheless, he couldn't let his heart depend on her. It was better that way. Would hurt less if she let him down.

"You don't have to choose between us."

She looked at him like he'd lost his mind. Maybe he had. She made him feel that way. "How can you say that? You consider my father your enemy."

"He's not my enemy." This much was true. Forbes represented the competition. The enemy was whoever had sent him. "We've agreed to help each other. That's why he went to Denison. This assignment will give him a chance to impress the board."

A shake of her head told him she didn't believe him. "I know why *he* went. Because he's a good man. He cares about the future of the railroad. Why would *you* agree to help him?"

Henry got the point. It was so sharp how could he miss it? He wasn't *good* therefore his motives were questionable. He wasn't sure which stung worse—his conscience or his pride.

There was no such a thing as a "good man." Not in the altruistic sense of the word. However, he could be a *better* man. This was possible. For her sake, he would try.

"I agreed to help him because I want you."

Her eyes widened with astonishment. "That's…"

"Selfish, I know."

His response was met with a stunned look. When he'd finally decided to be honest, she didn't believe him.

"That's the truth."

Her expression turned thoughtful, an improvement over doubt. She hugged her wrap, which was nothing more than a fringed shawl. The night air had gotten cold.

Henry removed his greatcoat. "You never dress properly for the weather," he murmured.

She allowed him to drape it over her shoulders, even let him put his arms around her to adjust it. "You're saying, you worked everything out, all because you wanted—"

"To have you to myself, yes." He ventured a kiss on her cheek. "Guilty as charged."

Lucy twisted around with a wry expression. "That's crazy, Henry. You could've asked to court me and saved yourself the trouble."

"Your father wouldn't have agreed to it."

She searched his face. "Is that the only reason you sent him down there?"

Admitting he hoped Forbes would demonstrate his incompetence didn't seem a wise thing to say. He could give other reasons, ones that wouldn't earn him a slap. "Someone with authority had to go. He offered."

"And if he gets the injunction lifted, then what?"

Henry would take credit for sending him down there. What else did she think he'd do?

"If he's successful in negotiating a settlement with the Texas Central, I'll speak to Mr. Parsons about appointing him over our operations down there." This seemed a good way to keep his future father-in-law busy—and distant.

Lucy appeared to give his suggestion thought, although the questions in her eyes remained. He wasn't ready to go into deeper truths. There was only so much honesty she could take.

He offered her his arm. "It's getting late. We should get back."

They walked in silence for the next several blocks back to the hotel. He led her inside. Up the carpeted stairs. Gasoliers mounted on the walls spilled golden light into the hallway.

"I'll see you to your room."

She glanced over, suspiciously. "You needn't bother."

"I insist."

Henry tamped down his impatience. Her jitters were normal, as were her doubts, yet she'd kissed him like a lover. She might fight her feelings. Eventually, he would win this battle. He never accepted defeat.

He halted at the door to his suite. The thought of her sleeping in his bed ignited his blood. Would she let him kiss her goodnight? He shouldn't press his luck.

She rifled through her reticule. Thankfully, she hadn't taken along her book bag. He took the key to unlock the door, turned the knob and pushed.

She froze at the threshold to the dark room.

Did she expect him to force his way inside? To confound her, he stayed put.

Her brows knitted, confusion or consternation. "I'm flattered by your proposal, Henry. And, I do like you. I'm not sure a marriage between us would work."

That's not what her eyes were saying.

Henry propped his hand on the doorframe. "Who are you trying to convince? Me or you?"

"You, of course. You're the one who seems to think it's a good idea."

"It *is* a good idea. If you put aside your fears and think about it, I know you'll reach the same conclusion."

"I wouldn't bet on it."

A challenge he couldn't resist.

"I would." He leaned down to give her a light kiss. Her lips parted. She couldn't deny this intense attraction between them, and he wouldn't let her ignore it.

She trembled when he stroked her cheek with the side of his thumb.

"Lovely Lucy. You should know me well enough by now to realize I never bet on something unless I'm sure I'll win."

CHAPTER 17

*L*ucy rose before dawn the next morning. She started writing a new story about an intrepid young woman who set out to seek adventure and found unexpected romance. Last evening, she had been inspired.

Aroused. Titillated. Provoked. Electrified.

Many words came close to describing this heart-fluttering exhilaration. None of them truly captured how she felt.

The right word might be *love*.

Her mother had met and fallen in love with her father within the space of a few weeks. She'd left the stage and a brilliant career to marry a man she hardly knew. Wouldn't *Maman* find it amusing if history repeated itself?

Lucy smiled. Except the part about her career. She wouldn't have to walk away from being a writer. Henry hadn't mentioned anything about her giving up her job. In fact, he'd gone to elaborate lengths to arrange things so that she could work and spend time with him. He'd also put her fears to rest about his intentions regarding her father. If he was willing to share power, it might work out well for both men.

After an early breakfast, she set off in the direction of the newspaper office. She glanced over her shoulder. Yes, the depot was visible from here, as well. Henry's brilliant design. What other hidden talents did he have? She couldn't wait to find out.

This didn't mean she would jump right into marriage. Before accepting his proposal, and the alluring offer to travel with him across the West, she had to get to know him better. What drove the indomitable railroad chief? What forces had shaped him? Could he be trusted with her future? Her heart?

Last night, the solution had come to her, and it was *so* obvious. As the railroad correspondent, she could go along with him on business, observe him in action, draw him out, get him to talk about his past, as well as his dreams for the future.

In the meantime, she would discover more about the situation with the Katy. Henry might think he was fooling her. She knew he had something to hide. Soon, he would trust her enough to confide in her and let her help him sort through the problem, whatever it might be.

She gave a happy wave to the apprentices at the printing press as she sailed by on her way to the editor's office. She'd arrived early, eager to get started. Hopefully, her idea for a fictional series featuring the adventures of a handsome railroad chief would be of interest to Mr. Reynolds. In the meantime, she'd leave him with a short piece about her father's endeavors to resolve the Katy's legal dispute in Texas. Good publicity was one way she could help him.

The door to the editor's office had been pulled shut, except for a small crack. Through the space, voices drifted out, Mr. Reynolds and a deeper voice she immediately recognized.

"Give her two weeks' pay. I'll cover it."

"You came in here a week ago demanding that I hire Miss Forbes without the benefit of seeing a sample of her writing," the editor replied. "Now that she's produced excellent work, you want me to *fire* her?"

Lucy covered a startled gasp. Confusion, then dismay gripped her. Henry wanted her fired? Why? Out of spite, because she'd refused him, that had to be the reason. Even so, how could he be so cruel as to steal her dreams?

Tears flooded her eyes. Blinking them back, she reached for the handle, then hesitated. If she confronted him, he wouldn't tell her the truth. He had to give an excuse to Mr. Reynolds. She leaned closer to the opening, straining to hear his answer.

Footsteps sounded. She froze, fearing he would fling the door open and discover her. Before, she hadn't spied on him. She'd simply walked in on his conversation with her father.

His footfalls grew fainter as he walked away. "It's not safe. People keep disappearing."

"You've known about that," the editor grumbled. "I assumed you thought she would be fine if she was with you."

Lucy trembled as the firm steps drew close again. Henry paced when he was agitated.

"I can't guarantee her safety. Not while those scoundrels who attacked the depot are still out there."

"You didn't consider that when you asked me to assign her to the railroad?"

Precisely what she would ask.

"Of course, I considered it—" Henry halted in mid-sentence.

"You've learned something new." A chair squeaked. In her mind's eye, she saw Mr. Reynolds lean forward, anxious to hear the reply.

"What is it?" the editor asked softly.

She gnawed her lip, awaiting Henry's answer. Something had panicked him.

"I can't say. The sheriff doesn't want to tip them off."

"You know who attacked you?" Reynolds declared. He sounded astonished. As was she. Henry had never given the slightest hint he knew the attackers' identities.

"No, I don't know them. Frank found a witness, that's all. My risk isn't the problem. I won't endanger Lucy."

The knot in her throat thickened. Henry had known about this last night. Why hadn't voiced his worries? Instead of talking to her, he'd chosen to sneak around behind her back. As much as she appreciated his concern for her safety, he didn't have the right to

E.E. BURKE

control her life. Disappointment didn't begin to describe the crushing sensation.

"Let her stay here in town," Reynolds suggested. "She can still write stories for us."

Lucy blinked in surprise. Apparently, the editor valued her enough to contest Henry's decision. It soothed the pain, slightly.

"No, I want her out of Parsons." Henry's flat refusal drove a stake through her heart.

"She'll agree to go?"

"My sisters in St. Louis will take her in. I'll suggest a visit."

She clenched her fists. More manipulation.

"Won't her father have something to say about that?"

"There's no need to distract him. He has enough to worry about. I can take care of Lucy."

Her heart pulsed thickly. Bleeding, she was certain, from a thousand wounds.

Henry had *betrayed* her. He didn't want to alert her father to the dangers, which could only mean he intended to thwart an investigation into who was after him and why. There was no reasoning with the arrogant man. An appeal to Mr. Reynolds would be a waste of time. Henry had used his power to coerce and manipulate. With her, he'd used sweet words.

She swallowed a sob. Put one foot behind the other, then turned and fled the office.

She would pack up. Leave. No, he wanted her to leave. Stay. She didn't trust him enough to remain here, under his influence. She could send her father a telegram, warning him of Henry's scheming. The message might not reach him. Henry likely controlled communications just as he controlled everything else. That left her only one option. Go to Denison, find her father, tell him what she knew. Insist he come back to Parsons to finish his investigation on Henry.

Her heart thudded painfully as she slipped inside the hotel. She waved at Claire without stopping to visit and dashed up the stairs.

The moment Henry realized she'd fled he would come after her.

Somehow, she had to board a train bound for Denison without being noticed. She could adopt a disguise like the heroine in *The Hidden Hand*. If she purchased men's garments here, the mercantile owner might tattle on her. Henry had everyone in his pocket, it seemed. She'd pick up clothes in the next town. In the meantime, hide in a freight car and hitch a ride.

Her plan set, she hurriedly packed her satchel, cursing Henry while she wept. To think, she'd fancied herself in love with that...that odious puppet-master. He didn't care for her. He wanted to own her. She'd known men like that. Her aunt had been married to one. He'd been charming on the outside too, and had made her aunt's life miserable up until the day he died.

Henry wouldn't get the chance to cause more misery.

Lucy changed into a looser jacket and skirt, one petticoat. She would travel light. Move fast. That way, Henry couldn't catch up with her. She would not let him—or any man—run her life. Not now. Not ever.

CHAPTER 18

*T*he hotel lobby appeared deserted. No folks lounged on the sofa or in the comfortable armchairs. The hotel owner wasn't behind the registration desk either. Unusual. Maybe she'd stepped way for a minute.

Frank Garrity took another slow, cautious look around. A moment's inattention had gotten his wife killed. If he'd sent Sarah away as he should have, she would still be alive—and their child. The tiny, blood-streaked little thing no bigger than the palm of his hand had never taken a breath after the doc had carved her out of her dead mama's belly. Frank knew that nothing he did, in this life or the next, would ever make up for letting them die.

He'd come here today to make sure Henry Stevens didn't make the same mistake.

Everyone in town knew of the general manager's interest in the Forbes girl, which made her a perfect target for that outlaw. Stevens hadn't mentioned yesterday what his plans were to protect her. He'd run out of time to mull it over.

He hadn't been at the depot this morning. His assistant suggested he might be at the hotel with Miss Forbes. That young lady needed to be on the next train headed east.

Frank approached the registration counter. The rich mahogany desk with ornate carvings on the front had come all the way from New York, after being taken out of some fancy, now-defunct hotel. At least, that's what the owner of the Belmont House had told him. She liked to talk about her hotel. He liked listening to her talk—about anything.

He reached across the cool surface to grab a notebook and a pencil, intending to leave a note. His nose detected a familiar fragrance. Reminded him of the wild roses that had grown up around the front of the house when he was a boy.

The hotel owner's dark head appeared above the counter. Her brown eyes rounded behind a pair of spectacles perched on the end of her nose. She jerked upright. An attractive pink blush spread across her cheeks. "Oh, I'm sorry. I didn't hear the bell... I, um, dropped a key and was looking for it under the counter."

With brisk movements, she tugged at the fitted jacket and smoothed her skirt, both fixes unnecessary. Her hand went to her head. She patted her hair. As usual, the thick tresses were braided and pulled back into a style suited to a woman much older. Even so, it flattered her.

Frank itched to remove the pins, take her hair down to feel the texture.

"Is there something I can do for you, Sheriff?"

With a start, he yanked his mind out of the gutter. "Mr. Stevens. Have you seen him?"

She drew back at the unintended sharp tone. "Henry left early this morning. He didn't say when he'd be back."

Frank bit off an impatient curse. He didn't have time to track down the general manager. He had to lead a posse to search for those missing men. This case was the most frustrating, puzzling one he'd ever dealt with. How did folks vanish into thin air? At least with the depot attackers, he had the name of one of the criminals. Now, he had learned a little more, which was why he'd come looking for Stevens. To warn him.

"Could you convey a message?"

"Yes, of course." Mrs. Daines remained polite, as always. She retrieved a notebook.

Her enticing scent teased his senses. He'd noticed before how nice she smelled. An odd contrast to how dowdy she dressed, which didn't hide her natural beauty, if that's what she intended.

He tapped his fingers on the counter, doing his damnedest to hide his interest. Hell, she was a married gal. Even if she weren't, he sure as hell wouldn't be tying the knot again. Not after what happened to the last unfortunate woman he'd married.

She held the pencil with the most elegant fingers he'd ever seen on a working woman. He stared at her hand, mesmerized.

"Sheriff Garrity?" Her voice took on a note of concern. "Are you all right?"

"I'm fine." He tried not to make it sound like a grumble. Belatedly, he removed his hat, then wiped his damp forehead with the edge of his sleeve. She'd be appalled if she had the slightest idea of his inappropriate fascination. "Tell your brother that Jasper Byrne and his gang left the Territory. Not sure where they'll turn up. They could be headed here."

Mrs. Daines wrote quickly. She didn't employ the elaborate curlicues most women favored. Her writing looked neat and no-nonsense. Like her.

She lifted the pencil, frowning. "Who's Jasper Byrne?"

Frank preferred to keep such information to himself. It was safer that way. Then again, maybe she ought to know. If Byrne had been hired because of some personal vendetta, he might come after anyone dear to Stevens, including his sister. The thought made Frank's heart pound harder. "He's an outlaw. We suspect he's the one who attacked your brother at the depot."

Her smooth brow creased with distress. "You believe he'll come back after Henry?"

"Can't read his mind, but I'd say there's a good chance. And anyone who's important to Mr. Stevens is in danger, as far as I'm concerned. That includes you, Mrs. Daines. You ought to keep a gun handy."

She reached below the counter, laid a pistol on the desk. "I always do."

Frank couldn't stop his smile. Damn, she impressed the hell out him. "Smart gal."

Her gaze met his. The defiant spark wavered. "I haven't always been smart."

Somehow, he knew her comment had nothing to do with that gun.

The bell on the front door jangled.

Frank turned with his hand on his revolver. The Colt whispered out of its holster before Henry Stevens had gotten completely inside.

Stevens frowned, looking pointedly at the gun. "What's going on here? Caldwell said you were looking for me." He didn't pause before addressing his sister. "Have you seen Lucy?"

"She returned from the newspaper office then left again. She seemed in a hurry. I thought she was meeting you."

Frank didn't miss the alarm that flashed across the general manager's face.

In the tense silence, his patience gave out. Whatever was going on between the railroad chief and that girl wasn't his concern. Men had gone missing, a potential assassin was on the loose, and he was no closer to finding any of them than he had been yesterday.

"Came by to tell you Byrne left his hideout. He's on the move. Might be headed here." Frank replaced his hat, adding a warning, "I advise you to find that gal. Fast."

CHAPTER 19

*L*ucy crept alongside the stationary train. According to the schedule, its final destination would be Denison, with numerous stops along the way. This much she'd learned from the station manager, who'd asked if she wanted a ticket then looked at her oddly when she said *no*.

Odors worse than those in a barnyard assailed her senses when she passed by a car enclosed with wooden slats. A snort sounded near her ear. She scrunched her nose. *Hogs. Ugh.* Her plan to hide away in a boxcar might bear rethinking. At the next rail stop, she could buy a ticket under an assumed name. Even the smelliest passengers crowded into coach weren't this odiferous.

The next two cars were closed.

Ah, this one looked promising. Loaded with crates marked for delivery to Fort Gibson. That meant the car would be unloaded at the first stop in Indian Territory, about an hour away.

After glancing around to make sure none of the crew had noticed her, Lucy grasped a handrail to haul herself up. Inside, she squeezed between two of the largest crates. She stepped on something.

"Ow!" came a cry.

Startled, she backed up. "Who's there?"

"Who's askin'?" The owner of the high voice inched out from behind the back of a crate. Oversized bib denims hung on his lanky form. The hems were rolled up above his bare feet. He held his chin down, which hid his face.

It had to be the boy she'd seen in the rail yard. The one who'd run away from her. Henry had told her he had a home. Finding him here would suggest otherwise.

She recalled the name Henry had mentioned. "Billy?"

The boy pushed an engineer's cap upward and cocked his head. "You. How come you're after me?"

For both their sakes, she didn't want him to run. The crew might see him and investigate. She put her hands up, a peacemaking gesture. "I'm not after you. This car appeared to be empty—"

Three loud raps sounded on the side of the car.

Billy grabbed her sleeve to pull her behind a crate. He crouched down then held a finger to his lips. She went to her knees, quietly.

"All clear," someone shouted.

The door slid shut with a bang. Daylight seeped through cracks between the boards.

Billy remained still. Obviously, he was used to hiding in rail cars. Maybe he even lived in them. Some children ran away because of poverty or abuse. His uncertain situation roused her sympathy. She couldn't imagine being without a home and family.

Henry knew of the boy's situation. Maybe he didn't have a heart for children.

Her chest ached. He didn't have a heart, period.

A whistle sounded. The floor beneath Lucy's feet shuddered as the train began to move.

She squinted, trying to see. "It's very dark in here..."

Billy slipped away. In another moment, a match flared. Threads of black smoke curled upward. The sharp odor of kerosene stung her nose. He'd lit the wick inside a wire-framed globe. He plopped down, cross-legged, on the dusty plank flooring. Put the lantern within reach. The light played across his freckled features.

Eager to find out more about him, Lucy sat across from him. She tucked her legs beneath her skirts. "Where did you get a brakeman's lantern?"

"From a brakeman."

Not a trace of regret. Nor did he confess to stealing it. He had, of course. No one would've given it to him.

He eyed her, suspiciously. "You asked a question, now it's my turn. Who're you hiding from?"

She kept her answer as oblique as his. "Someone I don't want to find me."

The boy's lips inched upward. "Mr. Stevens, I bet. He's sweet on you."

Lucy tried to conceal her shock. "How would you know?"

"I listen." Billy touched a finger to his ear, which stuck out from between greasy strands of hair. "The fellers talk about the Chief. They say he ain't showed no interest in a respectable woman since one up and left him for an Injun."

Henry jilted, how surprising. And the woman had chosen an Indian over him, which would be humiliating for any white man, much less one in Henry's position. The report could be a nasty rumor. She ought not encourage the boy by responding. Then again...

Her curiosity won out. "Do you know who she was?"

"Parsons' daughter is what I heard. Katie." Billy shared the knowledge with relish. "You reckon Mr. Stevens named the railroad after her?"

That would be a romantic thing to do.

Jealousy burned in Lucy's chest. *Nonsense.* "The name is derived from the railroad's moniker, MK&T." She had no reason to care, regardless. "If anyone named the Katy after this woman, it was probably her father."

"Yeah, maybe." The boy gave her an impish grin. "You headed for the Territory to run away with an Injun?"

He was more imaginative than her.

"No, I'm..." She stopped short of lying by saying she wasn't running. She had indeed fled from Henry, and from her attraction to him. Despite the evidence of his deceitfulness, she still couldn't purge him from her thoughts. "I'm on my way to Texas to see my father."

Billy's face reflected doubt. "How come you didn't buy a ticket?"

Lucy hesitated. She didn't think he'd betray her. He appeared to be hiding out, as well. "You're right. I don't want Mr. Stevens to know I'm on the train. I can't explain why."

"All righty, then. I asked loads of questions. I'll stop for a spell." Billy dragged a bulging flour sack over. He dug inside, came up with a loaf of bread. "You hungry?"

"I don't want to take your food."

"Aw, I can always get more."

"The same way you got the brakeman's lantern?"

"A man has got to eat."

Lucy held her tongue. She had no right to scold him. After all, she had stowed away too. "We haven't been properly introduced yet. I'm Lucy Forbes. What's your surname, Billy?"

"Don't know 'bout a surname." Billy talked as he gnawed on the bread, which appeared to be hard as a rock. "The fellers call me Frye."

"The fellows?"

"Railroaders."

"Why do they call you Frye?"

He grimaced. "Short for *small fry*. My Pa had the same name."

"That means Frye is your surname."

He shrugged. "If you say so."

"What happened to your father?"

"He died afore I was born. Kilt in a card game."

"And your mother?"

"Sickness took her five years back. I don't got no other family. That's why they sent me to a place for orphans. Didn't like it none, so I ran away." He gave his heartbreaking story in a matter-of-fact tone. Somehow, that made it easier to share hers.

"I lost my mother when I was thirteen. My brother was killed during the war."

Billy wiped his mouth with his sleeve. "You still got your Pa. You ain't alone."

"No, I'm not alone." She swallowed her tears, knowing the proud boy wouldn't appreciate them. "Why do you loiter around the rail yard?"

He squared his shoulders. "I aim to work for the railroad."

"Aren't you a little young?"

His frown conveyed his opinion. "The Chief won't give me a proper job yet. He says I have to stay with the family he picked out and go to school."

Lucy's heart tripped. So, Henry wasn't disinterested. A comforting thought. "Mr. Stevens picked out a family for you?"

"Yeah, a couple different ones. Didn't like 'em."

Lucy nodded at Billy's sack of belongings. "And you've run away again?"

"I ain't keen to be a farmer..." He looked down at the floor, seeming very interested in a piece of straw. "Reckon the Chief might send me back to that orphanage...if he catches me."

Somehow, Lucy didn't think so. Henry had tried to help. A heartless man wouldn't care. Moving past her anger, she could admit he had good qualities, possibly even the capacity for love. He confused affection with possession, which could be due to his own impoverished past. And like Billy, he trusted no one.

"Mr. Stevens had to work to support his sisters after their parents died. He was a little older than you. I'm sure it was very difficult for him. He must've struggled for years. He wants you to have a better life. Why didn't you like the families he picked out?"

Billy lifted his chin in defiance. Hurt shone in his eyes. "They want a farm hand. *I* want to work on the railroad. Until I'm old enough, I can take care of myself."

"I'm sure you believe you can." She shuddered at the thought of Billy trying to make it alone in the world. Even with his pluck, he'd find it difficult to survive. Which made her wonder why he'd been so desperate he would leave behind food and shelter. She couldn't seek Henry's help, so she had to find a way to keep Billy with her until she reached Texas and could gain her father's assistance in resolving the boy's situation.

"How well do you know the railroad?"

"I know most everything." His cocksure attitude reminded her of Henry. Had he been like Billy as a boy, hiding his insecurities behind bravado?

"Well, I could use a guide to help me get to Texas without being discovered."

His head bobbed. "That's easy."

"I thought you might be willing. In return, I'll help you find a better place to live."

The boy's eyes rounded. "You'd do that for me?"

"I give my word." Lucy put out her hand. "Shall we shake on it?"

Billy brought his hand up to his mouth, spit in his palm then took her outstretched hand in a firm, squishy grip. "Lady, you got yourself a deal."

CHAPTER 20

"What do you mean, she isn't on the train?"

Caldwell took a step back at Henry's bellow. "She didn't purchase a ticket."

"That doesn't mean she isn't on it." Henry paced to the edge of the platform. He peered down the tracks leading out of town. A veil of smoke hung in the air. Number Four had left the station ten minutes before he'd arrived. He whipped out his pocket watch to check the time. Ten-forty. His blasted luck, today they would run on schedule.

Lucy had to be on that train bound for Texas. Where else would she go?

According to Claire, she'd gone to the newspaper office. She must've arrived to work early, overheard his conversation with the editor. She should've made herself known, given him a chance to explain.

Henry frowned as he recalled his sister's scold.

"If you'd talked to her first, this wouldn't have happened."

Claire had taken him to task after he explained what he'd done— for Lucy's own good.

"You can't toy with people's lives and expect them to thank you for it."

He'd walked out of the hotel after that remark.

Damn it, he wasn't trying to manipulate Lucy or run her life. He wanted to protect her, and knew her well enough to know she wouldn't have agreed to leave the newspaper. Besides, he couldn't share the details behind his decision without risking her father's involvement, which would only make things more complicated than they already were. If Lucy had accepted his proposal, trusted him, none of this would've happened.

"Have my car prepared." Henry issued the command to his assistant. "Send a telegram to the agent at Vinita. Describe her. She might be traveling under an assumed name. Tell him I'll be there in three hours or less. Do *not* let that train leave before I arrive."

"Right, Chief." Caldwell jerked a salute.

"I'm not a damn general."

"Yes sir." The younger man's arm swung to his side.

"Why are you still standing here? Get going."

His assistant executed a quick turn then dashed away.

Henry strode through the lobby. The heels of his shoes clacked on the marble floor. He'd pack a bag, catch up with Lucy at the first stop in Indian Territory. Talk some sense into her. Tie her up if necessary. She had to learn not to run off half-cocked.

He reached into his vest pocket where he'd stuffed a message left for Milt Reynolds, who'd wisely turned it over. In her precise hand, Lucy wrote she was aware the editor had been *strong-armed* into firing her. She went on to tell him she would continue writing stories about the railroad. If the *Parsons Sun* wouldn't buy them, she'd find another newspaper that would.

Henry swore under his breath. He could imagine the stories she'd peddle, the kind that put him in the worst light. He dashed across the busy street, thundered down the sidewalk.

"Stevens!"

Almost to the door of the hotel, Henry debated ignoring the hail. The sheriff had already told him about Byrne, another reason he couldn't delay going after Lucy.

"Hang fire..." The sheriff caught up. On his heels came a well-fed man dressed like a politician. Frank Garrity's face shone red. His eyes looked a little wild. "Mr. Stevens, this is Senator York."

No other politician would be a bigger thorn in Henry's side—or a pain in his ass. He stuck out his hand, unsmiling. "Senator, pleased to make your acquaintance."

York ignored the customary handshake. "I wish I could say the same. I understand you've known about these disappearances for some time and have done nothing. Even though a number of these men went missing near your rail line."

Henry understood York's concern for his missing brother. Hell, he was frantic to find Lucy. Even so, the politician had no call to make him, or the railroad, responsible for an unfortunate situation. "None of the men were on our trains when they disappeared."

"If they had been, perhaps you would've acted more quickly to repeated pleas from The Grange."

The Grange? Since when had that organization gotten involved?

Henry answered his own question. Since a Senator's brother went missing. And they called *him* an opportunist. "Our station agents have been alerted. I've assigned a crew to help the sheriff. We've offered a reward—two thousand dollars—to anyone who comes forward with solid information."

York harrumphed. "You put up that reward *after* my brother went missing. You and I both know why, so let's not bother trying to whitewash it."

Henry reined in annoyance rather than engage in an argument with a surly politician, which wouldn't benefit anyone, least of all Lucy. The more he delayed, the greater chance something terrible might happen to her. She had a knack for finding trouble.

"What do you want, Senator? You have my full cooperation. Search every inch of our property. Do whatever you deem necessary." The sheriff knew this. Henry said it for York's benefit. "I have to find Miss Forbes. Otherwise, I'd join you."

The senator's discontented frown turned to one of confusion. "Who's Miss Forbes?"

The sheriff answered first. "The daughter of the railroad

investigator. This morning, she left town. Mr. Stevens is worried about her safety."

"Has she gone missing, too?"

Henry's heart began to pound. Lucy had no reason to go north, which was where those men disappeared. Anywhere in the Territory was dangerous. Denison was as bad. If that outlaw intercepted the train and discovered her identity... Awful images filled Henry's mind.

By God, he couldn't waste another minute standing here debating. He grasped the brim of his hat and dipped his chin. "If you gentlemen will excuse me, I'll be on my way."

Two short whistles shook Lucy out of her slumber. She'd drifted off while leaning against one of the crates. Billy had curled up on the floor next to her like a large puppy. He smelled like one, too.

The car vibrated as the train began to slow.

She reached out to touch his shoulder. "Billy? Feels like we're stopping."

He came up to a squat. "You go wait at the station. I'll nab them clothes you want."

She'd told him her idea about traveling in disguise. He'd loved it. "We won't steal them. I can buy what I need at a mercantile."

"Ain't no mercantile here. They got a trading post. *You* don't want to go in there. Too many Injuns."

Lucy doubted the natives would bother them. Still, she might draw unnecessary attention if the trading post catered mostly to men. She pulled several bills out of her satchel. "Fine, you buy the clothes. While you're at it, get us some food."

Billy stuffed the bills into the bib pocket. "Whatever you say."

Lucy sensed ill intent. She took hold of his arm. "Use that money to purchase what we need. Do not think you can pocket it and I won't know."

His head jerked up. "I wasn't gonna—"

"Good. I'm glad to hear it."

The train let loose with a long shrill tone, then ground to a stop.

"Time to go." Billy got to his feet and secured his cap. He pulled a dangling strap over his shoulder. "They'll open the doors first," he whispered. "Then another crew comes by to unload. Afore that, we'll hop out."

He handed her the extinguished lantern before he hefted the sack over his shoulder.

Lucy followed him behind a crate. She crouched there, hiding.

In a moment, the door squealed.

Daylight flooded the compartment.

Voices from outside faded as the men went to the next car.

"Come on." Billy sailed out the open door.

Lucy ventured to the edge to look down—three, maybe four feet to the ground. She held her breath and jumped. Billy caught her arm and helped her to stand. She trembled with excitement. Their eyes met. They grinned at each other like cohorts in crime.

"Up there's the station. Be back in a jiffy." Billy pointed before he ducked beneath the train and disappeared.

Lucy peered down the tracks at a clapboard structure with *Vinita* painted in bold black letters on the side. They'd reached the first stop in Indian Territory.

The town appeared to consist of numerous freight buildings and tents, huddled around the intersection of two railroads—the Katy and the Atlantic & Pacific.

She'd heard from Mr. Reynolds about bloody battles that had erupted between competing crews when the A&P—conspiring with unhappy Cherokee leaders—illegally cut off the Katy at the new town site. Henry had ordered his men to tear up the competitor's tracks.

When questioned about the incident, he was quoted as saying, "We won't sleep on our rights." He hadn't considered how his rights conflicted with the rights of others. He'd charged ahead. He had no *rights* where she was concerned. She would give no quarter in this battle of wills.

She kept the lantern at her side as she picked her way through the tall, brown grass growing alongside the track. On her way past one of the passenger cars, she kept her head down to avoid eye contact with people who'd departed at the stop. No one would likely recognize her. She would remain cautious, just in case.

On the platform, passengers rushed a counter where a vendor doled out coffee and sandwiches. Her stomach rumbled. She hadn't eaten since breakfast, imagining she could buy food along the way. Hopefully, Billy would find something for them to eat.

"Can I help you, Miss?" A conductor in a crisp uniform stepped in front of her. "What've you got there? A brakeman's lantern?"

Uh oh.

Lucy held up the squat globe, blinking with feigned astonishment. "A brakeman's lantern? Is that what it is? I found it..." She gestured with her chin over her shoulder. "Back there. Thought perhaps someone left it behind."

"One of our brakemen, no doubt."

"Here, you can return it."

Billy would be disappointed. It did belong to the railroad. She couldn't afford to be detained over a stolen lantern.

The conductor took the brakeman's light in his free hand. He consulted a clipboard held in the other. "Where you headed, today?"

"Denison."

"We leave in ten minutes. If you want something to eat, better hurry."

"Thank you." Lucy eyed the lunch counter. She'd never get through that mob, nor did she care to. Railroads strictly enforced ten-minute stops at each station, which resulted in a mad rush for food that always turned out to be cold and soggy.

She crossed to the far end of the platform. A river of mud churned up by wagon wheels led to a log cabin with a low-slung roof. An impressive rack of antlers framed the doorway. Above it hung a wooden sign with crudely painted letters.

Oowatie's Trading Post.

At the hitching rail, sleepy horses flicked their tails. In one of the buckboards, a woman huddled in a sky-blue blanket cradled an infant. Her face remained hidden beneath a bright yellow sunbonnet.

Men seated on a split-log bench in front of the trading post, both dark-skinned and fair, were dressed like farmers, with dusty jeans and baggy coats. One man wore a long-tailed shirt embellished with embroidered patterns. From beneath a stovepipe hat, his black hair hung in neat braids. Somehow, she hadn't pictured the mix of cultures. With the expansion of the railroad bringing in an influx of white settlers, it made sense.

Lucy craned her neck to search for Billy. She tried to convince herself that he wouldn't have run off with her money. He'd made a deal and shook on it. Even thieves had a code of honor. He'd better hurry, though. The railroad crews had finished unloading and closed the doors to the freight cars. They couldn't sneak aboard. Her only option now would be to risk purchasing two tickets.

She gathered her courage. Inside the station, she approached the ticket window. "What is the cost of two coach fares to Denison?"

The bald, bespectacled ticket agent behind the counter looked up. He stared at her for an uncomfortable moment. Then his eyes narrowed. "What'd you say your name was, Miss?"

A tremor of unease passed through her. "I didn't. I asked you the price of two fares to Denison."

The man stood. He exchanged a meaningful glance with the telegraph operator hunched over his machine. Lucy took a step away from the counter. Something was wrong here.

"Never mind, I'm not interested."

She rushed back outside. They'd have to find another way to get on that train.

Footsteps sounded behind her. "Excuse me. Are you Miss Forbes?"

Fear struck in a cold wave. They knew her name. Henry must've figured out where she was going. He had spies at every station. Why he had this obsessive need to control her, she didn't know. This time, he would not get his way. She'd done nothing wrong—except steal away on a train without paying the fare.

She kept walking. They had no power to arrest her.

Voices followed. "I'm sure that's her."

"Fits the description."

Lucy angled across the platform to make a beeline for the trading post. She hitched up her skirts so she could walk faster. She'd alert Billy. He'd know the best place to hide.

"Wait Miss! We need to talk to you."

Lucy threw a fearful glance over her shoulder. They'd sent the conductor after her. Her plan had to change. She dared not lead her pursuers to Billy or he'd be packed off to an orphanage.

She veered into a copse of trees behind the trading post. If Billy didn't see her waiting, he was sharp enough to realize something was wrong and hide. She'd catch up with him after she lost her pursuers in the woods. That's what a brave heroine would do in one of her favorite books.

Lucy melted into the forest. As she fought through the thick underbrush, her skirt caught on a thorny branch. The fabric ripped when she pulled away. Henry's warning about the Territory being no place for a lady suddenly took on a more concrete meaning.

She hurled herself deeper into the woods, dodged trees, crashed through underbrush, every so often throwing anxious glances over her shoulder to determine whether anyone had followed. Years ago, she'd played hide and seek with her brother in the woods back home. She'd always been adept at evading him.

Her heart leapt at the shrill whistle of the train. Oh no! It was about to leave. When would the next one be through? Where had Billy gone?

She looked back—and collided with something hard, which gave way for a second.

A man, black-haired and bronze-skinned, caught her. His surprised expression turned to one of wicked delight. "What's the hurry, little lady?" he said in a rasp that sent chills down her spine.

Her mind went blank for a second before one terrifying word filled the emptiness.

Savage.

She shrieked. Tried to wrench her arms free. He didn't let go. Alone, with no one to hear or see, he could do anything he pleased to her. Nearly blind with fright, she went at him with her nails. One swipe left a bloody streak on his cheekbone.

With a furious curse, he caught her wrist and twisted her around, bringing her arm up behind her back. Pain tore through her shoulder. Frantic, she groped for his gun with her free hand. He grabbed her failing arm.

"Stop that," he growled.

She paid no mind to his command and kept fighting, desperate to break away.

He uttered a string of course words—some she understood, others sounded foreign. He cursed her in a Native language. Oh God, she'd read accounts of abducted women. What they did to them.

"Dammit gal, stop your struggling. Don't want to hurt you."

The fact he spoke English didn't make him civilized. Even his voice sounded menacing. Harsh, rasping, like she imagined a devil would sound, if she ever heard one.

He held her arms in a painful vise. "You fellas could help..."

Who was he talking to?

Lucy's panic soared at the sight of two other men standing close by. One had long black braids. The other was pale-skinned and stout, with eyes like a hog.

"You caught her," chortled the hog. "That makes her yorn."

Her heart seized. Savages or fiends, it made no difference. They were equally bad. If she couldn't get away, they'd molest her, at the very least.

With a screech, she fought back, kicking like a mule.

Her assailant grunted. He shifted his stance. "Crazy woman." He snaked an arm around her neck while still holding her numb hands behind her. "Don't make me do this."

Do what? Break her neck?

Cold sweat drenched her skin. God help her, she had to get away. Run back to the station. Nothing Henry could do to her would be this bad.

"Let...me...go," she gasped in between heaving breaths.

"Stop fighting." He squeezed his arm tighter, cutting off her air.

Oh God, she couldn't breathe. She writhed and twisted. It did no good. He squeezed harder. Dark spots danced in her vision. Her heart thudded in her ears. The monster was killing her. She would die. Never see her father again, never see Henry...

She tried to speak, to beg him not to kill her, couldn't manage more than a squeak. Heaviness settled into her arms and legs. Her knees gave way.

He caught her around the waist at the same time he let up on his chokehold.

She sucked air into her starved lungs and tried to renew her struggles. Her energy had drained away. He'd weakened her, not killed her. He must want her alive for some nefarious purpose. Dread shuddered through her.

From the woods came a sound, twigs snapping.

Her captor tensed.

Lucy's hopes revived. She opened her mouth to call out. He muted her with a smelly wad of cloth, then hauled her to his horse.

"You two stay here. Lay low," he instructed his henchmen. "Find out who's after her and why. We'll meet up at Cabin Creek."

CHAPTER 21

a grim trio met Henry when he arrived at the station in Vinita. Inside, two railroad employees stood watch over a sullen child with a bloodied lip. According to the men, Lucy had run into the woods. They hadn't been able to find her.

Henry fisted the brim of his hat, tempted to throw it on the ground in sheer frustration. He'd been so sure he could catch her. How had she gotten herself into trouble in three hours?

"Did anyone go after her?" he demanded.

The station manager nudged grimy spectacles up the bridge of his nose. "The Indians have jurisdiction in these parts."

"Have you notified Fort Gibson?"

The telegraph operator shook his head. "No sir."

Henry shot him a hard look. "Send a message—now. Tell them a white woman has gone missing at Vinita. We need troops to mount a search."

The aggravating man didn't jump to obey the order. "The army cleared out a few months ago. Only a corporal's guard left. Doubt they'd be much help."

Henry swore an oath. He'd told General Sherman that the Army should keep at least one company permanently assigned to the

Territory. Without soldiers, the railroad had to depend on the tribal patrols for protection, which most of the time meant no protection. He'd refused to put the security of his railroad in their hands. He'd hired guards, posted them on the trains and railroad property. Other than that, he couldn't take armed men off on a search. The Indians would raise hell. It left him only one option—to go after her himself.

Billy sat hunched in a chair with his head down. The men guarding him told Henry the boy had been skulking around the station, asking after Lucy.

"How did you get that bloody lip?" Henry asked.

"I fell," came the terse reply.

The scowls on the faces of the two men standing nearby told a different story.

Henry's anger quickened. He directed the next question to the bulky telegraph operator. "What happened?"

"Like he said, he fell while he was running."

Henry restrained the urge to knock that smug look off the man's face. He'd deal with these two later. He squatted next to Billy, kept his tone even. "Can you tell me where Miss Forbes went?"

Billy stared at the floor. "Don't know."

"Was she with you?"

"We ran into each other is all."

Henry knew that wasn't nearly *all*. He forced himself to be patient. The boy had been treated badly. "Is there some reason you can't tell me where she is?"

"I gave my word. She don't want nobody to find her." Billy's eyes shifted in a fearful sideways glance.

Regret knifed through Henry. *Nobody*. Meaning him.

He laid a hand on the child's bony shoulder. "Billy, I know you want to protect her. You know she isn't safe out there. We need to find her before someone else does. Someone who won't be as nice to her as you were."

"Don't know where she went." Billy blinked hard like he was trying not to cry. "That ain't a lie. She sent me to buy her some trousers. Was supposed to meet on the platform."

"That gal ran off after we called out to her, like I told you," the station manager added. "Sam went into the woods, said he heard something like an Injun yell. Saw a horse hightailing it out."

Henry shot to his feet with a glare. "You didn't mention she was abducted."

"I-I thought I did..." The station manager pushed at the nosepiece of his spectacles.

A chill swept through Henry, at the same time sweat broke out on his forehead. He wouldn't put it past these surly natives to kidnap Lucy.

Two years ago, when he'd been tasked with building the railroad through this godforsaken land, he'd butted heads with the Cherokee. The wily Indians had thwarted him at every turn. One of them, an outlaw who'd since become a lawyer—one and the same in Henry's mind—had even stolen the woman he'd planned to marry right out from under his nose. Kate, with her bleeding heart, had fallen for Jake Colston's woeful tale. Lucy was smarter than that.

"Send word to Fort Gibson," Henry commanded. "Tell them Miss Forbes was abducted. I'm going after her."

The two employees exchanged nervous looks. Henry didn't ask why. Everyone knew the danger. One didn't go off alone into the rough, uncivilized Territory. Besides unfriendly natives, bands of outlaws took refuge in the ungoverned hills. He'd risk the danger, rather than wait for help to arrive. Every minute counted, and he was already two hours too late.

Henry put his arm around the boy's slender shoulders. He ushered him outside. Waved his assistant over and explained what was going on. "Take Billy back to Parsons."

"Shall I return the lad to the Zeller's?" Caldwell asked.

Billy's panicked expression gave Henry pause. The boy had been reluctant to return the last time he'd run off. The farmer might've abused him. What about the family before that? Damn it, there wasn't time to explore options. He had to rely on someone he trusted. "Take him to my sister."

Caldwell looked doubtful. "Mrs. Daines?"

Twice, Claire had turned down Henry's request that she take the homeless boy. Henry suspected it wasn't his sister who'd objected. Frederick Daines could to go to hell, as far as he was concerned. The loafer sat around all day, did nothing around the hotel, and had become a burden on his wife. He could put up with a little inconvenience.

"Tell her it's a temporary situation. We'll work things out after I return with Miss Forbes."

"Those men inside took my food," Billy informed Henry.

"Mr. Caldwell, you'll retrieve Mr. Frye's belongings."

"Happy to."

Billy hung back with fear in his eyes. "You gonna send me to an orphanage?"

Henry knew he couldn't be soft or the undisciplined boy wouldn't take him seriously. He didn't want Billy to run away again. Next time, the child might suffer worse than a split lip. "If there was an orphanage that could hold you, I might. Can't think of one, so we'll have to come up with something else."

The anxiousness on the boy's face made Henry regret his harshness. He started to ruffle Billy's hair, decided against it. Young as he was, he was no longer a child. By age ten, Henry hadn't been a child either. By the time he was fourteen, he'd become a man.

He offered Billy his hand. "Let's agree, shall we? You stay with Mrs. Daines until I return. Then you and I will have a talk about where you'll go to live."

Billy eyed Henry's outstretched hand. Slowly, he reached up. "I swore to Miss Lucy I'd look after her. Tell her I tried to keep my vow."

"I will when I find her."

"What if you can't find her?" Billy's voice wavered.

"I won't come back until I do." It was his fault she was out there in the first place.

His assistant frowned as he glanced over Henry's shoulder at the station. "Who's accompanying you to search for Miss Forbes?"

"Nobody."

"Not even our guards?" Caldwell's tone implied only an insane man wouldn't take help along.

Henry swallowed his fear. "If I did, we'd get arrested for overstepping our authority. It's better if I go alone."

The young man's expression turned thoughtful. He nodded in the direction of the Trading Post. "Maybe you can find a friendly local who'll help you search for her."

Friendly Indians? There weren't any left. At least none who were friendly to the railroad.

CHAPTER 22

*L*ucy's abductor took her to a run-down cabin, deep in the woods. The one-room shack appeared to be abandoned. Cobwebs dangled from rough-hewn rafters. Dust had settled into every nook and cranny, most of it from the dirt floor. Two chairs fashioned from bent branches provided the only furniture.

He hadn't offered her a seat. After binding her hands and feet, he'd stuck her in the corner like a naughty child. Then he'd dragged a chair in front of the cold fireplace, taken a bone-handled knife from a sheath in his boot, and proceeded to whittle.

She studied him with a mixture of terror and fascination. Like most of the Indians she'd seen, his skin had the hue of a dull penny. His black hair wasn't completely straight. It lay in restless waves. He could be a mixture of white and Indian. She'd read about outlaw gangs headed up by lawless half-breeds, despised by both cultures.

Dear Lord, what had she gotten herself into?

As he hunched over the stick, the faded broadcloth shirt stretched over his angular shoulders. Worn jeans were tucked into knee-high boots made from a soft-looking leather. His coat—deerskin or something like it—hung from a peg hammered into the wall. The fringed sleeves and back were decorated with beadwork. Someone had put time and love into creating it. Someone cared for him.

He might not be as horrid as she'd imagined. Possibly, he thought she had rich relatives and he intended to ransom her. That being the case, she'd better keep her mouth shut. If he found out her father was with the railroad, he would assume they were wealthy.

She had money concealed in a hidden pocket in her satchel. The bag hung beside his coat. She might be able to barter with him for her release. If she could unclog the fear stuck in her throat.

From behind a cracked jug near the fireplace, a dark, slithering shape emerged. The reptile undulated across the room in her direction.

Her mouth worked until she forced out a terrified cry. "Snake!"

Her captor looked up. At the same time, he lifted his arm and the knife went flying across the room, impaling the creature. Without a word, he went over, dispatched the snake by cutting off its head, and tossed it out an open window.

Lucy sagged with momentary relief. The other, larger, snake was still in the room. It was past time she put her mind to work to find a way out of this mess. "Why did you abduct me?"

He swung around with a look of surprise, then with a wry expression. "Abduct you? I *rescued* you."

Rescued? Preposterous. He had to be unbalanced or meant it as a cruel hoax.

Lucy straightened her spine, prepared to play along until she determined how best to handle the situation. "Perhaps you should've inquired as to whether I needed to be rescued before you choked me and wrestled me onto your horse." She held up her bound wrists. "Do you make a habit of tying up ladies you rescue?"

He sank down on his haunches next to her. With the knife's tip he pointed to a scratch beneath his cheekbone where dried blood made a thin line. "I do when the lady in question has claws."

Lucy winced. She'd never lifted a hand to anyone, much less scratched someone's face. "Yes, that must've hurt. I'm sorry. You surprised me when you grabbed me."

"I told you I wouldn't hurt you. You weren't in the mood to listen." His odd, rasping voice made her shiver. He didn't seem to be doing it on purpose.

Maybe someone had crushed *his* windpipe. Although he hadn't done permanent damage to hers, not even when he'd squeezed her neck to subdue her. That implied some degree of civility, perhaps a dab of compassion. She would try to reason with him.

"If I promise to sheath my claws, will you untie me?"

"You'd run off the minute I wasn't looking." Amusement flared in his eyes. She'd thought them brown. Upon closer inspection they were deep green. Dark as the heart of a forest, would be how she'd describe them in a book.

"I won't run," she lied. She would if she thought she could get away.

His knowing smile sent a shiver through her. "Dangerous critters out there."

"What about the one in here?"

His chuckle sounded like sandpaper rubbed over rusty metal. "Good to see you got a sense of humor. Still can't let you go. For your own good."

His refusal riled her.

"You cart me away and tie me up because of some twisted idea it's the best way to *save* me? That ranks right up there with Henry getting me fired to protect me." She huffed in disgust. "I don't know which of you is worse."

"Who's Henry?" His question held a note of curiosity.

Drat. She should've minded her tongue. This outlaw, or whatever he was, might think he could blackmail the railroad chief. Henry would pay the ransom—of this much, she was sure—and that would put her deeper into his debt when she didn't want to owe him anything.

Too late, she'd accepted she shouldn't have run. Confronting Henry would've been better, no matter how smoothly he might lie. Deep down, she knew he cared for her. Despite the atrocious way he demonstrated his affection. If she were honest with herself, she'd admit she didn't fear him as much as she feared her own heart.

Her abductor leaned back on his heels. His eyes narrowed with speculation. "Tell me your name and who you were on the run from, then I'll untie you."

She wasn't about to reveal her identity, which would provide him with the means to get rich. The Good Lord had given her a creative mind. She could come up with a convincing story close enough to the truth that it wouldn't seem like a lie.

"Adelaide." She gave him her middle name, which had been her mother's.

"That's a mouthful."

"You can call me Addy."

"Where are you from?"

"Boston."

He ran a finger under a dusty bandana around his neck. "That's what I thought. You talk like a Yankee."

"You don't."

His lips twitched. "No ma'am. I'd rather be called a skunk than a Yankee. Who's after you? That Henry fella you mentioned?"

Her heartbeat pounded in her ears, so loud she wondered if he could hear it. "First, tell me your name."

His gaze went flat. "That wasn't part of the deal."

"It's a fair exchange. My name for your name."

He considered her for another moment, then appeared to come to a decision. "Jasper."

He'd offered no more than she had, a given name, probably an alias. Now it was her turn to answer his question.

"I'm on my way to Texas to find my father. I hitched a ride in a boxcar. Those men who were after me were with the railroad."

"They were chasing you because you didn't pay for a ticket?"

She lifted a shoulder in a Gallic shrug. "I thought they'd put me in jail."

Jasper fingered the lace on her high collar. "You're not poor. Or did you steal this dress?"

Lingering fear made her cringe away from him.

His mouth twisted in a derisive smile. "You afraid of me, Addy?"

His plan was still unclear. He might be toying with her, enjoying her discomfort. Some men gained pleasure from inspiring fear. She held his gaze refusing to cower. "Do you want me to be afraid?"

An emotion flickered through his eyes. Regret? He rested his arms on his knees, his hand dangled, still holding the knife. His gaze swept over her. This time, she didn't have to guess what he was feeling. Reluctant yearning.

Lucy swallowed, hard. "What to do you want from me?"

The hard lines in his face softened, slightly. "Told you, I won't hurt you."

Her nerves jangled. If he'd taken her for sport, he must've changed his mind. That meant his mind could be changed about keeping her. "Will you let me go?"

"Soon as the boys get back."

Delay only gave him time to reconsider.

"Must we wait for them arrive? Return me now, I'll give you what money I can scrape up."

Indecision showed on his face. He was no more trusting than Billy. Or Henry.

At last, he moved behind her. The knots loosened and fell away, then he untied the rope around her ankles. "There's a place not far from here where the train slows down enough for you to catch it. I'll take you there."

Lucy sagged with relief. *Thank heavens.* She rubbed her tingling hands to make the blood flow return. Her stomach let out a gurgling noise. Fear had overridden hunger. Now it came back with ferocity.

Jasper wound the rope, looped it over the chair. "Better rustle up some grub before we leave. How about roasted snake?"

Snake? Ugh.

"No, thank you. I'm not hungry."

His gaze rebuked her. "Your stomach's growling like a bear."

She rubbed her hand over her middle. Her body had a bad habit of betraying her. "I'm not hungry for snake," she amended.

He went to his saddlebags, which he'd hung next to his coat. Upon digging into one, he produced a thin piece of dried meat. "How about venison? From a deer."

"Thank you, I know what venison is."

She struggled to her feet on her legs that still felt numb. He offered her his hand. His calloused hand pressed against her soft palm. Henry's hands were toughened, though not as rough. Then again, he didn't live in a saddle, as it appeared this man did. Nor had Henry tied her up. She might've forgiven him for that.

Lucy took a bite of the dried meat. The gamey flavor tasted surprisingly pleasant. Although at this point, she would've eaten most anything—except snake. She gave her captor a grateful smile. "Thank you...Jasper."

He made a slight bow. "My pleasure, ma'am."

What a contradiction he was, half savage, half gentleman. Now that she feared him a little less, her curiosity returned. He would make an interesting character in one of her stories. His harsh, dark looks, while not classically handsome, would be compelling to some women.

She still questioned whether he'd *rescued* her. There was no question in her mind that he was dangerous. In fact, his furtive glances at the door made her wonder if he was a wanted man. He could've taken her back to the station. Instead, he'd brought her to an isolated place.

From outside came the clop of hooves and a high-pitched whinny.

Jasper thrust her behind him with the order to "keep quiet," before he moved to the door with a revolver in his hand. His actions struck her as strangely protective. A man who feared capture would be more likely to use her as a shield.

"It's us."

Whoever *us* was, Jasper apparently recognized the voice. He opened the door.

In came the two men she'd seen earlier. The beefy blond had on a bowler hat that looked familiar. He tugged on a rope. Another man with his arms bound to his sides stumbled across the threshold.

Lucy's disbelieving gaze fastened on the bearded prisoner. Her heart seized with fear.

Henry. He'd come after her. Jasper's men must've surprised him in the woods, taken his gun. Bits of dead grass were in his hair and clung to his suit. If his rumpled condition and that cut on his lip were any indication, he hadn't been easily subdued.

His gaze fastened on her, startled, and then with an anxious question.

She longed to reassure him. However, letting on she knew him might not be the right thing to do. Even though she was starting to believe Jasper intended no ill, she sensed in some ways he was like a wild animal. Unpredictable.

"Bagged us some big game," the hefty man crowed. "We caught him lurkin' in the woods. Looking for her, I reckon." He pointed to Lucy. "We got two to trade now. What do you think they're worth, Jasper?"

~

HENRY JERKED his attention to the man in front of him. *Jasper Byrne.* Had to be. How had the black-haired devil gotten ahold of Lucy? Fury tinged with a sharp edge of fear cut through his confusion. He had to get her away from these vultures.

"You're Jasper Byrne?" Might as well establish for a fact his identity.

"And you must be Henry," the outlaw drawled in a rusty voice. His gaze glittered with a calculating look that made Henry stiffen with alarm.

He'd never met this man, yet the outlaw knew him. In fact, he could've walked right into a trap. Either way, his life might end in this dilapidated cabin. And then, who would protect Lucy?

Desperate, he surged forward.

The man who held his traces yanked him back. He could jerk out of Fat Boy's grip. With his arms bound to his sides, he couldn't defend himself—or her. He had to negotiate, not fight.

"Damn you, Byrne, let her go. She's got nothing to do with this. What is it you want? Money? My hide? I'll give you both—after you release her."

The outlaw pinned him with a hard look. "Release her? Out here in the wild?" He swung his arm in a wide gesture. "Think she'll get to where she was headed?"

He had a point.

"Let me take her to safety," Henry urged. "I give you my word, whatever it is you want from me, you'll get it."

Lucy frowned as she looked at him then the outlaw. "You two know each other?"

Byrne snorted. "He's crazy. Never seen him before now." His gaze narrowed in on Lucy. "You have, haven't you? Who are you, girl? Don't lie to me."

Her chin went up.

Henry closed his eyes on a groan. Why did she always pick the worst times to be defiant?

"I didn't lie," she said pertly. "I left out parts. I am going to Texas, and Adelaide is my name—my middle name. Lucy is my given name."

Henry released a frustrated breath. Why the hell did she have to open her mouth? He challenged the outlaw to draw his anger away from Lucy. "She didn't lie. You're the one who's lying. You tried to kill me. Shot a conductor instead. There were witnesses."

Lucy gaped at the black-haired scoundrel. "*You're* the one? At the depot?"

"*What* depot?" Jasper Byrne swung an angry gaze from Lucy to his henchmen, who wore similar confused expressions. "What the hell are they talking about?"

The Indian shrugged. "Don't know."

"Me neither," Fat Boy chimed in.

Byrne glared at Henry. "Who are you?"

Henry's insides knotted painfully. Why would Byrne act stupid? If this was some sick joke, it had gone on long enough. "You know damn well who I am."

Byrne shot a questioning glance at Lucy. He advanced on her, apparently determined to make her talk.

Enraged, Henry strained against the ropes. "Keep away from her, you devil. It's *me* you want. I'll pay your price. Whatever it is. Let her go. She hasn't done anything. She's innocent."

The heathen crossed his arms over his chest. He appeared to be contemplating Henry's request. "You'll pay?"

"Anything, name your price." He met Lucy's anxious gaze, trying to reassure her with his eyes. He'd sell everything he owned, give his life. His voice came out rough, pleading. "Take me in exchange."

Her stunned expression broke. "Wait, there's no need for that. Let's talk first."

She sidled closer to the outlaw and put her hand on his arm in a tentative gesture. Her voice dropped, yet loud enough for Henry to hear. "Privately."

Henry tried to catch his breath. Was Lucy prepared to sacrifice her virtue, for him? God, no, he wasn't worth it. "No, don't. You can't," he yelled. "I won't let you."

She scowled, as if *he* were the naughty boy. "Don't tell me what I can and cannot do."

"Listen to me, for once," His demand came out in a frustrated snarl. He wanted her angry with him, wanted her to hate him if that's what it took to make her come to her senses.

Instead, she coolly ignored him, and whispered something in the outlaw's ear. He curled an arm around her shoulders. Lucy didn't recoil. Too terrified to move, she had to be, except she didn't look particularly fearful of her captor. She gazed up trustingly at the bastard.

"Take him outside," Byrne ordered, with a dismissive motion.

"Like hell you will. I'm not going anywhere." Henry fought the men holding the ropes. Surely, Lucy had broken under the strain of her captivity or the outlaw had somehow mesmerized her, or he'd controlled her with threats. She couldn't do this, she couldn't.

Lucy turned a disdainful eye on him. "Henry, stop pretending to be a hero. You'll get yourself killed for no reason."

Stunned, he stopped struggling. She'd only said those things so he would leave, to protect him. Still, he'd gone behind her back and crushed her dreams. She'd run away, hurt and angry. Possibly, the outlaw had taken advantage of her vulnerable situation.

God no, not again.

The last time he'd lost a woman to thieves, she'd fallen in love with one of them.

CHAPTER 23

*H*enry put up such a fight Lucy feared the outlaws would shoot him. She'd rather bite off her tongue than say those hateful things to him. It had been all she could think to say to make him leave peacefully. As it was, it took Jasper and both his men to shove Henry out the door, despite the fact his arms were bound.

She winced when they pushed him to the ground. The hefty man sat on him.

Jasper returned, closed the door. The soft thud made her nerves jump. She had whispered she would willingly give him whatever he wanted if he wouldn't harm Henry and would release them afterwards. He'd apparently decided to take her up on her generous offer.

His gaze roved her body. Unable to stop trembling, she clasped her hands together to keep them from shaking. *Dieu m'aider.* God aid her. Not to sin. To be brave.

"Henry must be important to you," Jasper's harsh voice took on a remarkably soft tone.

Lucy hesitated. She shouldn't confess anything he could use against them. As it was, she'd given him too much already. "Anyone's life is important to me."

The outlaw chided her with a look.

She dropped her gaze, unwilling to let him read the truth in her eyes. Yes, Henry was important to her. When he'd pleaded for the outlaws to exchange his life for hers, she'd realized how important. She would do anything to save him. The same way he'd been willing to sacrifice everything for her. Whatever his faults, cowardice wasn't one of them.

Her chest grew tight with fear. Regardless, she wouldn't be a coward, either.

Jasper crooked a finger beneath her chin to lift her face and look into her eyes. "Tell me the truth, Lucy Adelaide."

Fear prickled her skin. She could lie. It wouldn't do any good. He already knew the answer, so she might as well admit it. "Yes, Henry is important to me."

Jasper's features hardened into stone. He walked to the open window, but not before she saw his mouth twist with disgust. Perhaps he found her offer distasteful, or found her disgusting for her willingness to lay with him, or...

Lucy sighed with resignation. She had no idea what Japer might be thinking. For all she knew, he would take what he wanted then kill them anyway because Henry had called him out as one of his attackers.

He stood at the open window with his back to her. From outside came the sound of scuffling, followed by a grunt, then a curse from one of the other outlaws.

She bit back the urge to scream at them not to hurt Henry.

At last, Jasper returned to where she'd remained rooted. "Let me tell you something, Lucy Adelaide. No man is worth your virtue. No man is worth your sacrifice."

Lucy swallowed a surge of relief. For whatever reason, it appeared Jasper had changed his mind. She couldn't fathom his motives and had stopped trying to second-guess him. However, a rather major problem remained. "Why do you want to kill Henry?"

Jasper released an impatient huff. "I don't *know* Henry. Why would I want to kill him?"

"He recognized you."

"No. He didn't recognize me. He guessed my name. Somebody claiming to be me must've shot up your depot."

Criminals always denied their deeds. "Why were you lurking around the train station in Vinita? Were you planning to attack there, too?"

Jasper's annoyed frown conveyed his opinion of her assumption. He hooked his thumbs on his gun belt. "Why would I attack a depot? Too many people around."

"That's what I thought, too. I can't speak for your intelligence."

His stern gaze softened slightly. "You reckon you can sway me with compliments?"

Oh dear. Best to consider her words carefully before she opened her mouth again. At least she'd gotten him to start talking. If he revealed his motive, she could find some way to reason with him. "Apparently, Henry believes you tried to kill him. You must have a reason."

"If I wanted to kill him, he'd be dead," Jasper stated flatly.

She couldn't know for certain whether he was lying. He had the perfect opportunity to kill Henry without anyone being the wiser. He could dispose of her easily enough. Yet, he appeared reluctant to hurt either of them. He'd given her his word he wouldn't harm her, and seemed intent on honoring that promise. Again, she sensed he had a strain of decency in his soul. She would appeal to that part of him.

"If you release us unharmed, without ransom, it would be a demonstration of good faith. Proof you don't intend to shoot Henry or rob him. I would testify to that."

His expression turned wry. "You'd testify in court...on my behalf?"

"I would." She would sweeten the offer. "And I'm certain I can convince my friend not to file charges against you in connection with the shooting. You won't have to worry about that being added to your crimes. Assuming you're wanted for breaking the law," she added quickly. No need to point out his sins.

He shifted his gaze to a spot beyond her shoulder. Faith, he appeared to be considering her suggestion. "If I let you go, you'll swear I didn't attack that depot. And, if I'm arrested, you'll testify on my behalf?"

An outlaw requesting that his captive defend him. She would've found it amusing, if she didn't think he was dead serious. "Yes, you have my word."

"What can you give me to seal our bargain?"

She should've known he'd ask for money. "How much do you require?"

"Not money. Something else."

Government authorities smoked peace pipes when they made agreements with the Indian tribes. "Do you have a pipe we can smoke?"

His half-smile said she'd amused him. "No. Something more personal."

She carried precious few items of that nature, didn't imagine he'd consider a book valuable enough. After thinking for another moment, she removed a sapphire ring from her little finger. With regret, gave it to him. Henry's life was worth more than a memento. "You may have this. It belonged to my mother."

Jasper took the ring between his fingers, examined it. Wistful was the only word she could come up with to describe his expression. Instead of pocketing the treasure, he took her hand and placed the ring in her palm. "We have a deal. You keep this for me."

His sensitivity surprised her. She shook her head, confused. "I don't understand."

"Long time ago, an innocent lady sacrificed herself to save me. I never got the chance to repay her. Until now." He dropped a brief kiss on Lucy's cheek and straightened, his expression enigmatic. "Tell Henry he'd better treat you right. Or he'll have to answer to me."

CHAPTER 24

*L*ucy considered the deal she'd struck with Jasper as strange as his reason for abducting her in the first place. He had odd notions of chivalry and honor. So did Henry.

Good to his word, Jasper and his men escorted them back to the woods near Vinita and released them. Henry grudgingly gave his word he wouldn't sic the authorities on the outlaw. She would make sure he honored it.

The two of them went directly to the station. Henry had a message sent to Fort Gibson to call off the search for her. He asked one of the Katy employees to find them something to eat before escorting her to his private railcar, which was parked alongside the main tracks.

She cleaned up as best she could at the washstand in his sleeping quarters. Then, she waited in the sitting area while he went in to wash up. As soon as he showed himself, they would have a conversation and come to an understanding. No more running. No more manipulation. They would start over, beginning with the truth.

Someone knocked at the door.

It was a crewman with a tray laden with two plates covered with napkins and two cups of coffee. "Here you go, ma'am. Chicken and dumplings. There's some mashed taters to go along."

Her stomach did a happy dance. "Thank you. Please convey our gratitude to your wife."

The man's baggy face folded into a smile. "Aw, it's nothing. Happy to help. The Chief, he's done right by us."

Lucy had heard this from more than one railroad worker. They cursed Henry with one breath as a relentless taskmaster, praised him with the next for being their champion. "What has Mr. Stevens done, exactly?"

"He's hard, but fair. Don't ask us to do anything he's not willin' to do. Here, your food will get cold if I go into all my stories about the Chief." The man handed her the tray, touched the brim of his hat and left.

Lucy set the plates of food, along with the coffee, on a low table in front of the couch while she mulled over the glowing report. If the men loved Henry so much, why hadn't they accompanied him to search for her? Or had he refused help? He was proud, not stupid. There had to be a reason he'd set out alone.

The smell of food made her stomach roar. Jasper's dried meat had only eased the intensity of her hunger. Henry wouldn't mind if she started without him. She shook out a napkin and picked up a fork. The succulent chicken and light, fluffy dumpling melted in her mouth. Her eyes closed for a brief moment, as she groaned with pleasure.

"Henry," she called out, "They've brought us dinner. I'll eat your portion if you don't show yourself in the next two minutes."

In what seemed like less than a minute, he appeared, still rolling up his shirtsleeves. The embattled collar had been discarded, as had his soiled waistcoat. His trousers were still damp in places where it looked like he'd tried to wash off the dirt. His expression looked as flat as his plastered-down hair. She longed to run her fingers through it, if for no other reason than to get a reaction out of him.

Over the past two hours, he hadn't spoken to her, except to answer her question about what happened to Billy. She was glad to hear the boy had been sent to Claire. Henry's sister would take good care of him, and was sharp enough to be wise to his tricks.

Lucy shifted to one side of the sofa to make room. "Sit here, if you like. It'll be easier to reach the food."

He did as she asked, bringing with him the scent of soap, damp wool and something intriguingly male, which set off a flutter in her stomach that had nothing to do with hunger.

While he polished off his meal, her appetite waned. The fact that he'd risked everything to rescue her proved more than his courage. It also meant he cared for her. Deeply. So, why wouldn't he speak of it? Why hadn't he been honest with her?

She had so many questions she didn't know where to start.

After he finished eating, he leaned back and stretched an arm over the back of the couch. His warmth enveloped her without him even having to touch her. His mere presence sent her pulse racing. No other man had this effect on her. Somehow, she knew no other ever would. She'd stopped wondering why. That's how it was, and now she had to deal with it.

"Thank you for coming after me. What you did was very brave." Such a simple expression of gratitude wasn't nearly enough. Strong emotions bubbled near the surface. If she started in on how she felt, she'd be blubbering before they had a chance to talk. After they discussed what had happened, they could get around to the emotional implications.

He took a sip of coffee. His eyes never left her face.

Lucy's nerves twanged. "Well? Say something. Scold me, rail at me, anything would be an improvement over silence."

"What's between you and that outlaw?"

She gaped at him, speechless. No *thank you* for their safe return, no expression of concern, not even a solicitous inquiry about her wellbeing. Instead, he accused her, of all things, of harboring an affection for her captor. "You must be joking."

Henry's eyes narrowed. He shifted forward to set his cup down, hard. Coffee sloshed over the side. "You should've let me handle it."

His curt rebuke stung. As well, it reminded her about why she'd been angry with him in first place. "Oh, I see, and you were doing so well. Flinging accusations, making demands. You're fortunate he didn't take you up on your offer to give him all your money."

Henry jerked to his feet with a scowl. He crossed to an open window. Light from the setting sun illuminated the stark fury on his face. He folded his hands behind his back as he stared outside. "What did *you* give him?"

Her cheeks heated at the crude insinuation. Of course, he would assume the worst. She'd hoped they could approach the subject with more tact. "Not what you're thinking."

"It's a simple question, Lucy. What did you have to give him to get us out of there?" When he turned, his face was devoid of expression. The strain in his voice gave away his emotions.

He might be blaming himself. She wouldn't allow him to own her decisions. What he feared hadn't even happened.

She moved to where to he stood, considered putting her arms around him. He might not welcome the show of affection. Not yet. "Mr. Byrne didn't take anything," she replied softly. "He asked for a favor."

The tips of Henry's ears turned red. "What sort of favor?"

He made it sound as if she wanted to be ruined.

"She ran off with an Injun." Billy's earlier remark popped into Lucy's mind.

Was that what Henry thought? That she'd chosen another man over him? She couldn't decide whether to be hurt, offended or angry.

"You think I'm like that other woman, Kate Parsons?"

Henry stabbed her with a look. "Where did you hear about that?"

"Billy told me."

"Billy?" Henry appeared incredulous. "How did he—?"

"He overheard the workers talking."

"Christ," Henry muttered, then stared out the window. The flush on his neck and ears spread to his entire face. She hadn't meant to embarrass him, although it was a little too late to worry about that. His past had a bearing on the present. They needed to talk about it.

"Henry, look at me. I am not like her."

He gave a dark laugh. "Stubborn, independent, outspoken."

On the other hand, it sounded like she and Kate had some things in common. The thought she might be a replacement wasn't very flattering. "What I mean is, I am not in love with an outlaw."

He fisted his hands at his sides. "So you say. Yet, you granted him favors."

The accusation rubbed against nerves already raw. She could admit that, yes, she had offered her virtue and her mother's ring. Jasper refused both. Giving Henry all the details of their interaction wouldn't serve any purpose other than to enrage him and send them off into a meaningless discussion about things that didn't matter.

Lucy took a deep breath. She propped her hands on her hips. "*Not* the sort of favor you're implying. I agreed to swear in court that he released us without harm, and, to my knowledge, he had no part in the attack on the depot."

Henry's eyes narrowed suspiciously. "Why would you do that?"

"Because I believed him when he said he didn't attack the depot. Mostly, I wanted out of there." She grappled with the urge to smack Henry. "I wanted *you* out of there, before they decided to kill you after all."

He studied her a moment, as if to discern whether she was being honest. He had some nerve to suspect her truthfulness, considering his deceit. "Will you testify on his behalf?"

"I promised I would. And, he treated me with respect. Which is more than I can say for you right now."

In a flash, Henry grasped her arms. "Respect? What the hell, Lucy? He *abducted* you. That isn't treating you with respect."

She could struggle if she wanted to get away. Truth be told, she wished he would put his arms around her and never let go. The simple, frustrating fact that she longed for his embrace only fueled her frustration. "If you hadn't sent your trained hounds after me, I wouldn't have run into the woods. Jasper wouldn't have thought that I needed to be rescued."

"*Jasper?*" Henry's eyes burned with fury. "You're familiar enough to use his given name?"

"It's not like that."

"No? Then tell me what it's like." Henry ran his hands up her arms to cup her shoulders and draw her closer. At the same time, he bent his head. His breath feathered her lips as he brushed a light kiss over them. "Is it like this?"

She blushed at her body's trembling response. "Stop it, I said it's not—"

"Or this?" He took her lower lip between his teeth and gently grazed it.

The soft abrasion sent delicious quivers rippling through her. She put her arms around his neck, her eyes drifted shut. Why wouldn't he stop tormenting her and kiss her?

He cradled the back of her head with one hand while he splayed the other hand possessively across her lower back. As he lavished attention on her lower lip, his hand moved down to cup her buttocks. With fewer layers on, she could feel the intimate press of his fingers as they dug into her flesh.

"Henry," she whispered, leaning into him, hungry for his kiss, aching for his touch.

Desire heated the air. Their passion, like dry kindling, needed only a spark to set it ablaze.

She threaded her fingers through his thick hair, scraped her nails over his scalp. With a low growl, he ground his mouth against hers in a way that could've been punishing if she'd resisted. She didn't. Instead, she let him plunder and take what he wanted.

He lifted her up, pressed her against the hard evidence of his fierce hunger. "You're *mine*," he murmured against her lips. "I won't give you up."

His selfish declaration doused the fiery embers. This wasn't about sharing or trusting. It wasn't even about give and take. Henry intended to stake his claim.

"Stop." Lucy placed her hands on his chest. It was like trying to move a boulder.

He kept right on kissing her. "No. You want this. I want it. No reason to stop."

She pulled back until the kisses ceased. "There is a very good reason. We aren't husband and wife. We're not even betrothed."

"You could remedy that. Marry me." His eyes blazed with a relentless, rampaging energy. Passion, ambition, whatever it might be called, consumed him. The same force would consume her, too, if she let it.

Despite the danger, it was tempting. So very tempting. Her body thrummed with desire. Her heart ached with the need to hold him. Was this love? If so, God help her. She'd fought it every inch of the way. Henry had hammered down her defenses. He'd pursued her with the same ferocious determination that built a railroad in the face of impossible odds.

Yet, he hadn't spoken of love, only possession. He wouldn't allow himself to be vulnerable enough to love. He'd built up so many barriers, carefully attended. He rarely let anyone see the man behind them. She'd caught glimpses of him. It wasn't enough.

"Even if I desire you." She wouldn't admit to love. Not yet. That gave him too much power. "How can I give myself to a man I can't truly know?"

"You know me as well as anyone knows me." His hands moved up from her waist to beneath her breasts. Her nipples tingled, anticipating his touch. Dratted man, he knew precisely what to do. He thought to make her want him so badly she'd give in.

Lucy went on the offensive. Her gaze locked with his. She placed her hands on his face. With her thumbs she stroked his soft beard. "You hide, Henry. Behind your position, behind that implacable mask. You even hide behind this beard. How can I know the real Henry Stevens when you won't show yourself?"

Something flickered in his eyes. Fear? He shuttered it before she could tell.

"I'm afraid, too," she admitted. They had to start being honest with each other or there was no chance for a future, no matter how much heat they produced between them. "You haven't been truthful. You've manipulated me and tried to control me. You've done everything except trust me. How can you ask me to trust you?"

A hint of desperation flashed across his face. "Yes, well, I admit, I've been heavy-handed at times."

"Heavy-handed?" She breathed a soft laugh. "You browbeat Mr. Reynolds into hiring me, then you demanded he dismiss me, without consulting either of us."

"To keep you safe."

Lucy sighed with frustration. Always, he went back to the same refrain. How could she make him understand possession wasn't the same as protection? Perhaps a story might help.

"When I was little, I found a baby bird in the grass. I wanted to take care of it, keep it safe. I scooped it up in my hand, clutched it to my chest then ran home to find something I could use to make a nest. When I opened my hand, the little bird was dead. It had suffocated. *Maman* told me I'd held it too tightly."

She slid her hand down Henry's neck over his muscular shoulder. "I know men are created with the need to protect the gentler sex. For you, it's an obsession. Why do you hold on so tight? What are you afraid will happen if you let go?"

His grip on her arm loosened, then his hands fell away. He stood there looking at her, frowning. Then he turned and walked off, down the hallway toward his sleeping quarters.

A door banged. He'd gone out the other end of the railcar.

Lucy sank onto the sofa, fighting tears. Had she so offended him that she'd driven him away? All she wanted to do was to free him. Release the prince trapped inside.

After a few minutes, she heard the door again.

From the back bedroom, Henry reappeared with a towel over his shoulder, carrying the washbasin and pitcher.

She observed, baffled, as he moved a stack of papers to clear a spot on the desk. He set down the basin then pulled up one of two armchairs. What was he up to?

Curious, she drifted in his direction.

From inside the washbasin, he withdrew a shaving cup with soap, a damp brush and a gleaming razor, which he offered by the handle. "Careful. It's sharp."

She eyed the blade with confusion. "What do you want me to do with it?"

"What does it look like? Shave me." He drew his suspenders down, then took off his shirt, which he folded and laid over the arm of the chair.

Lucy stared in fascination at his bare chest. A sprinkling of dark hair surrounded dark, flat nipples and arrowed down the middle of his flat stomach to disappear into the waistband of his trousers.

"Are you going to stand there gawking or will you do as I ask?"

Blushing hotly, she jerked her gaze to his face. He couldn't be serious. "What is this, your idea of a joke?"

"Do I look like I'm joking?"

He wasn't smiling.

Lucy's heart fluttered into her throat. Somehow, the act of shaving him seemed even more intimate than kissing him. "I can't *shave* you, Henry. It's...not appropriate."

"Kissing me isn't appropriate, either, and you did that." He arched an eyebrow. "Very well, I might add."

Her body thrummed at the reminder of their burning kiss. Shaving him was far more dangerous, not only because of that sharp blade. She feared whatever it was that drove him to make such a strange request. "I might cut you."

This seemed to give him a moment's hesitation. "Have you ever helped your father shave?"

"Well, yes. A few times, when he was ill."

"Then I trust you know how to do it." Henry placed the razor in her hand, gave her the towel. Then sat down.

"Start off slow. There's no rush. May take a while to remove all this hair." He rubbed the beard, looking rueful.

Her hand trembled. "I don't understand. Why?"

"You said I hide behind my beard. So, we'll start by removing it."

Her conscience cringed. Even if she had told him that, she hadn't intended for him to take it literally. "You don't have to do this."

"Yes, I do." He grasped her wrist when she would've put down the razor. "Please," he said in a softer tone. "You'll soon understand why."

She bit her lip, more flustered than she'd ever been around him. "If you want to shave off the beard, why don't you do it?"

"Because...I'm afraid."

Henry, afraid? Well, yes, of course, like any human he experienced fear. She'd never heard him admit to it. Whatever scared him must be awful. She didn't want to dredge it up.

He drew her closer.

She shook her head. Didn't he know? *She* was the coward.

His eyes filled with stark desperation. He needed her to do this for some reason, and he *trusted* her. That, more than anything, pulled down the last of her resistance.

She could overcome her nervousness if it meant that much to him. She could overcome anything if it would release him from whatever demons tormented him.

Gathering her courage, Lucy picked up the cup and brush and soaped his face.

HENRY HELD STILL for what seemed like hours while Lucy methodically plied the razor to shave away his beard. She moved slowly, bending over him from different angles, focused intently on her task. A golden strand of hair fell over her shoulder, the end tickled his nose. At one point, her bosom came within an inch of his lips. He gripped the chair arms, fighting an inferno of desire. The more desperate battle he waged was the one against fear.

He hadn't seen his face bare for twenty years. Last time he'd looked, a constellation of discolored, pitted scars had marred his complexion. The pox had ruined more than his face. As soon as he grew old enough to grow a beard, he'd concealed his shame.

Now, he'd given Lucy a razor and the means to unmask him. She wanted to see the real Henry Stevens. This was the only way he knew how to come out of hiding. Only God knew what she'd find.

Dark bristles floated in the soapy water in the bottom of the basin. She kept murmuring she wasn't sure about what she was doing, yet she shaved him as neatly as any barber. He trusted she wouldn't cut him. He wasn't so sure she wouldn't hurt him.

"You're doing fine," she murmured.

She must be talking to herself. He had a death grip on the chair arms.

He exposed his neck so she could shave beneath his jaw. As the razor rasped over his skin, tremors shuddered through him. Gently, she wiped away the soap and moisture with the towel. Then she trailed her fingers over his sensitized skin.

He stiffened at what felt like an electric shock, followed by an explosion of lust. He swallowed, hard, struggling for control,

She stared at the place where his Adam's apple bobbed. With a dazed look, she slid her fingertips over his neck.

Henry nearly levitated off the chair. If lust didn't kill him, he might die from the agony of seeing her attraction turn to revulsion, as the monster was revealed.

He longed to grab the towel so he could cover his face. Except, she'd made it very clear he wouldn't win her if he insisted on hiding. He knew of only one way to come out of the shadows. Ask her to shed light on the darkest part of him.

She looked him over with the delicate care of a whittler creating a masterpiece. After few more careful swipes over his cheeks, a crease marred her brow. He fought the urge to shrink away as she lightly touched the exposed scars.

Her gaze softened in a look that drove nails through his heart.

After his illness, the crueler boys had made fun of him. Called him "oatmeal face." The girls had laughed. Not all of them. Some had looked at him the way Lucy did now. He'd hated their pity more than their ridicule.

"Are you done?" He locked his fingers around Lucy's wrist to push her hand away.

Her eyes rounded with surprise. "I believe so."

"Good. I have a crick in my neck from leaning my head back for so long." As he stood, he snatched up the towel, then mopped off the remaining soap.

She set the razor on the table. With a mild expression, she retrieved the towel and wiped her hands. His sarcasm didn't seem to faze her. Neither did his scowl.

His heart pounded. Desire pulsed through him, wave after wave. He wanted her to leave. He longed for her to stay. He couldn't endure her pity. He couldn't bear the thought of losing her.

Lucy lifted a length of hair, which had spilled over one shoulder, to swept it back. He followed her movements, yearning to touch her, yet too proud to reach out and risk rejection. This deprivation was a kind of poverty he'd never experienced. He had been penniless before, but he'd never felt truly poor. Not until now.

She cocked her head to one side, as she might study an oddity in a museum.

"Well? Say something," he snapped.

"Without the beard, you look—"

"Ugly?" He said it before she could.

"Younger." The side of her mouth curled up. "The difference takes some getting used to..." She reached for his face.

He fisted his hands at his sides, fighting the urge to block her touch. Hadn't he been the one to demand she shave him? Then he'd barked at her like a surly son-of-a-bitch. If she wanted to examine the cursed scars, she'd earned the right.

Her fingers felt cool against his heated skin. Soft. Gentle. Her touch drew out his anger and the poison infecting his heart. He had no weapons left to fight with, nowhere to hide. Never had he felt so naked. So vulnerable. God, he trembled.

"You had small pox," she observed. "When you were a child, I would guess."

He cleared an obstruction in his throat. "Fourteen."

"That must've been frightening."

"Don't remember being scared. I was too sick."

"When was the last time you saw your face?"

"Seventeen." He answered in choppy sentences. Couldn't manage eloquence.

"The scars have faded. I'm sure they're not as bad as you

remember." Her regard turned thoughtful, as she continued her exploration of his face. With every touch, his desire intensified. Trapped inside, it built up faster than steam in a boiler.

He took a deep breath. Released it. The beard was gone, his disfigurement revealed, thus far she hadn't rejected him. Yet. There was more ugliness to come.

"Vanity isn't the only reason I grew the beard. Every time I saw my face, those scars, it reminded me of what I was. A murderer."

Surprise flashed across her face. Her hand fell away from his face. He didn't know which was the worst torment, having her touch him or her withdrawal. He would explain. Although it wouldn't excuse him, she deserved to hear the whole story.

"After I came down with small pox, my mother sent everyone away and stayed to nurse me. She got sick...and died." His wooden delivery didn't hint at the wrenching guilt he'd lugged around. He'd never admitted to the crime before now.

Lucy's gaze reflected sympathy. "That's not murder, Henry. You couldn't help that you came down with an illness, and she did what any mother would do."

He suspected she might say that because she possessed a soft, kind heart, not a shriveled, hard one, like his. He cut off any further attempt to absolve him. "It could've been helped. I had sneaked in to see a friend in a ward with other small pox victims. My parents warned me not to go there. I did anyway. My negligence killed her. It should've killed me."

Horror filled Lucy's eyes. "Don't say that. That's not what God decreed. It's not what your mother would've wanted. I'm glad you lived. You should be glad, too. Thankful."

"Thankful? She *died* because of *me*."

"She died because of a horrible disease." Lucy reached for his hand.

He withheld it. "It didn't destroy only her life. My father had dreams. Big dreams. Dreams *she* believed in. No matter how many times he went broke, he'd say, *failure isn't an option*. After my mother died, nobody believed in him. He put a bullet in his brain. The ultimate act of failure."

Lucy blinked. Tears leaked from the corners of her eyes. He caught her face, rubbed the dampness away with his thumbs. He didn't want her grieving on his account.

"Don't cry," he ordered.

"I can't help it. I *hurt* for you."

"Tears won't change anything, believe me."

"You can't think your father's death was your fault, too."

"Not my fault, no. But my younger sisters needed parents, and I didn't know how to be one. I only knew how to work hard. It wasn't enough. If my mother had lived instead of me, my father wouldn't have abandoned his family. My sisters' lives would've been better."

Lucy shook her head. "You can't know that. You had no control over your father's decisions, or your mother's death, or your sisters' lives. Regardless of what you might think, you have little control over most things in this world."

"There you're wrong. I control the Katy Railroad. I oversee a company that holds title to thousands of acres of land. I have authority over hundreds of workers—"

"Henry, you don't have power over life and death." When she grasped his arms, he became achingly aware of his shirtless condition. Her touch on his bare skin was like a match to kerosene. Desire blazed up, hotter than ever.

He'd admitted to being a killer. Perhaps he ought to confess other mortal sins. Like lust. Or accept the fact he was damned and not bother to cleanse his conscience.

He snaked an arm around her waist before she could move away, then took her mouth in a desperate, brutal kiss.

Her lips tasted salty. Was she crying for him or for herself?

His heart shrank into a tight, aching knot. She'd gotten what she asked for. Now, she knew the *real* Henry Stevens.

CHAPTER 25

*L*ucy's head spun when Henry kissed her like it was his last day on earth. Then he lifted his head, breaking the heavenly contact. She blinked in confusion. "Why did you do that?"

He drew her up from where he'd bent her over his arm. "Because I wanted to." His eyes were once again hooded, his voice flat. "You should know by now I take what I want. Regardless."

She wasn't fooled. He'd exposed more than his face. Henry had revealed his soul to her. He could no longer hide. "I wasn't asking why you kissed me. I want to know why you stopped."

His fierce expression shifted into a look of bemusement. "You *want* me to keep going?"

When had she given him the idea otherwise? He must still think he was ugly.

She circled her arms around his neck, rose up on her toes to press a kiss on his lips. Then she lovingly stroked his clean-shaven cheek. "You have a beautiful face, Henry. A beautiful, masculine face. The scars don't diminish your appeal. They add character."

He stared down at her. Disbelief, hope, fear, it was all there for her to see. It had been there all along, if she'd only looked past his disguise. "There's more to ugliness than what's on the outside. If you knew what I was thinking half the time, you'd run like the devil was after you."

Lucy held him tight. She refused to let him retreat. Not after coming this far. At last, he had given her complete honesty. Now, it was her turn. "I know what you want. I want it, too. So there. What do you think about that?"

His eyes locked with hers. Slowly, he moved his hands to her hips. Without blinking, he drew her against the part of him that strained at his trousers. "You want sex? Or marriage? I can give you one or both. Your choice."

Her heart's rapid beat fluttered at the base of her throat. She yearned to experience sexual awakening in Henry's arms. More than that, she was fairly certain she loved him. What she wasn't so sure about was his ability to love her. Would a physical relationship be enough?

If she meant to pursue adventure, she had to take risks. In this way, at least, he appeared willing to let her make her own decisions. Before she had a chance to reconsider, she arched against him like a cat and brought his head down for a kiss.

"I'll take this, for now," she murmured, as their lips made contact.

Shock jolted him, or that's what she imagined shook him. She felt the force of it all the way down to her toes.

He seized her arms. The way he stared at her, as if she'd transformed into someone else. Maybe she had. The chaste Miss Forbes wouldn't have asked for sex. She'd become an adventurous woman, in part, because of Henry. She ought to thank him for that.

"Are you sure? This is *all* you want?" he demanded.

Her hand trembled as she raised it to his cheek. "You gave me the choice. Are you rescinding the offer?"

His lips parted as though he would question her again. Frustration was stamped on his face. So, this wasn't about giving her choices. He thought to shock her into agreeing to marry him.

Her disappointment lasted only a moment. If this was what she had to do to teach him to open his hand and let go, then so be it.

Lucy strained upwards. At the same time, Henry folded her against him, groaning into her mouth, no longer fighting her will. She kissed him with a fervent passion. Applied everything he'd taught her. The heat of their mouths, the touch of his tongue rubbing hers, sent her head spinning again. She listed forward.

He crushed her breasts against his chest. His jutting arousal rubbed against her, eliciting quivers. Her legs grew weak, as desire filled her with a warm, aching heaviness.

No question as to where this would lead. They would soon embark on a journey she'd never made. A twinge of uncertainty tempered her excitement. Her heart reassured her. With Henry as her guide, she had nothing to fear.

He dragged his lips along the side of her throat. Bent her back to frantically work at the buttons and hooks down the front of her jacket. She shrugged out of it. He tossed it aside. He trailed burning kisses along the low neckline of her undergarment, while he deftly untied the ribbons to expose her breasts.

She gasped when he captured a turgid tip with his teeth, biting gently, then pulling on the sensitive peak with his tongue and lips. Erotic sensations rocketed through her. She dug her fingers into his hair to pull him closer. She was desperate to have him kiss her there, everywhere. When she tried to tell him, all that came out was an incoherent moan.

He gave both breasts equal attention before leaving them to focus on undressing her. Next came the buttons on the waistband of her skirt. He dispatched that, along with her petticoat, with stunning swiftness.

Lucy flushed as he stripped her naked. She resisted the urge to cover herself. Hadn't she asked for this ravishing? Her legs trembled under the weight of her desire.

"Hold onto me."

She obeyed this command without question.

He slid his hand down between her legs. Her breath hitched as he parted the tender, damp petals of her sex. If she hadn't been holding onto his neck, she would've collapsed at his feet. As he fondled her, he kissed her neck, sending bursts of shivers over her skin.

She shifted her stance so he could reach her better and soothe the throbbing need. He purred his approval, then positioned her so he could open her more fully to his invasion. With his fingers he filled the slick cavity, at the same time using his thumb to stroke an intimate knot of flesh. She jerked at the unexpected jolt. Below, her body responded, muscles clenching, with every rhythmic thrust of his fingers.

"Easy," he murmured. "It's all right."

Oh, it was more than all right. With one hand, he created a frenzy of sensation. Such sweet pleasure.

"You like this. There's more." His heated words filled her ear.

She trembled at the promises, matched by his bold caresses. Her breathing hitched. Perspiration misted her skin. "Henry, please. I-I can't stand..." She begged him to give her something she didn't know how to describe.

He gathered her in his arms, lowered her to the floor. That wasn't what she meant. It didn't matter. She sprawled on the soft carpet as he dragged her limp legs over his shoulders. His mouth and tongue took over where his fingers had been.

Lucy blushed over every inch of her skin. Who could imagine something like this could be done? She didn't have the strength to stop him. The wicked woman who'd taken control didn't wish for him to stop. Every touch, every kiss, inflamed her senses and wrenched gasps and sighs from her lips.

"Please," she moaned. "Please." Her head thrashed as pleasure mounted. He didn't let up, not for a moment. He coaxed every sensuous ripple from her body. Sensations flooded her, wave upon wave, rising higher, higher, until finally, they spilled over.

Lucy cried out at the sudden release. The force of it seemed to fling her into space, splintered into a thousand glittering pieces.

Slowly, she became aware of his heated kisses on her inner thighs. She blinked up at the stamped metal ceiling. Odd, she would've sworn she'd been transported. Yet, she remained on the floor of Henry's railcar. He kissed his way upward, forging a trail up her stomach to her breasts. He braced his weight on his arms, bent over and placed a moist kiss on her mouth.

"Delicious, as well as beautiful." He spoke with heartwarming tenderness as she gazed up at him, awestruck.

"There aren't words to describe."

"A writer without words?" His dark eyes glowed with masculine satisfaction, along with a hunger she recognized. While she was new at this, she was also aware enough to realize he hadn't found his pleasure.

Lucy slid her hands over his shoulders, smooth skin over bunched muscles. She wedged her hands between them, going for the waistband of his trousers. "These should come off."

"Yes ma'am." Henry lifted his hips.

She groped for the concealed placket on his trousers, blushing at how clumsy and awkward this seemed, compared to how smoothly he'd undressed her. Determined, she worked a stubborn button loose. "If your trousers weren't so tight…"

His nostrils flared and his eyes darkened, nearly black. "The problem isn't the trousers. Let me do it."

"You undressed me. I want to undress you." To convince him of her sincerity, she molded her hand to the shape of his hardness.

He arched into her hand with a groan. "Lucy, you're going to kill me."

She pressed a comforting kiss on his shoulder. "Then we'll be even."

ANOTHER SHUDDER RACKED HENRY. *Sweet mercy.* He'd pleasured her, not tortured her. Even so, if she wished to undress him, he wouldn't deny her. Wouldn't deny her anything.

He fisted handfuls of golden hair spilled in disarray across the floral carpet. At last, she nudged the final two buttons from their holes. He groaned with relief.

She fumbled with the drawers then clasped him, squeezed gently. Trailed her fingers up the hard length. Fascinated, like a child with a new toy. Only, she wasn't a child, and he was definitely not a toy—though he was dying for her to play with him.

His entire body shivered as she stroked him.

His need grew intense. He'd come close to losing control earlier. To hell with patience, he wanted to take her here, now, rather than seek a more civilized place like the bed in the next room.

Henry struggled out of the trousers and drawers. His lungs pumped like pistons in an engine casing. Desperate as he was to plunge inside her, he had to make certain she was ready for him, or he might hurt her. He bent over to feast on her breasts.

With a moan, she groped for his aching length.

"Wait..." His command came out as a thick plea. "Need to make sure you're ready."

"Ready for what?" she murmured.

A rueful laugh escaped between gasping breaths. God, she was such an innocent. He was a devil for leading her into sin. Tonight, she'd thrown open the doors and walked in with her eyes wide open. He'd agreed to be her guide.

Slowly, he entered the threshold to her body. He longed to bury himself to the hilt in one quick thrust. Lucy deserved more consideration than that. He would exercise restraint.

The tortuous entry into her tight sheath took his full concentration. Lucy seemed determined to break it. She searched his chest with her fingers, shifted her hips restlessly. Her needy little moans acted like a dissolving agent on his self-control.

He pressed forward, met little resistance. Yet, she was tight. Extremely. With his weight braced on his arms, he hung over her, panting. "Does this hurt?"

She nodded. The tautness around her mouth confirmed it.

"I'll stop." He gritted his teeth as he began to withdraw. He might not control heaven and earth, but, by God, he could control his own body.

"Don't." She drew him down, showered kisses over his face, his neck, everywhere she could reach. Her hips lifted. The muscles that held him squeezed like a fist.

His control snapped. He groaned her name then surged inside.

She clasped him to her with a sharp cry.

The sound brought him back to his senses. He slid his arms beneath her shoulders to cradle her head. Kissed her gently until the tension drained from her body. Then he withdrew slightly and entered her again, this time in a slow plunge. Aching, teetering on the knife's edge of control, he nevertheless set a slow, steady rhythm. Soon, she met him thrust for thrust.

"Yes," she breathed. "Love me, Henry."

Her soft plea filled him with exhilaration. As he moved over her, he focused only on her pleasure. With each measured thrust, he lavished her with adoration. He loved her the only way he knew how.

Lucy glided her hands over the flexing muscles in Henry's shoulders and back, loving the feel of him. As he labored above her, his skin became sleek with sweat. She inhaled his scent. Tangy, musky, incredibly arousing. His hard length stretched her to almost painful fullness, yet the pressure was unbearably sweet.

She had almost retreated. Until he'd offered to stop. His concern, his willingness to protect her from further pain in spite of what it cost him, had galvanized her. She wouldn't have let him stop after that. Not for anything.

Pleasure swelled with the now-familiar rise of passion, Lucy arched upward and gave herself to it. Her muscles clenched in strong spasms, drawing his release out of him. She felt the moment when his power gave way to vulnerability.

With a shuddering groan, he collapsed on top of her.

She hugged him tightly through the aftershocks, held his head, stroked his damp hair.

After a timeless moment, his breathing slowed. The calm was a different type of closeness. If possible, even more intimate.

Comfortable, at the same time, far more disturbing than the storm they'd experienced.

Now what?

Lucy tried to ignore the insistent voice. Her brain started with a whirr, then her conscience began to chirp. She'd given in to a dangerous passion. No longer could she ignore her feelings for Henry, go on as if their joining hadn't happened. In truth, she didn't want to go back. There was nowhere else to go except forward, in the direction of her dreams.

Would he help her fulfill them? He'd only arranged her position with the newspaper to keep her close to him, then had her fired when he'd decided it was the best thing for both of them. She feared he would continue to exert control over her life, in the same way he tried to control everything else around him.

She knew now what drove him. He'd revealed more than his scarred face. He'd exposed his scarred soul. Finally, she'd seen the *real* Henry Stevens—a complex, tortured man, possessed of a fierce ambition that could destroy them both.

Even if she loved him, could her love free him?

Not if he didn't learn how to love her in return.

CHAPTER 26

*H*enry roused at Lucy's delicate touch on his neck.
"Are you asleep?"

"Mm." He couldn't manage much more. He'd never been so completely satiated. Beyond satisfied. He'd gone to heaven. Somewhere he'd never been before and hadn't dared hope to visit. Lucy had taken him there.

"You're heavy."

He lifted himself up on his arms, still somewhat disoriented. "Sorry," he muttered. "Didn't mean to crush you."

Her lips curled in a sweet smile. She circled a hand around his upper arm. "I'm not crushed. I am ready to go to bed."

"Bed?"

"You do know what a bed is?"

"Yes. I didn't expect you to say you wanted to go there with me."

"Why not?"

He released a soft laugh. "Why not, indeed."

Lucy had said, and done, many things he hadn't expected. That she continued to surprise him was part of the delight. He lurched up, then helped her to her feet.

"You look tired," she remarked.

"A bit," he admitted. He hadn't slept well the previous night, wrestling with guilt over getting her fired, which had sent her running from him. Even exhausted, he'd found the energy to pleasure her, and would do so again before the night was through.

Lucy slipped her arm around his waist. "I've never taken a man to bed before."

Henry shot her a questioning glance. She could mean she'd not lain with a man before or she was being literal. He hadn't breached a membrane, yet she'd been tight as a virgin. Or at least what he imagined a virgin would feel like, having not had one before. He'd made it a point to stay away from chaste girls. Those were the kind a man had to marry, and he was particular enough not to get trapped by someone he didn't wish to marry. Ironically, he wanted to marry Lucy. Badly. And all she wanted was sex.

He would give her what she wanted, until he convinced her she wanted something more.

She snatched her white shift off the chair where he'd flung it.

He took it away from her. "No need for that."

"I don't have a nightgown to sleep in."

"You didn't say you wanted sleep."

She released a disbelieving laugh. "Henry, we're both exhausted."

He'd be damned if he was going to pass out after getting her into bed. He wound his arms around her and nuzzled her neck. Her faint flowery fragrance mingled with the scent of sex and his desire reawakened. "I'm not exhausted. Not even close."

"You fell asleep on top of me."

"I was resting my eyes." To prove the point, he scooped her up in his arms and carried her to bed.

She burrowed beneath the covers. When he slipped in next to her, she cuddled up against him. Then nestled her head on his shoulder with her fingers splayed above his heart.

He released a sigh, content for the moment to stroke her bare skin. He'd established a personal rule not to sleep with a woman, which seemed more intimate than having sex. With Lucy, it felt natural to let down his barriers. After all, she had seen his ugliness, and she'd still come to him, which meant she must return his love.

His heart jerked like he'd been kicked in the chest. *Love?* Was that what this was? He'd thought he was going mad. Wasn't love another kind of madness?

Before he spouted off, he had better be sure Lucy shared his insanity. He wouldn't make the mistake of professing his love to a woman who didn't love him in return. Besides, he'd made it clear to Lucy how much he wanted her. Had asked her—repeatedly—to marry him. She could surmise from that how he felt.

Her fingers curled on his chest. The light touch started a slow burn. "Henry, I..."

He held his breath when she paused. His heart pounded. In the throes of passion, she'd begged him to love her. Meaning the act, not the emotion. He'd tried his damnedest to show her what he felt was much more than physical desire. Perhaps she'd understood and would tell him—

"I need to see my father."

Disappointment deflated his lungs. He retreated into sarcasm. "This trip would've been much simpler if you'd asked me to take you to Texas."

She shifted, propping her arms on his chest. In the darkness, he couldn't make out her expression. "Would you have taken me? Or tried to talk me out of going?"

He'd driven her away with deceit. Maybe it was time to try honesty. "Talk you out of it. Let me explain."

"I'm listening."

"Someone recognized one of my attackers. Identified him as Jasper Byrne."

"Who claimed he wasn't there, *and* he didn't kill you when he had the chance."

Henry's anger simmered. "Whether Byrne was there or not, those men weren't disgruntled farmers. Someone was hired to kill me. I didn't want you wandering around, catching a bullet meant for me. That's why I asked Milt to dismiss you."

"You could've expressed your concerns instead of sneak around behind my back."

He felt the need to defend his actions. "If I'd asked you to quit your job and go away somewhere safe until the danger was over, would you have?"

She went silent for a moment. "Whatever the decision, it's mine to make."

He struggled with that. While he acknowledged the fact that she was an adult, she was also a woman. Few women were entirely independent. Yet, Lucy longed for freedom. She wouldn't accept the bit. He'd lose her if he tried to force her to do his bidding.

"My intention was to protect you. However, I realize now the way I handled things was not ideal."

"Wrong," she said.

"What?"

"The word you were searching for. *Wrong*."

Lucy wouldn't let him off the hook. She did allow him to bring her back into his embrace. He kissed her hair before he gave her what she wanted. "Wrong. Yes. That's the right word."

She snuggled closer. "See? It isn't that difficult to admit to imperfection."

"Your turn. Admit you were wrong, too." He tried for a teasing tone even though it was too soon to find anything about the situation amusing.

"I'm sorry, Henry." She did sound contrite. "I should've confronted you instead of running away. Why did you come after me alone?"

Did she think he was stupid, as well as controlling?

"This is Indian Territory, not United States soil. If I had rounded up a band of armed railroad workers, it would look to the Indians like we were attacking. Men could've gotten killed."

"I hadn't thought about that." She rested her hand on his shoulder. "What you did was brave, but very dangerous. You should've waited for the army."

"When the Indians took Kate, I didn't act quickly enough."

"You blame yourself because you loved her?" Lucy's voice sounded strained.

Had he given her that idea? Maybe she'd assumed.

Henry released a heavy sigh. "No. I felt guilty because I didn't care for her as much as I should have. If I'd gone after her right away, she might've been rescued before she was compromised."

"That's why you set off alone after me? Because you felt guilty?"

"No. I..." The words stuck in his throat. He'd never been so terrified. So frantic. "In hindsight, I might've hired an Indian guide. I was in a hurry to find you."

He rolled her over on her back and held her hands above her head. Found her mouth, Kissed her, hard. "Don't ever run away from me again."

Her fingers twined with his. "I'm not running."

CHAPTER 27

*L*ate the next morning, a Katy train chugged across the Red River and steamed into Denison. A whistle announcing their arrival pierced through the comfortable silence in Henry's private railcar. He paused in front of a mirror to smooth his hair and straighten his tie before they disembarked.

He also had business to discuss with the Major. As soon as he got an update on negotiations with the Texas Central, he'd take Forbes aside and formally ask for his daughter's hand. She hadn't exactly accepted the proposal. What else would she do now that they were lovers? If she didn't marry him, she risked ruin.

He watched her surreptitiously in the mirror. She'd dressed then sat on the bed to read. Her battered satchel hadn't contained a second dress, only a change of underclothes and a few books. Lucy had to be the only female he knew who'd pack reading material instead of clothing.

She'd trained her hair into a soft style with loose strands curling around her face. With her natural beauty, she made even the rumpled traveling suit look elegant.

What would inspire a woman as beautiful as Lucy to love a monster?

Henry dampened his fingers in the basin, wet down his hair. He'd avoided looking in the mirror. Now, he couldn't resist curiosity. His heart thudded as he stared at a man he didn't recognize.

Lucy was right. The scars weren't as bad as he remembered.

He rubbed his hand over the marred skin on his cheek. Didn't help his looks any. She'd been kind enough to tell him it gave his face *character*. His lips twisted in a crooked smile. Another sin to add to the list. Vanity.

"What's so funny?" she asked.

He turned. Crossed his arms over his chest. In the daylight, her assessment of his face might be different. "Which do you prefer, beard or no beard?"

"Hm." She cocked her head to one side. He'd get an honest answer. People who had the integrity to tell him the truth usually didn't have the nerve. Lucy had both. "You're handsome either way."

She'd taken the easy way out.

"Don't lose your refreshing honesty now."

"I mean it." After setting the book aside, she glided across the room. Her touch on his face set off a sizzling response.

He put his arms around her to bring her closer. "Careful. Start something, we may never get off this train."

Her sultry smile increased the odds of his prediction coming true. "I wanted to assure you that I find you attractive, with or without the hair on your face." Her expression became thoughtful. "The beard does make you look dangerous. More like a villain."

Her comparison amused him. Somewhat. He arched an eyebrow in his best dastardly imitation. "You'd cast me as a scoundrel?"

She tapped her finger on his chin. "If I put you in book, yes."

Was she serious? She smiled. Yet, something in her eyes told him she might be telling the truth. "Don't look so worried. I like villains. They're much more interesting. I thought Capitola should've chosen Black Donald instead of Herbert."

Like most women, Lucy had a bad habit of changing direction in the middle of a conversation without providing a map.

Henry shook his head. "Sorry, I don't follow."

"*The Hidden Hand.* The book I was reading."

"Ah."

"Black Donald is a treacherous highwayman who wants Capitola in his bed. She outfoxes him when he traps her then she ends up with a kind-hearted fellow named Herbert."

"Herbert?" Henry scoffed. "Even his name sounds boring."

"And yours is better?"

"There were kings named Henry. None to my knowledge named Herbert."

Lucy sniffed. "Well, if I were naming you in a book, I'd call you Hank. Sounds stronger."

"Stronger, eh?" Henry couldn't resist flexing his arms to remind her he wasn't exactly a weakling. "So, Capitola liked this Herbert fellow?"

Lucy nodded with a rueful twist of her lips. "As I said, I would've preferred she end up with Black Donald and rehabilitate him."

Henry swallowed a chuckle. Lucy got very wrapped up in her stories, as if they were real people. He didn't want to hurt her feelings by scoffing at her seriousness. "Rehabilitate the treacherous highwayman?"

Her gaze softened. "Or redeem him—with her love."

The remark stopped Henry's heart. After a breathless moment, it lurched into motion, chugging hard. Was Lucy admitting she loved him? He ventured a question to confirm. Kept his tone light, in case he was wrong. "Is that what you'd do with me?

Uncertainty flickered in her eyes. "Are you in need of redemption?"

For God's sake, he was in need of love. Her love. Only, he wouldn't beg for it. She was a bright girl. She ought to know by now how he felt about her. "Doubt you could turn me into a kind-hearted fellow. Men like that can't run a railroad."

She studied him with a creased brow. "You can run a railroad without breaking the law. My father is proof of that."

Irritation pricked him. He was tempted to point out that her illustrious father had been given the sack. "I'm sure he didn't get to where he did without bending a few rules."

He regretted the remark the moment it was out of his mouth, even more when Lucy's eyes reflected disappointment.

"How many rules have you bent?" she asked softly.

"If I told you, you might think I'm a treacherous highwayman." The line came out sounding more like a confession than a joke. "You did say you *prefer* villains."

The unhappiness that filled her eyes should've warned him. "Only in stories."

DENISON, the first Texas stop on the Katy line, looked more like a rough cow town than a proposed railroad headquarters. In fact, by Lucy's count, they'd passed three cattle pens and six saloons since leaving the station. The only other businesses were a land office, a mercantile and an undertaker. From behind a row of clapboard buildings, the tops of canvas tents were visible. So many it appeared a second town had sprung up.

"What's over there?" she asked.

"Nothing you need to know about." Henry's paternal tone irritated her.

"I asked a simple question. You might answer it instead of treating me like a child."

"Brothels," he shot back.

"All of them?"

"Most. As you can see, there's plenty of business to go around."

A band of whooping cowboys rode past, their mounts churning through the muck and manure. They made straight for the canvas town.

"Indeed," she murmured.

"Any other simple questions you need me to answer?"

Lucy would've lost her temper had she not been so miserable. What had happened to the affectionate man she'd woken up beside?

He'd vanished—ever since she'd tried to get him to admit he loved her. Instead, he'd confessed to being a scoundrel. He'd even acted amused by the idea that a woman's love could change a man for the better.

She had to get past her romantic illusions when it came to Henry Stevens. He might be keen to bed her, even wed her, so he could bed her whenever he wished. He didn't seem as eager to give her his heart. Without that, she'd be a fool to marry him.

Last night, she had quite possibly made the biggest mistake of her life by giving herself to him. After he'd revealed his doubts and fears with such heart-wrenching honesty, she could no longer withhold her love.

The respectable thing to do would be to accept his offer, except she couldn't bear it if they wed and she had to be content with second place to his ambition. *Maman* had done that. Much as her father loved her mother, he'd put his work with the railroad first. She had given up a promising, privileged future as an opera star to marry him. If she'd ever regretted it, she never said. Lucy wished she could ask her mother now. She might be able to make a decision about what to do. Choose independence or the man she loved.

Gunshots erupted.

In a flash, Henry yanked her behind him, at the same time uncovering the gun beneath his coat. Her heart pounded as she peered around his shoulder.

In front of them, swinging doors banged open. A man stumbled backwards out of the saloon, with his hand clutched on his silk waistcoat. He pitched off the rickety sidewalk into a brown mixture that reeked. Seconds later, a furious fellow stormed out, his leather chaps flapping against his legs. He wielded the largest revolver Lucy had ever seen.

"That's what cheaters get," the shooter bellowed. He turned his head. Upon spotting Lucy, he doffed a wide-brimmed hat, revealing flaming hair and a face that looked too youthful for a killer. "Pardon, ma'am. Just throwin' out the garbage."

He turned on his heel and, spurs jangling, clomped back into the saloon.

Henry placed his palm on the small of her back. With insistent pressure, he veered her around the saloon doors.

The man in the mud crawled toward the sidewalk. None among the curious onlookers seemed inclined to assist him. Lucy's heart went out to him. "We can't walk by."

"We can, and we will."

Lucy threw a worried glance over her shoulder. "He needs help."

"We're not getting involved," Henry stated emphatically.

"But—"

"The sheriff's office is on our way. I'll notify him. That is, if there's a sheriff in residence. They don't last very long around here."

She understood why. They were packed onto the narrow boardwalk with a rough-looking crowd. Men openly gawked at her. Some even made crude suggestions as they passed by. Henry's features were rigid. He ignored their remarks. She did, too. The last thing she wanted was for Henry to get into a brawl. Much as she hated to admit it, he had been right to warn her away from here. She shuddered to think of what might've happened if she'd shown up with only a boy to accompany her.

True to his word, Henry stuck his head inside the sheriff's office. He told whoever was there about the altercation. Afterwards, they turned a corner, where he pointed across the street to one of the only brick buildings in town besides the jail. "There's our office."

"Why so far from the depot?"

"Less noise. Less smell."

Ah, yes. The stockyards were near the depot.

"You have a point."

"I generally do." His wry half smile made her heart constrict. *Heaven help her.* She loved this man, but she didn't know what to do with him.

With a firm hold on her skirts, she picked her way around the wagon ruts. Henry held her elbow, while his other hand encircled her waist. She wouldn't deny she enjoyed his protectiveness, if only he wouldn't smother her.

She hesitated at the door. Her father would not be expecting her. He'd realize right away something was wrong. If he learned any of what she'd done over the past day, it would send him into a frenzy of worry, and spark another battle of wills she didn't have the energy to wage.

She tucked a torn bit of lace beneath the bottom of her sleeve to conceal the damage. "Henry, I..."

His gaze went to her sleeve. "Don't worry about your outfit. I'll buy you a new one."

"No, that wasn't what I was going to say. I don't want you to buy me a new dress."

"Why not?"

She almost blurted out she wanted his love, not clothing. "I don't need one."

"Doesn't matter if you need it or not. It's a gift."

Now he was annoyed again. About something that wasn't even important. She placed her hand on his arm to reassure him. "It's not my outfit I'm concerned about. I'm worried about how my father will react when he sees me. I'm sure he'll be surprised. Worried, even. You won't share all the details?"

His eyes widened with incredulity. "Good grief, Lucy. I'm not that much of a scoundrel—or an idiot."

"No, no I didn't mean our r-relationship." She stumbled over the word. "I don't want him to know I ran away or that I was abducted. It will only make him fret. He doesn't need to worry. Not about me. Not anymore."

"Somebody needs to worry about you," Henry muttered.

Lucy released a sigh. While she didn't wish for him to take up that mantle, she was too tired to wrestle it away at the moment. "All right. You can worry if it makes you feel better."

"Thank you for the honor" He leaned his arm on the doorframe. Leaned over to touch his lips to hers. "And I'll kiss, but I won't tell."

The light touch pulled desire in its wake. Lucy pressed her hand to his chest, not sure if she intended to restrain him or her. "Don't, Henry."

He lifted her fingers to his lips in mock apology. "Fine. I'll wait until I speak to your father."

Panic surged through her. She snatched her hand away. "No!"

"No?" He looked confused, then frustrated.

She rushed ahead before he could forestall her. "I don't want you to mention marriage. Not, not yet."

The muscles in his jaw tightened. Without the beard, his facial reactions were more noticeable. "When will you *allow* me to mention it?"

"I don't know."

"You don't know," he echoed in a voice that was chillingly emotionless. "How about when your belly swells with our child? May I mention it then?"

Lucy's face grew hot. Hurt, fear, longing, and a myriad of other emotions she couldn't name, swirled into a scalding stew. She stiffened her spine and refused to give in to tears. "That's a possibility. Not a certainty. Or an immediate concern. I told you last night I wasn't ready to discuss marriage. I meant it. We'll talk about it later. Don't—please—don't involve my father."

She might've mistaken his response as indifference based on his flat expression. The reddened tips of his ears gave away the strong emotions churning inside him.

"As you wish." His cold tone made her shiver.

He reached past her, turned the knob then threw the door open.

It hit the inside wall with a bang.

HENRY HADN'T INTENDED to use that much force to open the door. Damn it, he was angry. The day had started out so promising, when he'd awakened with Lucy curled up beside him. After that, everything had gone straight to hell.

He put on a pleasant expression as they entered the office. He'd greet her father as if nothing more was going on than the two of them showing up unexpectedly—together. Forbes was bright enough to discern the rest, even if Lucy didn't tell him.

As for their conversation about marriage, Henry fully intended to continue it once they were alone. He'd bedded her. By God, he would wed her. Even if he had to drag her to the altar.

Her father was seated at a roll-top desk. Next to it, on the wall, a large map showed the Katy's operational and proposed rail lines across Texas. The Major spun his chair around. He came to his feet with surprise lighting his face. "Lucy!"

She flew into his arms.

After he'd embraced her, the older man tipped her chin to look at her. He had tears in his eyes, for God's sake.

Henry turned away from the touching scene. He hung up his coat while he waited for father and daughter to greet each other. One would think they'd been apart for years, not days. When was the last time he'd shown his emotions so openly? Never. He didn't even hug his sisters, hadn't since their parents died. He eschewed displays of affection. Perhaps because Fate had a nasty habit of taking away people he loved.

In spite of his fears, he'd ventured intimacy with Lucy, and still, she couldn't love him. She'd called him a villain. Granted, they'd been engaged in banter. Still, he'd seen the uncertainty in her eyes. Her skewed perspective on scoundrels annoyed the hell out of him. She'd defend an outlaw, then chastened *him* for bending the rules. He obeyed the spirit of the law, if not every letter. The real problem, as he saw it, had to do with her measuring stick. She held everyone up to an impossible standard—her beloved father, whom she believed was above reproach.

Henry knew better. Forbes hadn't been sacked because he was a saint. The Major couldn't have been ruined if he hadn't given his enemies something to use against him. Lucy must not know about it or she wouldn't keep holding her father up like an icon.

"Mr. Stevens," Forbes left Lucy's side to shake Henry's hand. "This is an unexpected surprise."

A knowing glint shone in the Major's eye. He'd taken one look at Lucy and realized something was amiss. Henry didn't intend to enlighten him. He'd made a promise. He was a man of his word, despite her low opinion of him.

"How are things going with the negotiations?" he asked smoothly.

"We have a deal. I am preparing a report."

A deal? So soon?

Henry concealed his surprise. He offered Lucy one of two chairs near the desk. She sank down, murmured thanks, still wouldn't look at him. He plopped into the other seat, determined to keep the sulky tone out of his voice. "What kind of deal?"

"A good one." Forbes leaned back in his swivel chair with his fingers laced across the front of his wool waistcoat. "We'll construct an interchange halfway between where we want it, here in Denison, and where the Texas Central wants it, in Red River City."

Henry's bad mood soured further. That wasn't a good deal. It was a lousy compromise. "Wonderful. We can spend money we don't have to lay track we don't need."

Lucy cast a frown his way. Henry ignored it. No one, including her, could convince him to agree to this nonsensical arrangement. Well, he *might* be persuaded if she sat on his lap. It was a safe bet that wouldn't happen.

Forbes lifted his hand. "I won't argue it's an extra expense. If we compromise, they'll get out of our way. We'll get that injunction lifted. Start moving cattle. That will more than make up for the cost."

"Henry would rather win," Lucy interjected.

She still wouldn't look at him. If she did, she would see he found her smart-alecky remark unamusing.

"Although I do think he's learned that sometimes it's better to meet halfway."

He released his frustration in a slow breath. *Halfway?* There wasn't a point somewhere in the middle when it came to marriage. The answer was *yes* or *no*.

"Who came up with this *halfway* arrangement?" He directed his question to Forbes.

"It was a joint effort between myself and the vice president of the Texas Central."

Henry knew who was really behind it. Andrew Pierce. The president of their archrival the A&P, who sat on the board of the Texas Central. No doubt, his minion had pushed this absurd agreement through as another attempt to drive the Katy into bankruptcy.

"Pierce holds the puppet strings," Henry pointed out.

Forbes retained an annoying serenity. "That may be. But if we can't come to an agreement, the Katy will remain nothing more than a well-built railroad leading to nowhere."

Forbes was right, damn him. If they didn't break the injunction and get more money flowing in, building a railroad empire from Chicago to the Gulf would never become a reality.

Still, the Major knew they couldn't afford to give up on Denison, which was the message they'd send by building an interchange out in the middle of nowhere. Why did he appear so confident in this absurd solution?

Henry launched himself out of his chair. He approached the map. Was there something he'd missed? He studied the winding lines that indicated the river. On the Texas side, sandy land sloped gently until it butted up against a bluff. He'd selected a town site on top of that bluff. The Texas Central had located a town closer to the river, which was easier to reach and more convenient. They'd auspiciously named it Red River City.

"Everyone thought I was crazy when I suggested this location for our town. At the time, it was nothing except sagebrush and unbroken forest. But it was the closest point near the river on high ground," Henry remarked.

The Major tipped his head in a nod of approval. "The Indians told me about floods in the old days, when the river reached almost to the top of the bluff."

Henry's respect for the old man increased tenfold. Forbes had talked to the Indians, too. Ah, now it became clear what he'd done.

The Major, taking a long view, had also deduced that Nature, if not God, was on the Katy's side.

"Flooding doesn't happen every year. According to the Indians it occurs in cycles. When it does flood again..."

The answer to the problem barreled into Henry.

"Red River City will be washed away," he said, finishing the sentence.

"That's right." To the Major's credit, he managed to sound humble while claiming the win.

Henry tipped an imaginary hat. He could still claim that it had been his idea to build a town at a safe distance from the river. With the injunction lifted and cattle money flowing in, he could afford to wait it out until he won. That is, if he could come up with enough money to pay for this ridiculous interchange.

"Very clever," he acknowledged. "Glad to see you've succeeded at bridling these ornery Texans," he added, to show Lucy he could be magnanimous.

The older man chuckled at his daughter's disbelieving expression. "Come now, Henry. Be honest. If my success was what you hoped for, you wouldn't have sent me down here."

The blunt retort took Henry aback. Was frankness an inherited trait or a regional peculiarity? Lucy and her father seemed to share the inclination.

Henry crossed his arms over his chest. He could be frank, too. "If we're being honest, I'd like to know how a clever man like you managed to get himself sacked."

Lucy exclaimed something in French. Henry surmised she might be cursing him. Too bad he didn't understand the language. Or maybe that was a good thing. "Why can't you concede graciously?"

"No, it's a fair question." Her father conceding graciously annoyed Henry to no end.

Forbes continued. "I was *sacked*, as you put it, after I disagreed with a powerful man. Jay Gould. You've heard of him, I'm sure."

The entire country had heard about the devilishly brilliant financier after he'd tried to corner the gold market some years back.

Now, he had his eye on the railroads. By most accounts, he snatched them up to make a fortune by bleeding them dry, as he'd done with the Erie. Now *that* was a villain.

Henry held Lucy's heated gaze though his response was directed at her father. "What happened? Did Mr. Gould bend too many rules to suit you?"

She narrowed her eyes at his reminder of their earlier conversation.

"He did more than bend them," Forbes replied. "He broke them, and flaunted every moral code. He's so clever at juggling finances, no one was able to prove him guilty of a crime."

Henry's blood chilled. He'd been playing a financial shell game for the past two years. Not on the scale that Gould played or for the same reasons. Still, if his cover-up were discovered, he'd be sacked. Ruined.

He studied Forbes' bland expression. The investigator couldn't know. He didn't have access to the evidence. "Let me guess. You had proof of Gould's wrongdoing, so he fired you."

Forbes cradled his elbows, although he didn't blink. "If I had that kind of power, why would I be sitting here?"

Interesting question. The Major had kept silent about whatever it was he had on Gould. More importantly, one of the Katy's directors had come to his aid.

"You have an influential friend in your corner?" Henry ventured.

"Not a friend, exactly. Someone who shares a mutual enemy."

Henry nodded with understanding. "Yet, you weren't able to vanquish the villains."

Forbes broke eye contact to glance at his daughter.

Lucy didn't notice his worried appraisal. She was too busy glaring. "He would have done so, if he could have. Villains *deserve* to be vanquished."

Henry's stomach muscles tensed at the hurtful thrust. He should've guarded his barbed tongue. He wouldn't give her the satisfaction of knowing her arrow had struck true, even if he'd brought about the attack. "I'm sure most of the country agrees with you, Miss Forbes. If you and your father will excuse me, I have something to attend to."

He ignored her startled expression. Strode to where his hat and coat hung on a rack by the door. His anger was directed at himself more than her. He needed to cool off before he said something he would truly regret. "We should get started on the interchange right away. I'll find Mr. Munson and have him make the arrangements."

"Henry?" Lucy spoke his name softly, her voice tinged with regret.

He paused, his hand on the knob, then swallowed a lump in his throat so he could speak. "I'll be back momentarily. Then you can have another shot at rehabilitating me."

CHAPTER 28

Merde. There were times she really ought to keep her mouth shut.

Lucy flew to the door right as Henry shut it behind him. She hadn't meant to hurt him. She'd lost her temper when he so rudely flung her father's misfortune in his face. Henry thought she detested him. She'd seen it in his eyes. She couldn't let him walk away believing a lie.

"He doesn't want you to follow him."

She halted at her father's astute observation. Henry's pride wouldn't allow him to accept her apology. Not yet. Regret swamped her.

For once, Henry's motives were utterly transparent. He'd hoped to wring a confession out of her father so he would look better. She ought to hate him for that. Instead, she ached for him. The crack in Henry's supreme confidence proved he was human.

She drifted over to the front window to watch him pass by. He leaned into the brisk wind, unwilling to let anything, including Nature, stop him. He would be back. He'd give her another chance, which she wanted. Despite knowing she would be better off without him.

Her father came to her side. "Is there something you need to tell me?"

He meant more than the reason for her dig at Henry.

"This morning, we had a—" *Fight.* "Conversation about villains. Silly, the way it started out. I was telling him about the characters in a book." She craned her neck to keep Henry in her sights until he turned the corner.

"Lucy, this isn't about a book."

She snapped out of her daze. "No, no it's not."

What could she say? Henry had betrayed her, then she'd fled. He had followed, and they had become lovers. Now, she was confused. So very confused. She couldn't tell her father all that. He'd go after Henry with a shotgun.

"I offended him." And felt perfectly miserable about it. More than insult him, she'd turned down his marriage proposal. Twice. Or was it three times?

Her father's expression became thoughtful. "You've developed an affection for Mr. Stevens."

Oh, what she felt was far more than affection.

Lucy lowered her lashes to hide the truth. "We both know Henry is ambitious to a fault."

All his rampaging energy made him a passionate lover, as well. She wasn't about to admit *that* to her father, of all people.

"He's controlling, manipulative, out to conquer the world."

"Reminds me of me."

She looked up, startled. "You're nothing like that."

Her father's blue eyes filled with what looked surprisingly like regret. "Before I met your mother, I was. Unbearably arrogant. Restless. Every bit as ambitious as Henry Stevens."

When *Maman* had given up everything to marry her father, he'd become a better person. Lucy had heard the story many times. Was she selfish because she wasn't willing to sacrifice her dreams for Henry's? Maybe she didn't love him enough.

"What about a man who doesn't think he needs saving?"

Rather than answer, her father ushered her to a chair. With a weary sigh, he sank into the seat next to her.

She recalled a time when he'd been filled with a vibrant, bustling energy that seemed to make everything around him come alive. After her mother passed away, he'd become quieter, more introspective. She had attributed it to grief. Maybe the change had more to do with carrying too many burdens.

Her father removed his spectacles. He took out a handkerchief to clean them. He always did that before he was about to impart words of wisdom—or deliver a lecture. "Much as we men like to think we're perfect, we're not. We make mistakes. Fall down on our duties. Let down people we love. That doesn't mean we don't wish to be better. To love better."

Lucy's breath caught. *Love?* Why had he jumped to love? What made him think Henry desired improvement in that part of his life or any other? Granted, she'd broken through several of his barriers. He still hadn't indicated a willingness to change. His determination to marry her had more to do with a desire for possession. Not love. She couldn't confide all that without revealing her indiscretion.

"Henry knows he's not perfect," she replied. "I don't think he cares. He has no intention to play fair. He wants to put you somewhere that's close enough to keep an eye on you, far enough away you won't be underfoot."

"Are you talking about me—or you?" Her father's voice held a hint of amusement.

She didn't smile. She didn't find this conversation the least bit funny. "He'd control the world if he could."

"Then he'll learn he can't."

"That's not a lesson I can teach him."

Her father held up his lenses to peer at them. He tucked the wires over his ears. "You may be the only one who can."

For some inexplicable reason, her father championed Henry.

She released a frustrated sigh. "It's obvious you like him, although I don't know why, given his manipulations."

"He does relish the game. I'll give him that. You won't let him get away with it."

"I have no special powers," she said, unable to hide her disappointment. Her father had warned away her brother's best friend from courting her. He'd gone on to be a war hero. Yet, her father seemed content to let a rascal pursue her. "Is Henry the kind of man you'd pick for me?"

"Are you asking for permission or my opinion?" The sharpness in her father's eyes alerted her. The master at maneuvers had backed her into a corner, which was why he always won when they played chess.

She made the next move with care. "You reserve the right to give me both, I suppose."

"I do. Knowing all along you'll follow your heart."

Follow her heart? That was the *problem*. In the past, she'd always depended on it. Her heart had never misled her—until now. She held her arms out, pleading. "This isn't helping. I need *clarity*. "

Her father's expression turned somber. "That's something I can't give you, much as I'd like to. Being your father, I don't think any man is worthy of you. That means, I'll have to rely on your judgment."

Lucy's gaze shifted to the window. "What if my heart leads me to the wrong man?"

Her father appeared to contemplate the question. "Henry might not be the right man, or even a good one. But I suspect you love him. Only you can decide if that's enough."

How annoying. When she finally asked for his advice, he wouldn't tell her what to do.

"You trust I'll make the right decision." She tried to smile. "Why? Because you think I'm smart, like you?"

His gaze filled with love and pride. "No. Because you're wise. Like your mother."

CHAPTER 29

*H*enry stood behind the desk in his railcar. He reached into his waistcoat pocket to check his watch. *Five o'clock.* The last train to Kansas would depart in thirty minutes.

With a low curse, he left unfinished paperwork to look out the door.

Passengers who'd been milling about the platform had organized themselves into lines to board. No sign of Forbes. Or Lucy.

Earlier in the day, after Henry had returned to the railroad office —a short time after departing with his damn tail between his legs— her father asked if he might keep Lucy with him for a few hours while Henry inspected the location for the proposed interchange. Henry had agreed, grudgingly. They were supposed to be here by now. Another ten minutes and he would go after her.

He shrugged out of his coat, turned up his sleeves. Checked the rifle to make sure it was loaded. He never traveled without weapons and ammunition. He rolled up the window shades and peered outside.

How galling, to be so anxious for a glimpse of her when she was eager to put distance between them. It was time he shifted the balance of this relationship to his favor. As it was, Lucy held a distinct advantage.

He couldn't force her to love him. Last night, he'd proved he could make her want him. However satisfying, sexual compatibility wasn't enough. To further tip the scales in his favor, he had to work on getting her to *like* him. That meant addressing things that rubbed her wrong—his personality to start with. If he went after her now, she'd accuse him of being impatient.

Henry rested his hip on the corner of his desk. He'd wait.

The last boarding call sounded. *Five minutes.* He leaned on the ball of his hand and drummed his fingers. "God, hurry up," he muttered.

The door swung open. Lucy sailed inside.

That was the quickest answer to a prayer he'd ever gotten. Maybe the only answer. He didn't pray very often, assuming God didn't want to hear complaints. He would be more grateful if the Divine saw fit to give him his heart's desire.

Lucy smiled. "Good afternoon, Henry."

His heart soared. Then it stopped altogether. *God, no.* Lucy wasn't his heart's desire. Granted, he hungered and thirsted for her, but what he wanted more than anything was to rule an empire built on iron rails.

"You look startled." She paused next to the hat rack beside the door. Her hands went to the bow at her cheek and she released her bonnet. "Did you think I wouldn't show up?"

The thought had occurred to him. Except Forbes had agreed Lucy should go back to Parsons. Since when had she done anything other than what she wanted to do?

"I knew you'd be here." He spoke with more confidence than he felt. "Even if you wanted to stay, your father wouldn't allow it. He's a smart man."

She hung her bonnet next to his bowler. "You called him clever earlier. If you aren't careful, I'll start to believe you mean it."

The jab wasn't meant to be amusing. Rather, it was intended as a reminder of his misstep. He didn't need reminding. He'd already decided that discrediting her father was a bad strategy.

"I've always known your father to be intelligent."

Lucy arched an eyebrow. "Always?"

Henry caught his mistake. She preferred truth, without sarcasm. "Almost always."

The car trembled as the train started forward. Black clouds rolled past the glassed windows. As they got underway, Lucy took a seat on the sofa. With her book.

Henry heaved a sigh. Either that story was more interesting than he was or this was her way to ignore him. Annoying, though not unexpected.

How to proceed... Force a conversation? That hadn't worked earlier. Go back to his paperwork until she was ready to talk. She ought to appreciate his show of patience.

He took his seat. Hunched over the dismal revenue report he'd been reviewing earlier. No matter how he figured it, the increase in the number of shipments over the past year didn't provide the expected improvement in income. He'd asked Caldwell to collect each station manager's ticket receipts. Once the painstaking task was complete, the numbers would provide the answers.

Over the next hour, Henry kept glancing at Lucy. He couldn't concentrate on work. Not while his mind was occupied with a problem that couldn't be tallied up or calculated. What he needed was insight into the female mind. In particular, Lucy's mind.

She appeared to be a bundle of contradictions. He suspected there was a kind of logic behind her actions. She'd been telling the truth when she said she preferred devils to angels. After all, she'd given him a taste of heaven before hurling him back to earth. His mistake had been his refusal to be repentant about his nature. He'd shown her the wretch, without offering her any hope of redeeming him. That was about to change.

He got up and crossed to the sofa. The sooner she forgave him, the sooner they could pick up where they'd left off in the wee hours of the morning. Her attitude toward him improved dramatically when they were unclothed.

"That book, how many times have you read it?"

"I'm not sure." Her attention remained riveted to the page.

"That many?" He stretched his arm over the back of the couch, inching closer. "Then you won't mind if I interrupt."

"What for?" Lucy eyed his hand warily.

"To give you an apology."

"I don't require an apology. If you feel you need to make one, you can offer it to my father."

"He wasn't offended. You were."

Only an inch of space remained. The true distance between them was much farther than that. Henry braced himself. He didn't know if he could leap the chasm with one vault, but he'd try. "This morning, you said you'd cast me as a villain..."

She closed the book. "I was joking."

"Not entirely."

At last, she met his gaze then set the book aside. "Well, maybe not entirely. I didn't mean to hurt your—"

He put his forefinger to her lips. "Hold on. I'm not finished apologizing. Once I'm done, if you need to clear your conscience you can."

Her lips curved beneath his finger. He couldn't resist stroking them lightly before letting his hand drop. "Much as I hate to admit it, I do have a nature better suited to a villain than a hero."

She gave him a perplexed smile. "Is that why you're apologizing?"

"In a sense." He grazed the back of his fingers along the silken curve of her cheek. Her loveliness went beyond face and form. She had an abiding goodness that glowed from inside, through her eyes. Even if she'd fallen to earth, she was still a pure soul. What right did Lucifer have to an angel? None. That wouldn't stop him from pursuing one.

"I'm not the kind of man you deserve. But I'm a better man with you than I am without you."

Her eyes widened in amazement. Oddly enough, he was surprised, too. Surprised to discover he meant every word.

He bent his head, bringing his mouth to within a fraction of hers. Her lips trembled. Color suffused her cheeks. Her breathing came faster. He hadn't even touched her and already she was aroused. He could tap her passion and use it to ensnare her, make her need him.

Need wasn't love.

It would have to be enough—for now.

He feathered a kiss over her parted lips, then across her smooth cheek to the delicate shell of her ear. With the tip of his tongue, he traced the edge.

She drew a sharp breath. Put her hand to the side of his face. Weak resistance. "Henry, no," she murmured.

"Lucy, yes." He guided her fingers to his hair. She seemed to enjoy fondling it, among other things. And he certainly enjoyed being fondled.

"When you touch me, I get confused." Her bewilderment wrung his heart.

"Don't be. It's not complicated. We belong together." He trailed kisses down her neck and felt her shiver. An answering tremor went through him. "Can you feel it?"

"All I can do is *feel*. You don't give me a chance to think."

Henry fought his damned impatience. If he seduced her without regard for her confused feelings, she'd end up resenting him. He wouldn't like himself very much, either. He'd already admitted to being a scoundrel. He didn't need to prove it.

He cupped her head with his hand, placed a gentle kiss on her forehead and looked deep into her eyes. "What you're feeling, it's nothing to fear. I feel it, too. We're...synchronized."

She gazed at him with a dazed expression. "Synchronized?"

What could he give as an example?

"Like the engine that's pulling this train. Steam propels the pistons, which move the drive rods attached to coupling rods that move the wheels. It's not as simple as that, but the point is, the engine won't work if one part resists the rhythm."

Lucy blinked. The dreamy look faded. "How interesting. I'd love to learn more about steam engines."

Henry dropped his hands to her shoulders, tempted to shake her. "I'm talking about us."

Her lips tipped up. "Yes, I know."

She was too generous to tell him she hadn't been swept away by the clumsy metaphor. "My romantic prose needs tuning. That's what you're not saying."

"No, you gave a good example, very precise. I liked best what you said before, about being better when you're with me." Her fingers moved from the edge of his mouth outward, over rough bristle.

His facial hair grew so fast he had a shadow by the end of the day. Maybe she would shave him again. The thought sent an electrifying current straight to his groin.

She held his gaze as her thumb slid across his lower lip. Desire fused with every cell in his body, generating enough heat to power a train.

He moved his hand to her neck, drew her to him for a kiss. Now they could get to the more enjoyable part of making up. And by the time her father showed up, she'd be more than ready for him to ask for her hand.

Yes, everything would work in perfect synchronization.

A series of loud cracks came from outside the train.

Lucy jerked back from the heated kiss Henry had been giving her. "What's that?"

"Gunfire," he said grimly.

Her heart had already sped up under Henry's sweet seduction. Now, it began to pound.

They were under attack or someone had fired from the train. At a herd of buffalo? She'd read about hunters shooting from the safety of railcars, although Henry had told her the buffalo that once roamed this area were all gone.

Lucy left the sofa. She started in the direction of the window where a velvet curtain had been rolled up. She might be able to take a peek to see if she was right, as long as she was careful.

Henry caught her with a single stride. His hand locked around her upper arm. "Stay away from the window."

"I won't make myself a target. I'll watch from a safe position."

"There isn't a safe position if someone is shooting at us." He thrust his finger at the couch. "Get behind there, in a case a bullet gets through a window."

"You want me to hide, but you'll remain out here where you can get shot? Why don't *you* hide? I'm not the one they're after." Lucy jerked her arm away. She tucked her shoulder beside the window so she could see out without being seen.

Henry hovered next to her. "If you recall, a conductor was wounded in that shoot-out. I don't think they give a damn who they hurt."

If he was cursing, that meant he was very angry, or afraid—for her. Her irritation fizzled. She couldn't fault him for wanting to protect her. How he went about it was something they would have to work out.

She'd already accepted she loved him, and might've said so, except she sensed it would be a mistake. Henry wanted to control his world and everything in it, including her. Being the first to declare love meant giving up power. If she took the initial step, he'd be content to possess her and give her passion without risking the deeper emotions. Love. Trust.

"Don't make me pick you up and carry you to the couch." His breath stirred her hair, setting off a burst of shivers.

"As lovely as that sounds, I believe I'll remain here."

The late afternoon sun had turned the horizon golden. The ground was a blur. A group of brown-skinned men on galloping ponies rode into view. Spiky red feathers adorned their hair. Their black braids whipped in the wind like banners.

"Indians," Lucy said in awe.

"Renegades." Henry took hold of her arm to restrain her. "Kiowa, from the look of them. We've been plagued by attacks from small bands along this stretch."

She kept her gaze fastened on the riders. They'd painted their faces and were armed with bows and arrows. Two appeared to have rifles. Although the window was shut, she could hear their yelps. "They don't appear interested in your car. Looks like they're chasing the engine."

"Once the engineer takes us to full steam, we'll leave them behind." Henry put his arm protectively around her shoulder.

As the car pulled past the shaggy ponies, she noticed that the men and their mounts were painfully thin. "They're starving, Henry. Maybe they only want food."

"What they want is for us to leave the Territory. Far as they're concerned, this land belongs to them and we have no right to be here. The government and the railroad disagree."

He'd summed up the problem succinctly enough. However, he didn't offer a solution.

She searched his stern expression. "What can we do?"

"Do?" He looked bemused. "Nothing, except avoid starting a war."

"No, I mean, what gives us the right to drive them out of their homes and destroy their culture? There has to be another way."

Henry shifted his gaze to the window with a thoughtful expression. After a moment, he shook his head. "You're asking the wrong person. I'm a railroad man. Not a philosopher or a politician. I don't begrudge these people their land, but I have to take my railroad through it."

The floor beneath Lucy's feet shuddered. The train began to slow.

Outside, the Indians pulled ahead, gaining on the engine.

A shot rang out.

One of the braves wheeled away, hunched over his pony's withers.

Another Indian returned fire.

"What the devil?" Henry exclaimed. "My orders are to outrun Indians, not engage them." He rushed to the door. "Stay here while I find out what's going on. Keep away from the window."

He was gone before she had a chance to argue.

Lucy looked outside the door in time to see him climb over the tender box. He'd be exposed until he reached the engine room. God forbid the Indians would shoot at him. His engineer and firemen didn't even know he was coming. Someone needed to cover for him.

Decision made, she pulled over a chair and climbed up to retrieve the rifle mounted above the door. A repeater, already loaded. She went out the exit then moved to the corner of the platform and leaned into the wind to see where the riders had gone.

Smoke billowed from around and beneath the train, heating the chilly air and stinging her eyes. Through the haze, she spotted the Indians on their ponies, about even with the front of the tender box. Where was Henry? Had he made it to the engine room?

She used the upright as a brace, and brought the rifle to her shoulder. The movement of the train would make it difficult to be accurate. Hopefully, the Indians wouldn't make it necessary for her to test her skills.

Her hands shook. She lowered the rifle and searched for Henry.

The train took a slight curve then the engine came into sight. A man crouched on the running board. He crept alongside the engine's boiler. Dark hair, gray trousers, white shirt with rolled up sleeves.

Her heart leapt in alarm. *"Quelle folie!"*

Henry clung to a rail with one hand while holding a long-spouted can in the other. He had to be headed for the steam chest. Normally, the fireman did that dangerous job. Every so often, he had to pour tallow over the moving valves so the engine wouldn't overheat and seize up. Henry must have realized that whoever went out there risked being shot. He would've insisted on being the one to do it.

Fear congealed in Lucy's veins. With the way the train bounded along, the airflow had to be battering him with the force of a hurricane. He could be knocked off. Shot, if the Indians got any closer.

Suddenly, the engine belched steam. As a tremor shook the train, Lucy grabbed the rail. She knew what had happened, her father having explained it once when she'd ridden with him. The engineer had turned the throttle off for an instant. In that pause, Henry had to pour the oil into the vent in the steam chest. He'd be distracted.

As the train slowed, the lead Indian exchanged fire with someone in the engine room. Meanwhile, another painted warrior drove his mount for the front of the locomotive where Henry perched precariously.

Lucy snugged the rifle stock against her shoulder. She purged her mind and emotions with a deep breath as her brother had taught her.

The brave stayed on his pony using only his legs, which allowed him to raise his rifle to better aim at his target, which had to be Henry.

She pulled the trigger. The force of the shot thrust her backwards.

The brave hurtled from his pony. He hit the ground as the train rushed by.

Lucy blinked furiously in a cloud of steam and smoke. She strained to see Henry. Her heart thundered so loud for a moment she thought it was the sound of the ponies' hooves striking the hard ground.

The thick black cloud cleared. At the same time, the train began to pull forward. She saw Henry crawl inside the engine room through the fireman's window.

Lucy sagged with relief, which was quickly followed by a sick feeling that surged up her throat. She dashed to the rail and emptied the contents of her stomach. She reentered the rail car, lightheaded and numb. Set the rifle against the chair she'd used to reach it, then staggered to the sofa. It wasn't until she sat down that violent tremors racked her body.

She'd wanted to see Indians and talk to them, not shoot one. Their anger was understandable. They were starving, desperate. Her heart constricted with remorse. She had done what she had to do to protect Henry. Just as he had done what he had to do to keep the train moving.

Moments later, the door flung open. He stepped inside. Soot stained his face and clothes, his hair stood out in wild disarray. To her, he'd never looked better.

Overcome with relief, she ran to embrace him. "Henry," she whispered, as her tears flowed. "Thank God you're safe."

He hugged her close, pressed her cheek hard against his waistcoat, buried his face in her hair. He reeked of smoke, oil and sweat. After a moment, he gripped her shoulders to pull her away from him. The fierce intensity on his face frightened her.

"Are you hurt?" he demanded.

"No. I-I'm fine." She lied to reassure him. The sick feeling still swirled in her stomach, and she ached with regret for shooting that man.

"Good," Henry ground out. "Because *I* want the pleasure of killing you."

KILL WASN'T the right word for what Henry wanted to do to Lucy. He wasn't sure, actually, it might involve tearing off her clothes. She must've seen it in his eyes, because she backed away. He fought to keep his hands off her, to restrain his emotions, which threatened to erupt in a stream of words unsuitable for a lady's ears.

At one point, as he'd been creeping along the side of the scalding hot boiler, he'd turned his head and had seen her on the platform of his railcar, leaning out to look at the Indians. He'd been so shocked he nearly lost his grip. While he'd given his full attention to getting oil into the valves, he hadn't known who'd taken down that brave. Not until his men told him the shot came from behind the engine.

After he'd regained control of his temper, he posed a question to her. "Did you fire a gun?"

Wordlessly, she pointed behind him to a rifle propped against a chair near the door.

Henry's stomach did a slow flip. So, as he'd feared, it was her. How the hell had she made that shot? Only by some damn miracle. "What madness possessed you to get my gun, go outside and open fire on a band of armed Indians?"

Her eyes narrowed. Then she whirled away, muttering something in French.

He followed her, furious. "I don't understand that language."

She tossed her response over her shoulder. "If I want you to understand, I'll use English."

Henry fisted his hands, tempted to yank her into his arms and kiss her into submission. Although he couldn't imagine why he thought that would help. He'd made passionate love to her and it hadn't tempered her recklessness. Might've made it worse.

"Why?" He grasped her shoulders and turned her toward him. "Why did you go out there? Why did you shoot? You could've drawn their fire at you. My God, Lucy," he rasped. "They could've—"

"Killed you," she finished. Her chin went up in defiance. "That Indian, he would've shot you if I hadn't...hadn't *killed* him." Her voice tapered off to a whisper. Pain flashed in her eyes an instant before tears spilled down her cheeks.

His anger couldn't hold against the onslaught of tenderness. He folded her in his arms then held her as she wept. Even a hardened man couldn't kill without feeling something. A kindhearted woman like Lucy would agonize over it for the rest of her life. He shouldn't have left the gun, shouldn't have left her alone.

"I was trying to p-protect you," she stammered between breaths.

The only other woman who had risked her life to protect him was his mother—with disastrous consequences.

He buried his face in Lucy's hair, breathed in her sweet, womanly scent. His heart constricted. She'd done only what he would've done under the circumstances. His anger stemmed from fear. No, more than that. Abject terror, at the thought of losing her.

Lucy, sweet Lucy, so warm and youthful, so full of life. He ought to send her away before God, or Fate, snatched her out of his arms. He couldn't. He was too selfish.

"If anything happened to you, I'd never forgive myself."

She clung to him. "If I stood by and let you die, do you think I'd feel differently?"

He wanted to explain it wasn't her responsibility to protect him.

He wouldn't allow her to put herself in harm's way. Except he couldn't speak. Certainly, not to scold her. Instead, he scooped her up in his arms and carried her into the other room.

Rationality fled. Emotion ruled. He half expected her to fight when he set her on her feet by his bed and tore at her jacket. Instead, she went for the buttons on his shirt. In between kisses, their clothes were flung off.

He took her to bed. Beyond thought, beyond anything except the throbbing, maddening need surging through him, he pressed into the cradle of her hips. She wrapped her legs around him and grabbed handfuls of his hair, arching up to receive him as he buried himself to the hilt. He groaned as pleasure ripped through him. He desired nothing except to possess her.

As he drove himself into her, over and over, his breath came in wrenching huffs. Some bit of sanity told him to slow down so he wouldn't hurt her. That fleeting thought was swept away when she dug her fingers into his buttocks, urging him to thrust deeper.

She gasped his name. The muscles surrounding his engorged cock clenched. His body took control. His hips jerked as he reached his release. She held him in a splendid vise, wringing his seed out of him, demanding everything. He shuddered and didn't even think about holding back. Whatever she wanted, he'd give her—even his soul, should she find any use for it.

Spent, he collapsed in her arms.

When Henry came to his senses, he wasn't sure how much time had passed. He was sprawled on top of Lucy. Her fingers played through his hair. She caressed his neck, fondled his ear. Every touch sent a pulse coursing through him, as if her fingertips were somehow connected with a line running directly to his heart. Could she feel it beating? He felt hers, comforting in its steady rhythm. He could've lain there forever, sharing heartbeats.

"Am I crushing you?"

"Mm," she murmured.

"I take that as a *yes*." He couldn't bear to let go. When he rolled away, he brought her with him and settled her warm, soft body atop his. He smoothed his hand over her shoulder, idly toyed with golden strands that would've made Midas envious.

With his body satiated, his mind started to work again. He had dragged her in here, taken her without a single thought to her comfort or pleasure. That she seemed to want him as much as he wanted her didn't excuse his insensitive behavior.

Chagrined, he pressed a kiss on her hair. "I'm sorry."

Lucy braced her arms on his chest. She gazed at him with a mixture of tenderness and bewilderment. "I count that as three apologies in less than two days. You must be catching up on past debts. What's this one for?"

"Ravishing you."

Disbelief flashed across her face, followed by a soft laugh. "You don't owe me an apology for that. Not unless I beg your pardon, as well. That was a mutual ravishment, in case you weren't paying attention."

She did look pleased with herself. Her comfort with sensuality might've offended some gentlemen. He appreciated it, just as he treasured every aspect of her unique personality.

Henry gave her a wicked smile. "Then consider my apology an advance on future misbehavior. I plan on ravishing you again very soon."

"I should hope so. After you forgive me for scaring you, and I forgive you for treating me like I have no sense." She kissed his chin.

"You're very intelligent," he acknowledged.

"Thank you."

"Sometimes, too spontaneous. You could've lured those Indians to you, instead of driving them away with a lucky shot."

"It wasn't luck. I'm very good with a rifle, thanks to my brother." Lucy crossed her arms, causing her breasts to rub against his chest.

Henry's body roused. That she didn't seem to be doing it deliberately increased his excitement. He grazed her arm with the pads of his fingers while he tried to focus on their conversation. "Even a gifted marksman has a hard time being accurate from a train in motion."

"Then call it a combination of skill and God's hand moving."

God's hand hadn't moved too many times on his account. He was beginning to wonder if her faith and purity of heart formed some sort of protective barrier. Or was he deluding himself again because he didn't want to accept the fact that he was cursed?

"You shouldn't have risked your life. My men had rifles. They were told to shoot if necessary."

Doubt flickered in her eyes. "You believe it wasn't necessary?"

She'd be tormented by guilt if he said so. "I believe that Indian intended to kill me."

"I didn't want to shoot him." Her solemn gaze held his. "Don't expect me to apologize for coming to your aid. I'll do it again if need be."

Fear coiled in his belly. Henry cupped his hands around her soft shoulders. "Don't Lucy. Promise me you won't. If you—" He caught himself before he said the wrong thing. She'd never told him she loved him. "I would blame myself if something happened."

A frown creased her brow. "Stop taking responsibility for my actions."

"But—"

She silenced him with her fingers over his mouth. "No more arguing. I'll promise not to take unnecessary chances, and to guard my life. You promise to do the same. We'll both sleep better."

Her lips replaced her fingers. Henry gave in. Nothing he said would change her mind anyway. Stubborn woman. Independent. Brave to a fault. He wouldn't change her for the world. He adored her as God had made her, which meant it was up to him to do a better job protecting her. In doing so, he would find a way to become worthy of her love.

CHAPTER 30

*R*ain set in over the next three days, turning Parsons into a glorified mud hole. From the window in his office, Henry looked down on three men covered in brown slime who strained to dislodge the half-buried wheel of a covered wagon.

For months, Kansas had suffered drought. Now, God sent a deluge. Did it portend disaster? Only if one's name was Noah.

Henry observed the drama below through rain-streaked glass. He wasn't afraid of a little rain, though he wished it wouldn't pour on the morning he had to travel to a meeting. Part of the trip could be made in the comfort of his rail car. The last two miles he'd be on foot. Even with an oilskin poncho, he'd be soaked by the time he reached the farm where the negotiations were to be held.

Bad weather had kept Lucy inside and out of trouble, the one silver lining in that dark mass of clouds. He'd cajoled her into holing up at the hotel where she could write to her heart's content while he locked horns with surly settlers. She'd concurred, thank God, that it didn't make sense for her to become embroiled in what promised to be a contentious gathering.

It was the first time they'd come to an agreement on something other than sex. Must mean they were making progress. Maybe the sex had helped.

The entire trip home, he'd kept her busy in the sleeping quarters of his railcar. In between heated bouts of lovemaking, they'd chatted —about nothing and everything. Their comfortable intimacy satisfied a longing he hadn't even realized he had.

By the time they arrived back in Parsons, he'd felt certain that things would work out. However, timing was key. She wouldn't be badgered into marriage. He would focus on wooing her, instead. Once he finished these blasted negotiations.

Henry turned at a knock on the door, half expecting to see his assistant. He'd sent Caldwell after a case that would keep his documents dry. If he managed to wrestle an agreement out of those farmers, he'd be damned if he let rain wash away their signatures.

Frank Garrity took long, swinging steps into the office, sending droplets flying from the bottom of a long oilcloth coat. The brim of his hat dripped water. Mud caked his jeans. His boots left damp, dirty marks on the polished oak floor. He didn't seem to notice the mess he was making. "We need to talk."

Henry fished out his watch. "Don't have much time."

"Then I won't waste it," the sheriff groused.

Resigned, Henry propped his hip on the corner of the desk. He nodded to one of two leather chairs. "Take a seat."

The former soldier didn't sit, he paced. "That damn Senator York is causing an uproar. He's torn down fences. Dug up fields. Searched barns without permission. Farmers are howling. He vows he won't stop until he finds his brother. Says he has your full support."

Henry swore under his breath. He'd offered men, supplies, whatever the powerful politician needed to search for his missing brother. He hadn't expected the senator to lose a screw. "Those are his constituents, for God's sake. And why is he dragging me into it? If he wants to start a war, he can call in the military."

"He'd like that, I'm sure. The President told him they won't waste troops to search for a few men gone missing." The sheriff dragged a wrinkled handkerchief out of his back pocket and blew his nose.

"Get into some dry clothes," Henry suggested.

"Yeah, I'll be fine." Garrity coughed. "You have to join the search party. Control the senator. I can't babysit him and do my job at the same time."

Henry balked at the order. How the hell was he supposed to do *his* job if he had to coddle a politician? He had his hands full. "I'll join you after I hammer out this land deal."

The sheriff swung around with a look of disbelief. "Did I hear you right? You think those farmers are going to parlay with you while your *friend* the Senator plows up their fields? They'd as soon shoot you."

"What's this about Henry getting shot?" A familiar baritone came from the direction of the door. Lucy's father slouched at the threshold, top hat in one hand, traveling case in the other. Had he come straight from the train?

An idea struck Henry. Forbes had a talent for soothing ruffled feathers. Let him deal with Senator York. It would keep him busy doing something important while Henry got back to being general manager. He made a grand gesture. "Come in, Major."

After he'd run through a quick summary of the situation, Henry ended with, "You understand why I can't put off this deal. First, we need to get the Senator calmed down..."

This was a hint for Lucy's father to volunteer.

Forbes acknowledged with a slight nod. "Yes, I do see the problem. I'd be happy to go to the settlers' meeting in your stead. Then you can join the sheriff."

Henry knew there was a reason he shouldn't have left his door open.

He suspiciously eyed Forbes, who looked back at him with the innocence of a lamb. The old fox. He hadn't misunderstood. He'd chosen the assignment most likely to win him accolades with the board. Two wins in less than two weeks. He'd be promoted to general manager in no time. Maybe even president.

"Sounds like a good plan to me." The sheriff stuffed his

handkerchief in his back pocket and started for the door, his boots squishing. "We'll leave within the hour."

Henry simmered while the Major got comfortable in one of the leather chairs.

"I know you'd prefer for me to go with the sheriff. But you, Henry, have an image problem. And the senator is making it worse. Go out there. Be the voice of reason."

"How can I argue when you put it that way?" Sarcasm aside, Henry acknowledged the problem belonged to him. He'd unwittingly given York permission to wreak havoc. On the other hand, to give Forbes control of the settlers' negotiations would be a strategic error. He'd correct course to manage the outcome in advance.

He took the chair opposite the Major, placed his hands on his knees. "It's time you and I reached an agreement."

"I thought we had," Forbes replied blithely.

Henry would've applauded that great bit of acting, except he'd lost patience with this game. "There's one thing I should make clear. My job isn't on the table."

Forbes regarded him steadily.

Henry sighed. The older man seemed to make it appear that *he* was being unreasonable. He would have to concede some ground. He couldn't oppose Lucy's father *and* win her hand. Somehow, he had to come up with an equitable arrangement that the board would support.

Forbes had done well in Texas. It paved the path for a perfect suggestion.

"We don't have to fight over my position," Henry explained. "How would you like to be a vice president like Mr. Denison?"

When Parsons had made that decision a year ago, the board had supported it. Henry had been infuriated at the time. Until his boss explained they only gave Denison a fancy title in return for investments. He'd promised to elevate Henry to President at the right time.

About now would be the *right time*. Parsons was due back from Europe within two weeks. Upon his return, he would certainly shut down this investigation. He'd need to appease the board. A job for the Major that offered more than a title would do it.

Henry put his cards on the table. "I'll speak to Mr. Parsons. See if he'll appoint you to oversee our operations in Texas. We need a competent man down there to see to it that our line gets built."

Forbes removed his spectacles, pulled out a handkerchief to clean them. He had to be stalling to give himself time to come up with a counter offer. His face revealed nothing, other than deeper lines and dark circles beneath his eyes. His color didn't look good, either.

Lucy's father needed to get some rest, not jump into another contentious negotiation. He was pushing himself too hard, and he wasn't getting any younger.

Henry set aside his priorities to talk to Forbes as he would to a friend—or future father-in-law. "Forget business. I can manage. Take some time off. Spend it with Lucy. I know she'd like that. Have you been to see her yet?"

Forbes replaced his spectacles. "I was on my way. First, I wanted to stop in and give you the final changes to our agreement with the Texas Central." He withdrew an envelope from his case and handed it over.

Henry took it without opening it. Forbes wanted him to believe that he'd delayed his reunion with his daughter because of a report? Lucy's father wouldn't make her wait while he discussed some dry agreement. "What else is on your mind?"

"You don't need to speak with Mr. Parsons on my behalf."

"It's no bother. I want you to have that position in Texas." Surprisingly, Henry meant it. He liked Forbes. Moreover, he respected him as a businessman. Not to mention, he wanted to forge a good relationship with Lucy's father. They would be family, soon. He smiled wryly. "Vice President sounds better than General Manager anyway."

Forbes leveled a direct look. "Levi Parsons is a personal friend of mine. He contacted me a few months ago. Asked me to come out here and clean things up."

A chill swept through Henry, followed by an intense burning in his chest. *Friends. The Major and the Judge.* Of course... Why hadn't he guessed? He knew the Major had powerful connections.

Dazed, Henry stood and went to the back of the desk. He'd blamed the board. Come to find out, they weren't the ones who'd initiated this investigation. Like him, they were pawns, moved by the hand of the master. The rich, powerful financier who'd controlled him by promising him the things he coveted.

He sank into the expensive swivel chair Parsons had given him when the new depot was finished a year ahead of schedule. He had assumed his boss's generosity conveyed approval. The Judge had even offered his daughter at one point, suggesting Henry marry her and further the dynasty. Maybe that's why the Judge had turned on him. Because he let Kate get away and helped her save that Indian, who she later married.

"He spoke highly of you." The Major's unexpected praise penetrated Henry's musings.

He lifted a dull gaze. "Did he? Then why send you?"

"Remember, I told you we had a common enemy. Jay Gould has his eye on the Katy. He'd like nothing better than to swoop in and scoop it up. The only way to forestall that is to improve the railroad's performance. Make it more difficult for him to gain control."

Questions whirled in Henry's mind. Why hadn't Parsons mentioned a possible takeover? Why hadn't he communicated his concerns, confided in his right hand man?

"Mr. Parsons said he gave you two years to fix the problems."

That last remark shook Henry out of his trance. "Let me guess, the problems he told you *I* caused?"

Forbes's head moved in a barely perceptible nod.

Parsons needed a convenient scapegoat.

A dark thought flickered through Henry's mind, one involving a gun. The appropriate target was a continent away. He jerked forward, spreading his hands out on the desk. He'd be damned if he let that old geezer misrepresent what had really happened.

"When Mr. Parsons hired me away from the Union Pacific, he told me to build him a railroad. Fast. Our competitors had big a head start.

More manpower. More money. I rounded up the supplies, planned the route, and got the best tracklayers in the business. Drove them day and night. Never let up. Drove some of them so hard it..." Henry's words trailed off. He couldn't say it. He couldn't admit his decisions had been tantamount to murder.

"He signed off on cutting corners, whatever it took. He looked the other way. My foreman warned us about the dangers of slamming down track without proper grading. Trains derailed. Men died. But the Katy won the race.

"We slogged through constant rain in the Territory, tormented by mosquitoes, the mules weakened from blood loss. Nearly every man fell ill. The crew leader begged me to ease up."

Sick to his soul, he nevertheless demanded they keep going.

"Then, that bridge we built in record time collapsed." Henry leaned on his elbows and put his head in his hands. All that night he'd waded through the black water, frantically searching for survivors, finding only bodies. They'd lined up the dead along the muddy riverbank, while the wounded wandered around with bewildered expressions, like lost children.

"If I wavered, Mr. Parsons would remind me about what he expected. *'Stevens, I know you'll do whatever's necessary.'*" Henry lifted his head to meet a steady gaze. "And I did."

The Major remained silent. He knew.

Henry did too. The directives might've come from Parsons, but he had carried out the orders. In doing so, he'd brought about his own damnation. The choices had been his to make. He'd gone to work for an opportunist who cared for nothing except money and power, and had become like him. Yes, he deserved his fate. That didn't make the pain of betrayal any less.

Slowly, he leaned back in the chair.

Forbes regarded him with an expression that might be construed as concern. How did one discern its authenticity? The Major had been masterful at playing the game, as good as his *friend*, Mr. Parsons.

"Congratulations on your new job, sir." When in doubt about how to respond, scathing sarcasm was always a good option. Henry gave a careless wave. "Go handle the meeting. Take Caldwell along. *Clean things up.*"

Forbes didn't leap to the challenge. He remained planted in that damn chair. Had the gall to wear an apologetic expression. It was a little late for that.

Finally, he spoke. "You asked me why I kept silent after being dismissed from the Erie."

Why bring this up?

"It wasn't only because I knew too much. I participated in the cover-up."

Henry wasn't surprised by the admission as much as the timing. He'd assumed from the start the Major was hiding something. Ironic as hell, but... "Why tell me now?"

"I don't want your job, Henry. You won't believe me unless there's trust between us. For that, we have to be honest with each other. Especially now that we have a common interest. Lucy."

Henry didn't point out that they were at the opposite ends of trust, even with their *common interest.* "What is it you want? To be president?"

Amusement flickered across the older man's face. "If I wanted that, why would I give you information you could use to ruin me?"

That was puzzling. "Mr. Parsons doesn't know about your collusion?"

"Oh, yes. He knows. I was clear about that before I took the job."

Stunned was too soft a word for what slammed into Henry. His boss had knowingly hired a fraud to replace him? *Good God.* "He didn't share that information with the board?"

Forbes heaved a sigh. "I don't believe so."

Henry folded his arms over his chest. The Major had given him a weapon. Why? Had to be some sort of test. "Does Lucy know?"

Forbes fixed his gaze on a distant point. "No, I never told her. She's always idolized me, and it was easier, safer, to let her see me as the man she wanted me to be." He offered Henry a rueful smile. "You'll understand one day, if you have a daughter."

Fatherhood wasn't required for comprehension. Forbes guarded his pride. Mostly, he protected Lucy.

"I do plan to talk to her." Forbes's voice grew soft. "Should've long before now."

A dull throbbing started in Henry's chest. He'd wanted Lucy's eyes to be opened, hadn't he? He'd thought how much better he would look when compared to a worse sinner.

Clearer vision wouldn't make her love him.

He stood and came around the desk, took up his favorite perch on the corner. He liked it because from here he could look down on others, feel important. More self-delusion. He was no better than Forbes or any other man. They were all lost, groping in the dark. Angry. Resentful. Hopeless. Lucy had shone a rare light into his bleak existence. He couldn't allow her spark to be extinguished. "Don't tell her."

Doubt shadowed the older man's face. "She deserves the truth."

Henry was tempted to shake some sense into him. "That might clear your conscience. It's not what she deserves."

Lucy had lost so much in her young life—her brother, her mother, even her security when Forbes lost his job. Loyal and loving, she'd become bound by duty when what she yearned for was freedom. Despite everything, she hadn't become jaded and cynical. She believed that ultimately life would not let her down because the man she worshiped was still on his pedestal.

"She needs to believe in heroes."

"Yes, I know." Her father's pained expression conveyed he knew it all too well.

Henry wanted nothing more than to be Lucy's hero. But like a fallen angel longing to get back to heaven, that wasn't going to happen. "She already knows I don't fit that bill."

Forbes' gaze became searching. "You could change her opinion."

"How?" Henry came off the desk to go the window. The stranded wagon was still there. Stuck in the mud. He was making about as much progress in his goal to become worthy of Lucy. A good place to start would be to let her father remain her hero.

Henry checked his watch. Less than half an hour before he had to meet the sheriff. "You'd better get going or you'll be late for the meeting." He retrieved a poncho from the coat rack near the door, tossed it to Forbes. "Take my oilskin or you'll be waterlogged by the time you get there."

"Won't you need it?" Forbes held it up.

Henry shrugged on his greatcoat. "Don't plan on staying out in the rain. The senator has to be tired and hungry by now. I can ply him with whiskey then send him to bed."

"Sound plan." Forbes retrieved a notebook from his case. He placed it on Henry's desk. "Take a look at this when you return. I'll need your help to finish the investigation. Although, if things work out the way I hope they will, you won't have to give up your position."

Henry wasn't one to waste energy on pointless pursuits. Parsons had decided to discard him. Once his boss made a decision, he couldn't be moved. "Is this your way of getting me to cooperate?"

"I believe you'd do that, regardless," the Major said with a slight smile.

Ever the diplomat. Under his persuasive influence, the settlers would sign away their life savings by sunset.

Henry eyed the leather-bound journal. Curiosity propelled him to the desk. It was the ledger he'd turned over a few weeks ago, with extra notes in the margins. He could try to explain it away. He knew better than to think the Major would be fooled. Lucy's father had played this game perfectly—and he'd moved into checkmate.

The sense of a weight being lifted came as a surprise. Secrets were surprisingly heavy. When a man carried them for so long, they seemed to become part of him.

Now, the Major's confession made more sense. The significance was stunning. Humbling. Forbes had shown him that he trusted him to deal fairly with the truth.

Henry wouldn't have picked his successor to hear his confession. It appeared he didn't have a choice. Regardless, it was over, his dream of running the railroad.

Odd. He'd expected to feel crushing disappointment. The same kind of misery his father had experienced when he'd finally realized his pursuits had been meaningless and had ended his life. Henry had refused to accept failure. He'd been guided by a singular belief. Wealth and power would give him security. Fulfillment. Instead, he'd felt empty. Desperation had driven his father to take greater and greater risks. Hadn't he done the same? He'd never accepted how alike they were. He'd run from it all his life.

Henry dropped the journal on the desk. Lucy was right. There was freedom in letting go. Of his obsession, his guilt, even his stubborn refusal to admit he was as much a dreamer as his father. Strangely enough, giving up control felt like the best decision he'd ever made.

He glanced up at Forbes. "What do you need from me?"

The Major's gaze turned sharp. "The names of employees who have access to your ticket receipts. I believe someone is siphoning funds and altering the reports."

CHAPTER 31

*L*ucy paused with pencil in hand to take a look outside. At last, the rain had stopped. She hadn't been particularly bothered by the inclement weather because being stuck inside meant she had time to work on a new story. This one, a fictional adventure featuring a handsome railroad chief who braved danger to ensure the safety of his crew and passengers. One, in particular.

She smiled, remembering Henry's face when she said she would cast him as a villain. Of course, she couldn't. He was firmly planted in her mind as a hero. She imagined his surprise when she showed him the finished story. A few details were changed. He could easily recognize himself, pick up on the heartfelt message between the lines. If that didn't spur him to speak of his love for her, nothing would.

Since returning to Parsons, he hadn't brought up the subject of marriage. He'd pestered her endlessly for days, and now, when she was ready to accept, he'd gone silent.

Had he been too busy to think about it? Not a flattering thought. Or—her chest grew tight—had he decided he would rather find someone easier to manage? She would never be easy. Or managed.

She checked the timepiece pinned to the pleated bodice of her dress. Half past five. He'd promised to return by candlelight. He wasn't late—yet.

Lucy put her pencil down, too distracted to write and tired of waiting. She grabbed her hat and cape and headed downstairs.

"Hey Miss Lucy!" Billy Frye intercepted her in the lobby. His hair, which turned out to be as light as hers, had been neatly trimmed above his collar. After several layers of dirt had been removed from his complexion, she could see every freckle on his face. There were many.

Lucy smiled. "Hello, Billy. My, you look nice."

He tugged at the collar of the green flannel shirt. "Don't feel nice. This here shirt 'bout chokes me to death."

"I'm sure it takes some getting used to." She did sympathize, disliking her corset as much as Billy disliked his collar. "You might want to tie your shoelaces."

He made a face. "Shoes pinch my feet."

At least he was wearing shoes. Perhaps he didn't know how to tie them.

Lucy bent down. Having no younger siblings, she'd missed out things like this. Helping Billy brought out her nurturing instincts. Or, was it possible she could be with child?

She stood and took a deep breath, feeling almost lightheaded. Her dreams might be over before they began if she carried a child. Or would they? Her hand dropped to her middle. She cradled it against her flat stomach, excited and fearful at the same time. She loved Henry. She would treasure his child. He could take them, her and the baby, on that trip he'd promised, and she could still write...

"Miss Lucy? Are you all right?" Billy's note of concern snapped Lucy out of her musings.

"Oh, yes. I'm fine. Tell me how you're doing. Do you like Mr. and Mrs. Daines?"

He sneaked a glance at the registration desk where Claire sat, pretending not to watch him. "Reckon she's tolerable. I like her cooking. Her man ain't sociable though."

Lucy's heart went out to the boy. She understood his reluctance to form a bond with Claire and her husband, if he thought his stay would be temporary. Henry said Claire wanted children, badly. Her husband wasn't able or inclined to give them to her. How sad to long for children but not be able to have them. Another possibility Lucy hadn't dwelt on. No point in mulling over what ifs.

She slipped her arm around Billy's thin shoulders to give him a hug. "I'm glad you like Mrs. Daines. I can tell she likes you very much."

"Guess so." Billy didn't sound convinced. "You goin' out?"

Over his shoulder, she could see Claire shake her head. She held up a sheet of paper. Henry's sister had mentioned the boy's tendency to disappear whenever he had schoolwork.

Lucy made a rueful expression. "I'm sorry I can't ask you along. I'm off to Mr. Stevens' office for a private meeting."

Billy's crestfallen expression nearly broke her heart. "All right, then. But when you see the Chief, you tell him I ain't so sure about this deal."

Lucy cocked her head. "What deal is that?"

"He said he'd get me a railroad job if I stayed put and learnt to read." Billy huffed. "That'll take forever."

Lucy laid her hand on the boy's shoulder. "I understand. It's difficult to be patient. At the right time, you'll get what you really want. Then, the waiting will seem worth it."

"You didn't wait. You ran off."

Children had a way of going straight to the truth.

"Yes, and I'm a poor example. I should've waited and worked things out. Running away only delays problems. It doesn't solve them."

Billy turned away, appearing deeply disappointed. She wasn't sure she'd convinced him. Nevertheless, he went back to where Claire was seated, accepted the paper and pencil.

Lucy left his temporary guardian to her difficult task and hurried out the door.

Henry had offered her the same advice she'd given Billy. Be

patient. Wait until things settle down before venturing out. That didn't mean she should lock herself in her room. She had to speak to him, be assured he still wanted her.

Her boots squished through the accumulated water and filth on the sidewalk, as she trudged toward the depot. Some thoughtful person had placed boards across the street in front of the depot. Without the bridge, she might've been swallowed up in a sea of mud.

No passengers waited in the lobby, which meant no more trains were running this evening. She picked up her skirts and swept up the stairs to the second floor.

Henry's office was also empty.

Lucy heaved a disappointed sigh. He might've gone back to the hotel. Or perhaps he hadn't returned yet. He'd dropped by at noon to tell her there had been a change of plans. Her father would be taking care of the settlers' negotiations.

How unlike Henry to hand over control of something so important, even if he felt it necessary to join the sheriff to look for those missing men. It had to mean he was beginning to trust her father. If only she could convince him to trust *her* enough to open his heart.

She walked over to his desk and ran her fingers along the smooth surface. Letters and documents were arranged in neat stacks. Henry preferred order and routine. She'd brought chaos into his life, but also, spontaneity. Together, they balanced each other's extremes.

Exquisite synchronicity, he preferred to call it.

She smiled, recalling his adorable description of pistons and drive rods. Henry had a romantic soul. He'd be appalled if she told him so.

A leather journal lay near a corner, as if he'd tossed it onto the desk in his hurry to leave. Curious, she picked it up. Columns filled with numbers. Must be the railroad's accounts. She wrinkled her nose. Figures were so very boring. Not at all like words. The handwriting in the margins she recognized. Her father had made notations, something about discrepancies.

She caught a sharp breath. He was a genius at puzzles and numbers. He'd discovered a complex financial scheme perpetuated by the owners of the Erie Railroad. This looked like another scheme —one perpetrated by Henry.

A knot formed in her throat. The discrepancies could be honest mistakes. Even so, how could Henry hide this from her, after all they'd been through? He'd told her so many things. Intimate details he hadn't shared with anyone else. This, he'd kept a secret.

She clutched the book to her chest, fighting tears. This discovery didn't change her love for him. It might change everything else.

Footsteps sounded on the stairs. She looked up, expecting Henry. Instead, George Caldwell appeared in the doorway. Surprise flashed across his face. "Miss Forbes?"

Lucy's pulse jumped. She quickly placed the notebook back on the desk. "Hello, Mr. Caldwell," she chirped to cover her nervousness at being caught nosing around.

"Good evening." Henry's assistant removed his hat before he made a polite bow. His neatly trimmed beard reminded her of the one she'd shaved off Henry. No more secrets, he'd promised her. Then he'd kept the most important one.

"I didn't expect to find you here." The frown on Mr. Caldwell's face would've told her that.

"Nor was I expecting you." What an absurd reply. He was Henry's assistant. Why wouldn't he be around the office? "Have you seen Mr. Stevens?"

Her voice had gone back to normal, although the flutters in her stomach hadn't ceased.

Caldwell's furrowed brow smoothed. "He's with the sheriff and Senator York, I believe."

"Do you know whether my father has returned?"

"We've been in negotiations with the settlers all day, I'm afraid." Caldwell folded his hands behind his back. "Your father decided to stop at an inn for supper."

Her father wouldn't have stopped. He'd told Henry he would soon be home to see her. He'd returned from Texas and hardly had time to catch his breath before he was off again. "You said you were with him? Why didn't he return with you?"

"Oh, well, I meant, we've not come to an agreement with the Grange leaders. Only taken a break. He sent me back to retrieve an important document." Mr. Caldwell entered the room. He peered around her at the desk. "Ah, there it is. Would you hand me that notebook, please?"

Lucy lifted the journal in slow motion. She searched the assistant's bland expression. Did he know about the financial discrepancies? He might be in on it, too.

"Miss Forbes? May I have the notebook?" Caldwell held out his hand.

Henry owed her an explanation. They had agreed to be honest, which meant giving him the opportunity to tell the truth before she decided what to do with the evidence. She tucked the leather journal against her chest. "I believe I'd prefer to keep it. At least until Mr. Stevens returns. It is, after all, on *his* desk."

Caldwell observed her through hooded eyes. He appeared to ponder her response. "You might want to rethink your decision. I've spoken with your father. Told him everything."

"Everything?"

"About Mr. Stevens. He's been altering the accounts. I've known about it all along. He threatened to implicate me if I said anything. Your father figured it out. He's promised me I won't go to jail if I cooperate in the investigation."

Lucy's pulse accelerated. Could it be true? Her heart rejected the suggestion that Henry was a liar and a cheat. She'd seen the *real* Henry Stevens. That man wasn't a villain. He was brave, chivalrous, generous and loyal.

Caldwell took a step closer, his gaze locked with hers. "I noticed you were looking at the accounts. Do you doubt what I'm telling you? If so, come back with me. Talk to your father. Learn the truth."

It was a tempting offer. Even her father had admitted he wasn't certain Henry was a "good man." He could answer her questions, while Henry might deny it and come up with some plausible sounding story

Who did she believe? What did she believe? At this point, she could only do as she had vowed. She'd promised Henry she would never run from him again.

⁓

"Did I tell you how we caught Pomeroy?" The senator swayed to one side and bumped into the exterior of the billiards hall.

Henry shot out a hand to steady the drunken man. "Twice, this evening."

Senator York delighted in telling everyone how he'd exposed a congressman for accepting bribes from the railroads. Had he forgotten who'd been buying his drinks?

Earlier in the afternoon, York had finally agreed to take a much-needed break from their search for his brother—after farmers wielding pitchforks had run them out of a field. The senator had become more manageable after being plied with expensive whiskey and promised a nice dinner.

Henry hated spending one more minute away from Lucy, but she would understand. Afterwards, they'd have time to themselves. He wanted to wash up before he went down on one knee. His clothes reeked of soil and manure.

"Here we are, the hotel." Henry pushed open the door.

The Senator reeled inside.

Claire looked up from behind the registration desk. Her features froze. She wouldn't be happy about coddling a drunk.

He'd explain later.

With obvious reluctance, she came over. Billy Frye trailed behind her. She'd taken to mothering as naturally as a duck to water. The duckling appeared content with the arrangement, as well. Although she'd warned Henry the boy couldn't stay, he'd been cleaned up, given a fresh suit of clothes, and she'd undertaken his education. Those weren't signs she wanted him gone.

"Billy, take Senator York's overcoat," Claire said firmly.

The boy held out his arms. His gaze lingered on Henry,

accusingly. The boy was a tough customer when it came to approving families.

The senator struggled out of his soggy greatcoat. He jerked at the lapels of his black suit and smoothed his hands over bushy muttonchops. "Where's the young lady you told me about? I'd like to meet her."

Henry stifled a groan. He shouldn't have brought Lucy into the conversation. "I'll see if she's available, if you'd like to wait for us in the dining room."

"She left," Billy stated.

Henry frowned at the unexpected news. "Where did she go?"

"Said your office. For a private meeting."

He'd told her when he would return and asked her to wait. Apparently, she'd grown impatient. He'd be annoyed with her if he thought it would do any good.

Henry rushed to reply before the senator got the wrong idea. "She must've thought we wanted to meet her there. I'll go find her. Make yourself comfortable." He turned to his sister. "Show the senator to the dining room. Bring him a drink. I'll be back."

He didn't miss the eye roll.

Henry started out the door, not noticing his shadow until Claire called out.

"Billy, get back here."

As Henry jogged down the sidewalk, he silently gave thanks for his longsuffering sister. He didn't have time to wrangle a wild youngster. She made it look easy. Billy had thrived under her care. He'd have a talk with Frederick about keeping the boy around.

He sprinted across the street, yanked open the door to the depot. What remained of daylight came through the dome overhead and cast a soft glow on the marbled floor. His footsteps echoed around the empty room. The last train had left at five.

He stopped at the ticket window to speak to a station agent about preparing his car for the morning. If he had to be stuck with the senator, he might as well travel in comfort.

The agent rushed off to do as he was bid.

Henry's men knew how to obey orders. Why couldn't Lucy?

He'd started to smile when he bounded up the stairs. Soon as he found her, he'd send her back to the hotel. How many times had he told her it wasn't safe to be out alone, especially after dark? She wouldn't mind. He'd look into obtaining a pistol for her, maybe a very large dog.

The door to his office hung open. He slowed as he approached the threshold. She'd left it ajar, although he didn't see her inside.

Something soft, like a whisper, drifted out.

Unease crawled up his spine.

"Lucy?" He stepped into the office.

"Henry, look out!"

He twisted at the choked warning.

Behind the door stood Lucy, pale and wide-eyed with terror, with Caldwell's arm wrapped around her neck. He had a pistol pointed at her head.

Henry's confusion turned to cold fury. He tensed, his hand hovering over the place where the handle of the revolver jutted beneath his coat.

"Don't!" Caldwell's eyes burned with the crazed fear of a cornered animal.

The hair on the back of Henry's neck stood up. His fingers itched to shoot the rabid dog for touching Lucy. He didn't dare make a move for his gun. Instead, he straightened, and modulated his voice to project calm authority, the best approach when men had lost their reason.

"What the hell is going on?"

Lucy clutched a notebook to her chest. The movement drew his attention. She held the expense ledger he'd left behind.

His furious gaze flew to Caldwell's reddened face. So, that's what he was after. By God, *he* must be the thief, the one who'd siphoned funds and underreported ticket sales. Had to be. He'd been outside the office earlier. Must've overheard Forbes then come back to get his hands on the evidence. Lucy had found it first.

"Let her go, Caldwell. It's over." Henry fought to keep his voice calm. Every instinct told him to leap on the man and tear him apart.

"You don't understand. I tried to tell her it was *your* fault. She wouldn't listen. She won't give me the book." Caldwell's hand trembled. His trigger finger twitched.

Fear sluiced through Henry. Caldwell could be insane or desperate. At this point, it didn't matter. Lucy's life depended on what happened next.

Henry lifted his hands in surrender. "You're right. It is my fault. All of it, *my* fault. "

Lucy's gaze hung on him, questioning. He didn't blink. It *was* his fault she was in this mess. Had he not been concerned about covering up his wrongdoing, he would've detected his assistant's crime sooner. He hadn't protected her, as he should have. Agony ripped through his calm demeanor. "I'll sign whatever confession you want. Let her go."

Caldwell glowered at him. "I don't believe you."

Because he knew his boss was a liar. The truth tore another hole through Henry's heart.

"George, think about this. You don't want to kill anybody. It's not worth it. You'll hang." Henry inched forward, his hands up, buying time as he tried to figure out a way to get the gun without harming Lucy. "I'll make a deal with you. Take me to the sheriff. I swear, I'll confess. Lucy can be our witness. You'll go free."

He was lying about Caldwell going free. No way in hell would he let that bastard get away. The rest of it was true. He'd confess to his sins. He'd give up his job, his freedom, even his life. He would burn in hell for eternity if it would save Lucy.

"She won't testify against you," Caldwell spat. "The bitch won't even give me the damn notebook. She and her nosy father ruined everything. You know what had to be done, even if you won't admit it. You told me yourself you wanted to get rid of him."

Henry's heart slammed against his breastbone. *God no.* "What have you done?"

Lucy choked back a garbled exclamation, something in French. Her eyes darted to one side as though to see her attacker's face.

"Shut up!" Caldwell pressed the tip of the barrel to her temple.

Stark terror shone in the blue-green depths of her eyes.

Henry strained against the bonds of his self-control, the effort making him tremble. He had to do something before this madman killed her.

The ledger. That would distract him.

"Give him the book, Lucy," Henry ordered. He prayed she'd obey this time.

She hesitated, only a second, long enough for Henry to notice she looked pointedly at his gun. Slowly, she lifted the journal in one hand.

To take it, Caldwell unwound his arm from around her neck.

She dropped like a puppet whose strings had been severed.

In that instant, Henry launched himself at Caldwell.

A shot resounded.

Fire burned through his side. Lucy's scream echoed in his ears. He jerked at a sharp pain, but his momentum carried him forward. He struck the surprised man with his shoulder, taking Caldwell to the ground.

They grappled for the gun. On a surge of fury, Henry locked his fingers around the other man's wrist and slammed it against the desk leg. The weapon spun away. Caldwell hammered his free hand against Henry's injured side. Sharp, splintering pain made Henry jerk, unable to catch his breath.

He clenched his teeth, grabbed Caldwell's hair, pounded his head on the floor. "You bastard!" Rage coursed hotly through Henry's veins. He slammed Caldwell's head on the floor again and again.

"Henry, stop." She pulled at his shoulders. "I've got his gun."

He shook her off like a troublesome horsefly. Slammed his fist into Caldwell's slack jaw.

Lucy threw her arms around him. "For God's sake, stop. He's unconscious."

Her pleas penetrated the haze.

With a curse, Henry released Caldwell's limp body. He staggered to his feet. His side burned as if someone had thrust a hot poker through him. He groaned as his knees gave way, unable to resist the pull of gravity.

"Henry!" Lucy caught him, braced him with her shoulder, held him up. She was stronger than she looked. Her hand went to the fiery place on his side. She gasped, then stared at her hand, wet with blood. Strange words flowed from her lips in a rapid stream.

"Don't understand," he mumbled. His tongue felt thick.

"Oh my God. He shot you. I-I thought you'd go for your gun. That's why I pretended to faint."

Henry used the desk to prop himself up to avoid putting his full weight on Lucy. His body felt heavy, his head light as dandelion fluff. He blinked, trying to make sense of what she'd said. Go for his gun. She'd imagined he could draw his revolver and get off a shot—much less a well-aimed shot—in an instant. Her faith in his ability astounded him.

"I'm not...a gunslinger," he said, in between panting breaths. "Not like...in those books."

"You leapt at him." Her tone accused. "You let him *shoot* you."

"So you," he caught his breath, "could *escape*."

She gazed up at him, her face streaked with tears. "Thick-headed man—" Her voice broke. "You don't have to act like a hero."

What was that? He'd gone from villain to hero? Nice to know. It would make a more admirable epitaph on his gravestone, should he happen to die.

Darkness crept into the side of his vision. Weakness flooded his limbs.

The last thing he heard was Lucy's panicked cry.

CHAPTER 32

*I*n the wee morning hours, Henry's low moan woke Lucy with a start. She sprang out of the chair and stumbled in the darkness to the bedside table. After she'd found the candle, she lit it.

"Lucy..." He muttered and thrashed. "Get away! Run!"

Poor Henry. Having nightmares. Or it could be the result of the laudanum the doctor had given him.

"I'm here," she said soothingly. "It's all right."

He attempted to get up and gave a pained grunt.

"Don't struggle. You'll start bleeding again." She sat on the side of the bed, put her hands on his shoulders and forced him to remain prone. Healthy, she couldn't have held him down.

He stilled beneath her touch His chest heaved from his exertions and a light sheen glistened on his skin.

Awful scenes from the previous evening played through her mind. He'd fallen to the floor, unconscious and bleeding. The railroad staff had carted him over to the hotel with his blood dripping off the plank they'd placed him on. As the doctor removed the bullet and bits of fabric from the wound, Henry's every groan had sliced through her heart.

She'd feared he would die, which was why she'd stayed. His fever seemed to have broken. He might be past the worst.

Come daylight, she would leave to join the men searching for her father, who still hadn't turned up. Caldwell had admitted to nothing, except to say he'd left after the meeting and hadn't seen the Major since.

Lucy sent up a prayer for her father and a second one for Henry. Her hand trembled as she stroked his damp hair away from his forehead. Warm, not burning up, and sweating, which the doctor said was a good sign.

"What time is it?" he muttered.

Always worried about the time, even though he couldn't alter a single minute.

"Almost dawn." She rubbed her eyes. "I must've drifted off."

He raised his hand and touched the thick braid dangling over her shoulder. It slid through his fingers. "Rapunzel," he rasped. "Let down your hair."

Henry, quoting fairy tales.

"You are delirious. Here. Have a drink." Lucy cupped her hand behind his head then brought the glass to his lips.

He gulped water so fast most of it ran down his neck. She mopped his bare chest with the edge of the sheet.

"Your braid." His voice sounded slightly less gravely. "Reminds me of a story. My sisters made me recite the prince's lines."

Tenderness pressed against Lucy's resisting heart. She should've known better than to fall in love with a scoundrel who pretended to be a prince. "I have an easier time seeing you as a bear. Claire told me you played the part in Snow White and Rose Red."

"Had a varied acting career." His tongue was thick. He might not even be aware of what he said. His earlier ravings hadn't made sense.

"She said you were very sweet."

He licked dry lips before he spoke. "I have never been *sweet*."

"That's not true. You've been tender and sweet with me, unless you're going to tell me it was all an act."

His confused frown might've annoyed her if he hadn't been drugged.

Lucy set the glass aside. While caring for him, she'd been distracted from the rising tide of doubt. She could ignore it no longer. Henry's desperate confession haunted her. She didn't want to believe there was a grain of truth in it. He would've said anything to convince Caldwell to release her. Yet, she had seen the journal with her own eyes. Her father's notes.

"Did you...?" The question stuck in her throat. She tried again. "What you confessed to Mr. Caldwell."

"Caldwell?" Flames lit in Henry's dark eyes. "What happened? Where is he?"

Henry wouldn't be aware of what had transpired after he was shot.

"Mr. Caldwell is in jail where he belongs. I hope he rots there. He regained consciousness about the time you collapsed. I held a gun on him and screamed for help until one of the ticket agents came running. They brought you here. The sheriff rounded up some men. They went to look for my father."

"And?" Henry's voice held the same dread and tension coursing through her body.

"He's still missing." Fear closed her throat.

Henry shifted onto one arm. He caught his breath before he spoke. "I'll find him, Lucy, I swear. If that bastard hurt your father..."

If this concern was all show, it was a great act.

She quashed the awful thought. Henry would never have sanctioned any harm to her father. She knew that as certainly as she knew she loved him.

She planted a hand on his shoulder. "You aren't going anywhere. You've lost a great deal of blood. The doctor's dosed you with laudanum. All you'll accomplish is falling down the stairs, if you make it that far."

Henry gripped her arm. She'd never seen such stark despair on his face. "I sent him to handle the negotiations. It's *my* fault he's out there."

Lucy's heart came to dead stop. "You sent Mr. Caldwell after him?"

"*No.*" Henry's denial sounded like it was wrenched from his throat. His gaze turned into a plea. "God knows I should've figured it out. I didn't realize he was the one."

"The one, what?"

"Right before your father left, he told me someone had been skimming money from ticket sales." Henry swayed as he struggled to stay propped up. "I thought it was a station agent."

Lucy's emotions swung between relief and despondency. Her father must not think Henry was guilty, or he wouldn't have shared that information with him. She took comfort in that. Even still, for some reason Henry had sent her father to handle something he should've done.

"Why did you send him in your place?"

"Senator York. Somebody had to manage him before he started a riot."

"You should've let my father deal with the senator."

"Yes." Henry's arms gave way. He sank back onto the bed. "I know. And I should've told you. Everything. Before it was too late."

Judas had regretted his actions, as well. When it was too late.

A knock sounded.

Her heart trembled. She bounded off the bed and flung open the door. "Claire?"

Henry's sister had gone to check on Billy, and had promised to see if there was any news. Hope warred with dread in Lucy's heart.

Claire wiped her hands on an apron stained with Henry's blood. "They've brought in your father. He's hurt, but he's alive."

HENRY HEARD Claire's voice then Lucy's soft cry. She ran past his sister, out the door.

"Claire?" His voice sounded strange. Lucy had told him he was drugged.

The room smelled of camphor and sweat. He remembered being shot. The doctor digging into his side. Excruciating pain. Then nothing, until he'd awakened with Lucy's hair tickling his nose.

His sister hovered over him. Her face had more lines than before. She looked tired. Sad. "How are you feeling?"

To hell with how *he* felt. "Her father. How is he?"

"He's...conscious." Claire's voice caught.

"What happened?"

"When he was walking back to the railway station, someone struck him on the head then pushed him down a ravine. After he came to, he crawled up to the road. That's where the searchers found him."

Her words fell like hammer blows on Henry's conscience. He should've taken charge of that damned meeting, insisted Forbes return to the hotel. Instead, he'd sent him off with a killer.

"Will he get better?"

Claire pulled up a chair and leaned in. "I don't know. The doctor is with him now."

Henry swallowed a knot in his throat. Had his heart gotten stuck there? Lucy's father couldn't die. He was the only good man in her life. Her hero.

"God knows, I can't lay claim to that title. Not redeemable."

"What are you babbling about, Henry?"

"I should've told her the truth," he said thickly.

"What truth?"

"I'm as bad as she thinks."

Time and again, he'd been given a chance to come clean. He hadn't been willing to set aside his pride. Oh, he'd given Lucy glimpses of truth. That didn't change the fact that he was a liar and a cheat. A fraud. Only, *he* hadn't paid for his crimes. Her *father* had.

Claire took his hand. The gesture seemed awkward, probably because he'd never welcomed affection. For some foolish reason, he'd taken pride in remaining distant. Even from his sisters. Tonight, her tight grip was his lifeline. "You're not bad, Henry. Lucy doesn't believe that."

"How could she not?" He closed his eyes. His spirit plummeted to the depths of hell. Lucy might lose her father because of his poor decisions. He should've seen through Caldwell. Caught the discrepancies. Done the audit sooner. But he'd been too focused on his own financial juggling, and holding onto his position. He deserved to burn for what he'd done.

"Success is all I care about," he choked out.

"I know you care about more than that." Claire rubbed her thumb over the back of his hand. His mother had done that when he was a child. How amusing that his baby sister would use the gesture to soothe him. He would've laughed if he hadn't been close to tears.

"You, of all people, should know better."

His sweet little sister had been six years old when they'd lost their parents. He should've held her. Comforted her. Made her feel safe. Loved. Instead, he'd dumped the girls off on relatives they hardly knew then left to look for work. He'd been determined to prove he wasn't a failure like their father. Prove he could provide for them. He'd refused to give of himself.

"I'm sorry, Claire." His voice cracked as emotions he thought he'd conquered battered his crumbling defenses. "Should've been there for you."

"Henry, you've always taken care of us. We know you love us— and we love you." Claire's gaze filled with tenderness.

He reached up to cup her cheek. She'd always had a soft heart, too soft. She would hate him if she knew the truth, yet she deserved to hear it. "You shouldn't. Our mother died because of me. I brought smallpox home."

His sister's face registered surprise, then scrunched with distress. "You're not to blame. Mother didn't take only care of you while you were ill. There were others she helped. Neighbors, just as sick. She cared about people. You do, too. Even if you have a hard time showing it."

That his mother had been an angel came as no surprise. That didn't make him one. The person he'd always cared about most was himself.

He squeezed his sister's hand before he released it. "Don't make me out to be something I'm not. Warm and tender."

"You're too hard on yourself, Henry. Tell Lucy you love her. I'm sure she'll forgive you for whatever it is you think you've done."

Although Lucy had a merciful soul, even she had her limits. She'd heard him confess to Caldwell. Even if she hadn't, he wouldn't try to cover up what her father had discovered. Soon she'd know the depth of his deceit. His lies would be exposed. His true nature revealed. The trust and love that had sprouted in her heart would be ripped away.

The ache in his side spread to his chest. The truth hurt like hell. Nothing he did could make him worthy of Lucy's love. Even if he lived the rest of his life in a monastery, he couldn't atone for his sins. He'd endangered her at every turn, had lied to her, used her. He'd lusted after her, longed to possess her, pursued her until he wore her down, so sure she was the right woman. Never once had he asked himself if he was the right man.

She deserved so much more. If he could dredge up the courage to let her go, she might find what she was looking for. Find *who* she was looking for. Not a pretend prince. A real one.

CHAPTER 33

*B*y the next day, the sun was out. It's afternoon rays slanted across the low-slung roof of the front porch at the Bender place.

Frank dismounted and secured the reins to the hitching post. No other horses. No one sat in the rockers out front. Not a soul, unless one counted the skinny goat nosing around the bare yard.

Something felt weird about this place. The old Dutchman and his family, who ran the inn and grocery, did a big business with travelers who passed on the Osage trail. At suppertime, the owners ought to be here, as well as customers.

The sheriff stepped up to the door. He knocked. While he waiting, he read a painted sign nailed to the wall.

Dry goods, Meals, Professional Healer, Fortune-teller.

He shook his head. The Benders were strange birds. Part of the Spiritualists movement. He didn't care about their odd beliefs, only what they'd seen.

Henry's shady assistant had claimed the Major had stopped in here for dinner the night before and was fine when Caldwell left to catch a train. It was a bald-faced lie, of course. Caldwell had confessed to Miss Forbes and Henry—before he shot his boss. Still, it was always good to tie up loose ends. It would make the trial go quicker. And if the Major died, the sooner they strung up that killer, the better.

"Anyone here?" Frank called out.

When no one answered, he tried the knob. The door swung open with a creak. Frank recoiled when an awful stench wafted out. Smelled like something rotten...or dead.

He drew his revolver before he crept into the dim one-room cabin. No one behind the counter to his right. Strange, the shelves had been emptied. Maybe someone had robbed them.

Behind a rough-hewn table to his left hung a canvas sheet that separated the public area from the family's private quarters. Cautiously, he pulled the curtain aside.

The bed linens had been stripped off the ticking mattress. Drawers in a pine dresser hung open, also empty. If they hadn't been robbed, they sure had left in a hurry.

Frank's confusion intensified, as did his sense of wrongness. He checked through the house, found no one, dead or alive. On his way out the door, he paused to look behind him. *Something* had caused that stink.

From his position, he could see beneath the trestle table. The family had left behind a braided rug. Strange, when they'd taken everything else that could be easily packed.

He lifted one end of the heavy table to move it. Flung the rug aside.

A hinged door in the floor, which probably led to a cellar, had been nailed shut. Stains around the edges looked like—he got down on his knees—dried blood.

The smell got stronger. He recognized it, having smelled it before.

A decomposing body.

On his way to the barn to look for a crow bar, he scanned the property, in case whoever was responsible for what was shaping up to be a slaughter might still be around. The cornfield had been freshly harrowed. Wasn't an uncommon sight. There was something odd about the way the dirt looked depressed in some places, raised in others.

Dread lifted the hairs on the back of Frank's neck.

He veered into the field. His boots sank into the soft, damp ground.

At a raised spot, he bent down and used his hands to dig away loose soil. His breath caught when he exposed the bottom of a foot.

Shit.

Within a few minutes, he'd uncovered the remains of a man, buried face down. His shoes and most of his clothing had been removed. The condition of the corpse would indicate he'd been dead a couple weeks, after being hastily covered up.

Frank's stomach roiled. He put a handkerchief over his nose to block the stench from the rotting corpse. He'd likely find more bodies in the cellar—and out here.

Eight, maybe more.

He'd bet his badge he had discovered what happened to those missing men.

CHAPTER 34

For days, the entire town had been in an uproar over the grisly discovery at the Bender farm. They'd found six bodies already. More were being dug up every day. Everyone in Labette County, newspapers across Kansas, even reporters from as far away as Chicago, speculated in morbid fascination about the details surrounding the brutal murders. Any reporter worth his—or her— salt would be all over the story.

Not Lucy. She hadn't left her father's room since they'd brought him in a week ago. Although his head wound had started to heal, he'd succumbed to pneumonia. The doctor said it was from being out in the cold in a weakened state, and had declared there was nothing more he could do. God would decide.

Lucy resisted the pull of grief. She'd made a deal with the Almighty. Why wouldn't her father cooperate? He'd made it this far. He had to keep fighting. "Would you like for me to read to you?"

He lay in bed propped up by pillows. His eyes remained closed. For the past hour, he'd been drifting in and out of restless sleep.

She closed the book in her lap then went over to kiss his grizzled cheek. He mumbled through cracked lips.

"Are you thirsty? I'll get you something to drink."

His eyes opened. He blinked, then stared at her with surprise. "Adelaide?" he gasped.

Lucy's heart gave a violent twist in her chest. "You must be dreaming, *Papa.*" She used the childhood endearment. "It's me, Lucy."

His forehead wrinkled in confusion. "I thought you were—"

"If I sang, you'd know I'm not *Maman.*"

It was something of a joke between them, her lack of talent. He'd tease her, saying she was allowed only one trait from each parent. God chose to bestow her mother's beauty and her father's brains. She didn't feel very smart right now.

"*Papa?*"

He reached out a trembling hand, his fingers brushed her face. "Lucy, my darling girl," he whispered. His gaze sharpened. "You look unhappy. What's wrong?"

What a silly question. One he wouldn't ask, if his mind weren't addled by illness.

"I'm afraid," she admitted.

"You needn't be. I'm not." His cracked lips stretched into a smile. "I look forward to seeing your mother again."

Lucy had to swallow fast to hold back a sob. "Please, don't talk like that."

He bestowed a paternal pat on her cheek. "You'll be fine, my dearest. You're young and strong, and very smart, like me."

Ah, the joke. He made light of the darkest moments.

"And," he took another labored breath, "you've found someone to love."

She turned away before he could see her tears. Couldn't bear to tell him. Her love hadn't been enough. At one time, she thought it might be.

Over the past week, Henry become a different man. He'd recuperated remarkably fast, then had stayed busy tracking down Caldwell's paper trail and helping the sheriff unravel an atrocious murder. At least, that was the excuse he gave. She assumed he wished to avoid being confronted with what her father had discovered about the railroad's finances.

Caldwell claimed Henry was the fiend, and had ordered her father's death. Henry had told her Caldwell was the culprit. However, he acted as if he was guilty, too. She'd wrestled with doubts, but she hadn't been willing to leave her father to seek Henry out alone and demand an explanation.

Someone knocked on the door.

Lucy checked the timepiece she'd set by the depot clock. Henry's watch would keep the same time. He was right on schedule for his evening visit. The only time she'd seen him was when he stopped by her father's room each day. Fifteen minutes each morning, fifteen minutes in the evening.

She opened the door, freezing her features to hide her longing. She couldn't stop loving him, even if he had stopped loving her.

Henry stood at the threshold. He gazed down at her. For an instant, stark misery darkened his eyes. Then he concealed it. He hadn't shaved in over a week. Apparently, he'd decided he needed the beard. After all they had been through and everything they'd shared, he was hiding again. She had a strong urge to slap him. Instead, she stepped aside.

"Come in."

He entered with a worried look at the bed.

Lucy bowed her head to hide her distress. She noticed the condition of his shoes. They were caked with mud, and the hems of his trousers were filthy. He wasn't one to show up unkempt. "Where've you been? Traipsing through a cornfield?"

"What?" He looked surprised, then glanced down. "Oh, sorry. I was out at the Bender place earlier. The field's been dug up. It looks like a graveyard."

Now, the mud made sense. The senator's brother was reported to have been among the victims. Henry must've gone to find help find him.

"What about the people who owned the place?"

"They left town in a hurry. The governor has offered a reward for their arrest."

Lucy shuddered. A family of killers. Never had she heard of such a thing.

"One of them is a young woman, a fortuneteller. She advertised her services around town." Henry's lips twisted in a wry expression. "Word is, she offered to conduct a séance to help find the missing men."

"I heard about that." Lucy was glad she hadn't decided to attend. The woman had to be crazy or a she-devil.

"It appears the Benders have robbed and killed people for the past couple years. Nobody suspected them. Their place is near the Osage trail. Lots of people pass through there on their way west. When men go missing, it's easy to blame outlaws or Indians."

"Or the railroad." Lucy felt slightly ill. "I should apologize for accusing you of having anything to do with it."

Henry's frown became troubled. "Save the apology. You might decide I don't deserve it."

"Why would you say that?"

He rubbed his fingers over red-rimmed eyes. He looked so weary, so miserable. She would've taken him in her arms if she thought he'd welcome it. His gaze softened. "How's your father doing?"

Lucy bit back a negative report. Words had power. She would not admit defeat. "He's asleep."

"I'm awake." came his rasping answer from behind her. It seemed he always rallied whenever Henry showed up. She tried not to resent it. Her father didn't want to appear pathetic in front of another man and would dredge up his strength.

"You're welcome to sit down." She gestured to the chair next to the bed. "I'll go freshen his water and make some tea."

"Wait." Henry caught her arm, then released it as if he'd grasped a hot iron. "Stay a moment longer. I have something to tell him. There should be a witness."

She frowned, confused. "A witness? To what?"

Rather than answer, he dragged the chair over by the bed.

She went to stand behind him so the two men could visit without her between them. This close, she could easily reach out to touch him.

His hair hadn't been cut recently and had started to curl over his collar. A few strands of gray threaded through the rich brown. She hadn't noticed it before. He still had the lean, athletic form of a man in his prime. Her heart ached at the thought that she wouldn't be around to see how gracefully he would age.

Her father struggled to sit up. She hurried over to plump the pillows behind him, went back to stand behind Henry.

"What is it?" her father asked, breathless from the exertion. "Have you discovered how Mr. Caldwell stole from us?"

Henry leaned forward, braced his arms on his knees. "The original records from each ticket office show that he altered the numbers when he entered them into the books. He skimmed a few dollars here and there with each deposit. Not enough to be alarming, but enough to give him a tidy sum. Eight thousand dollars over the past year. To pay off gambling debts, is what he said. He feared to ask his family for money. Would rather steal it."

"Good work," her father acknowledged.

She couldn't see Henry's face. She could tell by the stiff set of his shoulders that he didn't feel very good about it. He withdrew something from inside his coat pocket.

"There's more." He held out a small notebook.

Her father took it with a trembling hand. "Will you find my spectacles, Lucy?"

She snatched them off the dresser. Why was Henry wasting precious time making her father work, for God's sake? On the way to the bed, she glared at him so he'd know how she felt. She ought to throw him out. Except, she also wanted to know what was in that notebook.

"Perhaps I could read it to you?" she offered, as she helped her father with the lenses.

"That's an accurate record of our expenses over the past two years," Henry's tone was as flat as his expression.

Her father laid his hand over the coverlet, still holding the notebook without looking at it. His gaze remained riveted on Henry. "The ledgers I reviewed?"

"Altered...by me."

Lucy's throat closed. So, this was what he'd been hiding. No wonder he could hardly look at her. She wanted to see the truth in his eyes, so she went over to sit on the edge of the bed.

"Did you," she forced out the dreaded question. "Conspire with Mr. Caldwell?"

Henry remained stone-faced. "Natural that you would think that. As I told you, I had no idea Caldwell was stealing from us. Although now I understand why our revenues weren't what I thought they should be."

Her father thumbed through Henry's notebook. "Where did you get the extra money to pay for these expenses?"

"I sold land, stocks, whatever liquid assets I had."

The answer startled Lucy. Henry had used *his* money?

Her father didn't appear surprised. "What did you spend it on?"

"Repairs along the southern branch," Henry explained. "That line was built in a hurry. We had to go back to grade it properly so the track wouldn't wash out. Or fall apart beneath the wheels of a train."

"There wasn't enough capital to cover those costs?" her father asked.

"Everything we had, I spent to win the race then get us through Indian Territory."

Lucy tried to recall what she knew about the construction race. Impossible odds. Only one railroad earned the right to pass through Indian Territory. Had Henry not won and taken the railroad on to Texas, the Katy would not exist.

Her father closed the notebook. "I see."

Henry propped his elbows on the armrests. His hands hung over the ends to expose his long-boned wrists. "We've teetered on the edge of bankruptcy for a year. I didn't want the directors to know."

He slumped forward, his posture conveying more than his words. To see him like this, in abject defeat, broke her heart.

"You covered the cost of the repairs and kept it a secret," she confirmed.

Henry stared at the floor, though it seemed he looked inward. "The men doing the work had to be paid. I could've let crews go, pushed the remaining workers harder, delayed paying them, but..." He shook his head. "I'd already asked so much. I couldn't."

The tension in Lucy's chest eased. Henry wasn't a killer or a thief. He wasn't even a greedy railroad baron. He'd been guided by the goodness and compassion that was as much a part of him as his pride. "You couldn't cheat them because you care about them. Your men know this. So do their families. They've told me they can count on you to do right by them."

He frowned. "Don't make me out to be a saint. The Katy made me rich. I wanted to make sure I'd get richer. I knew once we opened Texas then finished the Chicago extension, we'd be flush. Then I would recoup what I'd loaned the railroad. With interest."

Lucy's heart sank. Henry refused to acknowledge the man he truly was—deeply flawed, yet possessed of great courage and honor. Her father had been right. The two men were much alike.

She turned to see his reaction.

His eyes had drifted shut. He'd exhausted his strength.

She slipped the notebook out of his hand, held it out to Henry, who took it as he stood. The despair in his eyes wrung her heart.

"When your father wakes, tell him I'll write a full report. If he's unable to sign it, you can witness it. I'm turning in my resignation."

This was why he'd distanced himself. He was racked with guilt. Over the concealed expenses, her father's dire situation, the fiasco with Caldwell. Worse, Henry thought she held him responsible.

Her resentment didn't stem from those mistakes, which, for the most part, had been made by others. She was bitterly disappointed he couldn't trust her with the truth. Given the betrayals in his past, coupled with the fact that he'd been on his own for so long, she might've expected this. He wasn't going to reach out, so it was up to her. If she didn't, he might never forgive himself. Then she would truly lose him. Forever.

Desperate, she stopped him at the door. "What happened with Mr. Caldwell, what he did to my father, I don't hold you responsible."

Henry drew up to his full height. The haunted man vanished behind the haughty general manager. "My authority over this railroad makes me responsible."

~

HENRY MOVED SLOWLY down the stairs and left the hotel. His side still ached. Not nearly as bad as his heart. If he fell to his knees, begged for Lucy's forgiveness, she might weaken and give him another chance—one he didn't deserve.

It was too late for confessions of any kind. Like a long line of rail cars pulled by an engine, every miserable thing that had happened to her since she'd arrived could be linked to actions he'd taken because of his cursed pride. He might be a better man with her, but she would be better off without him.

Outside, the air remained heavy with moisture. The damp weather hadn't helped the Major's condition. Not that a change would improve anything. According to the doctor, Forbes wouldn't live out the week.

Henry's shoes sank into the wet mud as he started across the street. He threw an agonized glance over his shoulder at the closed window on the second floor of the hotel.

The curtain moved. Lucy appeared. From here, he couldn't make out the look in her eyes. He already knew what he'd see. Confusion. Misery. Grief. In the end, that's all he'd brought her.

He fought a vicious longing to go back up there to offer her his love. It wasn't enough. If he did it, he'd be doing so because he was weak. He wanted her to love him in spite of everything he'd done. He had to be strong for her sake, ensure justice was done on her father's behalf. He owed her that. She owed him nothing.

Henry turned away, swallowing his regret. He came to an abrupt halt as a wagon sloshed past then rolled to a stop. Loaded in the bed were pine boxes.

305

The sheriff, who'd ridden beside the driver, hopped down. "Found more."

"More?" Henry echoed. That one word had been repeated over and over, as searchers had fanned out across the Bender property and started digging.

First it was six victims, including the senator's brother. This made three more.

"Nine bodies, so far," Frank Garrity confirmed. "We're checking the orchard. Can you spare more men so we can work faster?"

Henry nodded solemnly. "Whatever you need."

Within moments, a crowd of onlookers had gathered. The sheriff gave his deputy orders to remove the boxed corpses to the undertaker.

As the wagon creaked away, the curious followed.

Pretty soon, the sidewalk had emptied.

"Any sign of the Benders?" Henry asked.

"Not yet. There's a posse searching for them. I would've gone, too —except somebody's got to finish collecting bodies." Garrity mopped his brow with a dirty shirtsleeve. The lines in his face were deeper than ever, as were the shadows under his eyes.

Henry understood the ingrained sense of responsibility that kept a man going even when he was about to collapse. "Have you discovered anything new?"

"A hammer that belonged to the old man. Fits with how the victims were killed. Bludgeoned in the back of the head. All their throats were slit. We found a kitchen knife in the cellar." Garrity relayed the information in a monotone voice. That told Henry, more than anything, how deeply he was affected.

"Were there bodies in that cellar?"

"No. Just a whole lot of clotted blood. Stunk to high heaven."

Henry's stomach rolled over. "You think they killed them down there?"

"That's what I'd guess. The table was situated in front of a canvas. The old man probably hid behind it and whacked the dinner guests on the back of the head. They dumped them into the cellar and cut their throats to finish them off. Left the bodies there until they could sneak them out to bury them. One of the neighbors mentioned seeing the old man out plowing by moonlight. Didn't think twice about it. Said the old German was eccentric."

Eccentric wasn't the right term. Fiendish fit better.

An awful thought took form. "Didn't Caldwell say he left the Major at the inn? You think he had anything to do with...?" Henry gestured in the direction of the departing wagon. He couldn't finish the sentence. Not only had he doomed Lucy's father, he might've unwittingly turned a madman loose on the community.

The sheriff rubbed his forefinger over his mustache with a thoughtful frown. "Don't think so. From what I can piece together, the Benders had already left when Major Forbes got attacked. Although," Garrity's expression turned sly. "I might've mentioned to Mr. Caldwell that I considered him a suspect."

An admirable strategy, and Caldwell was smart enough to know if word got out of his involvement in those murders, the townsfolk would lynch him. "Wish I could've been there to see his face."

"Yeah," Garrity said, with a humorless smile. "He got real cooperative after that. Admitted he lied about stopping at the inn. Confessed to taking the railroad's money and trying to cover it up. He swore he's no killer."

Henry snorted with disgust. "He tried to kill the Major. Lucy. Me. Twice, I think. You ought to talk to that witness who identified Jasper Byrne as one of the attackers. I met Byrne."

"What? You *met* him? When?" It wasn't often Henry surprised Frank Garrity.

"Outside Vinita." Henry didn't provide more details. He'd promised not to send the authorities after Byrne. He would honor his word. He still hadn't figured out why the outlaw let them go. Regardless, Lucy had a made a deal and he wouldn't undo it. "If someone hired him to kill me, I'd be dead."

The sheriff's gaze turned speculative. "Caldwell prompted the witness?"

"Or paid him off." While Henry had been abed, he'd thought

more than a few things through. "Six weeks ago, I asked Caldwell to collect the station receipts for an audit. I'm sure he panicked and hired some local thugs more than willing to take shots at me."

"You want to interrogate him?"

"I want to look him in the eye when I tell him I'll make sure he roasts in hell for what he did to Lucy's father." Henry gripped his aching side as he marched towards the jail.

The other man easily kept pace. "We'll get to the bottom of whatever Mr. Caldwell did. I won't rest until we have the truth."

Indeed. The whole truth would come out—eventually. Henry preferred that Frank hear it from him first.

He halted in front of the sheriff's office. "Thought you ought to know, I'm resigning my position."

The sheriff turned a perplexed look on him. "Why would you do that?"

Henry shifted his attention to a spot down the street. It was hard to look an honest man in the eye and confess. "Caldwell's my problem. I should've seen what he was up to before he hurt anybody. And...I haven't dealt honestly with the board."

After a moment of silence, the sheriff spoke. "You aren't saying I need to arrest you. Because Claire, uh, Mrs. Daines, would have my hide if I did."

His slip was impossible to miss. Henry chose to ignore it. Garrity's question, however, couldn't be ignored. "Far as I know, I haven't broken any laws, other than moral ones. If I am charged with a crime, you won't have to do the honors. I plan to leave Parsons."

What little was left of his pride wouldn't let him stay after the board announced his replacement.

Garrity removed his hat. "Too bad. I was starting to get used to you."

That was as a close as the sheriff would get to a declaration of friendship. It came as something of a surprise. Beyond business associates, Henry didn't have many friends.

He returned a wry smile. "I was starting to get used to you, too."

The sheriff's gaze strayed to the hotel. "What'll she do? Miss

Forbes, I mean."

"I don't know." Henry stared at the second-floor window, the room where Lucy had sequestered herself. He'd pondered that question, too. He wasn't the one who could answer it.

Up until now, Lucy's entire world had revolved around her father. As much as she longed for adventure, she wouldn't leave him. Not willingly. If by some miracle he lived, she'd remain at his side for as long as he needed her. If he died...

Henry's throat tightened. Lucy had never been alone. Who would help her through her grief?

He would return to the hotel later, sit with her, take care of anything she needed, with the exception of what she deserved. Fulfillment, happiness, a wonderful future—those things he couldn't give her.

One day, she'd find a man who could give her all that and more. Someone who'd know how to hold on gently, protect her without suffocating her. Someone who wouldn't hurt her. Someone she could trust. For a time, he'd thought he could be that man. He'd tried. And failed. Miserably.

Despite her attempt to absolve him, she'd hardly been able to look at him. Whatever respect, whatever affection she might feel for him, would die with her father. Lucy deserved to love with her whole heart. Pursue her desires. Write her stories.

"You want adventures? We can have them. We'll travel the West together." Henry's heart jerked as his promise to her came back to mock him.

He'd meant every word. He would do anything for Lucy. Take her anywhere she wanted to go. Give her everything within his power. Letting her go meant he also gave up the privilege to grant those wishes.

Still, there had to be something he could do beyond offering meager comfort. He'd climbed out of poverty when he was little more than a child. He'd built a railroad across an unfriendly land, despite the odds stacked against him. Surely, he could come up with a way to help Lucy realize her dreams.

CHAPTER 35

*I*n the lamp's low light, Lucy strained to read what she'd written. Tears blurred the words. The ending wasn't sad. She cringed at the harsh, rattling sounds from her father's bed as he fought for every breath. Her father's ending was a different story.

In between caring for him, she been writing, mostly to escape crushing despair. Tonight, even her writing failed to soothe her.

She'd bathed her father to cool the fever, spooned drops of broth, water, medicine and tea down his throat when she could get him to swallow. She'd read to him. Even sang to him. If her voice didn't rouse him, nothing would. He'd withered away before her very eyes, almost as if he wished to die. With a choked sob, she set the page aside and dropped her forehead on her arms.

Hopelessness yawned, as cold and dark as an open sepulcher. If she succumbed, sorrow would bury her, then what good would she be to him?

A soft knock sounded at the door.

She sat up, wiped her eyes with the handkerchief she'd kept beside her manuscript. "Yes. Come in."

The door opened. Henry stuck his head inside. He hesitated,

apparently not expecting to see her sitting at a table in front of a pile of papers. "Is this a convenient time?"

Each time he showed up, he twisted the knife in her heart, and still she eagerly awaited his arrival. She stacked the pages neatly, pushed the chair back. "You always ask that. This time is no more or less convenient than last time."

"I won't stay long." He always said that, too, and honored his word. To her great disappointment.

He went to where her father lay in bed, bent to greeted him, assured him things were being put in order, as if he heard or cared. Then he pulled up the covers, something he hadn't done before. He laid his hand on her father's forehead almost like he blessed him or said goodbye. When he straightened, his throat convulsed.

Lucy hugged her arms, fighting a strong urge to weep.

Henry studied her. His expression, once again enigmatic. "Do you mind if I sit with you?"

"Not at all," she choked out. She wanted to say she would be glad if he would sit beside her forever. He'd made it more than clear he didn't intend to do that.

She gave Henry the chair then sat on the bed next to her father. "*Papa?* Can you hear me? Henry's here."

His eyes remained closed, sunken. His hands, once so strong and powerful, were limp, the skin spotted and wrinkled. He'd aged since they'd arrived. Perhaps he'd been aging all along, but she'd refused to notice. She took his hand, as she'd done whenever she sat beside him. "I keep hoping if I hold on, he can't leave."

Henry cleared his throat. "How long has he been like this?" His low voice vibrated with concern.

Lucy blinked until her eyes stopped stinging. No crying. Not now. If she dissolved into tears, he might run away. Weepy women flustered him for some reason. "He hasn't spoken since dawn. I can't get him to take anything, not even water."

Henry nodded, solemnly. He pulled the chair closer. "Claire asked me to see if you wanted her to bring you a tray."

"Thank you, I'm not hungry." She didn't care about food. She was starved for Henry's love, and he'd withheld it from her. Before, she'd tried to absolve him of blame. Her assurances hadn't made any difference. During the brief periods he visited, he hadn't broached the subject of marriage, hadn't spoken of his feelings about her at all. Not even when she'd prodded.

Today, she wouldn't ask him if he no longer loved her. She was losing her father. She couldn't bear to hear she'd lost Henry, too.

She could think of only one thing that might make him reconsider. She went to the table, gathered the pages of her masterpiece, then took it to him. She'd poured her heart into the story with every bit of her love. "Here, I finished."

Henry took the stack, straightened the pages, and set them on his lap. "You want me to give this to Mr. Reynolds, I assume."

"No. It's not for him."

"Who then?"

A sob crawled up her throat. She swallowed until she could speak without losing her composure. "You. I wrote it for you."

His dark brows formed a question as he gazed up at her. "For me?"

"I hope you like it." Lucy turned her face away. It was impossible to talk. If he put his arms around her, she could hold him, say without words what was in her heart.

He stared down at the pile of paper in his lap, appearing vaguely confused. She prayed he would read it, then worried it might not change his heart even if he did.

She took up her spot on the bed beside her father. How long Henry sat there, she didn't know. She'd stopped counting the minutes. She wanted time to stop.

"Lucy?" Her head came up at the sound of her father's voice. Her heart leapt in a frenzy of relief. He'd woken up. He would get better.

She squeezed his hand. "Yes, I'm here."

He gazed at her with his eyes half-open, clear as a blue sky. "I love you," he rasped.

Tears flooded her eyes. She leaned over to kiss his grizzled cheek. "*Papa*, I love you, too."

"Must go. Your mother is calling me." He released a shuddering breath.

He was gone.

CHAPTER 36

The day Lucy left Kansas looked nothing like the day she'd arrived. For one, the sun was shining and the air felt warm. To the west, the prairie showed signs of life—delicate shoots on once-bare trees, hints of green peeking through the humps of buffalo grass. No rain. No snow. All that marred the expansive blue sky were clouds of black smoke that poured from the diamond stack of a steam engine waiting by the platform.

Other passengers crowded the platform close to the train, anxious for the conductor to begin boarding. Lucy took a seat by herself on a bench beneath a chalkboard marked with the day's schedules.

The *Prairie Star* would soon be northbound to St. Louis. From there, she would transfer to an eastbound line. She'd purchased a coach seat to save expenses, then had discovered when she arrived at the station that a ticket for the more comfortable parlor car awaited her. Henry's final gift, no doubt.

She hadn't seen him since her father passed away. He'd stayed by her side through that awful night. The next morning, he'd taken charge, notifying the undertaker, telegraphing her aunt on her behalf with instructions for the funeral. After that, everything became a blur. She'd gone through days without remembering half of what she'd done.

At some point, she would break down, maybe never get up again. That time wasn't now. She had to take her father home to where he wanted to be. Beside her mother. Lucy had watched over him as best she could. She'd stayed with him until the crew loaded his coffin into a boxcar and slid the doors shut with a resounding bang.

Unlike their trip here, he wouldn't sit across from her, read his newspaper or tease her about her books. She wouldn't see wry amusement flash in his blue eyes, or feel the warm security of his arms when he held her and told her how much he loved her.

Grief swelled suddenly, the tears coming so fast she couldn't stop them. It happened like that. One moment, she did fine, the next, she sobbed uncontrollably.

She dug through her sizable bag to retrieve a handkerchief. After mopping her eyes, she put her head down until she regained her composure. She took a deep breath, sat straighter, but tucked the handkerchief under the sleeve of her jacket where she could easily reach it.

This traveling suit was the same one she'd had on when she arrived. Had it only been a month ago? In some ways, it seemed like a lifetime. So much had happened. Funny how she couldn't recall anything except the moments she'd spent with Henry. Maybe that was because he'd monopolized her time. Until recently.

"Hey, Miss Lucy!" The familiar voice pulled her out of the trance she'd slipped into.

"Hello, Billy." She forced a smile. "I didn't know you'd be at the station this morning."

He stood straighter. Proud. "Mr. Stevens allows me to come here in the mornings. I help the porters before I go to school."

Ah, Henry had listened to her when she'd suggested he find some small job to keep Billy's hopes up. "That was very wise of Mr. Stevens. You'll do a good job, I know."

Billy peered at her from beneath the short-billed cap, his

expression solemn. "Sorry to hear about your Pa. Now you're an orphan, too."

Lucy sniffed. She was *not* going to break down in front of the poor child. "Thank you, Billy. It's good to know someone understands."

Anxious to change the subject, Lucy dug into her satchel for one of her dime novels. Thus far, Billy had balked at learning to read. This might spur his interest. "I'd like for you have one of my books. It's a novel by Mr. Buntline. Very bloody, and exciting."

"Thanks, Miss Lucy." Billy tucked it into the large pocket on the side of his coat. "When will you come back?"

She looked around at the sturdy stone building, recalling Henry's tour of the facilities and his pride in the railroad he'd built. Another wave of sadness washed over her. "I have things I need to do, to get my father's affairs in order."

"And after that?"

Go to bed. Stay under the covers for a year. "I'm not sure."

Billy pecked a kiss on her cheek. Then his face turned bright red. "I'll miss you."

Lucy touched the spot the boy's lips had touched. She couldn't keep the tears out of her eyes this time. "Oh Billy, I'll miss you, too."

The warning bell sounded. A conductor announced boarding would soon begin.

Late arriving passengers hurried past.

Billy nodded at her larger case. "Want me to take that? I can put it on the train for you."

"In the parlor car would be fine." She tried to give him two bits. He refused to take it.

As she watched him lug the bag toward the train, a shadow fell over her.

Lucy turned and looked up. Her heart tumbled to her feet. She caught her breath, then concentrated on keeping her expression polite. "Good morning, Henry."

He removed his black bowler. Motioned with it. "Mind if I sit?"

After a week of swinging between fury and distress, her emotions had finally centered on dull resignation. Now he had to show up. She would start the whole process all over again. Should she tell him to leave? Or ignore him?

She scooted to make room. "Please, sit."

He sat rather stiffly, turned his hat in his hands. He was never still, except for when he was sleeping. Lucy squelched the unbidden image. Too late. Her body's craving for him was something she couldn't control.

"Did they give you the ticket I left?" he asked.

"Yes, thank you. That was very thoughtful."

Lucy studied him while he pretended to focus on the train. He looked much the way he had when they'd first met—tousled hair, close-cropped beard, wearing his favorite gray suit. From the pocket of his waistcoat hung the ever-present watch fob. Yet, something was different.

He turned his head to look at her.

His eyes.

When she'd first seen him crouched by the depot door, gun in hand, his eyes had snapped with anger. Afterwards, when he came to find her, they'd brimmed with concern. She'd seen them flash with amusement, grow warm with tenderness, darken with passion. When he'd saved her from that madman, she'd looked into his pain-filled eyes and had seen a hero. Now, his eyes reflected intense unhappiness.

That made two of them.

He reached into his coat and fumbled with something in the inside pocket. Withdrew a folded piece of paper, offered it to her. "Here's a list of all the editors I know. I've written to them. Told them about your writing. Suggested they consider buying your stories."

She took the paper, unfolded it. Granted, at one time he'd agreed to help her. Before he'd started ignoring her. Out of desperation, she had put her manuscript in his hands. The story she had written about him. She foolishly thought if he read it, he would know she loved him, and would realize he loved her. He hadn't said a word since she'd given it to him. He hadn't even indicated whether he liked it.

Her mouth fell open with astonishment. The list Henry had given her contained more than a dozen names. "You wrote all of them? About my writing?"

"Yes. I don't know if that's proper protocol." Henry rubbed his hands over his thighs. For some reason he was nervous about what he'd done. She would've been ecstatic if she weren't so miserable. "You'll have to contact them, I suspect."

Stunned, she stared at the names and addresses. His thoughtfulness seemed in sharp contrast to his utter thoughtlessness throughout the previous week. If he'd had a change of heart, he would've spoken up before now. He'd done this out of guilt or some notion of obligation.

The rush of emotions caught her unprepared. A sob escaped.

His uncertain expression turned to one of horror. He yanked a handkerchief out of his pocket. "Here, I'm sorry. Didn't mean to upset you. I-I didn't want you to go home and give up. On your dreams."

"How..." she spoke haltingly. "How can you say that?"

Didn't he know *he* had become a big part of her dreams?

His answer was to press a handkerchief into her hand.

She bowed her head and screwed her eyes shut. Held his handkerchief to her face, caught his scent on it. The tears wouldn't stay in. She struggled so hard to hold them back that her shoulders began to shake.

"Lucy." The way he said her name, like it had been pulled out of him. Not as if he meant to say it or even wanted to say it. He embraced her anyway.

Unable to fight any longer, she turned into his chest and clung to his coat. All her pent-up longing, her grief, the wrenching loss, pushed its way up and out in uncontrollable sobs.

Henry held her close. He made senseless, soothing comments, and rubbed comforting circles on her back. All she could think was how perfect it felt to be in his arms. She didn't want him to let her go. Ever.

The final whistle shrilled, sending a jolt through her. The illusion shattered.

"All aboard!"

She jerked away. In her flustered state, she stuffed his handkerchief into his hand then grabbed her bag. "I have to go."

Henry shot to his feet. "Wait—"

"No, the train, it's leaving. My father is on it." She didn't stop to explain. There was no need. Henry had pushed her away then retreated to some place she couldn't reach him. Nothing said or wrote, nor all the tears she cried, would change anything.

Lucy grabbed the rail and hurried up the steps. She found her seat as the train pulled away. Finally, she allowed herself to look out the window.

Henry remained on the platform, gazing up at her. He walked alongside the slow-moving train, keeping pace as it picked up speed. Perhaps he'd wanted to apologize, or make awkward excuses for not coming around to see her.

She sat back in her seat. It was time to stop dreaming. Face reality. Get on with her life—a life that didn't include Henry. The future she had in mind would not require a man. At one time, she hadn't even wanted one. They tended to get in the way of a woman's freedom.

Was he still out there? She scooted over to draw down the window and stuck her head out.

He jogged alongside the train as it rushed away. Maybe he was worried about her after she'd fallen apart in his arms. He wasn't hard-hearted. She had to let him know she would be all right.

"Adieu!" She thrust her arm out the window.

"Farewell," she cried, and opened her hand to release him.

HENRY RAN FASTER, panting with exertion. He grimaced when his side caught. He was getting old if he couldn't run the distance of the platform without fatigue. It might have something to do with the still-tender wound from a bullet. That didn't explain the pain in his chest, which had worsened when Lucy broke down and wept in his arms.

At that moment, he'd realized he couldn't let her go. Actually, he had realized this many times before. Foolishly, he had done nothing about it because he'd kept telling himself it was for the best. He ought to have learned by now that Lucy, not him, knew what was best for her life. And she'd told him in the most unique and exquisite way possible.

He picked up speed along with the train. She'd boarded before he could say he wanted her to have a man she could truly love. Like the one in that story she'd written for him. If she hadn't been so obvious in her descriptions, he might not have recognized himself because the character was so damned chivalrous. It was how she saw him—as a knight, her very own prince.

If *she* could believe he was like that, then he could *be* that man. He couldn't do it without her, though. That's what he'd come here to tell her. Only, he hadn't gotten it out because he'd started off by talking about that damned list and her dreams, and had made her cry.

His vision blurred. He blinked to clear it, noticed the cars rushing by. Soon, the train would be moving too fast. Lucy would be beyond his reach.

With a final burst of speed, he leapt and caught hold of a handrail on the side of a boxcar. He was nearly pitched off before he grasped the metal rung of a ladder. With no little effort, he hoisted himself onto the top of the train.

The wind caught his hat. Took it airborne.

Damn, his favorite bowler. Should've held onto it.

He sprawled atop the rumbling rail car, paused for a moment to catch his breath. It'd been years since he'd clambered onto a moving train. He'd been a brakeman at one time. Ten, no, more like fifteen years ago. Time moved faster than this train.

With careful deliberation, he stood and gained his balance on a board that stretched the length of the car. Brakies used the "coon walk," as railroaders called it, to traverse the top of the train to reach the hand brakes.

He glanced over his shoulder. At the end of the train, in a cupola on the caboose, a brakeman would be peering out, wondering what fool had decided to jump on the train. Or maybe he knew which fool and was afraid to come out to ask the Chief what the hell he was doing.

By God, he was being heroic. Like the man in Lucy's story. The *handsome, clever railroad chief* didn't let fear or doubt or even reason slow him down. He saved trains and rescued damsels. He wasn't afraid to tell the woman he loved exactly how he felt.

Henry made his way forward, using his arms to balance. Soon, he hopped from one car to the next. Now, he gotten the hang of it again. No thrill equaled that of sitting atop a moving train, looking out over the prairie at vast herds of buffalo, feeling the sun on your face, the wind whipping through your hair.

In his peripheral vision, the flat landscape seemed to stand still as the train zipped past. The sensation disoriented him. He jumped onto the slight rounded top of a passenger railcar. His foot slipped. He flung himself face forward. His heart pounded so hard he felt it in his temples. If he fell, he could go under the wheels. Or break his neck when he hit the ground.

Henry forced the gruesome images out of his mind. Up here was no place for fear.

He stood again, braced his feet. The train rumbled and rocked. Black smoke rolled over the few cars remaining between him and the engine. He blinked, momentarily blinded.

Enough heroism for one day.

He eased off the roof that overhung the back of a passenger car and climbed down. It would be easier, and less dangerous, if he went *through* the inside of the train rather than *over*.

As he passed through the coach section, he nodded in greeting to the startled conductor. "Mr. Kelly."

The poor man gaped at him. Had to be wondering how he'd suddenly materialized.

Finally, he reached the parlor car.

He craned his neck to peer over the backs of cushioned benches. Lucy sat near the front. He could see the top of her head.

What would he say to her? Tell her he'd learned to dream again —of love, rather than power. Of passion instead of ambition. Then go down on one knee, pledge his heart, along with what little was left of his material possessions. Ask her if she'd take a reformed villain.

She might toss him off the train. She'd already leaned out the window and bade him farewell. Maybe she meant it.

He forced his feet to move, to go forward through the compartment. While he walked, he threaded his fingers through his hair, which, as usual, was a mess. It was a lost cause. So was saving his job. But winning Lucy back, he'd succeed at that if it took him the rest of his life.

He halted beside her seat. She had her back to him, her neck craned, as if to look out the window. Might be too much to hope for. He had to ask anyway. "Looking for me?"

She jerked around with a gasp. Her eyes grew wide. "What? How?"

"I jumped on the train. Came over the top." He gestured to the space beside her where her collection of books had been piled up on the seat. "May I?"

Her lips parted. No words came out.

Henry gathered up her belongings, set them aside, and plopped down next to her.

Lucy continued to stare at him. Did she fear he was an apparition?

He reached out to take her hand, sandwiched between his, as he'd done on that first day they'd met. "Your hands are cold. You're trembling."

She snatched her hand away. Her eyes flashed. "Have you lost your mind?"

"Might have." He gave her a rueful smile. "Lately, I can't think straight."

"Neither can I." The anger in her expression faded and her features twisted with anguish. "I wish you'd stop confusing me."

Her plea tore into him. If he hadn't been so damned prideful and thick-headed, he could've saved them both a great deal of pain. "That's not what I want."

Lucy heaved a sigh. "What do you want, Henry? Because I'm sure I don't know."

Fair enough.

"That story, the one you gave me. I read it."

"You jumped a train to tell me you read my story?"

Better stop equivocating and get to the point.

Henry rubbed his hand over the rough bristles he hadn't gotten around to removing. *No, let's be honest.* He'd let his beard grow back because he felt more comfortable behind it. He used that, among other things, as a shield. Undaunted, Lucy had charged through his defenses. Then he'd gotten scared and put them back up.

No more. This time, his surrender would be unconditional.

"What I want is to tell you, I should've told you before. You see, I love you." Henry held his breath.

Lucy didn't throw her arms around his neck. Didn't declare she loved him, too.

He'd said it wrong or in the wrong order.

"Apology first," he conceded.

She shook her head slowly. "No, no more apologies. I'd rather hear why you've suddenly decided you love me after you ignored me for the better part of two weeks."

Henry's neck grew warm at her blunt reminder of his bad behavior. "It wasn't sudden. I've known for some time now. I'd decided you were better off with a man who isn't selfish. Someone who'd never hurt or disappoint you."

The gut-wrenching sadness he'd seen earlier crept back into her eyes. "That kind of man doesn't exist."

"The man in the story you wrote, he's like that."

She lowered her gaze and laid her hand on a closed book in her lap. "That's fiction, Henry. Maybe, at one time, I did think there were men out there like that."

His insides knotted. Lucy couldn't retreat. Not now. Not after she'd sounded the charge and conquered him. He'd laid down his arms. There was no turning back.

"Don't tell me that." He gripped her shoulders, growing

desperate. "I know you believe in heroes. For God's sake, you turn villains into heroes. Remember what you wrote? You're so damn convincing, you've got *me* believing in fairy tales. You want to know why I jumped this train? Because you make me believe I can be a hero."

Her eyes rounded. "My story did that?"

He ran his hands down her arms, took her hands and poured everything he felt into his voice and his eyes. "It helped me see myself through your eyes. Lucy, I feel like a hero when you look at me. When you kiss me. Whenever we're in each other's arms."

Whispers came from the passengers behind them. They'd overheard. He didn't care. Let them listen. He'd shout it from the treetops.

"Lucy, you changed me. I can't go back to being a villain. God knows, I tried. It's more comfortable than this new suit of armor. Except, that part of me has been ripped away. There's nothing left of the old Henry Stevens. Not his position, not his power, not even his money. He's gone. But *I'm* here. If you want me."

"Yes." Her answer came out on her released breath. She threw her arms around his neck. "I do want you, and I do believe. I believe in *you*, Henry. I love you."

Her passionate declaration was far more eloquent than his rambling speech. Good thing he didn't have to make his living as a writer. He enfolded her against his heart and buried his face in her sweet-smelling hair.

"I'm going to kiss you," he murmured, "Before I do..." Henry dropped down on one knee in front of her and cradled her hands. "Miss Forbes, will you do me the honor of becoming my wife?"

"Yes, Mr. Stevens, I will gladly marry you." She sniffed.

He dug his handkerchief out of his pocket. "Keep it this time."

Rather than use it, she withdrew a lacy hankie from a beneath her sleeve and wiped her nose. Then she took his large handkerchief and held it to her face. "It smells like you. That's what made me cry before, when you gave it to me."

Henry grimaced. Had he given her a dirty—?

"No, I don't mean it smells *bad*. I mean it reminded me of being with you." Her gaze turned dreamy.

"Ah, a good memory." He took his seat next to her then gathered her against him. Now that she'd let him hold her, he couldn't keep his hands off. However, he owed it to her to make sure she understood what she'd be getting into.

"What's left of the land I own is jointly held by a railroad interest. It's complicated, was meant to be. That's how Mr. Parsons and I set it up, so we could move money back and forth, as needed—"

"I don't want your land, Henry. I want you." She looked up at him. "I'm curious, though. What was Mr. Parsons' part in all this?"

A stray curl on her cheek distracted him for a moment. He twined the feather-soft strand around his finger. It would be easier to blame his boss. He wasn't looking for an easy way out. "Nothing. I didn't tell him what I was doing. He didn't ask."

"He must've known."

"Parsons is no fool. He knew something was up. Didn't trust me to take care of it. That's why he sent your father out here."

Lucy went still and silent. Too silent.

Henry bent his head to see her face so he'd know what she was feeling.

Grief.

A knot formed in his throat. He had no idea how to help her with that. It wasn't a problem to be solved or an obstacle to overcome. The unexpected loss of her father, the violent cause of his death, would leave a wound. Even if it healed, the scar remained. This much Henry knew from experience.

"If it's any consolation, the sheriff says Caldwell will probably hang for murder."

Lucy turned her face into his shoulder. "Someone's death is never a consolation."

True enough, a hanging didn't lessen her grief. It did provide him with a measure of satisfaction. Lucy might not find that to be the case. She had more mercy in the tip of her little finger than he did in his entire being. That was part of the reason he loved her. There were many other reasons and, happily, they would have the time to explore them.

The coming days and months would be difficult for her. At times, agonizing. If he couldn't banish her pain, he would move heaven and earth to ease her path through it.

"My report sent to the board contains a recommendation that they honor your father by naming the next new engine after him. *The Major*."

"He'd like that," Lucy replied in a somber tone.

That wasn't all.

"Next month, the city council will vote to change the name of the town. From Parsons to Forbes."

Lucy drew back, searched his face. "You're serious?"

"Of course, I'm serious. It was only named Parsons because I recommended it. The old goat didn't do anything for that town. I hope your father will be remembered for his dedication to the railroad that founded it. And for his integrity."

"Thank you for that." The gratitude in her eyes was thanks enough.

She rested her head on his shoulder, after a moment, smoothed her fingers over his lapel. "He told me about the talk you two had the day he went to the settlers' meeting. How you pressed him to spend time with me. He was touched by your concern."

Concern? Was that what it was? Henry recalled he had been suspicious of Forbes' response, distrustful. "I should've pressed harder. Sent him home."

"He wasn't your employee."

"I know, but—"

"Don't. You didn't make the decision. He did. Even if you had the authority, you couldn't predict the future."

It was a gentle reminder of something she'd told him before. "I'm not God."

"I'm glad you've finally acknowledged it."

"You won't let me forget."

"Why do you put up with me?"

"It's only fair. You put up with me."

She snuggled next to him. The silence that descended this time felt more comfortable. His thoughts turned from the past to the future. He had resigned. Once the board reviewed his report and word got out about how he'd covered up the Katy's true financial situation, his reputation would be in tatters. No railroad would hire him.

He fought a surge of panic.

"What's wrong, Henry?"

"What makes you think something's wrong?"

"I feel it. We're synchronized, like a steam engine. Remember?"

He closed his eyes on a groan. "Don't remind me. Awful metaphor."

"I like it. Would you mind if I used it in a book?"

"Yes."

"All right. I'll probably use it anyway. Now tell me what's wrong." She'd made him smile while insisting on sharing his burdens. Two more reasons he loved her.

"The lack of employment prospects."

"You're concerned about unemployment?" She sounded almost amused. He had a difficult time finding humor in the situation.

"*My* unemployment, to be precise."

"You'll find something. I'm not worried. You found a way to support your sisters when you were fourteen. I'm sure you know a great deal more now."

Her confidence in him eased his mind. She was right. He'd provided for others all his life. He excelled at working. Opening his heart had been much more difficult. He wouldn't have learned how without Lucy's patient instruction.

He hugged her tight, kissed the top of her head. "You're right. I'll find something."

"If we need money straightaway, I can always go back to work in my aunt's hat shop."

"Hat shop?" He couldn't imagine anything more stifling. "There's no fun in that. Keep writing. I can work anywhere. If you'd like, we'll go further west. Find those adventures you want."

Lucy shifted and sat straight. She gazed at him with so much love in her eyes it made him certain he could move mountains. Or, at the very least, build another railroad.

"The day I came to Parsons, an hour or so before we arrived, the train had stopped at a barricade. After traveling for so long, I was eager to see what was over the next rise. I was sure when we got there, I'd find the greatest adventure of my life." She leaned forward and whispered against his lips. "I was right."

EPILOGUE

Six months later

"What you got there, Mrs. Daines?" Billy came up to the registration desk. He peered around Claire's arm at the open pages in her hand.

Perhaps this could be used as a bribe.

"It's a letter." Claire held it out to the boy. "Here, you can read it."

Billy had been making wonderful progress on his schooling. The trick was finding things he liked to read, like that dog-eared book Lucy had given him. Over the past few months, he'd settled down and seemed happier.

She'd been able to convince her husband to allow him to stay on, claiming he was wonderful help around the hotel, and could even assist her with the desk. She hadn't admitted her heart would be broken if she had to send him away.

In no time at all, Billy had burrowed his way into her heart. He'd become *her* child, the one she'd never thought she would have.

Henry's farewell gift. Without her brother around, having Billy in her life had become even more important.

He perused the first page, knitting his brow in concentration. "This handwriting is hard to make out."

"It's cursive, not printed."

He flipped the pages until he reached the end, then his face lit up. "It's from Miss Lucy."

Immediately, he turned back to the beginning and applied himself to working out the words. "Says here, she's in San-ta-fee," he sounded it out as she'd taught him.

"Santa Fe, it's Spanish."

Billy huffed in disgust. "Well, how come she's gone and written this thing in Spanish. I just got good at English."

"That's all the Spanish she uses, I believe." Claire took a seat on the stool. She rested her arm on the counter, waited patiently while Billy to finish reading the letter.

She'd been relieved, delighted really, to receive the update on the couple, and about how they'd fared after being wed for six months.

Billy turned the page, a moment later, he looked up with surprise. "Miss Lucy is having a baby."

"Yes, indeed." And that was only part of the good news.

Through her father's connections, Lucy had put Henry in touch with Cyrus Holliday, president of the Atchison, Topeka and Sante Fe Railroad. Being *a visionary man,* to quote Lucy, Mr. Holliday had offered Henry a job planning town sites along the line as it expanded westward. In the meantime, Lucy had sold a series to Harper's Weekly titled *Tales of the Katy Railroad.* She would continue to write while traveling with Henry on his new job.

Despite their earlier difficulties, things had turned out well.

Claire celebrated in her heart.

Previously, Henry had sent a lengthy tome about why he'd left in such a hurry. How he'd resigned his position because of inconsistencies with the books, which he'd explained in excruciating detail. In a strange twist of fate, it seemed his departure had been timed right. The Katy's president had resigned suddenly in August.

The railroad had been taken over by new management in September. Jay Gould and his investor companions cleaned house.

Henry went on to say he'd wed Lucy in her hometown. The two had remained there for a few months getting her affairs in order. Henry's uncertain situation had added to their stress, yet he praised Lucy as being *the most courageous woman* he'd ever known. He'd added he wasn't certain about what the future held, but was optimistic that with Lucy at his side, he could conquer the world. Figuratively, of course.

Claire could read between the lines. Her brother had, at last, found love. The kind that could slay dragons, scale castle walls, and turn bears into princes.

AUTHOR'S NOTE

Welcome to the series *Steam! Romance and Rails*, which features stories from America's golden age of steam railroads. In this book, I continue the saga of the Missouri, Kansas and Texas Railway, affectionately dubbed, "the Katy."

The main character Henry Stevens was inspired by the actual general manager of the Katy Railroad, Robert S. Stevens. Described as a man with "dark flashing eyes and a meticulous style of dress," he was a larger-than-life persona in the history of this legendary railroad.

In 1870, Stevens was hired by the Katy's president Judge Levi Parsons to help build a railroad empire that would stretch from Chicago all the way down to Mexico City. The Katy's birth and impressive growth is largely attributable to Stevens, who took a "never surrender" approach to just about everything he attempted. Many of the events in this book are based on exploits written about this fascinating man and the railroad he built.

Another historical tidbit featured in *A Dangerous Passion* is a series of mysterious murders that took place near Parsons, Kansas. From a period stretching between 1871 and early 1873, numerous travelers through southeastern Kansas were reported missing. There were theories as to what happened to them, including one rumor that the railroads were to blame for their disappearance.

When a well-known doctor went missing, his brother, a U.S. Senator (A.M. York) tore through the area on a frantic search. Authorities ultimately discovered nearly a dozen bodies (including the doctor's) buried in a field behind a cabin that doubled as a wayside inn, serving meals to travelers.

The Bender family—Johann Bender and his wife, daughter Kate and a "halfwit" son (possibly Kate's common-law husband rather than her brother)—fled before the authorities could arrest them. The father and "son" were never seen again. Two women were arrested years later, but never tried.

Kate Bender had widely advertised her services as a fortune-teller. Her pretty face lured many a man to his death. Grisly descriptions reported in the newspapers describe how the victims would be seated in front of a curtained partition where the father would be hiding with a large hammer. He'd bash the guest on the head, and one of the women would cut the victim's throat to make sure he was dead. Once stripped of clothes and valuables, the unfortunate victim would be dropped through a trap door into the basement until the family could sneak the body out to bury it. Neighbors reported seeing the old man plowing by moonlight, but they attributed it to his eccentricities.

Special thanks to Mike Brotherton and David Beach for their kind assistance in uncovering a wealth of research materials, including David's meticulous transcriptions of old newspaper articles, as well as the wonderful images and collections at the Iron Horse Historical Museum.

Other primary sources for research include Images of America: Parsons (Arcadia Publishing), as well as The Katy Railroad and the Last Frontier by V.V. Masterson (University of Oklahoma Press), and The Story of American Railroads by Stewart H. Holbrook (Bonanza Books).

I'd also like to thank Jill Marie Landis for her encouragement and mentoring. I've long admired her writing and she's inspired me in more ways than I can list here. To my friends at Midwest Romance Writers and Mid America Romance Writers, I couldn't make this journey without you.

E.E. Burke

FUGITIVE HEARTS

BOOK 4, STEAM! ROMANCE AND RAILS

A fugitive "Black Widow" challenges a lawman's notions about duty and justice—and love.

Parsons Kansas, 1873

Everyone in Parsons considers hotel owner Claire Daines a respectable, decent woman. Until she shocks the entire town when she rushes into a saloon in her nightclothes to confess to an inebriated lawman: "Sheriff, I shot my husband."

Is it an accident, as she claims? Or is it murder? When Claire sneaks out of town on a southbound train, Sheriff Frank Garrity follows. He's determined to unravel the widow's subterfuge, despite his soft spot for the town's most compassionate resident.

But the truth doesn't produce justice, it only puts Frank in a difficult position. To protect Claire, he must betray her trust.

Take wild ride along the Katy line with a persistent lawman and a desperate woman, who will let nothing get in the way of love. Read Fugitive Hearts today.

ALSO BY E.E. BURKE

SERIES AND BOOKS

The New Adventures

Tom Sawyer Returns

Taming Huck Finn

Steam! Romance and Rails (New Edition)

Her Bodyguard

Redbird

A Dangerous Passion

Fugitive Hearts

The Bride Train

Valentine's Rose

Patrick's Charm

Tempting Prudence

Seducing Susannah

American Mail-Order Brides

Victoria Bride of Kansas

Santa's Mail-Order Bride

The Brides of Noelle

Twelve Days of Christmas Mail-Order Brides

Jolie, A Valentine's Day Bride

The Drum (Twelve Days of Christmas Mail-Order Brides)

ABOUT THE AUTHOR

E.E. Burke is a bestselling author of historical fiction and romances that combine her unique blend of wit and warmth. Her books have been nominated for numerous national and regional awards, including Booksellers' Best, National Readers' Choice and Kindle Best Book. She was also a finalist in the RWA's prestigious Golden Heart® contest. Over the years, she's been a disc jockey, a journalist and an advertising executive, before finally getting around to living the dream--writing stories readers can get lost in.

Find out more about her books at her website: www.eeburke.com.